TRAPFICTION PRESENTS

WE MADE LOVE

IN THE

80'S

BY

ARABIA

TrapFiction Books

www.TrapFictionBooks.com
TrapFictionBooks@gmail.com
FB/IG/TW: TrapFiction Books
Please sign up for our mailing list directly from our website for
exclusive content, contest, and giveaways.

About the Author
Arabia is on the rise as an up and coming author. Striving to leave her
mark on the publishing world and with her Coke Dreams and From the
Beginning series', she is well on her way. Writing for her has always
been about having fun and making every thought a reality. Her pen
bleeds with gritty tales of love and deceit all while remaining true to her
unique writing style. In a class of her own, she is setting the tone for
authors not looking to conform but looking to set their own standard.

Connect with Arabia for future fun, sneak peeks, games and giveaways
on any one of the following platforms!

FaceBook/Twitter/Instagram: ArabiaWrites

I just wanna take a moment before y'all dive in, to say thank you. Thank you for supporting me and the brand. You guys really be showing out for me and it has never gone unnoticed. It took me a little over a year to write this book, but subconsciously, I've been writing this book for over ten years. It has always been on my heart to write an 80s love story. There were plenty of stories I've started over the years, thinking *this is the one* and never finished them, for whatever reason. However, this particular story just felt so damn good and the timing couldn't have been better. Within these pages lies the best parts of me and I'm so eager to share them with you. I definitely took my time with this one making sure you were able to capture every emotion, that the characters were relatable and most importantly that the story depicted what it meant to live and love in the '80s…So from me to you, signed, sealed and delivered!

WELCOME TO THE ZOO

A true '80s story....

This book is for the bamboo earrings, four-finger rings and gold chains...For the around the way girl rolling her neck with an attitude, and for the dope boys using pagers and payphones. This book is for everyone who lived, loved, and died in the '80s. With the explosion of hip-hop, crack and timeless fashion, the eighties were not only an era but a statement. A statement that resonated with people from all walks of life. If ever there was a time to be alive, the eighties were it. It was the definition of what the kids today call "lit." The sweaty basement parties, long summer nights on the Ave., to back when you just had to like a guy enough to give him some. The good ole days...relive every moment of it in We Made Love In the '80s.

TRAPFICTION PRESENTS

WE MADE LOVE

IN THE

80'S

BY

ARABIA

Chapter 1

"You can call me a crook, a robber, a thief…But I'll be your butcher if you got beef." The ladies rapped their hearts out as the new Salt-N-Pepa song blasted from a nearby boom-box.

It was officially summer, and the beautiful weather brought the whole hood out. Down the street, a group of young girls played Double Dutch, a little further down the block there were about ten neighborhood boys on the corner shooting dice, and cars were rolling up and down the street with guys wanting to be seen. In the midst of all that was going on, three young women sat on the stoop of a six-story building, taking it all in.

"Why is it so hot?" Keisha asked, waving her hand as if her fingers were the blades of a cooling fan. "I'm about to pass out."

"It's summer, duh." Faith joked, bumping her with her shoulder.

"Shit, I'm about to go into the house. Plus, these damn steps are hot." Keisha continued to complain.

"Girl, relax." Janae was over the dramatics. Yeah, it was hot. Shit, they were all hot, but saying *it was hot* every five minutes wasn't going to make it any cooler. "Soon as Lynette pull up, we out anyway." Checking her watch, she looked back at her friends. "She should be about to pull up any minute…"

"A minute my ass, shit, my ass gone be melted into this damn concrete in a minute."

Friends since elementary school, the girls bickered like they always did. The day wouldn't be complete if they didn't almost come to blows at least twice. Their personalities clashed, and they argued a lot, but the love was real, and they were bonded by the everyday struggle of living in the hood.

"That's probably her right there." Faith pointed, eyeing a cab bending the corner onto their block.

Before Janae could say anything, about ten dirt bikes came flying down the street, scaring them half to death. The loud sound of engines revving pierced the air as one of the guys lifted his motorcycle on the back wheel. Shaking her head, Janae was pissed. She watched in disgust as the guys obnoxiously disrupted traffic with their show. "Fucking animals."

"Yo', don't talk about my man like that." Faith cut right into her. She didn't play about her boo, Stacks, or his homeboys, Zoo Crew. Even if he technically wasn't her man, everybody in the hood knew her name held weight in his heart.

"Whatever." Janae waved her off as the traffic was able to continue, and the taxi stopped right in front of the building. "There, my bitch, go!"

The girls all hopped off the porch as the back door of the taxi opened, and Lynette stepped out. They looked her over and nodded their heads approvingly. Her door knocker earrings were so big they almost touched her shoulders, and the rings that adorned her fingers glistened in the sun. Finger waves lined one side of her hair while the other side was curled to perfection. Lynette was fly, just like them, and Janae was sure she'd fit right in.

"Damn, sexy, can I rap to you for a minute." Keisha joked, complimenting her look.

Lynette was all smiles as she shook her head. "I see y'all still crazy."

"And you know it!" They said in unison before bursting into a fit of giggles.

They all hugged her and stepped to the side. Patiently, they waited for the taxi driver to get her bags out of the trunk. Lynette thanked him when he was done setting her things on the curb and turned her attention back to her cousin Janae.

"Where you get all this from?" Janae grabbed at her ass and then her tits, making them all laugh. "You ain't that little girl that came up to visit for spring breaks no more."

"Nah, I ain't been little for a good minute now."

Janae could feel irritation creeping into her bones at the sound of those damn dirt bikes again. Immediately, her eyes shifted to

Faith, and she mugged her right back. "Let's take ya bags in the house before these animals come down here and snatch ya shit."

Lynette looked at her, perplexed, "Animals?"

"Yeah, and they'll snatch anything that ain't nailed to the ground." Bending down, Janae grabbed one of the big bags, and Lynette took the bags that were already in her hand. "So, you here for good? Auntie Kelly told my mother you were at home wildin'."

Sighing, Lynette shook her head, "Nah, I was chilling, them other hoes were wildin'. But you know how my mother is, so I ain't even gonna go back and forth with her." Together they stepped off the elevator and headed to the apartment Lynette would now call home.

"Well, I'mma make sure you have a good time before school starts. We about to fuck the whole summer up."

"Nah, I'm chilling, but y'all have fun. I ain't trying to get into no trouble out here."

"Ain't no trouble out here." Janae smiled wickedly as they placed the bags in her new room and headed downstairs for the rest. Soon as they walked out the front door, Janae huffed. "I lied, there is trouble out here because this bitch keeps feeding the animals." Faith looked from Stacks to Janae and stuck her middle finger up. "You wish."

Lynette slowly walked down the stairs taking in the scene. All the guys were cute, from what she could see, and they were ruff-necks; and that for her was trouble. She was so glad she decided to get dressed today because she would've been mortified if they'd seen her in the sweats she planned on wearing.

"Why ya attitude so fuckin' nasty?" One of the guys named Tech asked, resting on his bike.

Not letting up, Janae responded, "Why you smell so fuckin' nasty?"

Shaking her head, this was the type of shit Lynette didn't want to be involved in. She knew her mouth, and she knew her hands, and the Lord knew she lacked patience and understanding; so, she grabbed her bags and headed for the stairs.

WE MADE LOVE IN THE 80'S

<><><><><><>

Zoo Crew sat on their bikes posted in front of the building while Stacks kicked shit to his girl. One look at them, and you understood the name. They were young, wild, and getting money by any means. Feared by a few, but respected by many, they were definitely making a name for themselves. The gang was led by Stack Dollas, Uncle Sam, and King Zoo himself, Rich Tony. Together they started Zoo Crew in the basement of Stacks' grandmother's house.

They were thirteen or so when The SugarHill Gang dropped Rappers Delight, and they made it up in their minds that they were going to be rappers. It wasn't long after that they noticed it wasn't the rappers with the fly cars, money and girls…It was the street niggas. Just like that, they decided they were going to make their money in the streets. Rich Tony was 20-years-old now and had already lived two lifetimes worth of bullshit. Once he came up, Rich swore he would do whatever he had to, to stay there.

For a minute, he zoned out but was brought back to reality when he heard Janae cry baby ass. She was always buggin' on them about something, but he just ignored her. For one, he ain't argue with women, that was some hoe shit, and for two, Janae was right. They were everything she believed them to be, and you can't argue with the truth.

Looking past Janae, his eyes landed on shorty walking behind her. *Damn*, he thought admiring her slender frame. For a minute, their eyes connected, and it seemed like Rich was stuck, but when she looked away, without even blinking, his heart dropped. "What the fuck?" he spat under his breath. Did she not know who the fuck he was?

Never had Rich ever been dismissed, and right now, he felt played. *Nah, I'm trippin shorty ain't play me like that. She ain't see me looking at her*, he told himself. That had to be it because one look from him had bitches drooling. Without another look from her, he continued to watch her movements. He noticed the luggage bag, she picked up and wondered if she'd just moved around here. Rich had never seen her before, and he knew all the chicks in the hood. Just when she walked back in the building, the pager on his hip alerted him that someone was trying to reach him. Quickly, he removed the pager from his jean overalls and checked the number. "Word," he nodded, not able to block his excitement. "Zoo, let's blow this joint."

At his words, all the guys started their bikes as Stacks kissed Faith goodbye. When she stepped back on the curb, they burnt rubber down the street and off the block. The page Rich had just received was the call he'd been waiting nearly a month on. Together, he and his crew were into all kinds of shit. They sold weed, dabbled in a little cocaine, stole cars, and had even stuck up a few stores. None of them were strangers to crime, but Rich knew if they kept this shit up, it wouldn't be long before they were knocked.

He was with them making money by any means, but their shit was getting sloppy. Uncle Sam brought the shit to his attention a few months ago, and now he couldn't unsee it. After putting their heads together, they had a plan that would set them straight for life if it all worked out, and that's where they were headed. Zoo Crew split up after putting their bikes up for the evening. With no plans to link up later, Sam, Rich, and Stacks headed to their meeting. The three of them hopped in Sam's car and prayed the shit worked out how they thought it would.

When they pulled up to the apartment building, they sat back, scoping the neighborhood. The men weren't familiar with the area, and they didn't want to take the chance of getting stuck up. Rich knew what an easy lick looked like, and right now, it looked like them. "Aight, y'all, let's do this," he said, reaching for the door handle. "And keep ya finger on the trigger."

The three of them exited the vehicle, and stepped on the curb, headed to the building. There weren't a lot of people out that they could see, but you never know who could be watching. Not wanting to be considered a mark, they nodded their heads to the people that were outside showing respect. It was just like walking into someone's house, the first thing you do is speak. The same rules applied when you rolled up in someone else's hood. It wasn't until they were in the building and on the elevator that they could relax just a bit. Just a few minutes later, they were standing in front of apartment 723 knocking.

"What up fool," Stacks cousin, Trigga Kev, answered, slapping him five.

Once they shook it up, Stacks walked past him into the apartment, and he greeted the other guys. Inside the small apartment, there wasn't much in there. A table, a small couch, and a little kitchen completed the space. Just as they were about to speak, a man came from the back, drying his hands. The man was average height and had a small beard that blended into his dark skin. Trigga did the honors and broke the uncomfortable silence.

WE MADE LOVE IN THE 80'S

"Y'all niggas said y'all was trying to make some real money and stop fucking around with that little kid shit, right?"

"Hell yeah," Stacks said, speaking for all of them.

"Yeah, that's what ya mouth say because it sounds good, but ain't no turning back after this shit. This my nigga Freeway, he came all the way from Cali to teach y'all little asses how to make real money."

Rich was growing tired of the little nigga talk, and before he lost his cool, he needed them to get to the point. "Aight and how we gon' do that because you doing a lot of talking, but you ain't said shit." Freeway looked at Kev, and they both smirked before he tossed him a vial filled with some little white rocks. Rich caught the bottle and examined it. The contents were like nothing he'd ever seen before. "Fuck, is this?"

"Money," Freeway said before merely taking a seat. "Cocaine money is cool, but let's be honest the shit is hard to sell. I know y'all heard about Free Base? Well, this is better, and fiends love it." Sitting up in his seat, he looked at Sam since he was the one holding the vial now, "How much you think we sell that little bottle for?"

"Shit, I don't know, five dollars?"

"Twenty dollars," Freeway said, causing the men to look at each other, not believing it. "How many times you think they gon' come back for another one of those small ass bottles? The average fiend is getting high at least five/six times a day. That's $100 right there, but then the shit so good they come back with a friend, and they coming back with a friend, and now these muthafuckas getting high all day…Shit nigga, you do the math."

The numbers all added up to them, nodding his head Stacks was in. "Aight, so where we get the shit?"

Smiling, Freeway rubbed his hands together. "You don't get it; you make it." He began explaining the process of turning cocaine into crack, and they were all ears.

Pulling out his supplies, including a pot, baking soda, a Pyrex cup, a spoon, and cocaine, they got to work. It took a few hours, but before long, they were whipping up crack like they'd been doing it all their lives. Freeway was a proud teacher at this moment, looking at his students successfully complete their task. Now it was time for the final test, getting a fiend to try the shit. Trigga went out for a minute and came back with a woman that lived down the hall. She was in her late twenties, and she wasn't bad looking at all.

"Aight, where it's at?" Freeway pulled out the crackpipe and placed two rocks in it, before handing it to her. "What the fuck kind of weed is this?" she asked, as she sat at the table.

"Just smoke the shit," Trigga pulled out the fifty dollars he promised her, and she took the pipe.

"I ain't trying to die, Trigga, shit." Regret was creeping into her pores as she eyed the glass pipe suspiciously. She loved to have fun, and there wasn't much she hadn't done in her 27 years of life, but this she was unsure of.

"You ain't gon' die," Freeway told her, impatiently.

"Well, you hit the shit." She pushed it his way.

"I don't smoke," he said casually, as he pushed it back to her.

"Shit, I got $100 for you," Rich said anxiously, pulling out a knot of money, and tossing it on the table.

Her eyes followed the money as Trigga tossed the $50 he promised her on the top. "Aight, but Trigga, if I wake up dead, I'm haunting yo' ass."

"Aight, bet," was all he said, as she held the pipe to her lips, and Freeway did the honor of putting the lighter to it.

They all watched as she sucked back the smoke, and it seemed as if time stood still. Suddenly, it was like she was moving in slow motion as she fell back into the chair. For a minute, they thought her ass was about to pass out, and then she finally moved.

"What the fuck yo'," she slurred, high as a kite. "Shiiiitttttt, I can't even." Desperately she tried to focus, but she needed a minute. Sitting back, she relaxed and allowed the high to take over her body. For the next five minutes, she was in heaven. It was almost like she had an out of body experience and had never felt so free in her life. Like a jack in the box, she sprang up and reached for the pipe. "Let me hit that shit again."

All the guys looked at each other and knew it was a rap for any other crew getting money after this. This was it, and it would solidify that Zoo Crew was officially them niggas in the streets. That night before they left, Trigga secured them a Coke connect, and Freeway had come up with the name ReadyRock for the product, and they were good to go. In a couple of weeks, their first shipment would come in, and they needed to be ready.

"Aight, we need somebody to whip this shit up," Rich said, rubbing his temples. They had already secured a spot to cook out of, but they had yet to think of anyone to cook for them. They could do it, but they had to push it and watch the corners, there was no way they could do all three. Nah, they needed another person.

"Shit, I'll ask Faith to do it." Stacks shrugged.

"Faith?" Sam asked to make sure he was serious.

"Yeah, Faith."

"You sure you wanna put ya girl out there like that?"

"It ain't like she gon' be selling the shit, don't nobody even have to know she cooking it but us three. I mean, who else can we trust with this shit? For right now, she's all we got."

Sam and Rich looked at each other, and they agreed with Stacks. "Well, as long as she leaves Janae's big mouth ass out of it, we cool."

"Definitely." Rich shook his head, not needing that headache.

"I'll make sure she knows what's up." Standing up, he grabbed the house phone to page Faith. "And once the money starts rolling in, my shorty gon' need her shit off the top." They looked at him with blank faces, and he scoffed. "Shit, what y'all thought? Off the top."

They laughed, nodding their heads agreeing. Rich was going to pay her anyway, but they already knew how Stacks was coming about Faith, so it was nothing. "Ya shorty?

"Oh, you claiming her now?" Sam joked as he nudged Rich to watch for Stack's reaction.

"Fuck y'all." He flipped them off as he sat by the phone, waiting for her to call back. Not even ten minutes later and the phone was ringing. When she called back, Stacks told her to meet them at Sam's spot, and she agreed, telling him she would be over there in like an hour. "Aight, she'll be here in a few."

"Cool." Rich nodded as he rolled a joint.

"All jokes aside, what's really up with y'all?" Sam asked for no particular reason other than he just wanted to know.

Stacks shrugged not really into gossiping, but he answered anyway. "You know I ain't into the whole relationship thing," he told them, having his reasons for shying away from the subject. "But we chillin'."

Sam nodded his head, understanding what Stacks was saying and changed gears. "Who shorty that be with them? The new girl?"

Rich perked up at Sam, asking about her as he kept quiet, waiting for Stack's response. A few times since that day they were in front of the building, he'd seen her in passing. He hadn't spoken to her yet, but he had his eyes on her.

"I don't know. She Janae cousin or some shit like that. I think she just moved out this way tho. Why, you tryna' talk to her?"

"Nah, my ass just being nosey."

Rich allowed his body to relax a little bit, knowing his man's wasn't trying to get at his girl. Of course, she wasn't his just yet, but he was sure he would get his chance to mack soon. They stayed in the house kicked back until there was a knock on the door. Stacks went to answer it. Sure, it was Faith.

Their eyes connected as soon as the door opened. Faith stood there, licking her lips as she gave him the once over. Stacks was just so fine to her, like, everything about him. His high-top fade had a slope and he had it colored, with a hint of honey blonde in the front. He dressed the best, and the gold tooth on his side tooth had her drooling every time he smiled. "What's up, baby?" Stepping up to him, she held his gaze as she pressed her lips to his.

Stacks grabbed her by the ass, pulling her close as he deepened the kiss. Now he didn't know if what he felt for Faith was love, but it was strong like, he knew that for sure. Besides, their budding romance, they had history. Faith knew his deepest darkest secrets, and he knew for sure that he could trust her with his life. On that alone, he knew she was just what they needed.

"Nothing, just chillin with the crew." He answered once he finally released her.

"Okay, I see y'all being bums." She joked, walking into the apartment, "What's up, y'all?" Respectfully, she spoke, waving her plum-colored nails in the air.

Faith was 5' 2", with almond brown skin and hazel eyes. She wore her hair with a bang and the rest back in a ponytail most days, but today she had it down. Nearly touching her shoulders, her hair bounced with every step. Once Stacks was seated, all the men looked up at her as she sat her bag on the table before leaning up against it. "So, what's up?"

"I need a favor," Stacks spoke up, looking her dead in her eyes.

"Consider it done." She smirked, winking at him.

The other guys rolled their eyes as Stacks tried not to blush. "Faith, I need you to be serious because this shit we about to get into is heavy."

"What shit?" She asked, and Rich tossed a vial of crack to her with a red top. Swiftly she fought to catch it in her hands. "Fuck is this?" Carefully, she examined the contents and rolled her eyes. "I know y'all ain't selling pieces of fucking soap. That's bullshit…"

"Yo'," Sam busted up with laughter. "Get ya girl, fam."

"What? That's what it looks like to me," Faith said before tossing the vial back. "So, what is it?"

"ReadyRock," Stacks spoke up. "It's some new shit we about to start pushing, and we need someone we can trust to cook it up for us."

Putting two and two together, she figured she was the someone. "So, you want me to fake and bake pies of whatever that shit is?!" She nearly yelled.

"Shhh, keep ya damn voice down." Jumping from his seat, he advanced on her.

"Fuck you, what kind of bullshit you on?"

"See, you gon' make me smack the shit out of you, over something stupid." Grabbing her by the arm, Stacks all but drug her into the bedroom. Faith snatched away from him once they were in the bedroom, and before she could buck up, he pushed her against the wall. "Yo', shut the fuck up and listen. You ain't even give me a chance to say the shit how I need to say it before you popped off."

"Because it sounds like you want me to make drugs for you?" Folding her arms across her chest, she waited for him to tell her she was wrong. Her eyes challenged him, and he just looked away, confirming what she knew. "Fuck, Landon." She pushed him back and walked away from him.

Stacks knew she was mad for real when she pulled out his government, and his tough-guy act faded. "Babe, just hear me out." He turned her back around and made her look at him. "It's just temporary, just until we can get someone else to do it. Just this one favor?" Taking a deep breath, Faith shook her head. "Won't nobody know except me, Rich, and Sam. We were gon' pay you and everything…"

"Fuck the money, I ain't trying to go to jail."

"Faith, I ain't gon' let shit happen to you, and you know that. I'mma be right there." Walking closer to her, he wrapped her in his arms. "You know you the only one I got, and I need you to come through for me." Stacks grabbed her by her hand as he gently tilted her head up so that their lips met. "You trust me, right?"

Looking in his eyes, Faith couldn't deny that she did. "Yes, but…"

"Ain't no but's, if you trust me, know that I got you, and I ain't gon' let shit happen to you." Leaning down, he kissed her lips, hungrily seeking her tongue.

Deep inside, she could hear her mother telling her she was going to fuck up her life running with a no-good nigga, and maybe she was right. Whatever he wanted her to do, she was going to do it because she loved him, and she trusted that he wouldn't do her wrong. "Okay, I'll do it," she said, as every bit of her resolve chipped away, and she melted in his embrace.

Stacks wanted to jump and scream for joy, but he kept his cool. "Thank you," he kissed her lips again.

"But Stacks, I'm telling you…"

"I got you."

Nodding her head, she agreed, and the deal was sealed. They stayed in the room a little while longer before Stacks came out and walked her to the door. He kissed her lips once more, and she was off with promises to get up with him later. When Stacks closed the door, he turned around and walked back into the living room. Anxiously, Rich and Sam were waiting for the verdict.

"She's in."

"Smooth operator." Rich dapped him up laughing before Stacks slapped hands with Sam.

Chapter 2

Once Faith agreed to cook the drugs for Zoo Crew, she might as well had signed her life away. Every day, all day, Stacks had her cooking up dope for them. It took her a few times, but she got the hang of it. Once she made the batch right, they had the girl Trigga introduced them to test it for them. She came through with one of her friends, and like the first time, she was high as a kite. They had even sold her a few vials telling her to tell all her friends, and Rich was also kind enough to toss in a few extras.

They just knew for sure; the shit would be flying off the shelves. But things like that must only happen in the movies because here it was nearly a month later, and they still had product sitting. They were so excited to get started. They had Faith cook all the dope they had, and now they were waiting for the shit to start moving. For the moment, Zoo Crew was at a standstill, and they didn't know what to do. Never had they ever had to sell anything like this, and they didn't know the first thing about this particular drug.

"Fuck it. We gon' have to hit the streets and put the shit out there," Uncle Sam said, lost on ideas. "We gone have to get out there and find the customers."

Nodding his head, Rich agreed. The shit they were trying to sell was new around their way, and niggas weren't fuckin' with it. They had a few customers from ole girl, and her people, but shit was moving slow. "I need some fuckin' fresh air, this shit blows."

"Now, I'm with that shit." Stacks stood up, stretching his arms above his head. "Let's slide through the hood for a few."

"Cool beans," Rich said before heading to the bathroom. Once he was done, he grabbed his car keys, and together, the three of them left his apartment. "I need a damn drink."

"Oh, hell yeah, LQ still open, right?" Sam asked, just as they sat in the car.

"Should be," Stacks answered as Rich pulled off.

Neither of them were 21 yet, but on any given day, they could go to the liquor store and get whatever they wanted. Store owners were lax in the hood, and as long as you weren't a kid, you were considered old enough. In the store, they grabbed a pint of Hennessey, three forty-ounce bottles of Private Stock, and a pack of rolling papers. When they pulled up on the block, they parked a ways down and could see everyone was standing over by the park. After grabbing their things, they walked over there too. When they made it over to the small crowd, they said what's up to everyone because they knew just about everyone out there.

"Oh, shit, Zoo posted up. Y'all must've been bored," a girl name Amina said, and everyone chuckled at their expense.

"You know we had to fall through and bless you." Rich winked at her just as he took a seat. He allowed his back to rest against the park bench before he spread his legs wide. Before he took out the beer he'd bought, he took out the liquor bottle and tapped the top. Next, he held it out to Sam and Stacks, and they did the same. Every time they opened a liquor bottle, everybody who planned on drinking some had to tap the top.

"Yeah, whatever," she smiled, rolling her eyes. "Thought y'all would be over there at Leroy spot."

"What they got going on over there?" Sam asked.

"You know how he do; random-ass, sweaty ass parties that never end."

"And you ain't wanna go?"

"Nah, I ain't feel like all that tonight. I'm just trying to chill and catch some of this night air."

"I hear that," Sam agreed.

"I might slide through in a minute," Rich said, ready to see what he had going on. Leroy's basement parties were well known around the city. One thing for sure, you were guaranteed to have a good time.

"Well, I'm about to slide on this dice game real quick, tap me before you go over there," Stacks said, as he walked over to the other end of the benches from where they were sitting.

ARABIA

Rich tuned back into the conversation around him, half-listening to what everyone was talking about. The liquor was supposed to give him a much-needed break from work, but sitting here, that's all he could think about. Every now and then he would chuckle or throw a few words in, but his mind was elsewhere. Rich figured, tomorrow bright and early, he would distribute the work to his crew and post them up on every corner in the neighborhood. Everybody who was looking for coke was now going to get Ready Rock.

"Aight, I'm about to slide over to LeRoy spot." Rich stood up and tossed his empty beer bottle in the trash.

He walked down a little until he stood at the edge of the fence and tapped Stacks on the shoulder. Rich came over to tell Stacks he was ready to leave, and that's when he saw her. Rich took in her caramel skin that seemed to be illuminated under the streetlights and licked his lips. Her hair was different from the last time he'd seen her, but she still looked good. His eyes traveled from her neatly tucked ponytail to the jewelry adorning her neck and ears, down to her Adidas tracksuit, even her shell toes were crispy…She was so fresh, he had to have her.

"What's up?" Stacks looked up to him, breaking him from his trance. "You ready to go to Roy spot?"

A little caught off guard; Rich was stuck. There was no way he was about to miss this opportunity to kick shit with his future boo. "Uhh, nah, I'm trying to get next," he said, thinking quickly on his feet. Swiftly, he patted his pockets for cash, but before he could pull it out, the girls were walking up on him.

Rolling her eyes, Janae wasn't even in the mood to pop shit like she usually would. It was just one of those nights, and bullshit wasn't on her list of things to do. Without a word, she walked past Rich and Stacks, heading into the park.

"Oooh, Baby Father, I ain't know you were here." Faith smiled as she walked right over to Stacks, hugging him from behind.

Lynette was slowly strolling behind Faith as she took in the scene. One thing she could say about their neighborhood was there was always something jumping off and much to get into. Her eyes darted to Faith, who took off when she noticed Stacks playing dice, and she smiled. Their relationship was the cutest thing she'd ever witnessed. It was then she looked ahead of her and saw the guy she now knew as Rich Tony standing there. Tall and handsome he was, and from what little she knew, he was a lady's man. From Faith, she also knew Zoo Crew was in the streets, and Rich Tony, aka King Zoo himself, was the leader. If Janae was telling it, he was the devil himself.

The moment their eyes connected; she could feel flutters in her stomach. The feeling was almost comparable to riding a roller coaster, and the feeling in your stomach right before the ride drops, that's how she felt at that moment. Ignoring the feelings she was getting, Lynette politely smiled as he hit her with a head-nod. Shaking her head, she looked away, knowing she needed to cut the shit. A sorry ass nigga was the reason she was living with her aunt now, so the last thing she wanted to be was caught up. But she figured it was cool to at least look and that she did as she glanced over her shoulder once more.

"What up, Rich?" Faith smirked, watching him check her homegirl out.

He pulled his eyes from Lynette and looked down at Faith, "What's good, sis?" Smirking, he pulled her in for a hug.

"Yeah, aight, I see you, nigga." She laughed as she fell into his embrace.

"What? I ain't do nothing."

"Aight, I don't wanna have to fuck Zaria up, but I will behind that one." She nodded her head towards Lynette.

Rich looked over to where she was, and his eyes landed on her quietly, playing the background as usual. "Nah, you know ain't shit going on with Zaria ass. I don't even fuck with her no more, not even a little bit."

"Mmm-hmmm, I hear you talking." Faith knew better, but she let him make it. Zaria was bat shit crazy about him, and he was just as dumb about her. No, he probably didn't love her, love her, but something kept him fucking with her all these years later.

"For real, but what's up with ya homegirl? She gon' stay around here for good?"

"As far as I know," she shrugged.

"Cool, she got a man?"

"Look at you, like you care." Laughing, she tossed her head back.

"Right, I'mma still try to talk to her, but she seems like the one nigga at a time type." Rich didn't know her from a can of paint, but he could tell by the way she carried herself that she wasn't on that.

"Honestly, I don't know."

Nodding his head, Rich was done drilling her for info and was ready to chat with Ms. Lynette, when Stacks tapped him on the shoulder. "Yeah?"

"You up," was all he said, as he grabbed Faith by the hand, and pulled her over to the benches.

Turning around, Rich had forgotten all about getting next in the dice game. Looking back to the benches, he shook his head and reached in his pocket, pulling out a few twenties. "I'm in."

When Faith and Stacks made it to everyone else, they mixed and mingled until they sat down. Smiling at Lynette, she beckoned her closer. "Tony asked about you," she whispered in her ear, pulling her closer.

Licking her lips, she held back a smile, forcing her dimples to dent her cheeks. "No, he didn't, did he?"

"Yes, he did, don't tell Janae because she a hoe, but I mean he is THE NIGGA out this way, so you might wanna jump on that one."

Lynette looked his way, pondering if she wanted to go there, and she didn't. "Nah, I'm just chilling right now. After all that shit with Hines, I ain't even got the energy." Her eyes found him again, and she moaned. "He fine anyway, but nah." She laughed with Faith, who understood what she was saying, but knew Rich wasn't having that.

Stacks wrapped his arm around Faith's waist before kissing her ear. It had been a few days since he'd seen her, and he really missed her. He wasn't sure if she knew it or not, but he needed her on some real shit. "Where you been?"

"Around," she smiled, falling into him.

"See, here you go wit that shit." He tightened his hold on her. "You gon' make me spazz."

Giggling, she surrendered to his strength. "Nah, I just been kicking it in the house and chilling with the girls…Nuttin' really. What y'all doing out this way?"

"Shit, we been so busy lately, figured we'd pop out. We were supposed to be sliding through Roy spot; I guess we gon' go when Rich finishes."

"Oh, he having a party?" Faith asked, thinking she was about to go slide to the party with them. Nodding his head, Stacks answered her question.

While everyone was mingling and minding their business, Uncle Sam was kicked back, peeping the scene. He sat with one leg extended, and the other tucked by the bench, as he looked to Janae. "This the quietest you ever been. You feel alright? Are you sick?"

Holding her head back, Janae fell into a fit of giggles. "No, I'm not sick."

"Well, shit, something wrong with you."

"Nah, I'm just chillin. I'll fight with y'all tomorrow." For a minute, they went back and forth, surprisingly falling into a pleasant conversation.

Janae was a piece of work. "You ain't too bad when you kicked back."

"Yeah, and you ain't too bad when y'all ain't terrorizing the neighborhood." Rolling her eyes, she remembered how much she really didn't like Zoo Crew.

Now it was his turn to laugh. "We ain't half as bad as you make us out to be."

Turning her cup up to her lips, she peeked at him over the top. Her eyes scanned his fade, then fell on to his thick lips. Sam wasn't skinny, but he was far from fat, and Janae liked her men a little chunky and tall. Thankfully, Sam was both. He could dress, and he had money, and that was a bonus in her eyes. "Yeah, yeah, I hear you talking." After actually chilling with Sam, she could admit that he may not have been that bad, but the rest of those niggas were canceled.

"Yeah, but I need you to feel me." His eyes bore into hers, letting her know he was serious. "Let me take you out?" Immediately, she began to choke on her drink. Chuckling, Sam shook his head. "Damn, you wild."

Getting herself together, Janae was utterly taken aback. "Out? Like, on a date?" The words barely escaped her lips. Just the thought of her dating a dude from Zoo repulsed her.

"Nah, not a date. Just us kicking it, on some low-key shit, away from the hood for a minute."

Her eyes squinted as she looked at him seriously; all jokes were aside at this point. "Kick it with me? You must be drunk," she laughed. "You've had enough." Janae went to snatch his cup out of his hand, and Sam seized her arm.

"Don't disrespect me like that."

The authority in his voice made Janae back down, and her heart flutter. "You really wanna go out?" She looked in his eyes and asked after a moment of silence had passed between them. The look he gave her answered her question without him ever saying a word. "Okay."

<><><><><>

Initially, Rich really didn't want to play dice with the guys, but now he was up about $400, and he was into it. He held his arms out, asking the men gathered around to give him some room. "Aight, here we go." Blowing on the dice, he rolled them, and they landed on seven, causing the men to go wild. "Give me my shit!" He yelled, snatching all the money off the ground.

"Fuck that, bet it back?" A guy named Rome asked, trying to get some of his money back.

Before Rich could respond, he saw Stacks, and them walking his way, headed out the park. "Where y'all going?"

WE MADE LOVE IN THE 80'S

"To Roy's,"

"Aight, me too." Turning around, he looked at Rome and shrugged. "Maybe next time."

When he caught up, to everyone else, he was in the back, walking behind Lynette, with his hands tucked in his pocket. Rich admired her frame from the back and found himself intrigued by the way she walked. Her posture was perfect, causing her butt to sit up nicely, and it was always her right foot in front of her left as her hips swayed from side to side. His focus was on her, but everyone else seemed to focus on him. Every few steps, someone was calling his name or shaking his hand as he graciously accepted the love.

"I ain't know I was walking wit a celebrity," Lynette giggled, as she turned around eyeing him.

"Who me?"

"No, the owl behind you."

Laughing at her little joke, Rich shook his head, loving that she had a sense of humor. "Nah, I ain't that shorty."

"Mmm." Turning around, she continued to walk as he walked closer behind her. "Well, either that or everyone around here loves them some Rich, or is it King Zoo tonight?"

Nodding his head, it was clear that she'd done her homework on him. "Tonight, it's just Tony."

Smiling, she looked away as he walked beside her towering over her small frame. "Is that like a privilege?

Tony took a moment to think about his answer. "I guess. I mean most of these hoes out here only want Rich, and the streets only respect King Zoo, it seems like don't nobody give a fuck about Tony."

Lynette could hear the honesty in his words and felt kind of bad for him. She couldn't imagine being surrounded by all these people and still feeling alone. "Well, I've never been a hoe, and I could care less about the streets, so I'll take Tony." She finished just as they arrived at Roy's and was immediately whisked away.

ARABIA

Their eyes connected as she glanced back over her shoulder. The smirk that spread across his face caused her center to pool. He was beautiful, sexy, and alluring. She wanted to know more, but now just wasn't the time. Currently, her life was upside down, and dating was not the way to turn it around.

Like a moth to a flame, Rich's eyes followed Lynette until he couldn't see her anymore. Only then was he able to focus on what was going on around him. Rich stepped further into the party and took in the scene. People were packed from wall to wall as they bounced to the music. There were separate groups battle dancing and breaking all over the living room. Bopping his head, Rich spoke to everyone he knew as LL Cool J's Radio blasted from the speakers. Once he made his rounds around the party, Rich grabbed a bottle of beer and faded into the background.

While Rich and Uncle Sam held up the wall, the girls, along with Stacks, found their way to the kitchen. Soon as they walked in, their eyes immediately went to all the bottles of liquor decorating the counters.

"Oh shit, it's about to be on!" Faith yelled, clapping her hands together as she headed over to grab the cups. "Y'all takin' shots?"

"I'm in," Keisha shrugged, and Janae nodded, going with whatever they were doing.

Lynette walked in behind them as her eyes roamed the room. Faith went to hand her a cup, and she politely declined. Hopping on the counter, she took a seat and watched them take shots. They were all laughing and joking around, and every now and then she would put her two cents in.

"You don't drink?" Some random guy came out of nowhere, sliding beside her.

"Nah, not straight like that." Giving him the once over, he was alright looking, but he wasn't Tony, not even close.

Admiringly, he eyed her. "I respect that." After sitting his cup on the counter, he turned back to her. "Jeff."

For a minute, she watched his hand hanging in the air before her eyes met his again. "Lynette."

WE MADE LOVE IN THE 80'S

"Nice to meet you." His lips curved into a smile, and she turned her head rolling her eyes as she released his hand. "So, Lynette, you wanna dance, or you plan on holding up this counter all night?"

Before she could say no, Rich walked in the kitchen, and his eyes immediately fell on her. She could see the tension on his face as he looked from her to Jeff, nodding his head. Their eyes stayed connected as he walked over, and Lynette couldn't stop smiling.

"What's up, Jeff?" He spoke, sliding beside Lynette and wrapping an arm around her neck. Not batting a lash, Rich eyed him, almost daring him to jump bad.

Jeff squinted as he looked from Lynette to Rich and back again. He was confused as Rich's eyes stayed locked on him. "My bad, fam, I ain't know that was you."

Nodding his head, Rich let that be that and turned his attention back to the group.

"Mmm, don't come over here cockblocking like you got it like that." Lynette sassed as she unwrapped his arm from around her neck.

Smirking, Rich loved her feisty little ass. "Oh, I got it like that." After pulling his pants up, he looked to her. "I bet won't another nigga in here try to talk to you."

"And why can't another nigga talk to her Zoo?"

Rich heard the voice before he felt small hands mush him in the back of his head. Rolling his eyes, he definitely wasn't trying to do this shit tonight. "Don't hit me in my fucking head, yo'."

"I'mma do more than that in a minute." Placing her hands on her ample hips, "Now answer my fucking question; why can't another nigga talk to her?"

"Yeah, Zoo, why can't another nigga talk to me?" Lynette teased, giggling from behind him.

"Bitch, don't play with me. This shit between me and mine. I haven't addressed you, so you shouldn't be saying shit."

Rich looked over his shoulder to a smirking Lynette and then back to his ex. Well, she wasn't even really an ex, but he knew he fucked with her more than he fucked with any other girl. "Zaria, shut all that shit up because I don't belong to you."

"Since when? Everybody here knows what it is with us, so don't try to front because you got a new hoe on your dick."

"Move Tony," Lynette said as she went to get up, but he just backed into her resting between her legs so she couldn't move.

"Zaria, all everybody knows is that we fucked for a minute, and everybody knows that shit been a wrap."

The hurt in her eyes, couldn't be duplicated if someone paid her. Never had Rich ever in all the years, in all the fights, in all the arguments, had he ever played her in front of another female. That shit had her feeling smaller than small, and right now, she saw red. "Fuck you, nigga!" Before Rich or anyone else knew what was happening, she was swinging. "Stupid ass, you and this bitch."

Lynette saw her coming and just started swinging over Rich's head as she tried to get down to get to her. She had her all kinds of fucked up if she thought she was about to hit her. Even if she wasn't reaching for her, she was too fucking close. "Come on, bitch," soon as Rich moved just a bit, Lynette was able to get a hold of her hair, and it was over after that.

Once the other girls saw Zaria swing, they jumped on her ass too, and it was a full out brawl. It took Rich, Stacks, and Uncle Sam a minute to get them apart, but eventually, they did. They were still kicking, screaming, and yelling, but at least they had them separated.

"Y'all hoes wanna jump me!" Zaria raved, "I'mma catch all y'all in the streets."

"Bitch, I ain't no joke! Wherever, whenever hoe." In Rich's arms, she struggled to break free.

"Chill out," Rich whispered in her ear, as he held her in a bear hug. "She ain't worth it." Lynette heard what he was saying, and yeah, she wasn't worth it, but she was all hyped up now, and there wasn't any calming her down. She struggled against him until they were outside, and only then did he let her go. "Aight, aight, damn."

"Damn nothing. I will kill that bitch."

"And then what?" Rich looked down at her, smirking. His eyes were playfully dark, and the liquor that coated his breath gave her chills. "You wanna be sitting on murder charges before we make history."

With squinted eyes, Lynette didn't know what the fuck he was talking about. "History, nigga, right now all you doing is making me sick." This time she snatched away from him, and he let her go. "I don't even know you, and here goes the bullshit. Ain't shit but another nigga out here running around on his girlfriend, and I ain't got time. Shit, fucking with a nigga like you is why I'm up here now, and I ain't about to be caught up in no more bullshit."

He heard everything she said and just nodded his head. "I'mma come check you out later."

"Fuck you, Tony." With a middle finger over her head, she kept walking and headed home with the other girls.

Rich was used to her being quiet, laid back, and reserved. He loved that about her, there was a certain mystery he found sexy and appealing. But this shit she was on right now had his dick hard.

"You done fucked up now." Stacks walked up, shaking his head with Sam behind him. They all looked at each other seriously, before busting out laughing. "Yo', I couldn't stop Faith if I wanted to. Soon as Zaria swung, my bitch turned into fucking SheMan." Stacks joked, causing them to laugh harder.

"Man, I can't believe she came in here on that bullshit."

"Shit, you should've known it was gonna be some shit if she saw you all hugged up. You know Zaria ain't wrapped too tight."

"Well, she got wrapped tonight." Stacks continued to laugh. "Ole girl had her ass without the help."

"She ain't gon' fuck with you now." Sam continued to snicker.

"On Zoo, she gon' be mine."

At that moment, it was like everything stopped, and everyone was looking at him.

"Oh shit, Stacks, this nigga put that shit on the set." Sam slapped his shoulder, making sure he had his attention. Then he looked from Rich to Stacks, and again they burst out laughing.

Shaking his head, Rich couldn't stand their asses sometimes. It was late, and together they all decided to call it a night.

Chapter 3

After the fight that night at the party, Rich hadn't seen Lynette. She crossed his mind a few times over the months, but his main focus right now was hustling. They had a lot of work just sitting, and it was past time for them to move it. First things first, they had to map out exactly where they wanted to push. They decided that the alley right off the main street would be there stomping grounds. It was out of the publics' eye, and there wasn't much foot traffic out that way.

Next, they had to get organized. They separated their crew into three groups. First, they had their lieutenants, then they had the workers, and then they had the lookouts. Once they had everything ready to go, Rich, Stacks, and Sam went out to local parties, bars, and local events, practically giving their shit away. Sam rationalized that giving away samples would bring them more business and loyal customers in the end, and Stacks nor Rich was trying to hear it. Nevertheless, they went with it and was thanking him later.

In a matter of months, they had shit running like clockwork, and money was pouring in like water. To people around the way, it seemed as if they were getting money and had become the niggas to see overnight, but they knew this shit took hard work and dedication. They weren't where they wanted to be, be they were for sure on their way.

"Shit, we gon' need another apartment in a minute," Stacks said, as he tied the black garbage bag filled with money up and placed it in the closet on top of the other bags, they had in there.

"Hell yeah, we should move the shit to a house," Sam suggested.

"Nah," Rich was ready to chime in. "It's too many ways into a house and too many out. At least at the apartment, if they try to hit us, they might get in, but the muthafuckas ain't getting out."

Nodding their heads, they agreed that it made sense, but Sam had another idea. "Well, if we gon' keep all this shit in an apartment, we need two. Keep this one for the work and get another apartment out there in the Springs somewhere for the money. Having all this shit up here together is a setup. Somebody kick that shit in, and we gon' be fucked up."

"Niggas liable to take our head, they find out all this shit in here," Stacks said, as he closed the closet.

Rich figured they could do that. "Aight, Stacks get Faith to see if she could look out on that for us."

"Faith ain't got no real income to get it. She does hair and shit, but we need somebody with paperwork."

"Well, y'all already know Janae ass ain't having it." Sam shook his head, laughing. Rich laughed with him knowing it was nothing but the truth. Sam and Janae had been talking a little over the months, but she was damn sure feeding him with a long spoon. "What about Janae peoples, Lynette? She in school and shit."

Rich thought about it and nodded his head. It wasn't that they ain't know any females, but the bitches they fucked they couldn't trust. Not for no shit like this, nah, they needed the girls to come through for them. "I'll chop it up with her."

"Shit, you better hope she wanna talk to ya ass." Stacks laughed.

Shaking his head, Rich knew this shit wasn't going to be easy, but fuck it. He was Rich Tony, King Zoo, and women dropped their panties just to get a whiff of him. Surely, he could get Lynette to do him this solid.

<><><><><>

A few days later, Rich found himself posted up outside of the city college, Lynette attended. Gone were the good ole summer days with beautiful weather; they were long gone. They were into the brutal fall, the type of fall that felt like winter had already arrived but was still a few weeks away. No matter how harsh the wind was today, he was leaned up against his car with his fur hat pulled over his eyes, and his sheepskin and fur coat pulled tightly around his body.

Swiftly, he pushed his gazelle glasses up off his nose, and when he looked back to the entrance, there she was. "Damn," he said under his breath, before licking his bottom lip just a little.

Lynette walked out of the building, and when she looked to the parking lot, she wondered just who the hell was posted up like this was Harlem or somewhere. She could admit the whole look was cute, even the red Saab that sparkled playing the background. The closer she walked, and the person actually came into view; she noticed it was Rich and fell into laughter. Gripping her book bag tight, she walked over to him, continuing to laugh. "Who you all dressed up to see?" She looked in his eyes as her fingers gripped one of the two rope chains that dangled loosely on his chest in her hands playing with them.

Rich tried not to blush but being this close to her had him feeling all giddy, like a bitch. "I ain't dressed up."

"Oh, this just the tip you on now that you making real money then…Guess it's really Rich Tony today, huh?"

He laughed, shaking his head, "Nah, it's always Tony with you."

Nodding her head, she stepped back, not wanting to get caught up in his games. "Well, aight, I'mma let you make it before one of your little girlfriends call themselves getting froggy."

She went to step away, and he quickly grabbed her hand. "Nah, this ain't that, I'm here to see you." The way her lips twisted let him know she ain't believe him. "For real, and I ain't never really apologize for how that shit went down."

They stood there quietly, waiting on the other to speak, and Lynette was the first to sound off. "And you still haven't," she sassed, placing her hand on her hip. Rich looked away before he chuckled, flicking his nose with his index finger. "I'm waiting." When his eyes met hers again, she smiled, unable to help it. Rich Tony was just too fine, and he knew it.

Rich gazed at her, allowing his eyes to travel from her brown knee-length boots to her skintight jeans and her brown leather coat. Her hair was parted down the middle and laid straight on either side. There was a mole by her lip, he was almost sure wasn't there the last time he'd seen her, but it was cute either way. He was digging her like they could be exclusive type of stuff. Rich didn't know what it was, he couldn't tell you if you paid him, but he was drawn to her.

Stepping up closer to her, they stood chest to chest as he hovered over her. He was so close, Lynette had to look up to see him, and when she did, he grabbed her hand. "I'm sorry, and you ain't never gon' have to worry about no shit like that happening again."

She had to look away because the pull she felt when he looked at her was too strong. "I guess I can accept that."

"You guess?" He turned her face and made her look at him. "You ain't got no choice, you about to be Mrs. Zoo, and that means you're untouchable." Lynette couldn't stop the laughter that erupted from her soul. She was laughing, and Rich was standing there serious as a heart attack. "And you laughing at me like I'mma joke."

"Look, I think you're cute and everything. Hell, I might like you just a tad, but I ain't..."

Before another word fell from her lips, he hushed her with a kiss. A sweet kiss that wasn't rushed or forced. It felt natural, and he was so gentle and softer than she'd ever imagined. Whatever she was saying, Lynette was ready to take that shit the fuck back. What he say, *Mrs. Zoo*? Yeah, she was feeling all that. After teasing her with his tongue, he pecked her lips a couple of times before pulling back. Smirking, he licked his lips, "You sexy as hell. You know that?"

"Stop gassin' me." She smiled, showing all thirty-two of her pearly whites. Shifting her book bag on her shoulder, she looked up to him. "So, you wanted to see me?"

Nodding his head, Rich wrapped an arm around her waist. "Let's get out of here." She hesitantly allowed him to usher her to his car, and when they got there, he opened the door for her as well. Rich was a perfect gentleman on his best behavior, and she was waiting for a bitch to jump out of the woods, trying to fight her. "So, Tony, where we going?"

"I'm hungry, you hungry?" He cut his eyes to her, and she nodded. "So, I guess we going on a date."

Lynette rolled her eyes. "A date, huh?"

"Yeah, might as well mark this shit in your calendar." He laughed, and she fell into a fit of giggles.

Rolling her eyes, he was making her sick already. It was quiet in the car before Rich turned on the stereo and *The Message* played by

Grand Master Flash, and Rich began to nod his head. Lynette smiled as he rapped the words and jumped in on the second verse, shocking the hell out of him. After that, they laughed and joked all the way to the restaurant. About thirty minutes later, they pulled up to a little low-key spot on the west side of town. Still, on his best behavior, Rich hopped out and opened her door, before guiding her into the restaurant.

The restaurant wasn't that spacious and had an old school mom and pop feel to it. Lynette almost turned her nose up but caught herself. "You come here often?"

"A couple of times a week." He laughed as he took off his hat and coat. "It ain't much, but the food is good."

"It better be, since this our first date and everything." Lynette grabbed a menu and was looking over it when the little waitress walked up.

"What up, King Zoo?" She blushed nearly drooling over him. "Can I get you anything to drink?"

Rich didn't say anything. He just motioned his hand towards Lynette, looking directly at her, and paying the young waitress no mind.

"I'll have pink lemonade."

"Okay, and for you?" Rich told her, sweet tea, and she quickly jotted it down. "I'll be right back with your drinks."

When she was gone, Lynette tilted her head, looking at him knowingly.

"What?"

"Nothing."

"Shit, I can't help these bitches be dying for a chance to speak to me."

Shaking her head, she wasn't even listening anymore. "So, what's up with you?"

"Shit, ain't nothing up." He shrugged. "I'm just trying to take care of my people and live a good life." Rich kept his eyes on her and continued to speak. "Right now, I'm trying to get to know you."

Rolling her eyes, she blushed. "You can stop now."

"That's real shit though." He was going to ask her a question, but the waitress came back with their drinks and took their food orders. When she left, he continued. "So, ya ex nigga, the reason you out here?"

"Something like that."

"Nah, at the party, you were rolling ya neck, poppin' shit. You said he was the reason, so what happened?"

Laughing, she cringed at the thought of that night. His bitch had her way out of character. "I mean ain't nothing happen; not just one thing in particular. It was just always some shit." He egged her on, wanting her to elaborate. "Like he was running around on me, bitches popping up on me...Just bullshit. I would break up with him, and it never lasted long, so I moved to get away from all that."

"How long was y'all together?"

"Four years."

"Four years! How old are you now?"

"Nineteen."

With the wave of his hand, he dismissed all that she was talking about. "That's kid shit."

"It wasn't kid shit when ya bitch ran up on me...Y'all on the same shit to me."

Rich strongly disagreed. He wasn't on that type of time at all. "Nah, me and Zaria ain't never been on anything exclusive. We been kicking it for a good minute though, the same type of shit you were on...Fucking with each other on and off, saying I wasn't fucking with her anymore, and somehow, she'd end up back in my bed type shit. Yeah, we were on that for a few years now, but a few weeks before the party, she was wilding about some dumb shit, and I told her I was done fucking with her."

WE MADE LOVE IN THE 80'S

"So, you haven't fucked with her since?"

"Nah, I put that on Zoo." Rich held his right hand high above his head, and Lynette laughed.

"You ain't put it on Zoo, did you?"

"Shit, Zoo comes before God. If I put that shit on them, I ain't gon' lie."

Her face scrunched. "It's that deep with your gang?" he nodded his head, and she asked why.

"Because when I was out here fucked up, and I ain't have nothing or no one, I always had Zoo," Rich continued to tell her how they all came out of some fucked up situations, and together, they pulled each other up. "So, it ain't just a gang, this shit here is deeper than that. We have a brotherhood, and what we building right now is like our wildest dreams come true."

Tears nearly welled in her eyes as he spoke. There was so much pain in his words, yet he spoke so casually. She wondered how it was even possible. Looking at him, she wanted to love him and provide him all the comfort and security he never had. "I'm sorry."

"Don't be, it's cool, it's, life and shit happen."

"That doesn't mean it ain't messed up." She cut him off. "I don't know all of what you've been through, but if nobody ever told you, I'm sorry."

The waitress came over, cutting the tension that had accumulated in the air. She placed their food in front of them as they continued to stare at each other.

When she was gone, Rich spoke. "Thank you," was all he said before they dug into their food.

Lynette had to admit that the food was the bomb, and after kicking it with Rich, she didn't even care that it was a hole in the wall. He showed her that wherever they were, she was guaranteed to have a good time just enjoying his company, and she had done just that.

ARABIA

After dinner, Rich took the long way back to her building because he wasn't ready for her to leave just yet. Lynette wasn't complaining either because she was having the best date of her life, just being in his presence.

Finally, after spending hours together, they were parked in front of her building. "So, how was our first date?"

Smiling, Lynette nodded her head. "It was cool, really cool."

Rich grabbed her hand and intertwined their fingers, "So that means we can go out again, right?"

"Hell yeah, I'm Mrs. Zoo." They both laughed at that, and she looked over at him. "From now on, every Wednesday is date night, and you better not miss one."

"You got it." He looked at her, just studying her face. "Come here," Rich pulled her into him and kissed her lips. This time she was prepared. Lynette watched his lips like they were moving in slow motion as they approached hers. Sucking them up, she fed him her tongue and got lost in his being.

This time Lynette was the first to pull back. He smiled at the dreamy look in her eyes and shook his head. Rich didn't know if love was real, but if it was, he was sure it felt something like what he was feeling now. From his console, he pulled a pen and a piece of paper. Quickly, Rich jotted down his pager number, assigning her the code 1215, which was the date of their first date, and then he wrote down his house number. "Make sure you use it whenever, for whatever."

Lynette took the paper promising to do just that before he stepped out of the car. He bopped over to her side and opened the door before holding his hand out for hers. Together they walked to the entrance of the building and stood face to face.

"Well, I guess I'll talk to you later."

"You can bet that." He kissed her lips once more and stood back, allowing her to enter the passcode to get into the building.

Once the door was open, she turned to him and smiled. "Good night, Tony."

WE MADE LOVE IN THE 80'S

At the door, he watched Lynette walk through the lobby of the building until he couldn't see her anymore. Only then did he head back to his car. Once he was inside, he just sat there for a moment thinking. Smiling, he replayed his day with Lynette over in his head. Rich had a good time with her, way better than he expected. Now that he'd at least broken ground with her, he was really going to take their relationship seriously. Because of that, he couldn't ask her to put anything in her name for the benefit of their growing drug empire. Nah, he was going to have to find another way.

Chapter 4

When Lynette made it back home, it was well after eight o'clock in the evening, and she was sure Janae was worried sick. As quietly as she could, she turned her key in the lock and opened the door. She was trying not to disturb anyone, but it was no use because soon as the door opened, Janae flicked the light on.

"Where the hell have you been?" Janae ran over, hugging Lynette tight. "I was worried sick about you."

"I'm sorry, cuz. I ain't mean to make you worry."

"I'm sorry, my ass. Where the hell have you been?"

Lynette walked past her and headed for her bedroom with Janae right on her heels. "Hello!"

"I ran into Tony at school." Biting her lip, Lynette tried not to smile.

Rolling her eyes, Janae couldn't even say she was surprised. "Go figure. What he have you out there, knocking off banks?"

Chuckling, Lynette looked at her like she was crazy. "No, girl, bye!"

"So, where the hell you been? I hope you ain't let that heathen talk you outta ya little panties." Janae prayed her cousin didn't go out like that.

Holding her hands up, Lynette had to stop her rant. "You need to relax. No, I didn't sleep with him, and no, I wasn't out robbing banks. We went to dinner, and I had a really good time. It was our first date."

"Ugh," holding her mouth, Janae couldn't take the love in Lynette's eyes, "I'm going to be sick."

Shaking her head, Lynette continued to laugh as she undressed. "Well, get it all out ya system because Tony and I are going to be together a lot."

WE MADE LOVE IN THE 80'S

"A lot?"

"Yes, you're now looking at Mrs. Zoo." Lynette skipped down the hallway with her towel in hand, laughing as Janae fake passed out on the bed.

In the bathroom, Lynette took off her underclothes and prepared her shower. Never in a million years would she have thought this day would've turned out how it did. The smile that covered her face was genuine and stayed put the more she thought about him. For sure, she was attracted to Tony, but it was more than that. It was the way he towered over her. It was the way his eyes seemed to sparkle when he looked at her, the way his right eyebrow raised slightly when she caught him deep in thought, or the way her name rolled off his tongue effortlessly. Shaking her head, she didn't know what would become of them, but she was ready.

After Lynette showered, she wiped the mirror and looked at her reflection before she put her bed clothes on. She didn't understand Janae's beef with Zoo Crew, but she was kind of over the dramatics. Now she knew why Faith told her not to tell Janae about Tony and a part of her wish she hadn't. "Wheeeewww, good." She sighed with relief that Janae was no longer in her room. Quickly, she closed the door and locked it before hanging her towel up. Lynette didn't even bother to grab the remote as she plopped down on her bed. Over on her dresser was the piece of paper Tony had given her with his numbers on it.

Lynette debated if she wanted to call him or not. He had only left her just a couple of hours ago, and she didn't want it to seem like she was sweating him already. But Tony also said that she could call him whenever for whatever. Hours had passed before she decided she would page him. That way, if he wanted to talk to her, he would hit her back.

Her heart practically beat out of her chest with each button she pressed, and she nearly died when she entered the code, he'd given her. This was it. This was the test to see if he was all talk and no action. He had given her that code, so he knew it was her paging him, and he had better call her back, or their fake relationship or whatever they were was going to be over. Her mind was made up, so she pulled her covers back and climbed in the bed to wait.

"And it's midnight; he got thirty fuckin' minutes." Soon as she rolled over good, the phone was ringing. Her eyes ballooned as she kicked her covers with excitement. Calming herself, she had to take a deep breath. "Hello?"

"What's up, baby, you need something?" he asked, with the base in his voice rumbling into the receiver.

Laying back on her pillows, just the sound of his voice had her smiling. "Nah, I was just about to go to bed."

"And you wanted me to put you to sleep?"

Laughing, she said, "I guess so. What you doing?"

"With the crew, about to make a few moves, and I'm going in myself."

"Aight, well, I ain't gon' hold you. I just wanted to talk to you before I went to sleep."

Smiling, Rich nodded his head. "You got class tomorrow?" He listened to her tell him that she did, and he asked what time.

"Well, I don't have class until 10, so I'mma leave at like eight or so."

"Aight, well, get some sleep, and I'll talk to you tomorrow."

"Okay," she was about to hang up, but stopped. "Tony?"

"What's up?"

"Just don't hurt me, okay?"

It was as if time stood still. Rich was taken back by her request, and he didn't know what to say. He didn't want to lie to her and tell her that he would be a perfect nigga, so he had to be real with her. "Words gon' fail me; just know my intentions are good. I ain't gon' say, I won't fuck up one day, but I won't have you out here looking crazy. You, Mrs. Zoo, and I represent you just as much as you represent me. I done put you on the set, so you already know how I'm coming about you." Never would he intentionally hurt her, but he knew one day the shit was bound to happen.

She was scared their shit would end up how her relationship with Hines ended. Too many *what if's* and she'd promised herself that she would never be that girl again. "Okay," she said softly as tears welled in her eyes. Lynette didn't want to fall for him. She really didn't. Her mind was telling her to run and run fast, but one thing for sure, Tony had all the game, and she was eating that shit up.

"I got you, babe, stop thinking so hard, and get some sleep. I'll hit you tomorrow." They ended the call, and Rich stood there for a minute, thinking about their conversation. He knew what Lynette had been through with her ex, and he wasn't going to be that nigga.

"Aight, don't get lost on your way home from school," Janae warned, rolling her eyes at the naivety of her little cousin.

"Janae, I'm grown, and I'm good." Rolling her eyes, she was good on the warnings.

After kissing her cheek, Lynette was out the door. All the way downstairs, all Lynette could think about was that she was going to have to move sooner than she thought. The Lord knew she loved Janae, but she wasn't about to fight with her every day about Tony. It was only day two of their relationship; she didn't even want to know what it would be like six months or a year from now. Lynette didn't even want the headache.

Before she walked out of the building, she wrapped her scarf tight around her head and neck to brave the cold. She hated having to catch the bus and the train, especially when it was cold as hell outside. "Just two weeks and we go on break…just two weeks." She coached herself as she pushed the door open. "What are you doing here?"

"Waiting for you." Rich pushed himself off his car and walked towards the steps to greet her. "What else I'mma be doing here?"

"I don't know. I wasn't expecting to see you out here." He took her into his arms, and she folded into his embrace.

"You gotta go to school, and I ain't finna have you riding the train, so you rolling wit' me." Grabbing her hand, he didn't leave her any room to protest as he swooped her away. Rich had plans to take her to breakfast and then drop her off at school. He still had a few runs to make, but he planned on picking her up too.

Janae came downstairs just in time to see them pull off, and it annoyed her to see them together. But as Lynette said, she was grown, so she was finna let her ass be grown. All she could do was warn her, and from there, she was on her own. Janae wasn't no damn babysitter, and she wasn't about to start. From here on out, she was minding her business.

In the car, Rich and Lynette made small talk as he drove. She didn't have much to say because she was still sleepy, and she wasn't a morning person at all. Rich, on the other hand, wouldn't shut up. He was rapping the songs on the radio and saying random things, and Lynette couldn't do anything but laugh and shake her head.

"Why you always look so good every time I see you?"

Smiling, Lynette licked her lips. "What?"

"I'm just saying, I ain't seen you on a bad day yet."

"Because when you see me, I'm dressed to come outside."

"I wanna see you when you ugly…Hair all fucked up, dingy ass shirt. I need to see if you cute."

"Boy, shut up." She laughed, pushing his arm. "Shit, if I'm having that bad of a day, I ain't coming outside."

"Why it gotta be a bad day? Why can't you wake up all fucked up because we had a good night?"

Twisting her lips, Lynette tried to hide her excitement. "Well, that'll be the time you see me with my hair all fucked up in a dingy ass shirt."

Together they burst into laughter. "Shit, I ain't got no dingy t-shirts, nigga."

"The hell you don't, you in a dingy t-shirt now." She joked back as they continued to enjoy each other's company.

WE MADE LOVE IN THE 80'S

Not too far from her school, there was a little diner where they decided to have breakfast. Rich, still on his best behavior, opened doors and had even pulled out her chair. Once again, he let her order first and kept the conversation going. Lynette could tell that Rich was a natural leader. He had a take-charge attitude, and she liked it. Looking at the two of them together, someone would think they'd been together for years, but they were still just getting to know each other.

Rich took Lynette to school like he said he would, and every day after that. Like clockwork, he picked her up, they would have breakfast, he would take her to school, and then he picked her up. They had even maintained their Wednesday dinner dates. Rich promised her, and if nothing else, he was a man of his word.

Though he spent a lot of time wining and dining Lynette, Rich was still in the streets. Every day they had more customers and more territory. It took a little minute for things to get off the ground, but when they did, it was like a rocket had launched, and Zoo Crew was strapped to it. While Sam kept the crew in line, Stacks worked in recruitment, and it was up to Tony to map out new territory, while they all kept up with the money and product. Now, since Rich decided not to ask Lynette to put a crib in her name, it was up to him to figure that out too.

It took him nearly two months, but eventually, he found a coke head ass property manager that cut him a sweet deal on a house out in the country. The house was in a gated community, three bedrooms, and two baths. It was nothing too extravagant or too over the top, and that's what he liked about it. Rich was smart enough to know putting the house or anything in his name would trace shit right back to him if anything ever went wrong, so he thought ahead. Even though he was able to get keys and occupy the space, on paper, the house was listed as a model home, and the utilities were in the developer's name. It was all cool with him, long as his name wasn't on it, Rich didn't give a fuck. With this crossed off the list, he could breathe a little bit.

Briskly, Rich walked through the parking lot, kicking up snow with his Timberland boots. He was so over the cold weather and couldn't wait till warm weather rolled back around. He could see men patrolling the area as he approached the building and nodded his head in approval. Everyone was on point, and it was clear Sam was doing his job.

"Zoo," one of the guys said before whistling loudly.

ARABIA

That action let everyone know that one of their three bosses were coming through and that they'd better be on point. When Rich made it to the entrance, he nodded his head, and the other men saluted him, showing respect. In a matter of minutes, he jogged up the steps and was at the front door to one of their dope houses. Since they'd started, they had about five sprinkled over the city. They'd come a long way, but Rich knew they needed to get a little more organized. Shit wasn't sloppy, but they were still working out a few kinks.

"What up?" Rich greeted the guard before he stepped into the house. All the shit in this apartment was enough to land them under the jail, but this was just headquarters. In a minute, they would be moving and distributing the work to the other houses. "Shit, we need an old garage or something. It's small as fuck in here now."

"I told you," Stacks agreed, walking from the back.

"And, here you go with the I told you so's."

"Shit, I did." Stacks laughed. There was some other shit he needed to touch on, but he was going to wait until Sam got there.

The two of them busied themselves and small talk for a few before Sam arrived. Once they shook it up, they rolled a few joints and got down to business.

"Aight, so check it." Rich began, pulling out two sets of keys and tossing one to each of them. "I found a spot for the money. Low-key, real quiet area, a whole basement," he continued telling them about the details of the layout.

"That's what's up, good work." Stacks nodded, jingling the keys in his hands.

"About time you got Lynette ass on board." Sam threw in laughing with Stacks.

"Nah, I actually found somebody else to make that happen."

"Somebody else like who? I thought we already discussed this shit, and now you done switched up and put another muthafucka in our business." The last thing Stacks was trying to do was go to jail, and the way he saw it, Rich had just sealed his fate.

WE MADE LOVE IN THE 80'S

"Look calm yo' swole ass down! You forget if I fuck up, I go down too nigga." Rich based looking at Stacks like he was crazy. "And, I ain't want Lynette putting her name on that shit, so I made something else shake…"

"So, what you saying nigga? Ya bitch too good to put herself on the line for the crew, but mine ain't."

"Fuck are you talking about? You suggested ya girl do it, and I went along with it, shit ain't no deeper than that. You were cool with that shit. I'm not." He based with finality dripping from his tone. "Now, the house is out in Laurel Springs. The development manager sniffs coke and will do just about anything for a continuous supply. We don't have to worry about shit."

"Yeah, whatever nigga." Stacks twisted his lips, but the details were legit to him.

"Y'all fools crazy." Sam laughed, shaking his head.

Rolling his eyes, Rich wasn't bothered by Stacks little temper tantrum at all. "So, one of us gon' have to pretend to be a happy couple and move in that muthafucka. We can't look suspicious with different niggas running in and out." Both Rich and Stacks looked at each other and then to Sam.

"Oh, hell no, why me?" Sam asked, already wanting to say no.

"Because you be on that grown shit, this is just your speed."

"Nigga, we all the same age."

"Yeah, but you got maturity down packed. Me and Stacks keep too much shit going to be out that way."

Stacks agreed as Sam and Rich began to go back and forth. Now it was his turn to sit back and laugh.

"Shit, you ain't gotta stay there, but we need one familiar face coming through to take the money."

"Well, y'all can fight about that later. Faith wants to bring Keisha in to help her cook that workup. She said it's getting to be too much, and we need to find a warehouse, old garage, or something because we growing out of this shit."

"Why she wanna bring Keisha scary ass in?" Sam asked, already thinking it was a bad idea.

"You want her to keep cooking?" Rich asked, knowing the fuck he didn't. Not after all that shit he just talked.

Not even bothering to respond, Stacks stuck just middle finger up to him before he continued. "Because she trusts her."

Both Sam and Rich shrugged their shoulders, and Rich spoke up. "I don't think she needs to bring Keisha in. She scary as hell, and if shit goes bad, Faith gon' be responsible for cleaning that shit up."

Stacks sat back, thinking if he wanted her to take that chance. They were moving a lot of product now, and if even one person folded, they were all going down. So, he knew if Faith vouched for Keisha and she fucked up, Faith would have to kill her or worse something would happen to Faith. He didn't want to put her in that position. "I'll talk to her."

"If she doesn't wanna cook no more, I got a couple of people in mind to take over. Tell sis to let me know." Sam said.

"Who?" both Stacks and Rich asked.

"My sister was looking to get put on. You know her crazy ass ain't got nothing to lose."

"She moving back for good?" Rich asked, and Sam nodded his head. "That could work. So, get with Faith and see what she trying to do and let us know, but Keisha ain't gon' happen."

"Why don't we get the girls to move into the house," Sam suggested. Both stacks and Rich looked to him, wondering what the hell he was talking about. "I mean, what's more unsuspecting than two young women?"

Rubbing his chin, Rich thought just maybe it could work. "Faith and Keisha can work that out."

WE MADE LOVE IN THE 80'S

Stacks peeped how Rich once again excluded Lynette from the equation, but he ain't even say shit. He didn't like the pedestal Rich placed her on. They were taking that Ms. Zoo shit to the head and thinking her ass was too good to put her name on the line for the crew. All bullshit aside, they ended the meeting on a good note and planned to reconvene once Stacks had a chance to talk to Faith.

Once Stacks spoke to Faith, everyone was happy. She was more than happy to turn over the kitchen to Sam's sister and was sure to teach her everything she knew before she bowed out, gracefully. Not completely done with working with the crew, Faith and Keisha also took them up on their offer to fake move into the money house. Keisha, more than Faith, planned to be there because Faith was laid up under Stacks at his house all the time, and that was exactly where she wanted to be. For years they'd been rocking, and Faith wasn't letting him go. She would be telling a bald-faced lie if the no titles thing didn't bother her because it did. However, only she knew the reasoning behind it, so she let it rock. It didn't matter what title she didn't hold. He claimed her even if he hadn't claimed her. His actions claimed her, the love they made claimed her, and most of all, his heart claimed her.

"You coming out?" Stacks asked Faith as he bopped into the bedroom of his apartment.

Looking back over her shoulder, she rolled over on the bed. "Out where?"

"Shit, probably StarShips." It had been a minute since everyone had enjoyed a night out, and they had plans to step out and shut the whole building down.

"Oh, hell yeah, I'm coming." Jumping out the bed, her lazy day was over. "Why you ain't tell me earlier?" Faith questioned, hating that now she had to rush an outfit.

Walking back into the room from the bathroom to grab his towel, Stacks looked to her. "We just decided to go a minute ago."

Rolling her eyes, Faith didn't care. This last-minute shit got on her nerves. Walking out the room, she headed to the house phone hanging on the kitchen wall. Quickly, she placed her fingers in each hole and swirled them for each number to call Lynette. She knew if Stacks asked, was she going, more than likely Lynette was going.

"House of beauty, you're speaking to a cutie. How can I help you?"

"Grow up." Faith laughed, shaking her head at her, still answering the phone like that.

"Whatever, what's up?"

"Nothing, you going out with them?"

"Yeah, we about to go to dinner, and then we gon' meet y'all out there," Lynette spoke as she looked in the mirror, smoothing her hand up her sleek ponytail. "You coming?"

"I guess, but Stacks ass just told me. Now, I gotta find something to wear."

"Girl, it ain't nothing but StarShips…"

"Oh, please don't hit me with that because yo' ass gon' role out looking like the queen of the fucking crack stars and have me looking crazy."

Lynette looked down at her outfit. With a black silk blouse, Sergio jeans, and a pair of leopard print knee-length boots on her feet, Lynette figured she was right. "Well, maybe I'll leave my fur at home."

"Bitch, fuck you!" Faith shrieked, causing Lynette to bust up laughing.

"Shit, I'm serious! Tony bought them shits the other week and been waiting for us to step out, so we can wear them."

"Well shut that shit down, sis. You Mrs. Zoo, so you gotta hop out and show out on these hoes!" Faith yelled, hyping her up as Lynette just shook her head smiling.

She still wasn't used to the level of celebrity involved with dating Tony, but the title was growing on her. "Yeah, yeah."

WE MADE LOVE IN THE 80'S

"You ready?" Tony asked, walking in the room, clad in his fit matching Lynette to a tee.

"Yeah, just about." Swiftly she smeared her red lipstick evenly on to her lips and pressed them together. "Aight girl, we about to go. I'll see you later at the club."

After hanging up with Faith, Lynette looked at Tony through the mirror. She carefully put her earrings in, thinking maybe she should go ahead and give him some tonight. She wasn't a virgin or anything, but they'd been tiptoeing around sex. They wanted to get to know each other and let things between them happen naturally without sex complicating matters, but after nearly four months of dating, Lynette was ready.

"What's up, you good?" Tony asked as he slid behind her, wrapping an arm around her waist.

"Yeah, I'm okay." She smiled as he kissed her neck. "You look nice."

"Thank you." Looking up, his eyes met hers in the mirror, and he was still in awe of how fucking pretty she was. "Shit, you making me look better."

Rolling her eyes, Lynette smiled. "Cut it out," she blushed bashfully.

Rich told her how beautiful she was a million times a day, and he never got tired of it. "Nah, you cut it out," he whispered, bass heavy in his voice as he slid his tongue up the side of her neck and gently nibbled on her flesh.

Just a bit, she tilted her head, and he wrapped an arm around her waist, pulling her deeper into him. A soft moan fell from her lips, and it was music to his ears. Each moan was laced with immense passion causing his dick to brick up. Rich knew when they finally made love; it was over for any ounce of understanding he had. That's just one reason he wasn't too pressed that she hadn't given into him yet, Rich didn't want to become that guy. *Pussy be so good it'll have a nigga insecure, pulling up, flexing in broad daylight, ready to kill a nigga just thinking about someone else touching what was his.* Rich already couldn't go too long without seeing her or hearing her voice. He didn't even want to think about the kind of fool he was going to be once she blessed him. After finally letting her go, he turned her around and placed a kiss to her lips.

"Aight, let's be out before I have ya little ass sprawled out on that bed."

"Oooh, don't threaten me with a good time." Smiling she pushed herself off the dresser and pressed her chest to his. Their eyes stayed connected as they took in each other's features. "You know," biting her bottom lip, she reached for his belt. "We can skip dinner." Lynette was ready, she wanted him, and she wanted him now. Confidently, she pressed her lips to his and continued to undo his belt.

Rich kissed her back, but he didn't have any plans to sleep with her right now. Of course, he wanted her, but not like this. "Bring ya ass." He popped her on the butt and swiftly moved past her.

"What, come on, stop playing." She urged, grabbing for him, but he kindly popped her hands down. Sucking her teeth, Lynette was not trying to hear it. "You do this shit every time." Throwing her hands up, she was over it.

Rich smirked as he fixed his belt back, watching her stomp around like a child. She grabbed her bag and tossed that big ass fur coat over her shoulder, and he almost laughed. "Chill out." She went to storm past him, and he snatched her ass right up. Rich didn't play that being mad shit at all, especially when he didn't do shit for her to be mad about.

"What Tony?"

"You mad now."

"I ain't nothing." She went to snatch away from him, but he held her ass right there. Lynette looked right back at him as he peered down at her.

"What's up, because you ain't mad about no dick?"

"Why the fuck ain't I?" She bucked up, "Like, you just gon' deny me like that, and it's not the first time…What, you fuckin' somebody else?"

And there it was, just as he assumed. Rolling his eyes, Rich shook his head. "I gotta be fucking somebody else because I ain't pressing you for no pussy."

"Are you?"

Rich had to remember that she was only nineteen, and though she put on a brave face, her last relationship left her scarred. "No."

"Then what is it?"

"It ain't nothing, we gon' get there." The look in her eyes told him that wasn't enough, so he just kept everything one hundred with her. "Shit, I ain't never took the time to be with a woman without dicking her down. Every woman I've ever been with, sex was all I wanted..." he looked away before he held her attention again. "I just want something different with you."

Tears welled in her eyes as she took in all that he was saying. "Fuck Tony!" she yelled, pushing him. "Like, I swear I don't deserve you! Here I am, being a hoe, and you just trying to love me for me."

"Girl, get yo' ass out this room." He cut up laughing, pushing her along.

Lynette wiped her eyes dry as he draped his arm around her shoulder. Together, they walked out of the house and to the car. Tony opened the door for her, and before she got in the car, she turned to face him. "Thank you for real. I know I'm crazy, but I appreciate that."

Nodding his head, Rich accepted her peace. "I got you, just know that." He kissed her lips, and once she was seated, he closed the door.

Chapter 5

Stacks and Faith walked in the party with Sam and the rest of Zoo Crew behind them. Dressed to the nines, they were all looking like money as they floated through the crowd and straight to their reserved section. There were seats in the section as well as bottles of champagne, and they didn't waste any time getting straight to the bullshit.

The crew had been there for about an hour before Rich and Lynette walked through the door and shut shit down. Once they arrived, everything went up a notch. Everyone was dancing, throwing money, and living life. Not only was the music bumping, but there was also a surprise performance by Boogie Down Productions, and they went wild. The entire night was one for the books. When the concert was over, the crew decided to take pictures at the photo booth. The backdrop was red with a big bottle of champagne in the middle, and the prop was nothing but a whicker round chair.

First, the crew took pictures. Some were standing with their hands crossed in front of them. While others were bent down, holding large amounts of money in their hands. When it was time for the couples, Rich sat in the chair while Lynette popped her little ass right in his lap. With an arm wrapped around her waist, they were ready to flick it up. Stacks and Faith decided to stand to take theirs. She wrapped her arms around his neck, and his hands were resting on her ass. Once they finished taking the pictures, they hung around waiting for the photographer to develop them and staple them into the flimsy frame.

"I see you decided to come out in that damn fur anyway." Faith laughed as she ran her hands across the brown rabbit fur, loving how soft it was.

"Man listen, this all Tony doing." Lynette shrugged and turned towards the crowd. Just then, she spotted Janae. "I ain't know she was coming." She shrieked before she took off. Since she started seeing Tony, it was like she saw less and less of Janae. Lynette knew how Janae felt about Zoo Crew, so to keep the peace, she spent most nights at Tony's, and they hardly ever seen each other. "Janae!" From behind, Lynette wrapped her arms around Janae's waist hugging her tight.

Janae was caught off guard and was instantly heated. She was about to go off before she turned around and saw it was her grown-ass little cousin. "Why you grabbing me like that?"

"Because I miss you, and I'm happy to see you."

Lynette went to hug her again, and Janae stepped back, causing a frown to cover her face. "Miss me? I been in the same places, doing the same shit, so if you were really checking for me, you would've found me." Looking just beyond her, Janae saw she was with Zoo; and to add insult to injury, Keisha and Faith were there also. "But I see you all wrapped up now, living with those animals I see."

"Janae…"

"Nah, save it, you get out here and start acting real funny style over that cornball ass nigga…"

Lynette's blood boiled with anger the more she listened to her cousin talk down on her and her relationship. "You know what, you're crazy and fuckin' miserable." Stepping in her face, "I came over here to show love because we family, but I ain't gon' kiss ya ass."

"And I'm not asking you too, shit, you ain't even have to speak! Go back to ya lame-ass friends…"

"Yeah, aight, I'll do just that. I'm doing great. You keep being fuckin' angry and miserable, wondering why nobody fucks with you …" Lynette began but was pulled back by Rich.

He stepped in front of her and looked into her eyes. "Fuck her, it ain't even worth all that."

"Fuck me? Nigga, fuck you." She went to lunge at him, and Sam snatched her ass right up. "Let me go."

Sam held her tight as she fought against him. "Fuck is ya problem?" He asked once they were outside.

Janae's body shook as he held her shoulders, forcing her to face him. Shaking her head, she held back her tears. Sam looked at her and could see hurt, anger, and underneath all of that in the depth of her soul was fear. Without thinking, he pulled her into him hugging her tight as she broke down crying. He allowed her to cry on his shoulder, and after holding her for a moment, Sam pulled back. "Come on." He went to step away, and she stayed put. He looked back to her and their eyes locked on one another as he walked up to her. Sam grabbed her hands and pulled her along.

Reluctantly, Janae allowed him to put her in his car. Like a merry-go-round, her head spun as she rested back on the headrest. Silently, tears fell from her eyes as she allowed the vehicle to sway her to sleep.

When Sam pulled up to his house, he was glad there was an available parking space close to the entrance. It was late, and he didn't feel like walking a mile to get to his building. After parking the car, he looked over at Janae, and her evil ass was sleeping so peacefully he hated to wake her. Sam didn't understand why he was so attracted to her. He really didn't know. She was a straight bitch most of the time and swore she hated his guts the rest of the time, but he saw something else in her. Something that he didn't even think she saw in herself, but Sam was patient with her.

Stepping out of his car, he tucked his gun on his waist and checked his surroundings as he made his way to the passenger side. Once he opened the door, Sam nudged her awake. Heavy with sleep, Janae stepped out of the car and held tightly onto his arm as they walked into the building. Janae didn't know where she was, nor did she care at that point. All she wanted to do was climb in a warm bed and go to sleep.

Upstairs, Sam let them into the apartment and flicked on the foyer light. Janae took in as much as she could before they were in his bedroom.

"Make ya self at home," he said before he walked into the adjoining bathroom.

Janae looked around, and his room was clean, and everything seemed to be in order. She sighed, plopping down on his bed, before slowly removing her shoes. Looking down at herself, she didn't want to sleep in her party clothes, but of course, she didn't have anything else. Standing from the bed, she stumbled to the door, forcing herself to stand straight, before knocking. She wasn't sure if he'd heard her after a minute or two, so she knocked again. When the door flung open, Janae was stuck as her mouth hit the floor.

WE MADE LOVE IN THE 80'S

Sam opened the door in nothing but his boxers. He watched her eyes travel his body, and he smirked. Janae ass was always on that fronting shit knowing damn well she wanted to fuck with a nigga. "What's up, shorty?"

Her eyes were settled on his dick when she finally heard him calling her name. His voice pulled her from her nasty thought and stopped her from literally drooling over him. "I uh, do you have something I can sleep in?" Sam didn't say anything as he looked at her. When he stepped up to her, his chest gently brushed against hers, and he walked past her. Janae watched him walk over to his closet and go inside. From the top shelf, he grabbed a t-shirt and a pair of basketball shorts. "Thank you."

"Yeah, and I want my shit back too." He joked, causing her to smile a bit, then his house phone rung. "You can go ahead if you wanna shower." Janae nodded her head, and he went to get the phone. "Yo'," he answered the phone that hung on his kitchen wall.

"You good?" Rich asked, concern heavy in his voice.

"Yeah, man, I just got back to the crib." He told him, and he could hear Lynette ask if Janae was with him. "Yeah, she here with me."

"Oh good, because I'mma beat her ass." She laughed drunkenly. "Bitch done flexed on me in front of the whole hood…That hoe gotta see me."

"Aight, man." Rich chuckled, listening to her and keeping an eye on the people coming out of the club. "We'll catch up with you later." He hung up the payphone disconnecting the call as they posted up outside the club. The club was fun, and they all enjoyed the mini concert, but the parking lot was where the real party was. Everybody who was anybody, all the people that wanted to be seen, and everyone woman that wanted to be chosen was there.

Lynette and Faith laughed as they recapped the night. She was tucked right under Rich. His hand was wrapped around her waist as they kicked shit with the rest of Zoo.

"Aight Zoo, we out," Scott La-Rock said as he walked over with D-Nice.

ARABIA

"Fa sho." Rich smiled as they shook it up. "The show was crazy too, had the whole place rockin'."

"Hell yeah, The Bridge Is Over, shut all that shit down." Stacks added as he puffed on his joint.

"We appreciate it, man, you know we gotta let them know who started this rap shit." D-Nice joked, and they all fell out laughing. A horn sounded, and they said their final goodbyes before they left and hopped in the car on their way to the next city.

"You just know everybody don't you?" Lynette playfully rolled her eyes.

"Shit, I'm King Zoo, my name ring bells in any hood." On his cocky shit, Rich spoke nothing but facts. His name had been in rooms his feet had never touched, and to Rich, it was all a part of being on top of the game.

"Here you go," she said, wrapping her arms around his neck. She kissed his lips. While they were kissing, she moved her hand from around his neck and grabbed his dick. "I'm trying to fuck, Zoo."

He laughed as she continued to kiss on him like they weren't in public. Rich was bricked up, and Lynette had way too many drinks. "You're drunk."

"I ain't drunk." She slid her tongue up his neck and sucked on it gently before nibbling on his flesh. He grabbed her ass, and she moaned into his neck as she left a hickey. Then she swiftly moved to the other side of his neck. "What's up, you gon' come up off this dick or not?" Rich looked down into her eyes without speaking. The muscles in his jaw flexed as he watched her kiss his lips. "Please," she groaned, biting his bottom lip.

Pushing his tongue into her mouth, Rich kissed her deeply before popping her ass. "Let's go."

Lynette could hardly contain her excitement as she jumped on him, wrapping her legs around his waist. Rich nearly fell over as he struggled to hold her up and keep his balance. "Aight, we out." He dapped his crew up, and they were off to his car.

In the house, they locked up, and Lynette didn't waste another minute jumping his bones. They kissed hungrily from the living room to his bedroom, before he tossed her ass on the bed and told her to strip. Rich stood at the edge of the bed as he watched her remove her clothes, dick growing harder with every piece of clothing she tossed on the floor. After removing his clothes, he pulled her by her feet to the edge of the bed.

Rich looked at her naked body and swore his heart was about to beat out of his chest. "You so fuckin' beautiful."

Lynette looked him dead in his eyes as she sat up on the bed. She could feel the love radiating off of his body and falling all over her. Never had she ever felt a connection to anyone so keen. Water built up in her eyes, and she fought to hold it back. "I love you, Tony." Her voice cracked, and her lips trembled as she kissed him.

"I love you too, baby." He grabbed the sides of her face as they continued to kiss. "I love you so much."

Tony had all kinds of plans and thoughts of how he was going to twist her body when they finally had sex. But right now, he just wanted to be inside of her. Together they scooted to the middle of the bed, and Tony positioned himself on top of her. He kissed her lips and to her collarbone, before taking his manhood and rubbing it against her. She was so wet, and the feeling of his dick just sliding against her dripping center had him ready to cry out.

Rich gently pushed himself inside of her while they held eye contact, and Lynette cried in pleasure. Her legs tightened around his back, pulling him in deeper, and he damn near nutted. He pulled back, quickly bent her legs in his arms, and went to work. Never before had either of them felt anything so good. The way Rich commanded her body with just the thrust of his hips had Lynette shaking and cumming all over the place.

Their first time together didn't quite go as neither one of them planned. However, they couldn't have been happier about how it turned out. Lynette shed tears with each orgasm, and Rich was right there to wipe her tears and make her cum again.

ARABIA

Janae rolled over, and it took her a minute to remember exactly where she was. Just as the realization hit her, she could hear the front door close, and she sat up.

"I ain't think you was gon' be up just yet," Sam said, walking in the room with bags of food, he grabbed from the diner down the street.

"I just woke up," she told him softly before she slid from under the covers.

Sam nodded his head before sitting the food on the dresser. He removed his jacket and his shoes, then started spreading his reefer for a joint. Just as he rolled the paper between his lips, Janae came out of the bathroom. He watched her climb back in the bed and pull the covers over her body. "You cold?" She told him she was, so he walked over to the window and turned the radiator up. "I got you something to eat too."

She sat back, watching him as he grabbed one of the two plates of food out the tray and handed it to her. "Thank you."

"No problem," he told her before he walked out of the room and went into the living room. Her stomach rumbled as she opened the plate of food. Salmon cakes, grits, and eggs decorated the plate, and her mouth watered as she dug in. Janae didn't know what Sam was out there doing, but when he came back, her plate was nearly clean, and he hadn't even touched his.

"My bad, I had to run downstairs for a minute." Sam stepped back in the room eyes bloodshot red from the weed he'd just smoked, and now he was ready to eat.

"It's cool" Janae looked him over as she sipped the juice, he'd gotten her when he got her food. When she was done, she laid her head back on the pillows, and just watched him.

It was quiet for a while before Sam broke the silence. "So, what's up, what got you wildin' on ya people's?"

Just thinking about how fast her life was going downhill, had her on the brink of tears. "Nothing." Her voice shook as a tear slid from her eyes.

"Well, nothing ain't gon' make you cry, so what's up?" Now she had his undivided attention. All Janae had to do was tell him who did it, and Sam was ready to go to war for her. When she didn't answer him, he pushed his plate to the side and slid further down the bed so that he was next to her. The moment his hand touched her back, she broke down crying. "Come here, man." Janae sat up and cried on his shoulder as he held her in his arms. Sam gave her some time to get it out before he asked her what was wrong again.

Janae wasn't able to look him in his eyes, but she answered him as she turned her head. "I'm pregnant."

His heart dropped at the revelation. Sam looked from her then to her stomach before he looked back at her. "Damn, how far along are you?"

"Four months," she cried harder. "He doesn't even want the baby," Janae went on to tell him about her relationship with a guy named Kevin from out East. They'd been dating for a little over a year, and she thought their relationship was in a good place. He was a decent guy, had a job, and he wasn't in the streets at all. He was everything she was looking for. Then when she told him she was pregnant, he decided to tell her that he was married and already had a family. His suggestion to her was that she get rid of it because he wasn't messing up what he had at home and that it was best if she didn't contact him again. "I just feel so stupid. Like, after all this time, he just up and leaves me." Shaking her head, she was lost. "I don't know what to do."

Sam looked at her with sympathy in his eyes. It was fucked up how homie was doing her, but he knew single mothers that took care of their kids on their own after worse. "So, what you gon' do? You keeping it?"

Looking in his eyes, she nodded her head. "I was happy about the baby, and I don't wanna get rid of it because the father's a piece of shit."

"That nigga a clown, you know what you gotta do even if you gotta do it by ya self." He wiped the last of her tears from her eyes as he stared at her.

She felt everything he was saying and knew he was right. "I'm scared."

Her lip quivered, and he hated to think of how sexy it looked. He never thought he'd be playing stepdaddy to another niggas kid, but that's how it played out. "I got you," he told her, and she shook her head, ready to protest. "You hurt right now, but you gon' get on ya shit and handle ya business with ya baby, but if you need anything, I'm here." Sam couldn't resist as he leaned down and kissed her lips. A part of him thought she would deny him, and the other part of him didn't care. But when she didn't, he pushed his lips against hers and fed her his tongue. Slowly and methodically, he kissed her for a few and pulled back.

Janae looked at him and was not only thankful for his listening ear, but she was also grateful for his support. "Thank you, Sam."

"No problem," he pecked her lips once more and then slid back over to his food. "Shit, and you say we the bad guys." They shared a laugh as he shook his head. "What you say, homie name was again?"

"Kevin "*Sorry Ass*" James," she answered, rolling her neck, wiping her eyes.

"And he stays out East?" He thought of how far that really was. "Damn, you were ready to go to the end of the earth not to fuck wit me."

"Whatever, it ain't that far. He stays off Cambridge. That's like twenty minutes from here."

"Yeah, aight." He nodded his head, making a mental note of where dude be at. Sam was already thinking of ways to fuck him up.

"And Sam," she called out.

"What's up?"

Janae didn't speak again until he looked at her. "I'm sorry too. I'm sorry for being a bitch most of the time and for always talking to y'all crazy." Sam graciously accepted her apology, "I mean y'all are some hooligans, but I ain't have to come at you the way I did." She spoke her piece. Janae still didn't like Zoo Crew, but she could at least be cordial, she thought as she laid back on the pillows.

Sam sat in his chair, watching her until she fell asleep, shaking his head. "Fuckin' Janae," he said under his breath. Checking the time, it was a few minutes after noon, and he decided to take a nap with her. Once he took his clothes off, Sam slid under the covers. Carefully, he slid beside her and pulled her into him before smelling her hair. His chin rested on her head, and he relaxed as he allowed her breathing to lull him to sleep.

Lynette rolled over and felt an aching in her bones that she'd never felt before. The attempt she made to sit up was useless because she just fell back on the bed and buried her head in the pillows. "Oh, my god."

"Nah, oh, Rich nigga." He chuckled sleepily as he kissed her shoulder, then pulled her into him.

"Whatever." She giggled, relaxing into him.

He held her tight. "Mmm, mmm."

"Thinking about how I put it on yo' ass last night, ain't you?" Rich bust out laughing, and she did too. "I know you in love with me now."

"Shit, I was already in love with you. Now I'm *I'll smash ya fuckin' face in if I ever catch you on some bullshit* in love wit you."

He laughed, but Lynette knew he was serious. "Crazy ass." Slightly, she turned her body, so they were face to face. "But for real, last night was amazing."

Her eyes sparkled as Rich's eyes traveled her face. "It was, and all this ass is mine." He grabbed her ass, and she squealed as he kissed her lips. Rich sat up on the bed and slung his legs over the bed. He had to piss, but he turned around just as he made it to the door. "You really are cute."

"What?"

"When you ain't all did up, and ya hair all fucked up from us having a good night."

Lynette's eyes squinted, watching him smirk at her. "Shut up." She rolled her eyes before pulling the covers over her head. Thinking about that night had her blushing, and she was taken aback that he remembered.

Smirking, he grabbed his dick, shaking his head. Lynette's little ass was something else, and he was wrapped around her finger.

Chapter 6

"Feels like the weather is trying to break," Keisha said as she felt her edges, with the tip of her index finger.

"Nah, this fools weather. Hell, we were just in the club wearing minks the other week, and now it's nearly sixty degrees. That ain't nothing but pneumonia waiting to happen," Faith chastised.

"Okay, are you your mother or mine?"

They laughed, and Faith shook her head. "Y'all spoke to Janae?"

"Nah, and I still owe that bitch a beat down." Lynette joked.

"You know damn well; you ain't finna fight her." Keisha giggled, knowing better.

She hadn't forgotten about how Janae acted the other night at the party, and Lynette thought it was fucked up, but she wasn't going to beat her ass like she wanted to. "Only because she's my cousin, I'mma let that slick shit slide."

"Sam said she pregnant."

"What!?" Both Lynette and Keisha nearly screamed.

"Yup!" Faith sat up, voice high pitched, matching their tones. "I heard Sam talking to Stacks the other night, and apparently, the nigga she pregnant by ain't fucking with her and don't want the baby."

"The irony," Lynette snorted. "But you know what, I don't even feel sorry for her. Because she always kicking dirt on Zoo, and her nigga the one that ain't shit."

"Exactly," Keisha barked, shaking her head. "This might just humble her ass a little bit, though."

"It may have because I think she fucking with Sam now," Faith added, ready and willing to tell it all.

"He stupid," was all Lynette could say.

"Yeah, but you know he always had a little Jones for her."

Lynette's face instantly distorted. "And we know that she wasn't fucking with him. Now because she out here bad, she wants to? Like, nah, that's fucked up."

"Well, if he likes it, I love it." Faith shrugged, not caring either way.

"I know that's right!" Keisha and Faith slapped hands agreeing.

Lynette smirked as she sipped her drink, "Well, in other news, me and Tony finally did it!" She bounced in her seat as the other girls squealed with happiness.

"About fuckin' time!" Faith said, wanting all the details. "So, run it! Was it big, was it good?"

All thirty-two of Lynette's teeth sparkled as she smiled brightly. Just thinking about that night and every day after that had her spine-tingling. "Well, I'm not gon' tell you all that, but it was amazing!" Sighing, she shook her head, "I love him."

"That dick must've been good as fuck!" Faith shouted, and all the girls laughed as Lynette nodded her head.

"Shit, I been ridin' that dick ever since," Lynette howled, and the girls all slapped hands, knowing exactly how she felt.

They continued to giggle, and then Keisha sat upright, getting herself together. "I met someone."

"Oh shit, hell bout to freeze over." Faith fake panicked.

"Okay, so tell us about him." Lynette encouraged her to continue, wanting to know more. Keisha wasn't into dating like that and had crazy standards and ideals of what type of guy was right for her. So, to hear she was seeing someone had them shocked.

"Well, I met him a few weeks ago at Galleria," she explained how she met him while taking a lunch break at work. "He seems okay, I guess. He's nice, cute, decent conversation…"

"You don't like him." Faith knew it without Keisha having to confirm. This was how she was. Keisha would meet a guy, and the more she got to know him, she would start to pick apart everything about him and find one reason or another not to see him anymore.

"No, that's not it. I like him, kind of, I mean, I guess." Keisha stumbled over her words, unsure of how to articulate what she meant. "I'm just trying to keep an open mind and not let the fact that he chews with his mouth open annoy me." Rolling her eyes, it was clear that was one of the items on her list of deal-breakers.

It wasn't that Keisha was stuck up or anything, she was really cool. From being around the girls, you could tell that though she had grown up with the other girls, she wasn't like them. On more than one occasion, she found herself in a sticky situation, but the streets hadn't consumed her. She was still a little naïve and even possessed an innocence that was rare in girls her age.

"Well, I sure hope he makes it," Lynette joked, and they all laughed.

"Me too," Keisha sighed, pessimistically. She wasn't too sure, but she was going to try.

<><><><><>

While the girls were kicked back talking, the guys were on the block talking their shit. *I Ain't No Joke* by Eric B, and Rakim blasted from the speakers of Rich's car. There were a few girls on the set, but the guys weren't paying them any mind.

"Then 5-O ran up on us, and we had to hit the deck! Niggas got low quick as hell. Even had this nigga running." Stacks laughed as he recalled the story of Zoo being chased by the cops just the other day.

"Nah, not Sam." Rich had to see it to believe it.

"Shit, Sam, big ass was out. That muthafucka hit that corner and was ghost."

Shaking his head, Sam was slightly embarrassed. He couldn't stand cops, and he damn sure ain't no running type of nigga. But that day, he had work on him. The kind of work that could get him years behind bars, and he wasn't trying to get caught up like that. Rich looked to him, still not believing it, and he just shrugged.

"Shit, wish I had a video." Stacks chuckled as a nigga neither of them recognized walked up on the set.

Rich, Stacks, and Sam played the back as Tech, one of their lieutenants, stepped up. "You lost nigga?"

"Nah, nah, just looking for somebody. Maybe you can help me," the man said, eyeing the faces of all the men before him. He was searching for familiarity in all of them, but he saw none. "I'm looking for Tony Ricker. I think he goes by King Zoo nowadays."

"And who are you?"

"His father."

Tony's heart dropped at the revelation, but he didn't make a move to acknowledge the man or admit who he was. It had been years since he'd seen either one of his parents, and until this moment, he didn't care if they were dead or alive.

"His father, hunh." He spit on the ground before quickly looking over his shoulder to Rich, who slowly shook his head. "Well, if he comes through, I'll let him know you came by."

Nodding his head, the man sighed. Then he reached in his pocket, and just about everybody on the set pulled a gun and held it on him. "It's just a pen," not even fazed he set his bag down and tore off a piece of the edge. "My name is Larry, Larry Ricker, and this, this is my number."

When Larry went to hand it to him, Tech snatched it. "Get the fuck on."

WE MADE LOVE IN THE 80'S

The man looked him dead in his eyes without an ounce of fear or the slightest care as he nodded his head. For a minute, he unknowingly held eye contact with Rich.

Tech held the piece of paper tight until Larry was out of sight and off the block. After turning on his heels, he slid the piece of paper to Rich, and they carried on like nothing had ever happened.

Rich, on the other hand, was half-listening to the men around him as he twisted the piece of paper in his fingers. He wondered if the man was really his father, and if he was, what did he want? Rich looked at the number for a moment longer, before he slid it in his pocket and took a long swig of his beer.

The fellas kicked it for most of the day, and half of the night, before everyone but the third-shift workers went home. Rich walked into his apartment and looked around, thinking it was time for him to move as he placed his hat on the entry table. He removed his T-shirt as he walked into his bedroom. Just as he expected, Lynette was tucked tight under his covers. Rich loved she was always in place, and he didn't have to chase her all over the city. He could say with confidence that his girl was all his.

After he showered, Rich put on a pair of boxers and then tossed some basketball shorts on over them. He turned off the light and gently climbed in bed. Like every other night, Rich wrapped an arm around her waist and pulled her into him.

Sleepily, Lynette slightly opened her eyes. "You better not had let the sun beat yo' ass home."

Rich chuckled, knowing damn well he wasn't. "You know better than that."

"Yeah, you better know better than that." She giggled as she folded into him. "What you been up to?"

"Nothing, hanging with the crew," he said, and then he hesitated just a bit.

Lynette caught it and could sense a change in his demeanor. Turning around, she looked in his eyes until they were face to face. "What's wrong?" Rich watched her close her eyes, but he knew she wasn't sleeping. His eyes traced her facial features, and she wondered just what he was looking at. "Why you just staring at me?" She asked without even looking at him.

A smile slightly creased his lips before he closed his eyes. "My father came looking for me today." Her eyes opened, and it was her turn to watch him. "At least he said he was my father. He left his number."

"So, did you call him?"

Shaking his head, Rich told her he hadn't. "I haven't seen or heard from my father since I was like eight or so. I remember him and my moms got into an argument, she used to drink a lot, and they stayed arguing, but one day they got to arguing and fighting. I ain't even sure what happened. All I know is when I finally came to the living room, she was beaten bloody on the floor, and he was gone. A few months after that, my momma drunk herself to death. I ain't care either because she was no real mother to me anyway. All she cared about was the bottle, and I ended up raising myself."

"Where did you go after ya moms passed?"

"Bounced around in foster care until I was fifteen. Then one day, I just said fuck it left and never came back. For a minute, I was on the streets. Then Stacks started sneaking me into his basement and shit, and I just hustled until I had my place. Been on my own ever since. My father coming back now after I been through all that trips me out because now, I don't need him."

Lynette listened to Rich talk with tears in her eyes. She couldn't imagine surviving the life he had. Like everyone else in the hood, her father wasn't around either, but Lynette always had her mother. She couldn't remember a time when her mom wasn't there for her, and just thinking about all the shit she put her mom through made her sick. Mentally she made a note to call her and apologize, but right now, she focused on Rich. Lynette reached over and wrapped her arms around him, hugging him tightly. "You're not alone anymore, Tony."

When she pulled back, he stared in her eyes. "I know."

Sleepily Lynette smiled at him before gently pecking his lips. "Are you going to call him?"

"For what?"

"To see what he wants. I mean, if he went through all this trouble to find you, maybe it's something important." The look on his face told her he wasn't trying to hear that shit. "I mean, if, for nothing else, you can just stunt on that nigga."

They both laughed as Rich shook his head. "I'll think about it." He kissed her lips once more before he turned and laid her head on his chest. "Go to sleep." Sleep for Lynette came quickly while Rich stayed up a while longer thinking.

However long he stayed up didn't matter because the next morning, they were up with the birds. Lynette was off to school, and Rich was off to work.

"What you think about us pushing weight?" Rich asked Uncle Sam as he rode shotgun through the city.

"Shit, I ain't never thought about it." Glancing over to Rich, he quickly put his eyes back on the road. "Why?"

"Just thinking, you know me."

"Yeah, I do, so that's the next move?"

"I don't know yet. I mean, we getting money now, but if we make that move..." Shaking his head, Rich couldn't even imagine the type of money they'd be seeing.

Nodding his head, Sam begged to differ. "All money ain't good money, Rich. That type of money will have a target on our backs for real."

"I know," Rich sighed as he looked out that window.

"But at the same time, we gotta elevate and take shit to the next level. For us to stay on top, we gotta take risks."

Rich looked over to Sam and smiled. "My nigga." They dapped it up, pounding their fist into each other. They still had to talk to Stacks about it, but Rich knew if Sam was on board, more than likely, Stacks was with it.

"Shit, might fuck around and cop a mansion off this shit." Sam laughed.

"Hell yeah, I was saying that shit the other night. I was thinking about getting a house. I need a bigger spot."

"Damn, you ready to make big moves. Lynette ain't pregnant, is she?" Sam asked as he made a left at the light.

Rich smiled, "Nah, she ain't."

"Not yet anyway, right?" They shared a laugh.

"Yeah, not yet." Rich smiled because kids one day was definitely in the plan. "I just be thinking ahead. Like, I know what I want to build with Lynette, and I'mm a make it happen."

Sam nodded his head; he was proud of Rich. "That's what's up. I like you and Lynette together. She cool as fuck and balances you out and shit. Got you being all responsible and whatnot."

"Nigga, fuck you." Rich shook his head as he and Sam shared a laugh. "What's up? Where we going?" Looking around, he didn't recognize the area at all as he sat up.

"Gotta run down on this dude real quick."

"Nigga, when were you gone tell me?" Rich instantly went from lax to gangsta in an instant.

"I just did," Sam joked.

Zoo kept shit going, so Rich should've known better. He always stayed strapped, but now he was alert. Sam pulled up to a building, and Rich assumed he was going inside, but he just stood in the front. Not knowing what was going on, Rich stepped out the car and leaned up against the door with his hand resting on his pistol. His eyes traveled up and down the block, and nothing seemed out of the ordinary.

"Bingo," Sam said as he stood up straight, broadening his shoulders. "Hey fam, can I talk to you for a minute."

Rich eyed the man walking with a woman and two young children and wondered what was up.

WE MADE LOVE IN THE 80'S

"Umm, do I know you?" The man asked, looking at Sam as if he was crazy.

"Nah, you don't, but you're Kevin. Kevin James?" In his mind, Sam could hear Janae, *Kevin Sorry-Ass James.*

"Honey, what's this about?" The woman asked, confirming he was exactly who Sam was looking for.

"I don't know," he turned to Sam, "I think you have the wrong man."

"Nigga, is you Kevin or not? Janae told me some fuck ass nigga named Kevin James dogged her out, and I wanna know if I'm about to beat the right nigga ass." Sam said, grabbing him around the neck, practically lifting him off his feet.

"Janae, whoa, wait!" Kevin held his hands up. Recollection in his eyes, he was surprised. He thought Janae had done as he told her when he hadn't heard anything from her. Kevin felt his little slip-up should go to his grave. He had it in his mind that he would be a better husband and a better father, but he had it all wrong. "I haven't spoken to her."

Sam didn't say anything else before he smashed his fist into his face repeatedly. Shit happened so fast; Rich barely had time to react. "What you thought shit was sweet. Thought you would get her pregnant and live happily ever after, nigga?" Kevin couldn't say anything as he choked on the blood from his broken nose. He wasn't even standing anymore at this point. If Sam let him go, he would surely hit the ground. "Ya wife know, the type of nigga she married to?" Sam looked at her and continued. "You know he got a baby on the way?" She shook her head with tears falling from her eyes as she held her two children close. "Well, now you know the type of nigga you got!" Once more, Sam drew back and punched Kevin dead in his face knocking him out. Then he let his body fall. "Bitch ass nigga. Tell him, don't worry, Janae and the baby gon' be good. I'm daddy now." Smoothly, he stepped over his body and headed back to his car while Rich watched him shaking his head. "What?" Smirking, he got back in the car, and when Rich was in, they burnt rubber down the street leaving Kevin's wife to pick him up.

Chapter 7

Just as Rich suspected, Stacks was on board as they readied themselves to start selling bricks of cocaine. Because they had their area on lock when it came to drugs, they branched out to other cities and pushed the keys. To start off they got five extra bricks of cocaine, just to see if they could sell the shit. In just a couple of days, they made one-hundred-thousand dollars, and it was a done deal. They doubled the bricks on every reup. If they bought twenty to break down, they bought twenty to sell by the key and just like that, Zoo Crew was officially controlling the drug trade on the east coast.

To celebrate their newfound wealth, Rich thought it was a good idea to sponsor a block party. They wanted to give back to their hood someway, but Rich also knew as long as they were out here getting money, they would have to share their wealth and show love to the people, or they were going to start looking like food out here. So, Zoo Crew planned to have a neighborhood block party and give away some toys and shit for the kids. While the men handled the food and entertainment, it was up to the women to get the toys and other things needed for the neighborhood.

"I'm hot," Keisha complained, wiping her forehead as she stood bikes next to each other.

Lynette and Faith looked at each other and giggled. "Here she go!" Faith shook her head. "You was just crying about the weather breaking, and now you crying about it being hot."

"Well, shit, it's hot," Keisha sassed, placing the last bike in the row. "This a lot of stuff." Looking around, there was so much stuff she knew they paid a grip for all this.

They had like, forty bikes, she couldn't even count all the dolls, cars, and other small toys. The girls had everything separated by age and had even thrown in some things for the adults. Lynette knew folks always needed feminine products, laundry detergent, and other toiletries like deodorant. So, they threw some of that in there too.

Faith looked and the guys were hanging a banner that said, "Zoo Day" and she smiled. "This shit really dope." The other girls nodded agreeing. "Like, Zoo really got it out here. Like, niggas done really came up in a major way."

WE MADE LOVE IN THE 80'S

"Right!" Lynette remembered her first day on the set. It was almost a year to the day she moved up this way, and things had changed drastically. "Moving up here was the best move I've ever made."

"Okay! Bitch done came up here and became hood royalty and shit," Keisha joked, and they laughed as they continued to put the stuff out.

The block party was set to start at one and it was barely ten, so they had to put a move on it. Time was flying, and they knew it would be one before they knew it.

Lynette went to grab some more bags when she looked up, and her eyes fell on a very pregnant Janae. "Fuck she doing here?" Both Faith and Keisha looked up to see who she was talking about and shrugged. Neither of them had seen or spoken to Janae since she showed her ass the night of the party a few months back. She got closer and Lynette stood there with her arms crossed at her chest. "Fuck you want?"

Janae walked over to her cousin and her friends, a ball of nerves. She knew she'd been acting irrational and crazy these past couple of months, but she'd missed them. "Hey y'all."

Lynette scoffed and continued what she was doing, ignoring Janae all together. Faith looked at Lynette shaking her head, then looked to Janae. "What's up?" Removing her gloves, she leaned up against the table waiting for the apology she knew was coming.

"Nothing much, just coming to see what was up with y'all."

"Well, I'm posted in the same spot every day, so if you really wanted to know what was up, you knew how to get at me." Lynette rolled her eyes as she spoke.

Janae rolled her eyes, hearing the echo of her words to Lynette the night of the concert. "I deserve that," she sighed, biting her bottom lip. "Look, I'm sorry, okay? I'm sorry for everything," her voice cracked as she shook her head. This emotional shit just wasn't her. But she would be a fake ass bitch if she didn't admit when she was wrong, and she knew she was dead wrong, with how she carried her girls. "I was tripping, just going through a lot, and I ain't mean to carry y'all like that. Lynette you're my cousin, and I love you." By then, tears were rolling down her cheeks as she expressed how sorry she really was.

Keisha, Lynette and Faith looked at each other and then back at Janae.

"What about Rich? You sorry for how you spoke to him too?" Lynette asked, not batting a lash.

Janae swallowed hard, trying not to lie because she really wasn't sorry about that. "I, I, I mean, he said fuck me tho." No longer could the girls hold their laugh and had made her sweat long enough. Shaking her head, Janae wiped her eyes, sniffling and laughing too.

"We good," Lynette said walking over to her with open arms. "I love you, just know that." She kissed her cheek and hugged her tighter.

The other girls ran over and wrapped their arms around the both of them, and they were locked in a group hug.

"So, pregnant?" Faith smirked as she rubbed her round belly.

"Yeah." Her eyes fell to her stomach before she looked back to them. "Shit's crazy."

"How far along are you?" Keisha asked, taking her turn to feel the baby.

"Six months."

"Well, damn, that baby gon' be here in no time," Lynette swore as she looked at her, not believing she was so far along.

"Tell me about it. I finally accepted I'mma be somebody momma soon." She looked across the way to where Sam was and then looked back to the girls who were watching her like a hawk.

"You might as well go ahead and tell us all ya business because you know we know you fuckin' with Sam now," Lynette slid that in before she tried to tip toe around that part.

Blushing, Janae held her hands over her mouth to cover her smile. "I mean, we're just cool. I ain't fuckin' with him like that. But he solid."

"Well, welcome back. Might as well come on over here and help us set this stuff up," Keisha said once they were done catching up, and she happily jumped to it. After a while, the girls were back telling jokes and talking shit.

Lynette still felt a way about how Janae carried her that night at the club. Shit just ain't sit well with her. Whatever she was going through, is her business, but it wasn't an excuse. Family or not, Lynette didn't see them being close like they once were.

At one on the dot, they kicked off the festivities with food and games for the community. There was a DJ spinning all the latest music, a few local entertainers, and a community basketball game. The whole setup was dope and nothing they'd ever seen before.

Sam was sure to make sure the event was sponsored by a couple of stores and the local community center. They may have been on some shit, but they weren't dumb. Zoo knew if they did that type of event out of their own pockets, police would be on their ass. So, as always, they were thinking ahead.

By the end of the night they were all beat. Looking around they were glad they decided to hire a crew for the clean-up because there was no way.

Zoo stepped on the platform where the DJ was and Rich grabbed the microphone with one hand, while holding Lynette's hand with the other. "Yoooo, yooo, yooo" he shouted, and everyone gave him their undivided attention as they began to clap and cheer. "I just wanna take a minute to say thank you to everyone who came and supported the event. It was for the people and it was y'all that came out and made it a success…so give yourself a round of applause." He smiled as the crowd cheered for a moment. "Shoutout to Mike Layton for making this happen, he went out and talked to the sponsors and got them on board…give it up for him. And lastly, shout out to Zoo." Everybody clapped it up for them. "We all grew up in the neighborhood, shit terrorized the neighborhood." He joked causing everyone to laugh because they knew it was damn sure true. "And now we giving back. We'll do this shit again next year, Zoo!"

Rich along with the rest of the crew dapped it up and prepared to leave. He wrapped his arm around Lynette's neck, and they walked with the rest of their crew to their cars.

"What up Rich," a girl's voice called out and they all turned around. "This shit was mad crazy."

Rich turned around and saw it was his little cousin, Amanda. "What up, fam."

When Amanda ran over, she stopped dead in her tracks when she saw Lynette. "Ain't shit, this you, family?"

"Bitch don't fuckin' address me in any way." Lynette sassed ready to take off on her ass.

"Girl calm the fuck down, that's my cousin you wit, so I'll address you however the fuck I want."

"And I'll beat yo' ass too," Lynette was ready, and Rich knew she ain't do a lot of talking.

"So, what's up,"

"Yo', chill the fuck out." Rich stepped between them holding Lynette back. "Don't come over here with that shit."

"What shit! I was just saying hi, ain't my fault you can't keep ya bitch on a leash."

Lynette turned around him and slipped right between his fingers and punched Amanda right in her face. "You gon' stop playing with me!" She yelled punching her over and over, before Rich could get a hold of her. "Every time I see you bitch." She continued to shout as Rich tossed her over his shoulder. "She ain't tired of me beating her ass yet." Lynette swore as he tossed her ass in the car.

"Don't get out this fuckin' car." Rich told her and his tone let her know he wasn't playing. Pouting, she rolled her eyes and watched as he closed her door. Rich ain't know what was going on, but he had to make sure his cousin was okay. When he got back over to the where the fight happened, she was yelling and arguing with some guy and Rich stepped up. "What's up, you good?"

Amanda turned around pissed off, "Hell no, I'm sick of that bitch." She turned to the guy she was talking to. "And this shit all ya fucking fault,"

WE MADE LOVE IN THE 80'S

"Man, I done told you before to stop steppin to her, shit, she was my bitch, not you." He said mushing her in her head. "You keep up this dumb shit."

"Who was ya bitch?" Rich asked trying to piece this shit together. He just knew he wasn't saying what he thought he was saying.

"I ain't even talking to you for real homie…"

"Nah, nigga you cheated on me with her, that shit wasn't the other way around Hines."

Just then it clicked just who this nigga was, and Rich couldn't stop himself if he wanted to. Without warning or a reason anyone could see Rich took off on Hines and blanked out. Left and right, he was throwing haymakers to his face and body. So many that Hines couldn't even do shit but crumble to the ground. From there Rich was stomping him until the cops came over and broke it up. Hines crew on one side and Zoo on the other is how they separated everyone.

By now Lynette was back out the car and unbeknownst to Rich had jumped on his cousin again. "Bring yo' ass the fuck on," Rich yelled grabbing her by the arm. Like a rag doll, he drug her along and tossed her ass back in the car. After starting the car, he burnt rubber out the parking lot. "So, you fighting my cousin over this food ass nigga?"

"What?! Hell, no, fuck him and ya hoe ass cousin. I'mma beat her ass every fuckin' time I see her!"

Rich listened to her go on, and he was growing angrier by the minute. All he could think about was the fact that she was with Hines for four years and the history they had. That shit ain't sit well with him and he ain't like feeling insecure, that was for bitches, not a nigga like him. "You still seeing that nigga?"

"Oh, my fucking God," she yelled not believing he was making this situation that. "Now I gotta be seeing him…"

"Shut the fuck up," he yelled grabbing her up by her throat and scaring her half to death. "Are you still fucking that nigga or not?"

Tears welled in her eyes as she looked back at him. "No."

ARABIA

Tony could sense her fear, and thought she better be fucking scared. Letting her go, he pushed her away harshly. So hard that her head hit the passenger window. Shaking his head, he told her, "I'm telling you, if I ever find out shit different from what you just told me..." he ain't even wanna say what he was thinking.

"There ain't shit to find out," she began and the look he gave her if it could would've killed her ass.

The rest of the ride home was silent, besides Lynette's sniffles. Her feelings were so hurt. Not only had he put his hands on her, she felt like Rich totally misunderstood the situation. When they pulled up to the house, Lynette didn't waste anytime hopping out. Hurriedly, she pulled her keys and rushed to the apartment, while Rich hung back and sat in the car. Taking a deep breath, he ran his hands over his face. After about an hour and a joint later, he was calm and felt like he could be around Lynette without going off. He didn't really think she was still sleeping with her ex, but his ego held all the cards tonight.

Upstairs, he entered his apartment, and everything was silent. From the fridge, he grabbed a beer and headed to his bedroom. Lynette was in the bed wrapped tight in the covers and he just side eyed her. Walking straight to the bathroom, Rich placed his beer on the counter and prepared to take a shower. When he was done, Rich went and got in the bed.

"Don't touch me," Lynette stopped him just as he was about to wrap his arm around her waist. As far as she could, she scooted away from him. She was almost off the bed, but she would rather fall than to have his hands on her.

Rich breathed heavily as he moved back over to his side of the bed. He knew he was wrong on how he handled her, so he let her be and just went to sleep.

After that night, Lynette left Rich's house and was back staying with her aunt. Rich was sick without her, but he felt like maybe they could use the space. Shit for them, got too serious too fast and he could admit that was all him.

Right now, he was out running the streets and had even called his supposed to be father. He wasn't going to, but he figured he would at least see what he wanted. If for nothing else, it would at least give him a piece of mind. By himself he pulled up on the busy street and peeped his surroundings. Larry agreed to meet him at a little food spot out west. Somewhere low key on mutual ground where they could speak freely. Rich doubted he would be there long enough to eat, but nonetheless he was here. Stepping out his car, he wondered what Lynette was doing. He didn't know how he was gonna fix shit with her, but he was.

The restaurant was nothing more than a little chicken spot, so once he stepped inside it didn't take him long to spot the man he knew as Larry. When he walked over, Larry looked up at him and smiled before standing with an extended hand. Rich looked down at his hand and then back to him before he smoothly took his seat.

Larry held his hand in the air as he watched his only child sit before him. Rubbing his hands together, he clasps them and took a seat across from Rich. Before he could speak, Rich spoke up.

"How do I know you're my father? I haven't seen my father si..."

"Since you were about 8 or 9, I think." He tried his best to recall. "Ya mother and I got into it. That fight was the worst we'd ever had."

Holding his hand up, Rich wasn't trying to walk down memory lane of his fucked-up childhood. "I know what happened. If you remember all that, you remember I was there."

"Fair enough,"

"What do you want?"

Larry looked in his eyes, silently pleading with him. "To make amends," he sighed before he continued. "I know I ain't never been no type of father to you, and that's something I deal with every day. I'm not here to make any excuses for my absence because there ain't nothing I can say that'll justify it. I just felt like if I left, you and your mother would be better off. I was walking around talking big shit, but I wasn't no man. Men provide, support and are stable. I wasn't none of that, so I left."

ARABIA

Rich regarded him with no emotion, no love, no sympathy, no nothing. As a man he understood his dad was going through some shit. Even he knew how it felt to be out here fucked up, but as a man you find a way and you damn sure don't leave ya kid out here by himself. "Aight, so what, you want me to understand?"

"I just want you to know."

Rich chuckled shaking his head, "Aight then, I know." With nothing else to say Rich stood up to leave.

"Tony, please." He called out and Tony wasn't trying to hear that shit. Larry, called his name begging him to stay desperation soaking his words. "I'm dying!" Rich stopped in his steps just as he was about to push the door open. "Just ten minutes and you never have to talk to me again."

Rolling his eyes, Rich's first thought was to walk out and never look back. For all these years his father had been dead to him, anyway, so why did he care. Turning around, their eyes met, and Rich walked back over to the table and took his seat. Larry nodded his head as he sat down. After a few deep breathes he looked at Rich. "I have AIDS."

Rich's eyes squinted as his mind raced with thoughts. He'd heard of the disease, but he didn't know much about it. He looked his father over, and he didn't look gay or like an addict. From what he knew about the disease those where the only people that got it.

"I know what you're thinking, I'm gay or a dope fiend." Larry expected as much because he got it all the time. People he knew and loved had shunned and turned their backs on him since he was diagnosed. He knew what it felt like to be left alone to fend for yourself. It wasn't until his life flipped upside down, did he slow down enough to think of what he'd done to his own son. The heartache, the loneliness, the desperation he must've felt. Especially after his mom died. He'd known about that too, but even that didn't make him come back for him.

Larry explained all that to Rich, practically pouring his heart out and Rich didn't bat a lash, shed a tear or fake sympathy. "The irony in all this is pretty fuckin' funny." He chuckled as he rubbed his chin. "The fact that you got the balls to sit in front of me after ten years to make amends, makes me want to blow ya fucking brains out myself."

He held his anger, but Rich was steaming mad. So mad that his skin was hot to the touch.

"I know…"

"You don't fuckin' know! You don't know shit, you don't know what I had to go through. Sleeping on the fucking streets, eating out of fucking garbage cans…" Rich's voice cracked as the empty feeling took over. "You crying about what you couldn't do, nigga I was fucking ten and I made a way out of no way. See, I said fuck you a long time ago. I ain't never felt no type of way, never hated you, never wanted shit from you…I knew that shit would come back to you. The same way it came back to ma." He stood from his seat, "You just took a little longer." And with that, Rich headed out the restaurant. He didn't stop and he didn't look back.

Lynette walked into the money house after school and immediately kicked off her shoes, before dropping her book bag on the floor. The other girls sat watching her on the couch as she paid them no mind. She was officially a woman in mourning and didn't plan on doing nothing but sleeping. Every day since she'd left Rich's house had been dreadful.

It had been a week since the fight in the park and the last time she seen or heard from Rich. In that week she hadn't eaten much, slept any or talked to anyone. In the room with the curtains pulled back, and under the covers was exactly where she wanted to be.

"Bitch you still dead to the world?" Faith yelled as she cracked the bedroom door and poked her head in.

"Bye Faith."

"You been in the bed for a week."

"No, I went to school and then got in the bed." Lynette quickly clarified.

"Well whatever the case, you ain't done moping around? We about to hit the mall."

"Nah, I'm good!"

Rolling her eyes, Faith was over this fake depressed shit. "I need you to help me pick out some gear." She pleaded, "you know them other hoes can't dress."

Smiling Lynette shook her head. "Whatever, and I'm wearing this."

Throwing the covers back, Faith scrunched her face. "You ain't gon' do nothing to your hair?"

"I can stay home," Lynette said matter of factly, not caring one way or the other.

"Alright, alright!" Faith yelled throwing her hands up. "At least put a hat on."

"Whatever." Lynette rolled her eyes as she slid to the bathroom. She looked at herself in the mirror and shrugged. The jeans, oversized tee and sneakers she wore today wasn't her usual get up, but Lynette didn't care. She looked just like she felt, like shit. After turning off the bathroom light, she grabbed her baseball cap and threw it on her head.

"You ready?" Janae asked looking at her not believing she was going outside looking how she was looking.

"Yup, let me grab my sunglasses." They watched her put her glasses on and slide her feet in her flip flops with wide eyes. Girlfriend was really feeling away about her and Rich little fight and it showed. "Stop looking at me like I'm fucking crazy and let's go."

Lynette walked out the with her pocketbook hanging across her body and headed to the car. The girls looked at each other holding their laugh before doing the same.

"And Faith you know what?" Janae asked just as Faith bent the corner out of their neighborhood.

"What?"

"I can fucking dress bitch, I heard you." She giggled with Keisha and Faith.

Lynette on the other hand had tuned them out. In the backseat, she sat with her head resting on the window as she stared blankly at the scenery passing by. The bruises that once painted her neck had vanished awhile ago, but the pain in her heart still lingered. Never did she ever think Tony would put his hands on her. In the seven months they'd been together she'd seen him angry, but never had his anger been directed to her. Not only was she scared, but her fear was that if she pissed him off enough, he would hit her, and she definitely wasn't that type of bitch. A lone tear fell from her eyes and she wiped it, just as the car stopped.

In the mall, Lynette walked behind the other girls and window shopped. It wasn't that she didn't have any money, because honestly, she had plenty. She just wasn't in the mood. When they ate, she just sat there watching and when it was time to go, she was beyond happy.

"You could've just stayed home if you were going to be a zombie." Keisha said to Lynette as they slid back in the car.

"I should've," was all she said and left it at that.

Neither of the girls knew what happened that caused Lynette and Rich to fall out, so they couldn't really speak on it. "Well just because you and Rich on the outs right now, ain't a reason for you to be throwing the shit to us. We ain't do it."

Lynette knew she was right, "I know and I'm sorry, I am," her voice cracked. "I just need to be left alone, for a minute."

"Aww," Keisha pulled her into her and hugged her tight, but Lynette didn't break down the way she wanted to. Tears left her eyes, but she just couldn't cry.

They knew Lynette and being emotional wasn't even her. "Damn, so, you really quit him?" Faith asked.

Without a word, Lynette just shrugged. Once they got the hint that she wasn't in a talking mood, they left it alone. Faith and the other girls continued to drive, and unbeknownst to Lynette she had to stop and get something from Stacks. For sure Faith wasn't trying to piss her off, so she ain't even tell her. "Aight I'mma be right back, y'all can stay in the car."

"I ain't sitting in no damn car," Janae barked and unbuckled her seatbelt.

"I am," Keisha sat back getting comfortable and Lynette ain't say nothing. Just sat there with her head down. She had seen Rich's car and for sure she wasn't ready to talk to him.

Janae and Faith left the car running as they headed inside the house where the guys were. "Baby father!" Faith yelled out as she walked into the dope house.

"Shut up, he in the back." Sam said stepping out the back room.

"Bug head ass." Faith pushed him as she walked past him.

Sam allowed his body to sway as his flesh absorbed the impact of her hit. Smirking his eyes took in Janae and she blushed. "What's up."

"Nothing," she walked over and stood on her tip toes kissing his lips.

Sam grabbed her and deepened the kiss, before he pulled back. "What I tell you about coming up here?"

Janae looked away as he rubbed her stomach. "Well Faith had to come in anyway, so I wanted to say hi."

Shaking his head, he smiled as the baby kicked. "Just hardheaded."

"You already know that." Janae laughed.

Rich came out of the same room; Sam had come out of drinking a bottle of beer. Like always he ignored Janae and her rolling her eyes. Since she'd been seeing Sam, Janae never spoke to them crazy, but she still ain't fuck with them.

Sam looked at her knowingly and she sucked her teeth. "What, I didn't say anything."

WE MADE LOVE IN THE 80'S

"You ain't gotta say shit, fix ya fuckin' attitude." He corrected her grabbing her by her collar, Sam kissed her lips.

He didn't expect Janae to just start smiling and laughing in everybody face over night, but he ain't allow her to disrespect his crew. They ain't never disrespect her or come at her crazy, so he made sure she never did.

When Rich made it to the back room, he said what's up to Faith and leaned up against the counter. "Where ya girl at?"

Rolling her eyes, Faith was pissed at him and she didn't even know what he did. "I don't know, she ain't really fucking with nobody right now thanks to you."

Stacks pulled Faith into him as he watched Rich look at her. He turned his beer up to his lips as his jaw muscles clinched and Stacks wasn't feeling it. "Yo' don't be looking at my girl like that nigga." For a moment Rich just looked at them before walking away back down the hall.

"Ya girl, hunh." Faith smiled.

"Cut the shit, you already know how I'm coming behind you."

"Yeah but you ain't never came like this."

Stacks knew what she was talking about, but he wasn't ready to have that conversation. Never had he ever claimed her or anyone else as his girl, but he was slowly but surely warming up to the idea. It wasn't like he and Faith weren't together. Anyone with eyes could see they were a couple, he just couldn't claim it. "What's under…"

"Understood don't need to be spoken…yeah, yeah. Give me a kiss." Faith pressed her lips to his and passionately kissed her man. He just didn't know how much it meant for him to call her his girl.

When they separated, Stacks picked up the bag he had for her and walked her to the front. Janae and Sam were talking on the porch, and Rich was just coming out of the bathroom when they got to the car. He stepped on the porch, and when he went to turn the bottle up to his lips, he noticed Lynette in the backseat. He couldn't see her face, but he could tell there were four people in the car. It ain't take rocket science to figure one of them had to be Lynette. Hell, Faith lying ass only fucked with Keisha, Janae and Lynette.

For the rest of the evening the girls hung out and Lynette felt a little better. They went to dinner and had drinks, then they went walking around downtown. The area was full of life and good people, so Lynette couldn't help but loosen up a little bit. By the time they got home, she was laughing and joking a little at their usual silliness.

The only thing on Lynette's mind when she stepped out the car, was her leftover food from the restaurant. "This food about to be so good"

"Fat ass," Keisha joked, and all the women stopped in their tracks.

"Oh shit," Faith snickered as she looked from Rich sitting on their porch and back to Lynette.

All Lynette knew was she was not for this shit. She was having a good night and she wasn't about to ruin it. When the girls were in the house, Rich stood up looking at her. Nervously, he put his hands in his front pocket, from a lack of anything else to do. He began to walk over to her, and Lynette could barely look at him. "Bye Rich."

"Yo' chill out," he grabbed her arm stopping her from pushing past him. Violently, she fought her way out of his grasp. "Don't put ya fucking hands on me."

"Babe,"

"Don't fuckin' babe me, Rich."

"Stop calling me that shit, that ain't for you." He shouted growing angry at her calling him by his street name.

Lynette crossed her arms over her chest as the smell of liquor and weed swirled around her. A drunken mess stood before her and this wasn't the man she loved. "Nah, that's who you are. See I fucked up and thought Tony and Rich were two different people…but, nah y'all one in the same."

"Don't say that shit, you always got the real me."

WE MADE LOVE IN THE 80'S

Tears came to her eyes, "No, I didn't."

Tony approached her slowly, "Everything, I shared with you was who I really am. I'm in love with ya ass and…"

"So, in love with me that you would fuckin' choke me and bash my head into a fucking window." She screamed pushing him out of her face.

"I'm sorry," stumbling back a little, Rich rubbed his hands across his face. This shit was way harder than he ever thought it would be. Everything in him was saying fuck it and walk away, but he just couldn't. "Lynette please."

"Bye Tony," turning around she went to walk away.

"Please, I need you." Rich grabbed her from behind, wrapping her tight in his arms. "I'm sorry babe, I should've never put my hands on you. I been fucked up since, because I know I hurt you." Falling into his embrace Lynette allowed him to hold her, but she wasn't sold just yet. "I love you and you know I do."

"I don't know shit," her voice shook, "I know I was scared the other night. Scared that you might really hurt me." All of her resolve had diminished as she turned to him. "I never thought in a million years that you would hit me."

"And I won't," he looked in her eyes, "I was wrong as hell for what I did, but babe I didn't hit you."

"Well choking me like you did is bad a fucking nuff,"

"I know, I know, but listen, you ain't even give me a chance to make shit right. We been together seven months and shit been good, I been everything you needed me to be. I fuck up one time and that's it? It's over, just like that?" Looking away from him, she didn't know. "Babe, please," Rich got down on his knees holding her around her waist. He placed his head on her stomach, "You promised I wouldn't be alone." His voice cracked subtly but she heard it. "Ain't nobody ever gave a fuck about me. My moms and not even my pops gave a fuck. Shit, he came back just to tell me he dying. You all I got, babe."

Lynette was shocked to hear the news about his dad. She knew how hard it was for him to actually meet with his dad and just to find out he wasn't here to stay broke her heart. Rich had been through so much, so much shit that it was draining her. If she was emotionally drained, she knew he was. But together, together they were strong.

"Bitch, is he fucking crying?" Faith asked as the girls watched from the window.

"This shit got me about to cry." Janae held her chest with tears in her eyes.

"Oh, shut up, you don't even like Rich." Keisha waved her off.

"I still don't, but I mean I ain't heartless."

Both Faith and Keisha looked at her knowing better as they bust out laughing.

"It must be the baby," Faith offered knowing better as they tuned back into Rich and Lynette.

Lifting her hand, she placed it on his head. "I'm sorry, Tony. I really am." She hugged him going against everything she thought she believed in.

Relief washed over him like a tidal wave as he hugged her tight. Standing up he lifted her off her feet and held her in his arms. After a few moments he put her down and looked into her eyes. "I love you."

"I love you too Tony." He grabbed her face and she allowed him to kiss her. "You better not ever again in life, think about handling me like you did the other day."

"I swear babe, I won't ever put my hands on you like that again, ever." He promised and he meant that. Rich watched his mom get her ass beat just about every day for nine years and he refused to become his father. "Come on." Rich pulled her by her hands and after looking back towards the house one final time, Lynette was going back home to her man.

"Well I guess the action is over," Keisha sighed as they all got down from the window.

WE MADE LOVE IN THE 80'S

"I guess so," Janae rubbed her stomach, wondering when Sam was coming to get her.

"Well I know one thing," Faith said, and the girls looked to her wondering what. "That makeup sex gon' be bomb as fuck!!!" She howled and the other girls agreed as they slapped hands.

Chapter 8

Once Rich got Lynette back home, he promised himself that he would do everything in his power to keep her there. On any given day, he had her missing school, flying her out of town to go shopping or gambling, they often took trips to the beach, and next on her list was Disney World. Rich didn't stop there either. The more money he made the better her clothes got. Lynette could already out dress every bitch in the hood, but once Chanel and Fendi was added to her closet, it was a wrap. It was nothing for him to drop thousands on her at a time or for him to buy out a store for a day.

On the other hand, Lynette was in a whirlwind love affair. Rich just swooped in and changed her life in ways she'd never seen imaginable. She was officially that bitch, and she wore that title proudly. Every little girl in the hood wanted to be Mrs. Zoo, and every little boy in the hood wanted his bitch to be like her. At first Lynette opposed all the partying, shopping, and late nights. But now, it was like a staple in their small circle. Wednesday through Sunday, the girls were out either with the guys or without, and they loved it.

While Lynette and Rich were living their seemingly perfect lives, Stacks worked on making things with him and Faith official. Because of his past, he didn't really do titles and all that, but he knew it was something she desired. When Stacks met Faith, he was ten or so, and she was seven. They used to live in the same building when he stayed with his parents. Stacks couldn't remember a peaceful night from that time in his life.

Every night his parents were arguing and fighting. He watched his father claim he loved his mother and in the same breath, she would be a dumb bitch and he'd beat her ass. So many times, Stacks would beg his father not to hit his mom and then one day, his father turned his anger on him. He knocked Stacks around a little bit, and Stacks called himself running away. Only thing was he ain't have nowhere to go, so he ended up in the playground.

Not too long after he got there, Faith came over and began playing. At her age, she was very curious and wasn't shy about asking questions. "You're that boy that live upstairs."

Looking up, Stacks recognized the little girl from the building he lived in. "I don't live there anymore."

WE MADE LOVE IN THE 80'S

"I just saw your mother,"

He knew what she was getting at and he clarified. "I didn't say we moved, I left. I don't live there."

Nodding her head, she guessed she understood. "So, where you live at now?" She watched his shoulders shrug. "Well, you can't sleep on the streets." She thought that was crazy, and she couldn't imagine living in a park.

"Shit, it's better than staying there." Finally, his eyes met hers. "That's enough talking. Go home, little girl."

"I'm not a little girl."

"You younger than me, so you a little girl."

Rolling her eyes, she wasn't trying to hear it. She was ready to tell him off, but she could hear her mom calling her for dinner. Without a word, she ran off. Stacks watched her until he couldn't see her anymore. With nothing to do and no one to talk to, he busied himself throwing rocks and writing rhymes.

Faith left and washed up for dinner. Throughout the night she couldn't stop thinking about the little boy in the park, and she wanted to help. At her age, there wasn't much she could do, but she knew not to tell where he was. His mother was going around the building asking if anyone had seen him, and she lied like her pants were on fire. She didn't know what went on upstairs, but it was always a lot of noise coming from their apartment. She felt he'd run away for a good reason, and she wasn't going to tell on him.

Later that night when her mom went to sleep, she snuck some of the leftovers and grabbed a blanket. As quiet as she could, she opened the door to her apartment, and was sure to leave it cracked, as she took Stacks the food and the blanket. When she made it back to the park, she didn't see him and was disappointed. She called out to him and when she heard nothing, she turned to go back to her building.

"Didn't I tell you to go home." Stacks came walking out of the woods.

Quickly, she turned around, happy he was still there. "I did go home."

"Well, you should've stayed there. You ain't got no business out here this time of the night."

"Your mother is looking for you," she told him, as she walked over to the bench and put the things she brought him down. "I ain't tell where you were tho."

"Good." He smiled as she handed him a plate with aluminum foil over it.

"Here, I got you a plate of food, a couple of snacks, juice, and a blanket."

"Good look." He smiled before taking a seat. He was happy the little girl looked out because he didn't have shit at his house to take with him.

"You're welcome." She sat down with him and watched as he scarfed all the food down. Faith knew he must've been starving. "So, what's your name?"

"Landon," he said, in between bites. "And yours?"

"Faith." She smiled.

"Faith, I like that. Well, I mean it's different."

"My momma said, she couldn't have kids and then she got pregnant with me, and prayer and faith in God saved me...So, she named me Faith."

He nodded his head, believing that her momma named her right. "That's cool." He finished his food and drank one of the cans of soda she'd brought. "Thanks for the food and stuff, but you should get home."

She looked around, and it was the darkest she'd ever seen the sky at night. "Yeah, I should."

"Come on, I'll walk you." Together they got up and just like he said, he walked her to the building. Stacks snuck around back and waited until Faith made it to her apartment before he retreated back to the woods.

From that night on, Faith and Stacks met up every night for one reason or another. His running away, didn't last long. He eventually went back home. The fighting, arguing, and abuse continued, and he felt like losing his mind. The only thing kind and constant in his life was Faith. The little girl from downstairs, that wouldn't mind her business, kept him sane. In her own little way, she gave him something to look forward too.

WE MADE LOVE IN THE 80'S

About a year later, Stacks and his dad got into a fight, and he was removed from his parent's house and sent to live with his grandmother. His first black eye, he wore like a badge of honor. With a police officer in front of him and one behind him, he walked down the stairs without a care in the world. He saw Faith and smiled at the worry in her eyes. To be young, she was passionate, and he liked that about her. If nobody else cared, he knew she did.

"You're leaving?" She asked in her soft voice.

"Yeah, movin' to my grandma house for a bit." Stacks could see the surprise on her face as tears welled in her eyes. "I'm okay." he looked around him, taking in the building he hated for the last time. "I'll check you out from time to time." That made her smile as he moved along. "Aight, little girl, go in the house."

When Stacks moved to his grandma house, he linked up with Sam and Rich, and from there Zoo Crew was born. He settled in nicely, but he'd never forgotten about Faith and how much she meant to him. One day, he went back over there, and she was all grown up. Well, not grown up, but she was about thirteen or so.

When Faith saw him, she dropped everything she was doing and ran over to him. "Landon!" He held her up as she jumped in his arms. "I was so worried about you."

"I'm good." He hugged her tighter before he put her down. "How you been?"

"I've been okay, you know how it is around here."

He nodded his head already knowing. "I hear that, you look good; done grew up on me."

Blushing, Faith rolled her eyes. "Stop."

"I'm for real, you still young as hell, but you ain't no little ass girl no more."

They both laughed at that one as they walked over to the park. Together they sat on the same bench she used to bring him food and kicked shit for hours. They talked about everything and found themselves laughing more than they were talking. Neither of them had realized how late it was until Faith's name could be heard all across the courtyard.

"Ya moms still call you for dinner like that?"

Laughing, she nodded her head. "You know she be on it, soon as the streetlights come on." Standing up, she stretched, and he did the same.

"Aight, well, I'mma head home myself. I just came over here to check you out, let you know I ain't forget about you." He opened his arms for a hug, and she fell into them. "Aight, I'll come check you out next week or something."

Instantly, her smile faded. "We're moving next week."

"Damn." He stood back and looked at her. "You know where to?"

"Nah, I don't even remember."

"It's cool, here…" He pulled a pen and a piece of paper from his pocket and wrote his house number down for her. "When you get where you going, call me."

Smiling, she held the number in her hands like her life depended on it. Faith looked up at him and for a minute they just stared at each other. Without thinking, she leaned up and pressed her lips to his. Slowly at first catching him off guard. She pushed her body against his and deepened the kiss. Soon as he was about to kiss her back, they heard her name being called, and she pulled away. Faith headed to her apartment and when she was halfway, she turned and waved goodbye. Stacks shook his head, smiling, as he felt his lips. Faith was different from the other girls. He was sixteen now and had tested the waters a little, but he knew Faith was special.

Once she had the digits, Faith called him every night, and Stacks didn't mind at all. He made sure he was in the house at 9pm because that's when she would call. For hours, they sat on the phone, talking about nothing in general, but they enjoyed the conversation, nonetheless. When Faith moved it was like the stars aligned and blessed them because she was just a few blocks from his grandmother's house. It was like fate, when they linked up and from there, she was a part of the crew.

Thinking about their history, Stacks felt he owed her so much more than he'd been giving her. Faith was always down for him, and she never switched up. He thought of all the times he went M.I.A. on her, and all the females he'd ran around with, Faith ain't never trip. She let him do him and would always say, *"When you're ready, you'll slow down. I ain't going nowhere."* And she didn't, Faith was always there. She knew he was young, and she was even younger. But he ain't never fuck with no chick harder than he fucked with Faith. She was always it; it just took him a while to be ready to make that move. Stacks parents' relationship had fucked him up, but he was over it. Actually, he owed a lot to Rich and Lynette. Seeing them together and how Rich moved with her, made him want to do better.

Now here he was, walking around a two-story home for just the two of them. There were three bedrooms and two baths for them to do whatever they damn well pleased. "This is it," he said, just as he showed Sam and Rich the back yard. They'd been through every room in the house and the men were pleased.

"This real nice. Faith gon' love this shit," Sam said, as he stepped off the back patio.

"Yeah, you on your grown man shit right now." Rich proudly dapped him up. "Shit, I'm about to have to make a move myself because Lynette ass ain't gon' let me hear the end of this."

They all laughed knowing it was true. The girls loved each other, but they competed with each other just as much. Whatever one had, the other wanted one or something better, and that's how it was. Rich already knew once Stacks presented Faith with this house, Lynette was going to be thinking it's a good idea that they move. They chopped it up a little longer before they separated. Stacks went back to his apartment, Rich went to pick Lynette up from the hair salon, and Sam went to get Janae.

Janae had a late doctor's appointment, and he was going to take her. She was due any day now, and Sam was excited like he was the one having the baby. Ever since the night he took her home from the club, he'd been there. Sam was supportive in every way. He ran out in the middle of the night and got her food, he rubbed her feet, and he'd even footed the bill for baby stuff. Everything was good to him except one thing, Janae refused to make things with him official. No matter what he did, she was still on that we're good friends' shit, and he was over that. Before the baby came, he needed to know exactly what they were doing. If they weren't going to be together, he still planned to look out for her and the baby, but be available to her he couldn't be. Sam wanted a girlfriend. Shit, he wanted Janae, and today was the day she was gon' give him an answer.

When he pulled up to her building, she was sitting on the porch, watching the people in the neighborhood go about their day. Sam left the car running as he stepped out and headed over to her. "What's up babe?" Leaning down he pecked her lips and grabbed her hand, helping her down the steps.

"I'm okay. I just feel like a cow." She laughed already out of breath, and she wasn't even to the car.

Sam shook his head, laughing as he opened the door. "You look fine," he assured her, before he made sure she was seated and closed the door. He got in on the driver's side and they were off. They didn't say much on the ride over to the doctor's, and both of them were fine with the silence.

At the doctor's office, everything went okay. Janae still hadn't dilated any, so she was still playing the waiting game. She pouted all the way to the car. "I just want him out of me already."

"He gon' come when he ready." Sam laughed. "He just ain't ready yet."

"Well, he needs to get ready because I'm beyond ready."

"You wanna go get something to eat?" She nodded, and he made a right at the light, heading to her favorite restaurant.

Inside, they were seated immediately because there weren't that many people there, and that was good because Janae's stomach was growling. When the waitress came over, they both ordered, not even needing the menu. They had been there so many times they knew exactly what they wanted. Dinner went smooth even though Sam had a lot on his mind. The dinner table wasn't the right place to bring it up. But once they made it back to her place, in the confines of her room, he spoke his mind.

Sam sat on her bed, just watching her as she undressed. Having only been out the house for a couple of hours, she stripped from her clothes and hopped right back in the bed.

"Come lay with me," she told him, and Sam readily obliged her. After removing his shoes and jacket, he laid back on the bed. He was on top of the covers, and she was under them. Sam wrapped an arm around her shoulders, and she exhaled as her head fell on his chest. Sam was so comfortable to her, like a big teddy bear.

They were quiet for a moment, before Sam spoke. "So, have you put any more thought to what we talked about?"

WE MADE LOVE IN THE 80'S

Janae lazily opened her eyes. She loved the feeling of his hands in her hair. "What?"

"Us, what we gone do?"

Janae sighed as she moved her head from his chest. "Samuel," she used his government, and Sam knew it was about to be some bullshit, "we talked about this."

"No, we didn't, so we about to." He sat up and turned to her. "It ain't that hard, I'm right here." He looked in her eyes. "Either you wanna be with me or you don't."

"It's not that simple." She swore, tired of the whole conversation already. "Why do you keep pushing?"

"Because I want more."

"Why tho? Like, why can't we just keep chilling like we've been doing?"

"Aight." Shaking his head, Sam was over this shit with her. Right now, she had him feeling like a bitch, and he was far from it.

"Sam, I just got out of a relationship, and I'm not ready to just jump into another one." She went on to tell him that right now, her focus was on the baby, and he nodded his head.

"Cool," he sighed, as he slid his feet back into his shoes and grabbed his jacket.

"So, if it's cool, why are you leaving?" Her voice cracked just as her eyes filled with water.

"Because I'm out here being a good nigga. I took on all ya shit, beat a nigga ass, and even stepped up for the baby, and I don't regret none of that shit because I rock with you, hard. I ain't even been on no other bitches because I thought that eventually, you would come around." He looked down at her. "You ain't feeling a relationship and that's cool, but I ain't no sucka ass nigga. I ain't just gone be here catering to your every fucking want and need, and you can't even be with me. I ain't built for that shit, so you be good."

She heard what he was saying, and her heart was breaking with every step he took to her door. "Sam, please."

"Page me when it's time for the baby to come" was all he said before he walked out.

Janae fell back on the bed, and she cried. She didn't know what she wanted. It was like she spent so much time hating Zoo, she just couldn't do it. Messing with him from time to time was one thing, but to be the woman on his arm...That just wasn't it.

Rich was on his way to get Lynette when he got a page from her. On the block, he quickly located a pay phone and called her back. She told him that she was going to the mall with Keisha, and she would meet him back at the house. He fucked around a little bit, then headed home. It was after eight in the evening, so he knew she was home. Walking into his apartment, he stumbled over bags in the foyer. Bypassing the actual items, he went straight to the price tags. There were a pair of $4,000 Chanel shoes, t-shirts, jeans, and bullshit that was easily another $10k. Shaking his head, Rich was pissed. He told her before about shopping like she ain't have no damn sense, and her little ass ain't listen.

"Lynette," he called out to her as he removed his watch. She didn't answer as he made it to their bedroom, and he called out to her again.

"I'll be out in a minute," she said, from the bathroom.

"What I tell you about spending all that money on bullshit?" He cursed, removing his shoes and then his shirt, before sitting on the bed.

She knew he would be mad, that's why she didn't even try to hide the bags. "I know, but baby, they had a sale. I couldn't resist."

"I'mma start giving yo' ass an allowance, that's what I'mma do."

"I thought you like for me to have nice things." She purred, still talking to him from the other side of the door.

WE MADE LOVE IN THE 80'S

"Man, you heard what I said."

"Well, I bought you something too." The door opened, and Rich's eyes fell on her, causing his dick to instantly brick up. "You don't like it?" She twirled just a bit, so he could get a good look at her barely-there negligee.

"Shit, and how much you paid for this fucking piece of thread?" He cursed, running his hands over her nipples that poked through the holes in the bralette.

"Does it really matter, when what it holds is priceless?" She stood directly in front of him while unbuckling his pants. Rich bitched and complained, but she knew how to handle him. Anytime she overspent, she would suck and fuck him real good, and all would be forgiven until the next time.

The next morning, Rich rolled over and wiped sleep from his eyes before grabbing his watch off the dresser. It was after nine AM, and Lynette was still asleep in the bed. Nudging her, she stirred until she was awake. "What's up, you ain't going to school?"

Sucking her teeth, she couldn't believe he woke her up for that shit. "Nah, I'm tired." Rolled off her tongue just before she was back off to sleep.

Rich stood up from the bed shaking his head. "Lazy ass."

"I love you too."

He heard her say it, and he paid her no mind. These days Lynette hardly ever went to school and spend most of her days partying and bullshitting. Rich didn't mind the occasional club night or two, but Lynette was out every weekend. Wednesday through Sunday, her Keisha and Faith were somewhere being seen and getting into trouble. At least when he went out, he got back to work the next day or two. Lynette, however, that's all she seemed to want to do.

In the bathroom, Rich relieved himself and then jumped in the shower. When he was done, he came back into the room and searched for something to wear. Looking in his closet, he was shaking his head at how small it was getting. Hell, with all the shopping Lynette did, it was just a matter of time before his side was reduced to a corner. Yeah, he was definitely about to start looking for a bigger place. His two-bedroom apartment wasn't really small, but with the both of them now sharing it, they were growing out of it quick.

"Where you about to go?" Lynette asked, rolling over, not even bother to cover up her breast as she looked at him.

Smirking, he still thought she was the finest thing in the world. "Work."

"Why?" she pouted. "I wanna spend the day with you."

"We can kick it, just not all day." He told her as he put his clothes on. "Page me when you up and dressed, and I'll come scoop you."

Rolling her eyes, that's not at all what she wanted to hear. "See, if I had a car, I could just meet you."

"You don't even know how to drive," he laughed, "but I'mma get you right, when you ready."

Rich said that every time she brought up getting a car. "Yeah, yeah, give me a kiss." He buckled his belt as he walked over to the bed, and she sat up to meet his lips. Slowly, she took his lips into hers and swirled her tongue around his mouth. "You love me?"

"You bet ya ass I do." He smirked. Rich thought about fucking her before he left and quickly changed his mind. He would never leave the house fucking with Lynette, and he had shit to do. "Aight, I'm out. Page me when you ready."

"Aight, love you and be careful." She heard him say it back and laid back against the pillows, before pulling the covers up. It was too early for her, and she was going back to sleep until at least one.

On the front of his stoop, Rich looked around and took in his neighborhood. It was cool for the most part, full of hardworking middle-class families. Trees lined the streets, while cars zipped down the road. He jogged down the steps, loving the neighborly feeling of his neighborhood. Once he made it to his car, he hopped in and burnt rubber down the street. They had a shipment coming in today, and they were also switching apartments. They didn't want people to get too comfortable seeing them running, in and out the same spot, so they switched shit up every few months or so.

WE MADE LOVE IN THE 80'S

"What up?" Rich dapped his niggas up as he walked through the courtyard. Things for Zoo had been going well and if you asked Rich, they'd been going to good. He was almost paranoid because he anticipated some shit going wrong. They didn't have any known enemies but making the kind of money they were making, it was just a matter of time. "Y'all just about got shit set up." He nodded once he made it upstairs and into the new apartment.

"Yeah, we been at this shit all week," Tech said, as he pushed the table into the dining room. "It ain't too bad, and it's bigger than the last spot we had."

"Right." Rich continued to check out the progress they'd made. There wasn't much furniture in the two-bedroom apartment. They didn't keep much in there because they didn't want anyone to get too comfortable. If it looked like a house, niggas would get lax and start acting like they were home, and they ain't want that. So, in the living room there was a table with a small couch, in the bedroom there was a table for the work, and in the other bedroom there was money machines and shit.

"You up and out early," Stacks said, as he walked into the apartment and shook it up with Rich, followed by Sam.

"Hell yeah, the early bird gets the worm, nigga." Rich chuckled, before turning his attention back to what he was doing.

Before Sam could greet Rich, his beeper was going off, alerting him that someone was trying to reach him. Once he pulled it from his waistband, he was able to see that it was Janae. His first thought was to ignore her, but he decided against it. It had been a few weeks since he'd spoken to her, so his next thought was something happened to the baby. The last conversation he had with her, he was clear that he wasn't fucking with her, outside of the baby, but in the first few days, she paged night and day. He knew she ain't want shit, so he let they situation die down, and she stopped. Now she was paging him again, and he had to call her back. "What's up."

"Hey," her voice quivered, from relief because she didn't think he was going to answer.

"What's up, Janae?" He asked, irritated already. "The baby okay?"

Janae didn't like the tone of his voice or the attitude he was giving her. She gave him the space he'd demanded and hadn't been contacting him at all, and obviously that's how he wanted it. "You know what, never mind."

Sam could hear someone in the background as she was talking her shit, and his ears perked up, "You at the hospital?" His heart rate picked up as his breathing got heavier. "Janae!"

"Don't even worry about it, we're okay. I can do this, even if I have to do it by myself."

He was ready to respond, but all he heard was the dial tone. "Damn." He shook his head and put the phone back on the receiver. "I gotta go. I think Janae in labor."

"Word?" Rich raised a brow. "Well, congrats my guy." They slapped hands, and then Sam and Stacks did the same before he bounced.

Because Sam had attended most of her doctors' appointments, he knew which hospital she was planning to have the baby, and he prayed he was right. When he pulled up to the hospital, he hurriedly parked before running inside. After talking to the woman at the front desk he was able to get Janae's floor and room number with no problems. Upstairs, Sam told the people who he was and who he was there to see. Quickly, they congratulated him and gave him a gown and head gear to dress up in. Before pushing the door open, Sam took a deep breath to relieve the nervousness he was feeling, and he went in after one of the nurses.

Instantly, his eyes met Janae's, and the relief she felt was apparent. He could see in her eyes she was happy he showed up. Just as quick as their eyes connected, she fell back against the bed and screamed at the feeling of another contraction ripping through her mid-section. "Okay, okay, just breathe," he coached, kneeling down so that his lips were by her ear.

"Oh, it hurt so bad." She strained, while her teeth clattered, still unable to cry. The pain she was feeling was so vast, she couldn't even form an expression for it. Tears, screaming…Nothing was enough.

"Okay, on the count of three, I want you to bear down and push," the doctor said from between her legs.

WE MADE LOVE IN THE 80'S

"Aight, 1, 2, 3, push." Sam held her back up with one hand while the other held her hand. Once that contraction subsided, she was allowed a few minutes to breathe, and they were back at it. Just a few pushes later, and the most beautiful noise either of them had ever heard filled the room.

"It's a girl," the doctor said as they cut the umbilical cord and sat the baby on Janae's chest.

"Oh, wow," she marveled, as her chest heaved with excitement. Her arms cradled her daughter in disbelief. "I can't believe this." Janae looked from her daughter to Sam, and the excitement and love in his eyes made her cry.

"Damn." Sam was in awe, right along with Janae. It was crazy that at this moment he felt like a proud father. "She beautiful." He smiled running his fingers over her little head.

When the nurse came over to get the baby, Sam followed her over to the incubator they had set up for her. He watched as they cleaned her up and put a newborn hat on her head, before swaddling her in a hospital issued receiving blanket.

"You want to go to daddy?" the nurse asked in her best baby voice as she looked to Sam.

Sam nodded his head as he held his arms together, ready to receive their new edition. Nothing he'd ever done in life felt like this, nothing had ever filled his heart so much or had bought him so much joy. Stepping up to be her dad was most definitely his greatest accomplishment.

Janae watched Sam holding her baby and thought of how stupid she was being. This man had stepped up for her in ways no other man had ever, and she was ready and willing to fuck it all up. Janae didn't know how she was going to do it and right now she could hardly think, but she was going to put her little family back together again.

Later that day, Janae and the baby were moved to their stay room and were getting comfortable. Because the room was a double occupancy, there was little privacy, but they made do. Sam kept the curtain pulled and didn't let the baby out of his sight. He didn't want her to go to the nursery for anything and Janae couldn't help but laugh.

They were relaxing after Janae fed the baby. She was eating a plate of food Sam went out and got her, while Sam was sitting in the chair holding the baby. There really wasn't any tension, but they weren't really talking either. Janae wanted to talk to him, but it just wasn't the right time.

"Congratulations!!!" Lynette's screeching voice pierced the silence causing everyone in the room to look up.

"Eeeoooooowwwwww, where our first Zoo Baby at?" Faith shouted in an equally annoying tone as the crew piled into the room.

Sam and Janae were surprised and welcomed the company.

"Hey y'all!" Janae squealed happily as she eyed all the balloons and gift bags. "Thank you!"

"Shit, look at this nigga wit a baby and shit." Stacks laughed as they dapped Sam up.

"I know, right?" Sam smiled as he shook it up with his niggas. They all gathered around him as he held the baby up, allowing everyone to get a look at her.

"I wanna hold her, where the sink at?" Lynette asked when she was finished putting all her stuff down.

"Over there in the bathroom." Janae pointed her in the right direction before turning her attention to the rest of her visitors.

When Lynette came back, she was the first to hold the baby before they started taking turns washing their hands, so they could hold her. Quickly they split into groups, guys on one side with the girls sitting on the bed. Sam walked over, peeking at the baby, before he told Janae he was going to the café with the guys. The moment the men were gone, they started.

"So, how's that whole situation been going?" Keisha asked.

Janae knew what she was referring to but instead of speaking, she just shrugged.

"Y'all ain't trying to be together?" Faith followed up. "I mean, if he stepping up to be there for the baby, why not?"

WE MADE LOVE IN THE 80'S

"I don't know," Janae finally spoke. "We just gon' focus on parenting right now."

"Girl, what is it?" Keisha wondered.

"Hell, we already talked about you, if that's what you worried about." Lynette leaned back on the bed, adding her two cents causing the girls to bust out laughing.

Janae shook her head because they were so crazy. "I mean, honestly, I was feeling like I couldn't be with him like that. It's just since my dad...I just don't want to deal with people in that life." She shrugged, teary eyed.

They all knew how her dad was killed and could feel where she was coming from. When Janae was ten or so, her dad was killed by some neighborhood boys just being reckless. The young boys had stolen a car and were out speeding through the neighborhood. The driver lost control of the car and jumped the curb, killing her father. Faith would never forget the pain she felt of losing her father. His death, in her eyes, would've never happened had those boys acted like they had some home training.

Their little act of fun cost a man with a family his life, and Janae couldn't stand reckless folks since. It wasn't nothing personal against Zoo, but it was. In her heart of hearts, they were just doing dumb shit and acting like niggas, and she didn't like that. But she loved and respected Sam. She wanted him; she just really wanted a different him. Like, a him separate from Zoo. Tears continued to fall from her eyes as she conveyed this to the girls.

"Well, every nigga ain't the dudes that killed ya pops," Faith said, once she finished.

"Right, you can't put that on him. Sam really is a good dude, shit, Zoo ain't half as bad as you make them seem. I mean they young and been on some bullshit more than a little bit, but they all good dudes," Keisha defended the crew, looking at them like they were the brothers she never had.

Lynette wasn't even going to speak on how good Zoo was because Sam had already shown her what he was on. "Well, ya baby daddy ain't treat you no better. So, seems to me like an ain't shit nigga gon' be just that whether he in the streets, or not."

ARABIA

Janae heard all they were saying and knew it was truth. She just needed time to get her shit together, and she was going to make shit with Sam right.

Chapter 9

Janae was the only one of the girls who had a baby, but the rest of the girls felt like proud parents and wanted to celebrate. For almost two weeks, they helped Janae get settled, waiting on her, and helping with the baby. But it was time for them to step out. The girls were ready to party and bullshit. It was Saturday night, and out of all the nights of the week, Fridays and Saturdays were the biggest. They went all out on these nights and tonight was no different.

"Where my chain at, hoe?" Faith asked Keisha from the living room of her and Stacks apartment.

"It's on the kitchen counter, calm down," Keisha said, as she walked out of the bathroom, adjusting her breast in her crop top.

"It's almost ten o'clock," Lynette reminded them. It was getting late, and they needed to get a move on it. "I ain't trying to hear Tony shit, so we need to go before he pop the fuck up."

"Damn, he still tripping on you?" Faith rolled her eyes over Rich and his dramatics. "We been chilling these last few weeks; we deserve a night out."

"Exactly!" She quickly agreed. "Talking about, maybe I need a baby to slow me down. Like, I'm twenty, I don't need to slow down."

"Okay." Keisha high-fived her, knowing it was nothing but truth. "Aight, well come on before Rich come fucking up our night." Together, they all piled out the house and ran into the rest of Zoo.

"Fuck y'all think y'all going?" Tech asked as they walked out the building.

"None of your business." Lynette mushed him in his head as she walked by.

"Yeah, Aight, Rich know you out here?" He asked, knowing damn well he didn't.

Lynette laughed as she opened the passenger side door to Faith's car, "You let me worry about Rich."

Tech shook his head. Females wasn't nothing but trouble, and Zoo chicks were the worse. "Echo."

"I'm on it." He sat up and dapped everybody up, as he readied himself to play security.

"Shit, I'm rolling with you." Another Zoo worker by the name of Jay-Tap, stood up and together, he and Echo were out.

Tech didn't have to send Echo and Jay to watch the girls, but he knew if Rich was here, that's what he would've done. He was sure Rich ain't know they were going out, but he was minding his business, and he felt he'd done his part. Zoo Crew's reputation in the street had surpassed their neighborhood and all surrounding areas, everyone knew about them. Tech didn't understand how they let their women move so reckless. If anyone wanted to get at them, a sure way would be through the women. Tech was just glad his bitch was home, in place, and not out here running the streets.

At the club, the girls were able to walk right in because everyone knew who they were. Dressed in their best gear, they were dripped in gold and turning heads left and right, as they made their way to their section.

"Oh, shit, Ms. Zoo in the building, shutting shit down with the crew…Give it up one time for hood royalty!" The DJ yelled as the spotlight fell on them, and it seemed like the crowd split. Smiling, the girls all waved, putting an extra twist in their hips as they maneuvered through the crowd.

"Umm, excuse y'all!" Faith tapped a man on his shoulder as she walked over to their section.

Turning around, he was about to spaz, but his eyes landed on Faith, changing his attitude quick. "Damn, sexy, what's up?" He looked over the girls she walked over with and nodded his head appreciatively. "You trying to sit wit us, we got room for ya pretty ass."

"Nigga, this is our section. Y'all need to get y'all's shit and move around." Lynette stepped up and started taking their stuff off the table. She was going to move it to the section across from theirs, but she was halted in her steps when the dude grabbed her by her arm, spinning her around.

WE MADE LOVE IN THE 80'S

"You rude as fuck, shorty." He smirked, licking his lips. "You fine and everything, but put my shit back."

Lynette's eyes were trained on his hand as his fingers sat firmly planted into her skin. Her nose flared before her eyes met his and if looks could kill, he would've been dead right then. "Nigga, if you don't get ya fuckin' hands off me." She snatched away from him. "Don't put ya fucking hands on me. Do you know who the fuck I am?"

"Okay, you heard my girl, let's go!" Faith stepped up, backing Lynette up.

"First, we ain't moving shit, and y'all hoes ain't gon' make us. Fuck you think this is?" Dude snatched his shit out of Faith's hands and was coming for the bottle Lynette had, but she started pouring it out.

"Bitch." He went to lunge at her, but she turned the bottle around, ready to swing that bitch.

"I wish the fuck you would! I got niggas willin' to die behind me, and my bitches trained to go. Ask ya self if this section worth it." Smugly Lynette looked around and had she not been feeling herself; she would've noticed the look of death in his eyes, but nah, she was on a roll. "Nah it ain't worth it, you look like a bitch, and ya niggas look like bitches..." Before she could say anything else, he rushed her, grabbing her by her throat causing everyone to jump up. All hell had broken loose as the guys moved to grab him, and the girls moved to jump on him.

Echo and Jay-Tap had just made it upstairs, and couldn't believe what they were seeing, but had quickly sprang into action. Echo grabbed his gun, firing shots in the air, and everyone froze but the girls. Jay came over, snatching all they ass's up and cracking niggas over the head with the butt of his gun. He didn't stop until he reached the one with his hands on Lynette and without hesitation, he shot him not once but twice.

Quickly, he snatched Lynette up, and she just stood there. "Told you, dummy," she spat before Jay snatched her away, and the group took off running. She was hardly able to keep her footing as Jay drug her to the car. "Aight, damn, nigga, I can walk."

"Girl, get yo' ass in the car," he snarled before pushing her inside. "Y'all sit the fuck back."

Echo hurriedly pulled away from the scene, blending into the traffic as the rest of the party goers fled the scene.

"You okay?" Faith asked, checking Lynette's neck out. There were bright red handprints nestled into her caramel skin.

"Yeah, I'm good, food ass niggas, I tell you." She shook her head still pissed.

Echo and Jay looked to each other and back to the road. They were mad as hell, and this shit was way out of hand. Jay was beyond pissed because he'd just caught a body on some dumb shit. He knew it was something dumb because the girls always got into shit when they went out. But nothing ever to the point where hands were placed on them. Like, dude choking her was in direct violation and nothing else but death awaited him. Had they just been arguing that was one thing, but he fucked up putting his hands on her.

Echo took them straight to the block where they knew Rich and them were at. When they pulled up, the girls had miraculously calmed all the way down and were acting like they had sense. But nah, Jay was ready to tell it all. He stepped out of the car first and headed straight over to where their crew was posted. "What up, Zoo?" He dapped them up. "Let me talk to you for a minute."

"What's up?" Rich asked, with furrowed eyebrows as he peeped Lynette sliding out of the backseat with the other girls.

Jay began to tell him what happened, from the moment Tech told them to keep an eye on the girls, and how they walked up to them fighting with some niggas, then he ended with how he had to take dude's life. "Whatever the case, niggas had to go after that."

Rich's jaws tensed as he looked over to Lynette leaning against the car. Without a care in the world, she helped herself to a drink and had even hit one of the many joints in rotation. "I'mma handle it." Reaching in his pocket, he pulled out his keys and removed two. "Lay low at the safe house for now. I'll come through and let you know what the word is in a few days." They shook it up, and Rich pulled him in for a man hug. "Good lookin', don't worry about nothing, I got you."

"Zoo," Jay-Tap said as they released, and he went and did as he was told. Jay knew without a doubt, Rich would take care of everything.

Rich was so angry, he knew if he didn't breathe a minute, he was really going to fuck Lynette up. Closing his eyes, he counted back from ten then drank his beer down. When he was done, he tossed the bottle to the ground and coolly walked over to Lynette. Before she could react, he grabbed her by her jacket collar and drug her over to his car.

"Tony, what the fuck, nigga…"

He opened the door, paying her no mind, and tossed her ass inside his car before walking over to the driver side, and got in. Without a goodbye or see you later, he spent tires off the block and headed home. They didn't say anything on the way over and Lynette knew not to push him.

In the house they went upstairs, and Rich sat on the bed. "What happened tonight?"

Lynette looked to him and huffed before she leaned up against the dresser. "Well, we decided to go out…"

"How you get from going to help Janae to going to a fucking club?" He asked, making her start over.

"I mean, shit, I been cooped up for weeks, like I had a baby and shit. We wanted to go have a few drinks, listen to some music, and relax. So, we went to Eclipse and when we got there, this nigga was in our section."

Rich's face scrunched in confusion because they didn't even do assigned sections at Eclipse. "What section?"

"The section we usually sit in, like, everybody in there know that's our section, so we told him to move." Before, she could finish her sentence, Rich was chuckling a sinister chuckle. "Why are you laughing? That nigga tried to kill me, and you think it's funny? Look at my fuckin' neck."

"Yo', fa'real, this shit with you is getting old." He stood up, shaking his head as he removed his shirt.

ARABIA

"Excuse me?!"

"Every week, it's something with you. If you ain't fighting, you arguing with somebody, or into some other shit…And I'm fuckin' sick of it."

"What the fuck did I do?" Tears welled in her eyes. "He fucking took my section…"

"The fuckin' section wasn't yours!" He yelled furiously. "You taking this Ms. Zoo shit and running with it, like niggas out here owe you something. You forget you only Ms. Zoo because of me nigga! You stand on my name, embarrassing the fuck out of me every other day, and I let that shit rock because I love you." He shook his head holding onto his emotions. "But this shit tonight, this shit is unacceptable. Do you even care that Jay and Eco just killed a nigga for you? Their lives could possibly be over, and you sitting here talking about a fucking section. Fuck the section, fuck the club, fuck all this drinking and partying shit…Fuck all of it! Shit, on the real, fuck you too."

Tears poured from her eyes, as she listened to him read her ass for filth. "Fuck me," she couldn't even respond, she was shocked.

"Hell yeah! On some real shit, you becoming more trouble than you're worth." He put his shirt back on and looked to her. "Why you even with me? You ain't trying to do shit, you ain't in school no more, all you do is lay around and spend fucking money… Is that what you want?" Reaching in his pocket, he pulled out a knot of money, and took the rubber band off it. Licking his fingers, he began to flip through the bills. "Let's see, how much for you to buy a fuckin' clue." He began to count it out, then he just started tossing handfuls in her face. "Is that enough?" He taunted, "Here, here, here, take it all."

Lynette watched the money rain down all around her and fall on her feet. It hurt her to her core to hear Tony say such things about her, but what hurt even more is that she wanted to pick the money up. Had she really become the money hungry, superficial bitch he'd described? He was the one who made her Ms. Zoo. Before Rich, she didn't have money like this. Rich walked past her and slammed the door on his way out the apartment. Wrapping her arms around her body, Lynette cried harder than she could ever remember crying in her life. She didn't even cry this hard when he hit her. But the blow he delivered tonight was the toughest by far, and Lynette didn't think she could handle it as she broke down.

WE MADE LOVE IN THE 80'S

<><><><><>

Rich, Stacks, and Sam had gone through great lengths to make sure all evidence of the shooting had disappeared. In addition to paying off the club manager and security, they took the tape and hushed a few witnesses. They didn't know who the guys were or where they were from, but they were hoping they'd never hear from them. The last thing they needed was some retaliation shit going down. However, they were ready for anything.

The women on the other hand were all in trouble after that night. Rich wasn't the only one pissed, Stacks was equally as pissed. Lynette and Faith's asses were in deep shit, and Keisha wasn't exempt. Even though she wasn't dating a nigga from Zoo, they still took care of her and looked out for her, so she was swimming in shit, right along with them.

Since the shooting, everyone had been in the house for the most part, and the guys were clocking their every move. Little did they know, it wasn't even necessary; they had no desire to go out. Maybe, just maybe, things had gotten a little out of hand, and maybe their heads had gotten a little big.

"So, what y'all been doing?" Janae asked Lynette, Faith, and Keisha as they sat talking, on their three-way call.

"Shit," Faith and Keisha chuckled on one line.

"I had class today." Lynette sighed running her hands through her hair. She wasn't feeling the best, so her hair wasn't done at all.

"Whaaaatttttt…" everyone sang in unison.

"You back in school?" Faith asked.

"Yeah, something like that." She shrugged.

"I know that's right. Well, I have to pick the baby up from Sam's in a minute.

"Rich and Stacks came back today?" Keisha asked.

ARABIA

"I don't know," Lynette sighed because in all honesty, she hadn't really spoken to Rich since he cursed her ass out. A few days later he was off, gone for two weeks on a business trip. He called every couple of days, just to make sure she was okay, and that was it.

"I guess, I half talked to Stacks earlier, and he said they should be in tonight or tomorrow," Faith added.

"Aight, y'all. Well, let me go. I'll call y'all when I get home," Janae said as she hung up, then prepared to go and get her baby.

Shit with her and Sam had been real chill since bringing the baby home. They hadn't spoken about being together, but they were focused on parenting. Little Samantha Reign was the apple of both of their eyes. Even though Sam wasn't her biological father, you couldn't tell him that. When he stepped, he stepped all the way up, even put his name on her birth certificate, and Janae couldn't do shit but respect him. Never could she ever say shit against Sam. He was everything she and little Sammie needed.

Today, she had her six weeks doctor's appointment, and Sam kept the baby for her. The appointment was this morning, but she took a few hours for herself and was just headed over to his house around four. She was just thinking of how to approach him about being together when the cab pulled up to his apartment building. Quickly, she paid the cab driver and hopped out.

The door to Sam's building was always unlocked, so she got in with no problem and headed to the second floor. After knocking on his door twice it opened, and Stacks was standing there.

"What you want?" He asked, rudely.

"Not you, so move." Janae rolled her eyes, pushing past him and walking into the living room. On the couch, Rich was sitting next to Zaria and Janae scoffed shaking her head. "Let me get my baby and go because y'all got some serious bullshit going on around here."

She peeped Rich try to put a little distance in between him and Zaria but it was too late, she was already telling. "Bitch ass niggas," she hissed, heading down the hallway, when out of nowhere she was almost knocked down.

"Damn, Z…" Sam caught her before she could hit the ground. Once he stood her up, a look of perplexity covered his face when he noticed it wasn't Zaria, but Janae. Once she was upright and, on her feet, she was going to speak but a woman coming out of the bathroom behind him had her words caught in her throat. The look on Janae's face said it all, and Sam ain't want these types of problems. "Go wait for me up front Laya, while I talk to my kids' mom."

"I see you still fuckin' her." Now it all made sense, Nalaysia was Zaria's cousin. Shaking her head, Janae started laughing. "I gotta get the fuck out of here," she said, stepping to the side. She continued to his room and found the baby asleep on the bed. Grabbing her bag, she just started throwing her shit in it.

"Janae…"

"Don't fuckin' Janae me!" She nearly screamed. "This what the fuck you do when you get my child. Have her in here with these fucking bums and random ass hoes."

"Relax! They just got here…"

His nonchalant attitude didn't do anything but piss her off more, but she tried to remain calm. "Yeah, well, everybody real fucking comfortable to just get here," Janae barked, not believing him one bit. "Move!" She pushed past him to load up her bottles that were on the dresser.

Sam watched her as she angrily grabbed the baby's things and stuffed them into her bag. When she went for the baby, she snatched the blanket and to Sam, it looked as though she was handling her rough. "Calm all that shit down. You can be mad all you want, but you ain't gone handle her like that." He stepped up and bumped Janae out the way.

"Nigga, I know how to handle my fucking child." She pushed him back hard. "And don't put ya fucking hands on me!" Janae yelled, mushing him in his head so hard, it felt like a slap.

Almost immediately, Sam's reflexes kicked in and before he knew it, they were tussling. "Janae, stop fucking playing with me," he snarled, holding her up against the wall.

"Get the fuck off me!" She bucked her body, ready to take his fucking head off as she tried to swing.

"You better keep ya fuckin' hands to ya self."

"Fuck you, Sam. Get the fuck off me."

"Aight, Aight, let her go, let her go," Stacks said, as he and Rich came in the room and broke them up. Stacks held Sam back and Rich had Janae.

Tears fell from her eyes as she tried to break away from Rich and smack fire from Sam's ass. "You a dog ass nigga, and you ain't never gone see me or my baby again." Snatching away from Rich, she went to finish getting Sammie ready.

"You really want me to fuck you up." Sam pulled away from Stacks. "Don't fuckin' play with me when it come to my daughter, Janae." He grabbed her by the back of her neck, yanking her backwards, and she turned around swinging.

Janae wanted to yell from the mountain tops that Sammie wasn't his, but no matter how mad she was, she knew better than to play with Sam like that. More than anything, she ain't wanna play with her daughter like that.

"Just let her get the baby and bounce," Rich said, pushing Sam into the other room.

"Come on, Janae, I'll take you home," Stacks offered, as she snatched away from him. As fast as she could, she grabbed Sammie and her bag.

Up front, Zaria and Layla had left because they had other shit to do. Neither one of them was trying to be in the middle of whatever Sam had going on, but Zaria was disappointed her time with Rich was cut short. But she remembered his pager number and planned on hitting him up later.

While Sam and Rich were in the living room, Janae came storming past them and out the door. She ain't even look Sam's way, and Rich couldn't help but chuckle.

"The car unlocked; I'll be down in a minute." Stacks yelled behind her and looked to the guys before he and Rich bust up laughing.

"Y'all think everything fucking funny, I'mma crack her got damn jaw word to muthas." Sam swore pacing the floor.

"Chill out, I'mma run ya baby moms' home and then I'm going home my damn self." Stacks dapped them up before Rich did the same.

"Yeah, I'm out too," Rich said preparing to leave himself.

Stacks said his goodbyes and when they were gone, he locked up. Rubbing his eye, his shit was sore. Janae clocked his ass good and he had to laugh. She was lucky they had a child together, because the way he was feeling today, he could've killed her with his bare hands. Shaking his head, he removed his shirt. The only plans Sam had now was to shower, ice his eye and get some sleep.

It was funny to Rich how Sam had a baby, and all this drama with a bitch he never fucked. Like that shit was comical at the least. Rich couldn't laugh at their problems, because he had his own. He knew Janae was going to run and tell Lynette, he was talking to Zaria. So, he was already prepared for the bullshit when he got home. So, instead of going straight home, he rode around a little and handled a little business. Rich ended his night around nine after kicking it with his crew. When he walked into his apartment everything was still and quiet. He looked around and everything was clean and in order. One thing Rich appreciated about Lynette was that she kept a clean house, that was one thing she was good for.

Rich could see the light on in the bedroom, and he was prepared to deny everything. He had to laugh to himself because he was nervous. Pushing the cracked door all the way open, his eyes met Lynette's and he had to smirk at how cute she looked. Sitting up on the bed in one of his t-shirts, her hair was halfway down the other half pulled up, she had her glasses on and books scattered all around her. "Hey"

"Hey," she said giving him the once over as he stepped in the room. "I'll be done in a minute."

ARABIA

"Nah, you good. I'm about to shower anyway." Rich walked into the closet and removed his shirt and then his pants before placing them in the hamper. When he came out, Lynette was closing her books.

Rich honestly didn't know what to say to her, so he didn't say anything. In the shower, he thought of the argument they had. He loved Lynette deeply, but he wanted her to be more than just a kept woman. When he met her, she had goals and shit, and he didn't want her to lose sight of that. She was young so Rich understood that she was only really thinking about the right now, but he was thinking about the future. None of this shit was promised. This fast money was plentiful right now, but one day Rich knew it would come to an end and he needed her to know that too. His delivery may have been a little harsh, but shit wasn't no game out there.

When he was done, he quickly dried off and slid on a pair of boxers before turning the light out. In the bedroom, the television was still on and Lynette was wrapped under the covers. Rich knew she hated sleeping in the dark, so he left it on and climbed in the bed. After two weeks it felt good to lay down in his bed. Even if they were beefing, it felt good to lay next to his girl as well. Turning around, he wrapped his arms around her waist and pulled her into him. Lynette took a deep breath relieved to be in his arms. Rich just didn't know how much she loved him or how much she needed him. Honestly, Lynette didn't even think how much she needed him in her life was healthy.

Rich could feel her body trembling beneath his touch as she sniffed back tears. "Come here man," he pulled her on to him as he wrapped her into his arms, holding her tight. "You know I love you, right?" He asked after giving her awhile to cry it out and she nodded her head.

"I love you too and I'm sorry," she choked out, holding him tighter. They didn't say anything else as they lay there just holding each other. When she was sleep, Rich rolled her off of him and snuggled up next to her. It wasn't long before he was sleep.

The next morning Rich rolled over to an empty bed. Smoothly he ran his hands over the sheets where Lynette had been laying. He wondered where she was, but he didn't have to worry long. All the books she had piled on the dresser last night were gone, so he figured she was at school. A smile creased his lips. He was happy she was back on her shit. After stretching, he got up and went to the bathroom before heading to the kitchen.

WE MADE LOVE IN THE 80'S

On the table, there was a note on top of a plate covered with foil. Picking up the note it read, "I cooked breakfast before I went to school. I love you and I'll see you later." Nodding his head, Rich for sure appreciated it. "Finally got a reason to use this microwave shit," he mused uncovering his plate. The plate was covered with cheese eggs, grits and a couple of pancakes. Once he popped it in the microwave oven, he spent a few minutes pressing buttons trying to figure out how to work it. It took him a minute, but he was able to heat his food up enough to eat it and then he got dressed.

When Rich finally hit the streets, he planned to work until Lynette got home from school, and then he was gonna lay up and get some pussy. It was clear Janae ain't snitch him out and he was happy about that. Not that there was really anything to tell, but he ain't even feel like defending that shit. Sam had been chilling with Layla and Zaria before they got there and according to Sam, they just came through to get some weed. Sam used to fuck with Layla off and on, back in the day but as far as Rich knew he ain't fuck with her like that no more. Whatever the case, he was just shooting the breeze with Zaria since he hadn't seen her in a minute. It was truly innocent, but he knew Lynette wouldn't see it that way. It had been nearly two years since that fight at the basement party and Lynette still couldn't stand her ass.

Chapter 10

Keisha walked next to her man Nate all smiles as they held hands. At first, she didn't know if they could be a thing but here they were. They dated for a long time, before actually becoming official and Keisha was glad, she waited. The wait gave her time to get to know him without any pressure. Today they'd officially been together for almost five months and Keisha figured it was time she introduced him to the crew. She wanted the girls to see how fine he was, and she wanted the guys to feel him out. So, Keisha, asked Stacks to check him out…

"Stacks, can I talk to you for a minute?" She asked one day when he was on the block with the crew.

On this particular day, she was by herself and Stacks thought it was odd. The girls usually rolled together. Very rarely did you ever see one without another; so, immediately, his mind got to wondering, "What's up, everything good?"

"Yeah, it is. I just need a favor?"

He was relieved but his face remained neutral. "You know if you need something, just hit Faith…"

"Nah, nothing like that." Keisha giggled, "I'm kind of seeing this guy and…" she stumbled over her words not knowing what she wanted to say. "Shit, you and Zoo are the only men in my life that actually care about me and shit. I just need somebody to scope this dude out, you know."

Stacks was honored that Keisha would come to him for some shit like this. He didn't have any siblings or close family, so his gang and the girls became that for him. All of the guys looked at Keisha like a sister to the gang and whatever she wanted she could have, "So you want us to make sure the nigga ain't on no bullshit, I got you."

Smiling, Keisha was happy. "Thanks, Stacks,"

"No problem," he dapped her up before pulling her into a brotherly hug. "Now I need you to look out on something."

"Name it," she stood upright, popping her hand on her hip.

"You gotta keep ya big ass mouth shut,"

Playfully, Keisha pretended to zip her lips and throw away the key, "My lips are sealed."

"I bought a house, for me and Faith." *He paused at the sound of her gasping as she held her chest.* "I wanna make shit with her official and I need y'all to help me plan this housewarming party shit."

"Oh my gosh," *she screamed grabbing him as she jumped up and down.* "A fucking house, Faith is going to flip. Is she pregnant, oh my gosh she's pregnant!"

"What, wait, no." *He laughed bursting her bubble.*

"She not,"

"No, how the fuck you get she pregnant out of that."

"I don't know, a bigger house, more room, an extra person." *She was trying to rationalize what all this meant.*

Shaking his head, Stacks killed all the baby talk. "I'm just ready to make shit with us official. It's been a long time comin, but I'm ready to build with her."

"That's so dope, I'm excited." *Keisha beamed.* "Alright, so Faith doesn't know about the house and we're planning a housewarming party or is it an engagement party?"

Stacks laughed shaking his head, "Just a housewarming party for now."

"Okay, okay."

"I'll tell you what, you do me this solid and you can bring your little friend too."

"Hunh," Keisha squinted finally tuning back into what Nate was saying.

"I said, ya brother's house is all the way out here." He looked around the neighborhood they were riding through approvingly. It was nice and he had to admit he was impressed.

"Yeah, it ain't too much further." She recalled trying to remember exactly where the house was. The neighborhood was one of those cookie-cutter communities, where all the houses, for the most part, looked the same. "This it up here," she pointed to the house with cars parked all around it. Shaking her head, she laughed, "They already tearing up these folk's neighborhood."

Nate chuckled, laughing with her as he unbuckled his seatbelt and stepped out. Quickly, he moved to her side of the car. "You know how our people do," he said as he helped her out the car.

"Okay," Keisha laughed grabbing her gift as they walked to the house.

"This is real nice," Nate eyed the bungalow style house admiringly. The porch was huge and inviting as they approached the door. They were standing side by side as Keisha did the honor of knocking.

It was just a few minutes before Sam came and opened the door. "What up," he greeted eyeing her friend. Stacks already told them, she would be bringing a friend, so he was just checking him out.

"Hey," Keisha smiled before hugging him. "Sam this is my boyfriend Nate, Nate this is Sam."

"Hey man, what's up." Nate extended his hand to shake Sam's and Sam stared him up and down, before extending his fist for a pound. Nate didn't take too kindly to the disrespect, but he was going to make the best of his introduction to Keisha's family. Balling his hand in to a fist, he dapped him up really quick.

"Is everyone here?" Keisha asked removing her little jacket and offering to take Nate's.

"Nah," we still waiting on Net and them. He said watching Nate closely. Sam didn't think it was a good idea for them to meet Keisha's new man at Stacks house. But Stacks wasn't worried about it since everybody was going to be there. "They should be on their way, crew in the back tho."

Keisha nodded her head, and they headed to the back where everyone else was. Keeping busy, Keisha introduced Nate to the other people there and then made sure everything was perfect and in order.

WE MADE LOVE IN THE 80'S

The girls were responsible for setting up all the décor and cooking the food, the only thing Stacks had to do was foot the bill.

Nearly an hour had passed, when commotion could be heard coming from the front causing everyone to turn their attention to the door.

"Zoo!" Rich barked loudly as he, Lynette and Janae walked through the door.

The guys returned his greeting as Keisha walked over to the girls. "Let me see my baby," She cooed, "Come here Sammie. Gosh, she getting so big."

Janae handed the baby over and noticed Sam in the corner standing with his friends. They hadn't really said more than two words to each other since the fight at his house, and Janae ain't plan on talking to him no time soon. "I'mma run to the bathroom right quick."

Lynette and Keisha looked from her to Sam and then at each other, before shaking their heads. "Girl what time this supposed to start, shit I thought I was late?"

"They supposed to be on their way." Keisha told her as they chatted for a bit before she and Lynette walked over to the guys. "Here she heavy."

Sam's whole face lit up when he laid eyes on Sammie. "There goes daddy baby," taking her in his arms, he kissed her before holding her to his chest. Quickly, he scanned the room for Janae, but he didn't see her. "Where Nae?"

"She's in the bathroom." Keisha said before walking away.

He watched Keisha head back over to her little friend, before turning his attention back to Sammie. Right before his eyes she was growing up. A head full of curly locks covered her head and her chinky eyes melted even the coldest of hearts.

"You okay?" Keisha asked making her way over to Nate.

He nodded he was as he pulled her into him. After turning the beer bottle up to his lips, he spoke. "I'm good." He assured her before looking back at the people around him.

ARABIA

"Aight, they just pulled up. So, when the door opens, just yell surprise." Lynette said as she walked in with Janae.

"Man, we know how the surprise go," Tech joked, and everyone laughed as Lynette flipped him off.

Outside Stacks opened the car door for Faith and she stepped out. "Who the hell live all the way out here?"

"My homeboy having a little get together." He lied easily, "you don't like it?"

"I mean it's nice, real nice, it's just far as hell." She gathered as she checked out the neighborhood. "Quiet,"

"Yeah it is," after grabbing her hand, they walked over to the door and Stacks walked them in.

"Surprise." Everyone yelled as the women threw confetti in the air.

"Shit," Faiths breath caught in her throat as she grabbed her chest. Confused, she ain't know what was happening.

Her eyes met Stacks and he was smiling. "Welcome home!" He could tell by the look on her face she was still confused. "I got this house for you, for us…" Shaking her head, she started to cry as her hands covered her face. Stacks pulled her into his arms, "I got you forever." He whispered in her ear hugging her tight as she nodded her head.

Once he let her go, she was swarmed by the girls and the party began. There was food and drinks for them to enjoy, music to dance to, and everyone was having a good time.

"So, you like it right?" Keisha asked excitedly, the moment Faith came back from her tour of the house.

"Yes, I love it! It's so big," Faith beamed. "I still can't believe y'all knew about this and ain't tell me."

"Then it wouldn't have been a surprise." Lynette tossed in adjusting her Kangol hat.

"Yes, it would've, hell Stacks barely been talking to me as it is."

"Same," Lynette chuckled.

"Well my man talking to me!" Keisha smiled. All the girls turned to her date and gave him the once over. "He fine ain't he?"

"He looks alright, calm down." Lynette joked and the girls giggled.

Faith looked to her, "Where you meet him at again?"

"Y'all remember last year I was telling y'all I met that guy at the mall?"

"No," Janae answered quickly knowing she never knew Keisha was seeing someone.

Lynette squinted, "Vaguely."

Faith remembered them having a conversation once, but never mentioned it again. "So, you've been dating the same guy since then?"

"Something like that,"

Janae needed clarification. "For almost a year and we're just meeting him?"

"Nah, we were just cool. We just decided to make things official a couple of months ago."

All the girls looked at each other smirking, "well alright bitch we see you." Janae high-fived her. "Okay, give us the rundown on Mr. Nate."

"Well, Nate is twenty-five, he stays out west, no kids, got his own place, a freaking car," she huffed animatedly, because she was tired of meeting guys with no car. "He in the streets, but he real low key with it."

"That's all good, but how does he treat you?" Faith asked wanting to know what kind of man he was.

"He treats me good. He's always available for my emotional drama, and any man that can handle my mood swings is a keeper." All the women nodded their head agreeing before they bust out laughing. "Oh whatever, I'm not that bad." She laughed, "but so far he's been nothing but amazing. That's why I wanted Stacks to kind of feel him out...finding a good one out here, all about you, that got his shit together, is almost too good to be true."

"Shit we told you to snatch up one of them Zoo niggas, but nah, you wanna go out West!" Faith mushed her in her head laughing.

Rolling her eyes, Keisha wouldn't hear of it. "You already know them like my brothers. I couldn't even see myself dating a nigga from Zoo...and shit y'all took all the niggas in Zoo, what y'all want me to fuck with a worker?"

"Tech is more than just a worker, don't do him like that." Faith interjected. A while ago she called herself playing match maker and Keisha wasn't having it.

"First of all, he has a girl, and Tech is Tech, no."

Janae nodded her head agreeing as she and the girls continued to laugh and talk about Keisha's man. Her ears perked up when she heard her baby crying and almost instantly, her eyes found Sam's. He was talking to some chick and Janae wasn't even for the drama today. Reaching in her baby bag, she grabbed a bottle and a burp cloth before she walked over to him. "Hand her here, I'll feed her." She stepped right in between him and the woman standing next to him. Sam looked down at her and allowed his eyes to linger making her fidget. "I'll bring her right back."

He nodded before letting her take the baby and his eyes followed her to the kitchen.

"That's ya kids' mom?" The girl that just happened to be standing next to him asked.

"Yeah," he looked back at Janae and she was staring right at him. He wanted to talk to her but felt as if he'd put himself out there one too many times.

"You have a beautiful family," she smiled respectfully. Sam nodded his head thanking her, then she held her hand out. "Taneika."

He looked down at her hand, then back at her face. "Sam."

Rolling her eyes, Janae was using her breathing techniques to calm her nerves. This shit was Sam was blowing her and she was ready to go. Her mind was made up, once she finished feeding the baby she was out.

"What up, Nae?" Solomon greeted as he walked into the kitchen.

Looking up from Sammie, she smiled, "What up Solo."

"Shit, I can't call it." He walked over peeking at the baby. "You got the little one out, hunh?"

"Yeah, just for a little bit. We about to go tho."

"I hear that, I'm about to break in a few myself." Licking his lips, he propped himself up on the counter. "This was dope tho, got me ready to buy a house and shit."

"Right," she laughed agreeing. "It's definitely nice."

"Yeah, once I get a girl on some real shit, Ima make that move." He looked down at her feeding the baby and smirked. "So, you and Sam, y'all still rockin?"

Before she could answer, Sam came in the kitchen. "What up Solo," he greeted slapping a hand on his shoulder smoothly moving him out the way. He stood in front of Janae and noticed that Solomon was still on his neck. "Can I help you?"

Solomon looked from Janae back to Sam shaking his head, "Nah, I was just leaving." He slapped a hand on Sam's shoulder as he walked by and Sam had to fight not to swing on him. Solo wasn't Zoo, but they had all grown up together, so he was cool but not so cool that Sam wouldn't fuck him up. When Solomon was out of the kitchen, he turned his attention back to Janae. "Stop fuckin' fuckin' with me bruh." Sam snarled as he took the baby from her and put her on his shoulder.

"You got the nerve," rolling her eyes, Janae stood up adjusting her clothes. "I ain't even about to go back and forth with you, we about to go."

"Aight, let's go." He said moving back so she could walk out past him.

"I don't need you to get home. I got here by myself and I can get back."

Janae pushed past him and he quickly snatched her up. "Don't make me turn this shit out," he held her arm tighter as he brought her face closer to his. "Now get ya shit and let's go."

Her eyes didn't leave his and she knew not to push him. Besides, this wasn't the time nor the place to be acting a fool. Snatching away from him, Janae briskly walked over to the girls. "Aight y'all, I'm about to go."

"Why? We ain't even cut the cake yet." Faith pouted.

"I know, just save me a piece." Leaning over, she kissed Faiths cheek and said her goodbyes before meeting back up with Sam. While he held the baby, she put her little jacket on and then her hat before they were out the door.

"Mmm, mmm" Lynette snickered watching Janae and Sam with the other girls.

"Right," Faith added.

Keisha finished her drink, licking her lips. "I wish they just fuck and get it over with already!"

"Okay!!!" Faith high-fived her. "But when they do, I bet that shit gon' be good as fuck!"

"That part!" Lynette agreed.

Sam buckled the baby in the car seat and Janae hopped her happy ass in the front. Her plan was to not say shit until she got home.

WE MADE LOVE IN THE 80'S

A shower and her bed were calling her name. All this drama and shit, plus a new baby at home was just too much, she needed to relax. "Where you going?" She asked once she noticed he was passing the exit for her house.

"Don't you ever just be quiet?" Sam sighed as he turned the music up.

Licking her lips, Janae was fighting not to go off the way she wanted too. Her knee bounced as she folded her arms across her chest. This was exactly why she ain't wanna ride with his rude ass. A few minutes later and it was clear Sam was taking them to his place. When he parked, Sam jumped out and grabbed the baby from the backseat, before holding the passenger side door open for Janae. She looked to him rolling her eyes as she undid her seatbelt and stepped out. Together they walked to his apartment and he let them in the house.

As always Sam handed her the baby and walked in first. It was a habit of his, to check the house for any intruders before they came in and he did it all the time. Once they were all in the house, Sam took the baby to her room. Sammie was still sleep, so he gently removed her clothes before laying her in the crib. Back in his room, he found Janae sitting on his bed. She was still fully clothed with the baby bag resting at her feet. "You might as well get comfortable."

"Why did you bring me here?"

"Because, we need to talk." He said nonchalantly as he removed his shirt.

"Well talk," once his bare chest came into view, Janae diverted her eyes trying to look at anything else but him.

"I don't wanna talk right now."

Her eyes fell back on him and Sam was stepping out of his pants. "Sam for real,"

"Right now," he walked over to her and pull her to her feet by her arms. "Right now, I want you to stop acting like you don't want me…" he bent down kissing her lips. Just a peck at first as they gazed in each other's eyes. "Like you don't want this."

Janae's eyes stayed connected to his as he continued to kiss her. She felt him fumbling around with her jeans and couldn't stop him. She wanted to but she couldn't, because she wanted him just as much as she didn't want him. The eternal battle she was dealing with was something new to her and something she honestly didn't think she was strong enough to fight. Lost in her thoughts, she didn't come back to reality until she was stripped down to her panties and bra. With little to no effort, Sam picked her up and she wrapped her legs around his waist.

Sam laid her down on the bed and settled between her legs. "I love ya little ass." He whispered in between kisses to her neck and nibbles to her collarbone.

Tears flooded her eyes as she bit her lip holding back the cry that she so desperately needed. "Sam," she finally found her voice. He pretended he didn't hear her as he continued to kiss down her body. "Sam," she nearly growled his name as he pulled her panties to the side and ran his tongue up her silky slit. Almost instantly, her legs opened wider and her eyes fluttered from the rhythmic swirls of his tongue. "Oh, fuck," she sounded as he grabbed her clit between his lips, sucking and probing it with his tongue.

Her pussy ran water like a faucet and tasted sweet like it was made of honey. Sam became lost in her essence as he ripped her panties off and tossed them to the floor. His strong arms held her legs back as he smothered his entire face in her coochie lapping all her juices up.

Janae bucked her hips matching his strokes, fucking his face. Hands down, this was the best head she'd ever had, ever. Gripping the covers, she was practically running from this tongue lashing he was putting on her. "Ugh, uhhh, oh fuck," her pelvis lifted, and she came so hard she was choking Sam with her legs and he didn't stop.

Once her body fell back on the bed, she laid there sprawled out, eyes barely open. Sam unwrapped her legs from around his neck, then sat up. He looked down at her while wiping his mouth with his sheet. He took in her body and to him she was perfect. Sammie was a little shy of four months and it didn't even look like she'd had a baby. Sam continued to eye her, while grabbing her right leg and placing it in the crook of his arm. Steadily, he slid his dick over her warmth a couple of times before he slid inside of her.

"Damn," they both moaned in unison.

WE MADE LOVE IN THE 80'S

"Shit, you feel so fuckin' good." He pulled back and went back in, working his stiffness inside of her.

"Oh, my god, sssss," Janae was spent as his dick completely filled her up. Like this shit felt like she was having another baby.

"Relax," he whispered looking in her eyes. When she looked back at him, they locked eyes and there was so much love there, so much passion that eventually they began to move in sync. Leaning down he kissed her lips and she began to fuck him back. For every stroke he delivered she came back with one of her own. Janae wrapped her legs tightly around his back, then sat up on her elbows riding his dick from beneath him. "Hell yeah, ride that shit just like that." And, ride she did. Sam let her get her little shit off for a minute, then he started bangin her shit out. Relentlessly, he pounded into her and she screamed his name. "Tell me you love me." She didn't say anything, and he went harder. "Tell me!"

Voice caught in her throat; Janae could barely form the words he was dicking her down so good. Tears freely slid from her eyes, as he fucked her into submission. "I love you! Oh, shit I love you." Her voice cracked just as she came, and Sam came with her.

Staring at her, Sam had to catch his breath. Her hands were covering her face as she cried the ugly cry into them. Leaning down, he kissed her shoulder. "I love you too," he said into her ear and she snatched away from him.

"Get up," she pushed at his chest and he didn't budge.

Shaking his head, he slid out of her and rolled over on his back. Rolling his eyes, he just wanted to fuck and go to sleep. But of course, that was too easy for Janae dramatic ass. Looking up she was walking to the bathroom. When she closed the door, Sam sat up on the bed. Over in the ashtray was the joint he needed to finish his night. After lighting up, he hit it a few times before the door opened.

Janae was so flustered; she didn't even want to look at him. She was embarrassed, she was scared, she was too many things right now. Over by the bed she grabbed her clothes.

"Fuck is you doing?" Sam looked to her.

"I'm leaving, I'll pick the ba…"

"Put that shit down," he got up dick swinging as he stomped towards her. "Cut it out Janae and grow the fuck up."

"Sam just stop,"

"Stop what?" He snatched the clothes out of her hand and tossed them to the floor. "You keep fighting this shit with us, then wanna flip when you see me with another bitch." Letting her go, he stepped back. He was tired of doing whatever this was with her. "I'm not about to play these childish ass games with you for real. You don't wanna be with me, cool."

Shaking her head, Janae didn't like the finality in his voice. "I do, I just…"

"Ain't no me without Zoo, Janae. If you ain't willing to accept that we really ain't got shit else to talk about. I'll be the best father to Sammie, but I'm done with yo' ass." That was it, Sam had enough. "Lock my door on your way out."

Janae watched him walk away from her and her chest tightened as she gripped her clothes. She wanted Sam, she did. Hell, he just fucked an "I love you," right up out of her. So, she couldn't even lie about that anymore. But, loving him meant that she had to accept Zoo and she hated that. Sam was perfect in every way. He stepped up for Sammie and made sure Janae didn't want for anything…leaning against the dresser she thought of his one flaw. Then she thought of all she would be missing out on, if she let that one flaw stop her from being with him. When she thought of it like that, it just wasn't worth it. Sighing, she dropped her clothes back on the floor and headed to the bathroom. Janae turned the doorknob, but it was locked. Fisting her hand, she was prepared to knock, but she hesitated. Shaking her head, she went to walk away, but came back. She did this twice before she hurriedly knocked on the door three times. She waited a minute before she knocked harder and that time, Sam swung the door open.

His body glistened with water while her eyes traveled his frame. When their eyes met again, she slowly walked up to him. On her tippy toes, she kissed his lips. He didn't kiss her back, but it didn't matter she wasn't going to stop.

"What you want Nae?" He stopped her when her hands grabbed his dick.

Looking at him, her eyes watered. "I want you," she blinked back tears. "You already know how I feel about Zoo, but I don't even care. You got ya shit with you and I got mine."

"You sure? Because ain't no turning back after this Nae…"

She silenced him with a kiss and this time he kissed her back. "I love you, Sam." She told him just as he swooped her up in his arms.

"I love you too," he smirked stepping into the shower. He pushed her up against the wall and they were on for round two.

The housewarming lasted another hour or so, once Janae and Sam left. When everyone was gone, Stacks and Faith were left home alone. She couldn't stop walking around the house. Everything was just perfect, and she couldn't believe it was all for her.

"Come here sit down," Stacks chuckled.

"I can't, I just wanna keep looking at everything." Faith looked up to him as he pushed her down on to the couch. "Thank you."

"You welcome," he sat down next to her. Leaning back, he wrapped an arm around her neck and relaxed. For a minute the two of them were silent, then he spoke. "I know I ain't a real emotional type nigga and I don't always say the right shit, but I love you Faith." He brought his index finger to her chin and turned her face until their eyes met. "I appreciate how you always been down for me, like out of everybody I've ever known you the only one I know for a fact is solid."

"Shit Landon," Faith cried loss for words.

Scooting to the edge of the couch, Stacks smirked just a bit. "I bought this house to show you I was for real about us being together, and that I was ready to make you my girl." He stood to his feet then looked down at her. "But that wasn't enough, after all we been through you deserve way more than that…shit, I owe you more than just this house." Reaching in his pocket, he dropped down to one knee and pulled out a black box. "I owe you the world, but I'll start with giving you my last name."

ARABIA

Immediately, Faiths hands flew to her mouth and she was stuck in shock as water literally poured from her eyes. Since she was seven years old, all she ever wanted to be was his girl. Now not only was he asking her to be his, but to be his wife, "Yes, yes, yes," she shouted jumping on him knocking him over. "I love you so much."

Stacks laughed as he held her in his arms, "I love you too." Once she allowed him to sit up, he grabbed her left hand.

Faiths, fingers trembled as he placed the diamond princess cut ring on her finger. Her pupils dilated as the diamond sparkled in her eyes. Faith didn't know how many karats it was, and she didn't care. It was the biggest she'd ever seen, and she loved it.

Looking at Stacks, she grabbed his face with her hands and kissed him passionately. Her love for him flowing through as she parted his lips with her tongue. Stacks placed his hands on her ass and pulled her onto his lap as he continued to tongue her down.

"I wanna fuck you so bad right now." She moaned into his mouth, before she moved to his neck.

"I bet you do," he smacked her ass. "We only got a couple of days and I'mma tear that ass up."

This was the worst time possible she could ever remember having her cycle. "Ugh, I swear. I'mma get on some birth control just so I won't have one."

Once Stacks got up, he helped her up shaking his head. "Nah, you don't need that shit. Plus, you ain't gone have no period once I put my Jr in there."

"Oh, marriage and a baby?"

"Damn right, you mine now."

"Shit I was yours before all this." Faith let him know quickly. They were locked in for the rest of their lives and she wouldn't have it any other way.

Chapter 11

Lynette stood behind the purchasing counter watching the clock. Getting a job was the worst thing she'd ever done, but she felt it was necessary. Even though she and Rich were slowly moving past that bump in the road, the things he said didn't sit right with her. At this point, she felt like more of a burden than a partner. The little job she picked up, was okay for what it was, but it was just something she could say was hers. This whole situation with Rich showed her to never count what a man has as yours. So, here she was. Now more than ever, she was determined to finish school and make something of herself.

"I know you ready to clock out," her manager walked over checking out the empty store.

"I am," she said unable to hold her laugh.

"Go ahead, get out of here." She smiled as Lynette looked at her with questioning eyes. "Go ahead, I got it from here."

"Thanks Cheryl." She didn't have to tell Lynette twice. She went to the back grabbed her bag as she clocked out in record timing. On the way out of WoolWorths, she checked her watch and it was going on seven in the evening. This was seriously for the birds, every night she was getting home later and later. Since she got off early, she figured she would just catch the bus back home and that was going to take her another hour.

"You just getting home from school?" Rich asked when he walked through the door.

Lynette had just gotten in the house as well and was taking off her jacket. "Yeah, I had that study group and work."

"Oh, that's what's up." He walked past her and stopped to kiss her on the forehead before heading to the back.

Lynette's eyes followed him to the back surprised that he ain't have more to say about her having a job. She hadn't been working at the store long, as a matter of fact tonight made exactly two months. Either way, Rich hadn't noticed or mentioned it. "You want anything to eat?"

"Nah, I ate a little earlier." He said walking back into the kitchen.

"I shoulda' picked something up too." Lynette thought out loud.

From behind her, Rich wrapped his arms around her waist before kissing her neck. "You want me to go get you something?"

Shaking her head, Lynette couldn't think of anything she wanted. "Nah, I'll find something." After closing the refrigerator, she turned around wrapping her arms around his neck. "You missed me?"

Smirking, Rich nodded his head. "All day," he added palming her ass, and pulling her closer. "We still going to see ya moms tomorrow?"

"Yup, I spoke to her earlier and she already got her questions ready for you." Laughing, Lynette shook her head knowing her moms was crazy.

"I'm good, women love me."

He laughed but Lynette didn't. "Yeah aight," she rolled her eyes popping him in the back of his head. After she let his neck go, he turned her around and together they walked to the bedroom. "Ya birthday coming." She smiled stepping out of her shoes when they made it to the bedroom.

"I know." Rich sighed, "Nigga getting old."

"Boy, twenty-two is not old," after waving him off, she removed her shirt. "You want anything special?"

Shaking his head, Rich really wasn't into gifts and all that. "Nah, ain't nothing I really want." Walking over to Lynette he grabbed between her legs cupping her lady parts in his hand. "Some of this same pussy I been getting is good."

"You get on my nerves," rolling her eyes, she was not going to play with him. "Yeah, yeah, I'm going to shower." Lynette heard all that he was saying but it went in one ear and out the other. Last year for his twenty first birthday, they flew to Vegas and spent a week at MGM. Everything from gambling to shopping to eating at the finest restaurants was on their list, and to top the week off they went to see Mike Tyson fight. Vegas was the most fun that either of them had ever had and she had all kinds of plans to top that this year. But, no, this year, she wanted to do something a little more intimate and lower key. Lynette planned to do a quiet dinner at home, and she was sure he was going to love her gift. After that whole fiasco about her spending money, she was kind of penny pinching and holding back on a lot. His money was still available to her, but she barely wanted to touch it. When she got her first check, the very first thing she did was open a bank account. It was probably something small to other people, but she was proud of herself. It felt like she had taken a huge step to self-independence.

The next morning, they were up with the birds, Rich had a little business to take care of and Lynette had a few errands to run herself. However, they both made sure they were back at the house by two in the afternoon, because they were supposed to be at her mom's by four. It was Sunday and her mom planned this big dinner to meet Tony and to welcome Lynette back home. Since she'd moved, Lynette spoke to her mom often, but she didn't see her nearly as much as she should've.

"You nervous?" She asked looking over to Rich as he drove.

"Nah, I don't get nervous baby." Rolling her eyes, Lynette couldn't stand his cocky ass sometimes. He looked over to her and could see her mood had shifted. "You?"

Taking a deep breath, Lynette sighed. "A little," she looked out the window as they passed through her old neighborhood. "I just know my mom, and it feels like I'mma be a fuck up, no matter what I do."

Rich pulled up to her mom's house and turned the car off. After he set up, he grabbed her face making her look at him. "You ain't the same little girl that left ya moms house two years ago." Leaning in, he placed his lips on hers kissing her softly. "Besides, you wouldn't be my girl if you were a fuck up."

Blushing, Lynette rolled her eyes before pecking his lips. "I love you too."

Once she was cool, Rich stepped out the car and walked around to open her door. When she stepped out, they held hands as they walked to the front door. Rich looked around checking out the neighborhood and it looked cool for the most part. Lynette took a deep breath before knocking on the door, and then she stepped back. It took a few minutes, but it wasn't long before the door flew open and Lynette's mom was standing before them.

Smiling, she quickly pulled Lynette into her arms. "My baby," she had never hugged her daughter so tight. Rocking side to side, she didn't want to let her go. "Oh, lord let me get a good look at you." At an arm's length, she held Lynette as her eyes scanned her from head to toe. "You look nice and healthy."

"Thanks momma," Lynette beamed. "You look good too."

"Oohh, I'm so happy to see you." She hugged Lynette again before ushering them into the house. After closing the door, she turned to them both. "And who is this handsome young man?"

"Ma, this is my boyfriend Tony, Tony this is my mother LaVelle." Lynette introduced them.

"Hello, Ms. LaVelle, nice to meet you." Rich smiled putting on his best charm. Looking at LaVelle was like looking at Lynette twenty-five years from now. Rich could definitely see where Lynette got her good looks from.

"Oh, hush with that miss stuff, just call me Momma Velle." She opened her arms for a hug and Rich quickly obliged.

"Okay, well come on, before the food gets cold."

Together they all walked to the back of the house. After Lynette and Rich washed their hands, they took a seat at the dining room table. They passed around plates filled with fried chicken, macaroni and cheese, collards and there was even a lemon cake for dessert. Once everyone made a plate, they begin to eat and make small talk.

"So, how'd the two of you meet?" LaVelle asked causing Rich to cut his eyes at Lynette.

"Mutual friends," he shrugged. "Just kind of in the same circle, and we just linked up."

Sucking her teeth, Lynette knew better. "Boy please…He saw me and was sweatin me." She joked causing them all to laugh.

"I know that's right, daughter! I'm sure he was," LaVelle added.

Now it was time for Rich to blush, "Come on man…"

"Nah, Nah, don't be shy now." LaVelle continued to laugh. "Tell me, I wanna hear this."

Rich put his fork down smiling as he recalled their earlier interactions. "I mean when I first met her, we ain't really talk much. I would see her from time to time and she was always playing the background and whatnot. Then one day I was like I'mma pull up on her, and I did. We went out and she been mine ever since."

"Oh, just like that, huh?" LaVelle asked looking between them.

"Of course,"

"Oh my god," rolling her eyes Lynette smiled. "You need to calm down."

"What? That ain't how it happened?" He asked looking at her.

"Something like that," she laughed knowing it was true.

"So, what have you been up to Nettie?" LaVelle asked.

"Nettie?!" Rich asked.

"You better not," she warned, through her giggles before turning to her mother. Her mother was the only person she allowed to call her Nettie. Lynette hated that nickname. "Mmm, nothing much still in school and I have little job now."

"A job," both Rich and LaVelle said in unison, both shocked.

ARABIA

Looking to her mother, Lynette purposely avoided his gaze. "Yeah, nothing too crazy just a little cashier position to keep me busy."

"School is enough to keep you busy. If you needed money you could've called me." LaVelle looked to Rich, "That's a lot on you at one time."

"She don't need money," Rich's eyes were burning a hole in the side of Lynette's head, and if looks could kill she would've been dead. Like passed out, face down in her food dead. "Because, I provide whatever she needs or is that not enough."

Lynette licked her lips then looked to him. "Let's not have this discussion right now."

"Why not, you brought it up right now." He challenged and suddenly the atmosphere became a little hostile.

LaVelle could see it was about to be some shit and she didn't want it to happen at her dinner table. "Well I think it's a lot on you, but if it's what you wanna do then do it." Rich scoffed before excusing himself. Both Lynette and LaVelle watched him walk out, before anything was said. "He's not happy,"

"Nah," sitting back Lynette folded her arms across her chest.

"He didn't know you had a job?" LaVelle asked and Lynette shook her head. "Why would you having a job be an issue?"

There was so much Lynette could say, but she opted to play it safe. "He just wants to be the provider and thinks I should focus on school."

Nodding her head, LaVelle took what she said but knew it was bullshit. She was born at night, not last night and she knew the type of man Rich was soon as he stepped through the door. LaVelle knew his type all too well. In her day, she wanted a street nigga too, but it ain't always everything it's cracked up to be. Whatever the problem was, she could tell that her daughter had figured out that much. Instead of calling her on it, she simply said. "Never let what a man feeds you, be all you have to eat." Standing up, she began to clear the table. "I'll cut the two of you some cake to go."

WE MADE LOVE IN THE 80'S

When Rich came back to the table, it was clear that dinner was over, and he was happy. LaVelle was nice enough to make them to go plates with extra food and cake, and he thanked her with a kiss to her cheek.

"It was nice meeting you," she hugged him, and he told her the same. Turning her attention to her only child she hugged Lynette tight. "I love you baby,"

"I love you too momma,"

"Take care of yourself," LaVelle's voice cracked as she teared up. "You all grown up now, but you know I always have a place for you."

"I know momma, I'll call you later." Lynette kissed her cheek and her and Rich were headed back home. The car ride over was tense as they both rode in silence. They had been doing good. No arguing or fighting, and she wanted to keep it that way. To keep the peace, she figured it would be best to just talk it out, "Tony can we just talk about this."

"Oh, now you wanna talk," shaking his head, Lynette was always on some bull shit. "After you embarrass the shit out of me, making me look like a broke ass nigga in front of your moms. Got her looking at me like I ain't shit and now you wanna talk."

Rolling her eyes, she really didn't know what Rich wanted from her. "One minute you're yelling at me because I don't do anything and all I do is spend money, the next minute your mad because I'm working and making my own...I don't know what you want me to do Rich."

"So, you went and got a job for me?" He asked trying to make what she was saying make sense. "I ain't never asked you to work."

"You didn't have to ask me; I bought a fucking clue." she yelled rolling her eyes as she used his own words against him. Throwing her hands up she was lost. "Nothing I do is good enough for you. You made me Ms. Zoo just to hate me for it, I fall back, and you still hate me for it." Tears came to her eyes, because she didn't know what or who she was outside of being Rich's girlfriend. She didn't even know what it meant to be a girlfriend, hell she didn't even know what it meant to be herself at this point.

"Babe," He calmed down and softened his voice. It was clear Lynette was taking everything he said the wrong way and he wasn't feeling that. "It ain't about you working, I just want you to think." He had to put this shit in a way she would understand. "You need to know that being Ms. Zoo is about more than just spending money, partying, and sitting pretty. You represent a gang of niggas out here on their shit, making moves, getting money, and I'm King Zoo. As my queen, ya hustle should match mine. You supposed to know how to get out here and get money with or without me. Hell, one day, this life could take me and then what?" He turned to her, "You know how many women be out here fucked up after they lose, they man to these streets?" Lynette set back taking in all that he was saying and when he put it like this, she got it. She could understand him without feeling like she was being attacked. "I don't want you to ever think I'm trying to control you. I'm just trying to give you game, trying to make you see past all this flashy shit." He lifted the chain on his neck, then pointed to his clothes. "This shit ain't nothing but smoke and mirrors, don't really mean shit at the end of the day. All this money at ya fingertips and the only thing you can think to do with it is go shopping? All the ways you could be making more money and you wanna buy clothes you ain't gon' be able to fit next year." He joked and Lynette cracked a little smile hitting his arm. "If you wanna do something, open some type of business."

"A business?"

"Yeah, you wanna cashier open a store. Whatever you wanna do I'll help you make it happen. Hell, you like to dress open a boutique or something."

Lynette was hanging on to his every word as if it was the gospel. No man had ever taken the time to help her elevate herself, or really put her in a position to make something of herself. Hell, before this conversation, she had never thought about life past the day, but now Rich had her thinking about her future. Nodding her head, she was going to give it some serious thought. "Okay, I get what you saying and I'mma figure something out."

"Whatever you want just let me know." He looked over to her. "Give me a kiss." Lynette looked at the light that was now red, before leaning over the console and kissing his lips. "And I'm sorry for how I spoke to you too. I ain't mean to hurt ya feelings."

Lynette nodded her head, kissing his lips again. She accepted his apology and sat back in her seat when the light turned green. Already, she was thinking of what kind of store she wanted to open. A clothing store would be fun or a salon. Shaking her head, there were too many salons and she couldn't do a lick of hair. But Rich was right she could dress, and she knew how to get people to spend their money. "Thank you."

Nodding his head, Rich told her she was welcomed before grabbing her hand. He intertwined their fingers, turning her hand over he kissed the back of it. "So, you gon' quit that job, right?"

Shaking her head, Lynette laughed. Rich just never let up, "I'll put in my two weeks' notice tomorrow. I'll quit, but I don't just wanna never show up again…that ain't right."

Rich nodded his head, but in his mind, he was like fuck that job. "Aight, two weeks."

In just a few weeks, summer would be over, and it would be back to business as usual. After the conversation in the car, Lynette quit her job as promised and changed her major to business. She not only wanted to open a store she wanted to be successful and in order to do that she had to educate herself. Lynette might've fucked around a lot, but she was very smart. In addition to her changing her major, she picked up every book she could about starting a business. What to do and what to expect. Through her reading she was able to map out a business plan and was prepared to give it to Rich with his birthday gift. Her life was headed in a new direction and she was happy with her progress. It wasn't much but it was something and she was ready to brag.

"Soooo," she smiled as she sat down at the restaurant table with the other girls.

"Oh lord, what happen now?" Faith side eyed her.

"First of all, fuck you," playfully Lynette gave her the finger and the girls laughed. "Now my good news is I'm opening a clothing store."

"A clothing store?" The girls said together, baffled because this was the first, they'd ever heard of a store.

"Yes," Lynette smiled, "A store! I'm going to call it 55th Street…" she screamed with glee. "It's good right."

"I love it!" Keisha bounced in her seat happy for her. "I love the name."

"Yes, I wanted it to be something special to all of us. Everything they were building right now, started on 55th street."

"That's what's up!" Faith dapped her up. "Done put that shit on the hood and I love it!"

Janae agreed and was very happy for her cousin. Right before her eyes she was growing up. Anyway, she can, she wanted to help. "Can I decorate?"

"Sure, y'all can help me pick out everything. I kind of have an idea how I want it to look, but I need to put it all together."

"I'm with it," Faith nodded ready to do whatever. Then it was quiet for a minute while the waitress sat their food on the table. "Well I have good news as well." She began when the waitress left, and everyone looked to her. "I'm getting married!" Screaming she held her left hand up, putting her ring on full display.

All the juice in Janae's mouth flew out as she nearly choked from shock. Lynette and Keisha looked from her back to Faith and screamed their heads off.

"Bitch how you come to my lunch and top my news!" Grabbing her hands Lynette was so excited. "When did he pop the question?"

"The night of the housewarming party!"

"Bitch that was weeks ago," she yelled once she got herself together.

"I know, I know," she sighed looking at her ring, admiring the way it sparkled in the light. "But we been so busy with the house and getting shit together, I ain't seen or talked to nobody."

"Oh, shut up," Lynette rolled her eyes. "Well I'm definitely a bridesmaid."

"Shit I better be Maid of Honor." Keisha swore knowing better.

Laughing Faith held her hands up, "I'll let y'all know all the details in due time."

Before, either of them could say anything else, Sam walked in. They snickered as he walked over to the table.

"This is a girl only lunch." Lynette swore rolling her eyes.

"Girl, shut up," he said before mushing her in the head. "You ready babe."

"Yeah," she pushed her chair back. "Aight y'all I gotta go." Sam helped her stand from her feet, and she walked around the table kissing everyone in the cheek. "Congrats on the store and the wedding, I'll call y'all later." And just like that she was gone.

"You feeling okay?" Sam asked as he opened the passenger side door of his car for her.

"I feel the same as I been feeling." She huffed plopping down in the seat.

"Well maybe this doctor can figure out what's going on." Sam said one he got in the car.

"I surely hope so." Was all she said before laying her head back on the headrest of the seat Life post baby for Janae had not been a walk in the park at all. She constantly had headaches, her stomach was cramping and upset but her menstrual had been irregular. Sammie was almost six months and Janae just wanted her life back.

When they got to the doctors, Sam checked her in and took a seat right next to her. Sammie was with his mom for the weekend and together they planned on spending some quality time. Sam wanted to go out of town for the weekend, but they had to get this bit of business out the way first. It took about twenty minutes, but once they were finally called to the back Janae was happy. The doctor came in and she didn't waste any time telling him all that had been going on with her. In grave detail she described all the symptoms she'd been experiencing, and he was certain she was just having a little postpartum blues. It wasn't uncommon for women who'd recently given birth to experience what she was going through. But, to be on the safe side and to put her mind at ease he had her undress and he ran some blood work. After her exam, they just sat there waiting.

"See, I told you everything was cool, you just be stressing, making yourself sick." Sam shook his head knowing he was right all along. What the doctor just told her was what he'd been telling her.

"Whatever, I'm sure I need some type of prescription. I know my body and this ain't no damn postpartum blues." She knew better, "I need some antibiotics."

Shaking his head, Sam laughed. Janae ass was just dramatic and there wasn't a prescription for that. Just when he was about to speak the doctor walked in. He was holding his clipboard going over her results and for a minute he didn't say anything.

"I knew it, what is it cancer?" Janae's eyes watered as she gripped her chest.

"What, calm down." Sam sat up and look toward the doctor. "What's up? What's wrong with her?"

"Well it looks like you're expecting."

"Expecting what?" Janae's whole voice changed from worried to this nigga crazy in a second.

"Congratulations, you're having a baby." The doctor said way to happy and Janae felt like she was about to pass out.

"A ba...ba...by," jumping off the table she ran to the trash can and emptied the contents of her stomach.

Sam got up and went over to her rubbing her back. "Are you sure?" He wasn't feeling any pressure, Sam was actually excited.

"Yes," he closed his folder and looked to them. "I know it's probably a little bit of a surprise."

"A little bit," Janae screeched. "I just had a baby, like how is this even possible! Ain't it a reset button before you can get pregnant again." Janae was so lost and didn't know how this even happened. They never had unprotected sex, the only time was the first time nearly three months ago.

"Actually, after giving birth is when a woman is more fertile and stands a higher risk of conceiving. "When you're ready, lay back on the table and I'll have a nurse come and do an ultrasound."

They waited until he walked out before either of them said anything. Janae was about to pass out. The last thing she expected today was to hear that she was going to have another baby. Like, shocked wasn't even the word. "I can't believe this."

Sam saw the tears in her eyes and pulled her into him. "Cut it out, what I tell you about worrying all the time." He kissed her forehead as she walked over to the sink. "I got you babe."

After rinsing her mouth, she sat down on the table. It may have been a terrible thing to think and maybe it made her a bad person, but she wished it was cancer. That she would've been able to handle, but this, this just wasn't it. "Sam, two fucking kids. What am I going to do with two babies?"

"Shit, I don't know, but we'll figure it out." Lifting her head with his index finger, Sam kissed her lips. Usually his words comforted her, but not today.

The nurse came in with the ultrasound machine and Janae was annoyed as all hell. She didn't even want to look at the screen or acknowledge what the nurse was saying. It wasn't until the baby's heartbeat came blaring through the monitor that her eyes began to water, and she broke down crying. Holding her hands over her face, she continued to ball her eyes out as the nurse hurriedly finished up.

Sam's heart smiled looking at his baby on the screen, no doubt he loved Sammie and she was his too. But this for him was a little different and it warmed his heart to see his baby. Looking down at Janae, he shook his head. Pulling her up by her hands, he held her in his arms as she cried. He knew it was soon, real soon, and shit they were young, but fuck it. She was pregnant now and it wasn't nothing they could do about that.

"I'm okay," she sniffled wiping her eyes.

"You sure?"

Nodding her head, she dried her eyes and took a deep breath. "Yeah." Once the doctor came back, he told her that she was ten weeks pregnant and that she should follow up with her OB. Janae and Sam both thanked him as he passed them a couple of ultrasound pictures. After she got dressed, they headed back to the car. On the way, Sam stopped her causing her to look up at him. "What's up?"

"You okay with this?" He asked needing to know. Sam ain't wanna have to bash her face in later so he needed to know now how to move.

Sighing, she looked away from him. "Sam, I ain't gon' sit here and act like I'm over the moon happy right now. I need a minute, but, I'm okay with this."

She assured him as he pulled her into his arms. "Thank you," he lifted her off her feet. "I love you so much."

"I love you too," her voice cracked as she hugged him tighter. "I'm just scared."

"You ain't got shit to worry about. Just like I had you with Sammie, I got you this time." Now it was his time to assure her as she nodded her head.

Chapter 12

Today was officially Rich's birthday and Lynette could hardly sit still. She was so excited; you would've thought it was her birthday. To the tee, she had planned this evening and she wanted it to be perfect. While Rich was out kicking shit with his niggas, she was home setting everything up. Rich had already told her he didn't want anything, but that went in one ear and out the other. Like she said earlier, she wanted to celebrate with him intimately. Something nice and low key. So, she lit candles all over the house, had a tablecloth covering the table. She didn't cook, because she ain't know how to make all the fancy stuff; so, she had their dinner catered and it smelled so good while she was plating it, she snuck some of hers. Soft music was playing, and she was dressed for the occasion. Her nighty was barely there but it was cute, and she got it in his favorite color, blue.

"Okay," she huffed checking the time.

It was ten to eight, so she could breathe just a little. Looking around everting was perfect. This was some next level grown and sexy shit. Lynette was thinking they could do this type of stuff more often. Before she could get caught up in her thoughts, she heard the locks turning and she ran to get into position. Behind his seat, she stood with her arm resting on the chair. She swung her hair over her shoulder and squinted her eyes, popping her hip out as far as she could.

Rich walked into his apartment and a smile instantly covered his face. Lynette slick ass never ceased to amaze him. His eyes took in all the candles, the yellow, red and pink rose petals, and every few feet there was a card. Leaning down, Rich picked up the first one. "You're the best boyfriend ever" then he walked to the next one, "I appreciate the support you give me," the next one, "I love how you love me," the next one, "I love that you never let me be alone," the next one, "I love how you make me a better me," the last one, "No matter what, through whatever...I'mma always be here for you," when he rounded the corner, Lynette was standing there. Her skin glowing and flowing...her body looked broke from the pose, but she had never looked so beautiful. Licking his lips, he shook his head. Nobody had ever done no shit like this for him. On the real, he would take this over going out any day.

Rolling her eyes, Lynette stood up right, "Don't laugh at me, I'm trying to be sexy."

"And you are," he smiled as she walked over to him and then he pulled her into his arms. "Thank you." Rich looked down into her eyes, before kissing her lips.

"You're welcome." Standing on her tippy toes, she kissed his lips. "Aight, go wash your hands and have a seat."

Rich went to do as he was told, and Lynette strutted to the kitchen to bring the food in and make their plates. When he came back, his plate was full of a nice juicy steak, garlic mashed potatoes and gravy, with asparagus on the side. Rubbing his hands together he was ready to eat. Lynette pulled out his chair and once he sat down, she pushed it in. Carefully, she walked his plate over to him and sat it down right in front of him. Then she brought her plate over, their drinks, and took a seat herself. They sat across from each other as they began to eat, not really saying much because the food was so damn good.

"I really like your hair like that." Rich spoke chewing his food.

"Really," Lynette smiled as he nodded his head. It was a new little flip style she was trying, and she liked it too. "Well, I'll wear it like this more often."

Nodding his head, he hoped so. "You did a good job with the set up to. I liked the cards."

"You liked the cards, huh?" she playfully rolled her eyes. Lynette wasn't the overly emotional type, but she wanted to let him know how much she loved and appreciated him. "So, what you do all day?"

After chewing his food, he wiped his mouth. "Shit, drink, smoke and bullshit." He shrugged keeping shit real with her.

"Sounds like some Zoo shit." She laughed just imagining what they were probably out there doing. "Did you know, Stacks and Faith are getting married?"

Nodding his head, he confirmed he knew. "Yeah, we helped him pick the ring out."

"Well, why you ain't tell me?"

Rich tilted his head knowingly, "Why, so you could run and tell it?"

"Whatever," Rolling her eyes, she wasn't trying to hear that.

Rich finished his last bite of food and sat back, "That was good," rubbing his stomach, he finished his beer. "Come here?"

Biting her lip, Lynette shook her head. "No."

"Why not? I want my gift."

"This is not your gift."

"But that pussy is what I asked for." He bit his lip as he leaned to the side grabbing his dick.

"You get on my nerves." Lynette could barely hold her laughter as she stood up from the table. Walking over to the closet, she grabbed three boxes. Two were about the same size and one was significantly smaller. "I know you were opposed to me working, but I took the money and I wanted to get you something from me. Something I got for you all by myself," taking the largest of the boxes, she handed it to him. "Happy Birthday."

Rich watched her for a few seconds before he took the box from her hands. It may have been crazy to other people, but Lynette was giving him a lot of his first. Like this shit was really touching his heart. Clearing his throat, he sat up and tore into the wrapping paper before he opened the box. "Damn," he looked up to her and she was smiling. "Babe, no you didn't."

"Yes, babe, I did."

"Yooo, this shit so fresh." Lynette had gotten him a Dapper Dan jacket and he was so excited, he was about to piss himself. Jumping up from his seat, he put the jacket on, smoothing his hands over the front.

"It looks good on you, but it's missing something." She handed him the other box, and he didn't waste any time tearing into it. "Babe," he looked to her knowing damn well, "you got me the whole set!" he yelled, pulling the pants out. "Thank you, thank you," he pulled her into his arms kissing her lips, "Damn, now I gotta get you one."

"Now, you know," she started, and walked over to the closet and pulled out another box. "I did, however, use your money for this one."

Patiently, Rich waited as Lynette began opening it, and it was a girl version of his Dapper Dan set and he bust out laughing. "I should've known."

"You damn well should've," she laughed. "That set nearly cleaned me out, but I'm happy you like it."

"Like it, baby, I love it." He was in awe of the set, and he couldn't figure out how she had it made. Dapper Dan was booked for months damn near a year in some cases.

"I do have one more thing for you," he said as he looked up, and Lynette was standing there with the smaller of the gifts she had for him.

Rich removed the jacket and sat it on the chair before taking his seat. He ripped into the last of the boxes, and it was a folder. Rich looked up to her, and she encouraged him to keep going. The papers were bound together and on the front in bold letters read *55th Street*.

"It's my business proposal." She licked her lips, looking from him to the paper. Their eyes met again, and she got serious. "I heard everything you said in the car that day, and I put a plan together to let you know that I was serious. Being your woman is something I'm so proud of, I'm proud of you and everything that you're doing. And, now I wanna be proud of me." Her voice cracked as she shrugged. "You gave me the motivation I didn't even know I needed, to be something I never thought I would be, and I could never thank you enough for that."

Rich stood up from his seat and grabbed her in his arms. He planted both hands on her face and looked into her eyes before kissing her lips. "I love you,"

Tears slowly fell from her eyes as she kissed him back. "I love you too." She swore she did, and she would put that love on her life.

They continued to kiss as Rich grabbed her ass lifting her up in his arms. Lynette wrapped her legs around his back as he pushed her up against the wall. He needed his real gift right now. The other shit was nice, but he wanted what he'd asked for. While they were kissing, Lynette undid his belt and grabbed his dick out of his pants. Without any hesitation Rich slid into her and together, they released satisfied moans. Rich loved the way her body fit his like a glove. Lynette wrapped her arms around his neck as she rocked on his dick. He went in and out while she bounced up and down. Beautiful friction that would lead to nothing but bliss. The love they made got better every time. It's like every stroke brought them closer together and with every orgasm, they became one.

Just as they were about to catch their second wind, there was banging on the front door. The banging was so loud, Rich was sure it would wake the neighbors. When he made sure Lynette was good on her feet, he pulled his pants up, walking to the door. "Who the fuck is it?" He asked, swinging the door open, instantly he rolled his eyes. "Man, y'all need to get y'all some business."

"Ooooh, it smells good up in here!" Faith screamed pushing the door open. "And put a shirt on."

Rich stood back as the rest of the crew piled into his apartment.

"Yo', y'all had the mood set," Stacks joked, kicking rose petals and candles out the way.

"Yeah, you knock that wax on my floor, I'm a wax yo' ass," Rich said, closing his door and locking it. "Fuck y'all want?"

"Shit, we came to party." Stacks smiled, holding up two big bottles of Hennessy.

"And where ya clothes at?" Keisha asked, looking to Lynette wrapping a silk robe around her body.

"On the floor where they supposed to be, bitch." Rolling her eyes, Lynette didn't appreciate them stopping her groove. She looked to Rich before stomping to the back.

"Yeah, go put some damn clothes on," Stacks said, grabbing some of the extra steak out the kitchen.

"Y'all some niggas, for real." Rich shook his head before heading to the back to make sure Lynette was okay. "You aight?"

"No, they need to go back wherever they came from," She fussed before hopping in the shower.

Shaking his head, Rich agreed but they were here now, and they might as well kick it. Removing his pants, he jumped in the shower with her real quick. Together, they tossed some pajamas on and headed back up front.

"Bitch, you always trying to outdo us on some shit," Faith fussed.

"Girl, what are you talking about?" Lynette asked before plopping down on the couch. Swiftly she snatched one of the bottles of Hennessy and took it to the head.

"Why you ain't tell me you were getting Dapper Dan sets?"

"Because it was a gift for my man. Copying ass hoe." Lynette laughed as Faith mushed her in her head.

"Whatever! It looks cute in here." Faith looked around really liking the set up.

"Thank you." Lynette smiled before taking another swig.

"Aight, that's enough. Get a cup." Faith jumped in, passing out plastic cups to everybody.

Once everyone had liquor in their cup, they made a toast and clinked glasses. Together they laughed, joked, played cards, and told stories. At first, they didn't want the company, but it turned out to be a nice evening. It was well after midnight when everyone went home and when they did, Rich had Lynette's little ass bent over the couch.

Later that night, Lynette laid beside Rich, snoring. He dicked her down real proper and put her ass to sleep, not even an hour ago. Gently, he placed a kiss on her forehead before he slid from under her and headed to the bathroom. After relieving himself, he came out the bathroom and looked at Lynette sleeping on the bed. Shaking his head, he smirked, then headed out the room.

WE MADE LOVE IN THE 80'S

In the living room most of the candles had burned out, and the rose petals still decorated the floor. Since Lynette went through all the trouble to make his birthday special, the least he could do was clean up, especially after the crew came over and crashed the party. The first thing he did was clear his and her Dapper Dan outfits off the table. He took them to his second bedroom, which had become one big ass closet, then he grabbed a trash bag and started sweeping and tossing shit away. He kept his cards tho, of all the stuff she'd given him, they meant the most. Quickly, he washed the dishes, swept the floor, and wiped off the counters. After all that work, he needed a drink, so he grabbed a beer out of the refrigerator and took a seat at the table. When he sat his beer down, he picked up Lynette's proposal. He smiled at the front page,

55th St.

I had been to many places and had done many things in my life, but I didn't start to live until I moved to 55th street. I learned a lot about myself, who I am, and what I like. I found love, the purest of love, a love like no other...I found friends, the type of friends that become family. The happiest moments and the saddest moments of my life have all taken place on 55th street. So, I name my store, not only for me, but for everyone that has lived, loved, and died on 55th street.

Rich bit his lip as he swiped a tear from his eye with his index finger. Rubbing his chin, he sat there thinking about his life. He thought about everything that he'd been through that led him to where he was today. After taking a deep breath, he wiped his eyes, then took a drink of his beer before he continued. Reading over her proposal, he was very proud of her. Lynette had researched properties and how much they'd cost; she even compared her cost to similar businesses in the area. There were sketches of the types of clothes she wanted to sell, and even demographics of where her target base was. Lynette had everything mapped out, and whatever she needed, Rich was going to back her one hundred percent. Now this was the type of shit Ms. Zoo should be on.

Closing the book, he put it on the counter and cut off the light. He went to the bathroom one more time before he climbed in bed. Laying down, he pulled her into him and buried his face into her hair. When he met Lynette, initially it was her looks they got his attention, but he saw something else in her and now it was clear she saw it too.

ARABIA

Nate whipped his little Beamer recklessly through the streets while Keisha kicked back in the passenger seat. They had just left dinner and were now going to one of his people's house. Keisha liked when they kicked it with his people because it was like he was showing her off. And he was. Nate loved everything about Keisha. In his eyes, she was the total package. She had a little business about herself, she wasn't all in the streets fucking around, and she wasn't ran through. Shit, to him she was it. When they arrived at his homeboy house, Nate parked and did the usual opening of her door. After wrapping an arm around her neck, together they headed inside. Keisha wasn't really familiar with this part of town, but she felt safe with Nate. The way his tall frame covered hers, the way he knew everybody, and seemed to be well respected had her panties leaking. This was the type of shit she'd been missing out on.

"Where Rick at?" Nate asked as he walked up slapping hands with one of the guys outside.

"He in the back." The man eyed him before turning his attention to Keisha. "This you?"

"All me, nigga." Smirking, Nate moved right past him with Keisha connected to his hip.

Keisha took in the scene inside, and it wasn't much. The parties at Leroy's were better back in the day, but it was okay. The lighting was low, and everyone was coupled up, sitting on the couches or standing against the wall. She couldn't really see many of their faces because she was whisked to the back of the house. In the kitchen, there were a few guys posted up and a girl tucked away in the corner, talking on the house phone. Keisha gave her the once over and guessed she looked okay.

"What up?" Nate let Keisha go and locked hands with a couple of the men around the table. "This my girl Keisha, Keisha this Rocky and Bullwinkle." He paused, and everybody bust out laughing but her. Clearly, she was confused.

"Don't mind that nigga. I'm Spooky." He held out his hand, and Keisha just stared at it before looking to Nate. Gently, he nodded his head to her, and she reluctantly took Spooky's hand. "Damn, I ain't gon' bite you." Keisha didn't laugh or bat a lash. Something about his whole vibe was a little off. "You always fuck with them stuck up broads."

Keisha's eyes narrowed into slits, and before she could go off, Nate stepped up. "Yo' chill with that shit." He pushed past Spooky and back over to Keisha's side. "She ain't just some broad, this my girl."

Spooky looked her over as he took another sip from his drink and shrugged. "My bad," he said with little conviction.

"Never mind that nigga, he been drinking." Turning to the other man, Nate introduced him. "This my guy, Karl and that's his girl over there ShyKeema."

Unlike Spooky, Karl seemed a little nicer but at this point Keisha was ready to go. "Where's the bathroom?"

Nate could tell she was in a mood and hoped he would be able to rectify the situation. "Right through there." He pointed down a hall. "Last door on the left." He watched Keisha head down the hall before scowling at Spooky. "What the fuck is wrong with you?" he chastised when Keisha was out of site.

"Man, ain't nobody trippin' off ya girl." He joked, nervously. "I even said my bad, for real. I ain't mean no disrespect."

Nate wasn't trying to hear that shit, but he knew his friends and how they talked. "Don't let that shit happen again. That's my girl, not some bitch I'm fuckin'."

"So, my cousin was just a bitch you was fuckin'?" ShyKeema asked, stopping her phone conversation.

"Hell yeah!" Nate nearly yelled as he looked down the hall to make sure Keisha wasn't coming. "Fuck her." ShyKeema looked back to him and flipped him the bird.

"That's the chick that fuck with them Zoo niggas?" Karl asked, remembering a conversation they had not too long ago about a chick he was seeing.

"Yeah, them her people."

"Shit, see if we can link up with them niggas and do some business. Lil momma could be your way in," Karl said, thinking beyond the bullshit they were talking about.

ARABIA

When they heard the bathroom door creek open, all talking ceased as they turned back to what they were doing. Back in the kitchen, it was eerily quiet, and Keisha was ready to go. She didn't want to be a party pooper, so she stood quietly by Nate's side, ignoring the ugly looks she was getting from dude's girlfriend. The moment Nate asked if she was ready to go, she nearly jumped out her skin and beat her damn self to the car.

"I'm sorry about that back there, you know, what happened earlier," Nate apologized as he looked over to her.

"It's cool." She shrugged

Sighing, Nate didn't want this to fuck up their night. "Come on, don't be like that." He tried to tickle her, and she barely budged. "Aight, you ain't fuckin' with me right now. So, what you wanna do, you ready to go home?"

"Did I say I was ready to go home?"

"Well, you all attitude down. Thought you was ready to call it a night."

"Whatever, where we going now? Hopefully, not another one of your friend's house."

He laughed, shaking his head. "Nah, not tonight, we chillin'." Nate turned the music up and cracked the windows, letting a little air in. They rode around for a little bit before they ended up at his house. It wasn't Keisha's first time being over there, so she was really comfortable. Upstairs, she took off her shoes as Nate crept behind her and wrapped his arms around her waist, pulling her into him. "You still mad at me?"

Keisha bit her lip as his tongue tickled the back of her neck and then her ear. "Nah, but next time Spooky ugly ass calls me a stuck up broad, I'm fuckin' him up."

Holding his laugh, Nate buried his head in the crook of her neck. "I promise I checked him about that. He was just drunk tonight, talking out the side of his neck. He really a good dude."

"Yeah, yeah." She rolled her eyes, not caring to know what he was. "It's too late, I already don't like him."

"Noted," was all he said before he stopped kissing her neck and lifted her shirt over her head. Slowly, Nate turned her around taking her in.

"Don't just stare," she popped her shit with her hands planted firmly on her hips.

"Nah, but you know I can back my shit up tho." Nate removed his shirt, then tossed it to the floor.

Walking closer to Keisha, his heart beat out of his chest with every step. Once he reached her, he wasted no time pulling her into him and kissing her lips. Hungrily, they kissed as he backed her into the bed, and she fell back on it. Keisha looked up at him while unbuckling his pants. Once she pulled them and his boxers down, his dick sprang out as if it was saluting her and she smiled. Without hesitation, she gripped his dick in both of her hands and licked the tip. Swinging her hair back, she took the head of him into her mouth.

"Sssss," he hissed as she took more of him in. Inch by inch, she devoured him, and he fell deeper in love. "Damn, Keish." His mouth fell open, as his dick touched the back of her throat.

"Mmmm," Keisha began to hum as her mouth filled with spit causing her to gag a little. Saliva poured down his shaft, and she used it as lubrication to jerk him faster as she sucked harder. In and out, her mouth turned into a vacuum as she practically sucked the cum right up out of him.

"Fuck, fuck, fuck," Nate cursed as he shot his load down her throat. "Damn," he groaned as she swallowed every drop.

Pulling back, he looked down at her. He watched her intently as she leaned back, removing her pants and underwear. When she was done, he watched her spread her legs and that pussy was dripping. "Shit, stay just like that." He went over to the dresser and pulled out a condom. His dick grew in his hands as he stroked it back and forth. "Get that shit wetter for me." He ordered as she dipped and swirled her fingers in and out of her wetness. He put the condom on and stood at the edge of the bed. Keisha's legs were open wide, and her pussy was pulsating as if it had a heartbeat. Leaning down, he kissed her lower lips, tonguing her clit.

Keisha closed her eyes as she thrust her hips slowly into him, serving all that goodness on a platter. She was spent, then she felt him pushing inside of her. Cries of pleasure and pain bounced off the walls as they fucked each other silly. For over an hour, they skipped the love making and were straight fucking up that headboard.

Later that night, they lay in the bed listening to each other breathe. Keisha was wrapped in his arms, laying on his chest. Nate looked down and kissed her head. "I gotta go out of town for a minute."

Keisha shifted her head, so that she was looking at him. "For how long?"

"Just a few days, I gotta secure a new product." He told her, then he thought of what Karl had mentioned to him earlier. "You close to Zoo; you think they would fuck with me on some product?"

"What product?" Keisha was 'there's lights on, but nobody is home dumb' right now.

"Keish, you know what I'm talking about?"

Shaking her head, she disagreed. "No, I don't. I don't get into they shit like that, so if you got questions, you gon' have to ask them ya self." And with that, she turned over and was ready to go to sleep because she wasn't even about to go there with him.

A few days later and Nate found himself solo in Zoo territory. Keisha played dumb the other night, and that shit left Nate feeling a way. He didn't know what she was hiding or who she was protecting, but it showed him where her loyalty really lied. But she was right, if he wanted to know something, he had to ask them himself and that's why he was there. They had all hung out a few times, and Nate felt like they would be able to do good business together. He wasn't sure what they were selling but from the houses, cars, and clothes, it was something big, and he wanted in. Pulling up on their block, just like he suspected they were posted up outside on the benches. The apartment complex they ran wasn't bad looking or anything, it was actually kind of nice. Hopping out of his car, he fixed his clothes before he headed over. All eyes were on him the moment he stepped out of his car, but he wasn't the least bit intimidated. Stepping on the set, Tech stopped him in his tracks.

"You lost?" he asked, looking at Nate like he was crazy.

"Nah." He smirked. "I ain't looking for no trouble either. I just need to talk to Stacks and them for a minute."

"Stacks and them, huh?" Tech's eyes stayed locked on his. "Zoo, y'all know this nigga?"

Sam and Stacks looked up from the dice game they were playing and noticed it was Nate. "Yeah, that's Keisha nigga," Stacks answered, turning his attention back to the game.

Nate smirked at Tech as he moved past him and walked over to where Sam and Stacks were at. It was clear that Keisha held a little weight with them, and he was hoping it was heavy. "What's good, y'all?"

"Shit," Stacks replied as Sam remained quiet. "Keisha, straight?" Stacks followed up, turning his attention back to him.

"Yeah, she good. I was hopin' I could talk some business with y'all?" Nate asked, looking from Stacks to Sam, who hadn't taken his eyes off him since he walked up.

"We don't have no business with you?" Sam shrugged.

Nate's jaws tensed and Stacks could sense the tension, so he was ready to shoot all this shit down before it could get out of hand. "Yeah, we ain't got shit going on right now." He looked to him but turned away before he could respond.

"You ain't even gon' hear what I gotta say?"

"Fuck outta here," Sam said before nodding to Tech.

"Take a walk." Tech stepped up from the side of him.

From Tech and back to Stacks and Sam, Nate looked before nodding his head. "Aight, then," was all he said before he walked off the set. When he got to his car, he looked back to them, and they had resumed their game like he had never stepped up. "Bitch ass niggas," he huffed before he sped off.

When he was gone, Sam spoke. "That nigga really rolled up here trying to talk business? Fuck he get that from?" He couldn't explain it, and he didn't know why, but he just didn't like Nate. First of all, what nigga really named Nate. That shit just rubbed him the wrong way.

Stacks shook his head, wondering the same. "I don't know, but I ain't got shit for him."

Chapter 13

When Lynette decided to go into business for herself, she never thought about how much time would really be involved. Every other day she was out looking at suites, store fronts, and buildings, and she was tired. Ideally, she wanted to open the store in their neighborhood, but the realtor kept showing them storefronts uptown, and she wasn't having it. Rich told her to keep an open mind, and that she should at least look at the places before dismissing them. So, she looked at every property the realtor had, and she didn't like any of them. There was something wrong with every one of them, besides them being outside of her desired neighborhood. Today, she invited the girls to see a property that was just on the outside of the neighborhood. It was more on the downtown end and to her, that was close enough to where she wanted to be, so she was actually excited.

"Sorry I'm late." The realtor walked up buttoning his suit jacket.

"It's cool." Lynette lifted off the car and introduced the girls to Taylor her realtor. "So, let's see what you drug me out here for today. You see I brought back up just in case I had to swing on you."

Taylor laughed; he truly got a kick out of Lynette. Not only was she funny, he liked her charisma. "Nah, for real, I think you're going to like this place. It's right outside of your southward neighborhood…"

"Oh, Southward," Keisha mimicked. "I like how you put that." She laughed and so did the other girls.

"Yes, it sounds like a real place and not the hood, Southward!" Faith added.

Shaking his head, Taylor laughed. "After you ladies." He unlocked the door and held it open.

"Cute and a gentleman." Janae smiled as Lynette pushed her ahead.

"Don't even try it, Sam ain't finna kill me, messing with you," Lynette said as she stepped in, getting a good look at the place. There was plenty of light, and she was already in love with the exposed brick that made up the wall and four columns.

"As I was saying, the place has plenty of square footage for you to do what you like. The back room is spacious and would make a great stock room. There are two bathrooms and a loft area, I thought would be good for an office." He spoke as he walked over to the wall and cut on the light. "So, have a look around and let me know if you have any questions."

"This is nice," Keisha marveled over the white and black marble floors and the brick walls, it was a nice contrast.

There were built-in shelves and bright lighting, the girls were in love. The bathrooms were nice and updated, everything was clean, and it seemed to sparkle. Up the backstairs the loft area was huge and overlooked the main floor. It was cool because from downstairs you could only see the bottom of the balcony but from upstairs you could see down. Lynette liked that even though there was a balcony, there was still privacy.

"This is it; I'll take it!" She shouted from the balcony.

Taylor looked up, smiling. "You sure? You don't have any more questions about the property?"

"Nope, this is it!" Lynette told him and she was sure this was the one.

"Okay, I'll get in touch with Mr. Ricker and get the paperwork together," Taylor said, already calculating his commission. "I'll give you all a few more minutes while I wait outside." He didn't have another showing for a couple of hours and was going to use this time to take a little break.

"This shit about to be dope as fuck!" Faith rocked her hips with her arms in the air. "I can't wait until we throw the grand opening party, we gone have all the drugs, all the liquor, shit finna be crazy."

Janae cleared her throat, stepping away from them. "Well, won't be no drinking or drugging for me."

"Oh, what you on that healthy kick again?" Keisha joked, knowing Janae was good for her fake diets and cutting alcohol and carbs.

"No," she looked back to them, "I'm pregnant."

"Damn," the girls howled together as shock swept over their faces.

"Bitch, y'all ain't waste no time!" Lynette just knew her cousin had lost her damn mind.

"Shit, who's baby is it?" Keisha asked.

"Bitch, I'll beat ya ass, don't play with me." Janae rolled her eyes not even for those type of games. "I ain't no hoe that just sleeps around."

"I ain't say you was, but shit don't act like my question ain't valid." Keisha said, returning the same tone she was given.

"Bitch, fuck you." Janae flipped her off. "Anyway, since obviously I'm just a hoe that runs around fucking on niggas and getting pregnant…This baby is Sam's."

"Well, thanks for telling us this time." Keisha smirked.

"Aight, y'all quit." Faith stepped up, rolling her eyes at Keisha. "Congratulations." After pulling her into a hug, she knew she needed, Faith kissed her cheek. "You're okay, and we're here for you."

"Thank you," Janae said, swiping a single tear from her eye.

"What Sam say?" Lynette wanted to know, just for the sake of knowing.

Janae shrugged as Faith released her. "He's okay with it, I mean at this point, it is what it is."

Nodding her head, Lynette walked over to her, "Well, you know I got ya back." Hugging her, she kissed her cheek. "Well, I guess the loft gon' be a damn nursery now." They all laughed shaking their head.

"Well, if it's a girl, I give you permission to name her Keisha."

"I wish the fuck I would." Janae rolled her eyes, pushing her as they made their way out the front door.

They bickered back and forth in the car all the way back to the block. Lynette and Faith were so ready to get away from them, they ain't even know what to do. When they pulled up in front of the buildings, the two of them didn't waste any time jumping out of the car, leaving Keisha and Janae behind.

"What's up, y'all?" Lynette greeted everyone as she walked up.

"What up?" Tech greeted her with the official Zoo handshake while everyone else saluted.

"Unh unh, Tap don't be like that," she chastised, noticing he was the only one that didn't speak to them.

"Man, go ahead." He smirked, not fucking with her.

"Come on, I said I was sorry." Annoyingly, Lynette wrapped her arms around his waist and held him tight.

"Girl, if you don't let me go."

"No, not until you forgive me."

He tried to shake her off, but she wasn't letting go. Everyone laughed until Jay-Tap couldn't help but laugh too. "Aight, aight, I forgive you."

Lynette hugged him one last time before she let him go. "I love you too, Tap."

"Yeah, yeah." He waved her off. "You owe me lunch, nigga."

"And I got you." Lynette smiled as she turned around and headed to the back of the buildings with the rest of the girls.

WE MADE LOVE IN THE 80'S

When they made it to the back, they found the rest of Zoo posted and a few hoes scattered around. But the moment they walked on to the set, it was like everybody stopped and all eyes were on them.

"Don't stop talking now!" Faith yelled, mugging every female that was posted.

"Girl, shut up," Echo joked.

"You don't want none of this, you seen how these hands work," she let him know.

"Cut it out." Stacks walked over, meeting her halfway. He snatched her up kissing her lips before pushing his tongue into her mouth.

While they were practically fucking in the middle of the courtyard, Janae and Lynette went over to where Sam and Rich were. Keisha, on the other hand, pulled out a couple of dollars to get Stacks' spot in the dice game.

"Where y'all coming from?" Rich asked as he pulled Lynette into him and tucked her under his arm.

"From seeing that building, it's so nice. I can't wait for you to see it."

"About time you finally picked one."

"I know, right?" she agreed. "But it's right downtown, still on this side of town though, and it's so big and the loft...Oh, my gosh, you gon' love it."

"That's what's up!" He hugged her kissing her forehead. "I'll get with Taylor in the morning."

"Yeah, he said he was going to call you."

"I know, he paged me not too long ago, and I spoke to him."

"No, but why, Dap gon' make me some custom pieces?" Lynette nearly jumped out of his arms.

"Who the fuck is Dap?" Rich's face scrunched.

"Dapper Dan." She laughed at the look Rich was giving her.

"Yeah, aight, don't get that nigga head knocked off."

Rolling her eyes, she wasn't paying him any mind. "Nah, he gon' make me a couple of Zoo pieces for the store. He said if they sell, he'll do some business with me."

"For real?" Rich asked her, surprised she was able to pull that.

"Yup." Smiling, she nodded her head. "See, I been out here making moves."

"I see you." He laughed, letting her talk her shit.

They kicked it for a few hours before it was time for them to call it a night. It wasn't really dark, but the streetlights were on and Lynette was ready to go. She had been up all day and was ready to be home. Everybody else agreed to disperse as well. Sam and Janae were going to get the baby and go home while Stacks and Faith were going to get something to eat. Together, they all walked out the back, saying their goodbyes to the rest of the crew.

"Aight, bitch, I'll call you later…"

Faith began but Lynette had tuned her out and focused on the car driving down the street. She didn't know what about it had caught her eye, but the light hitting the silver barrel caused a glimmer that snapped her out of it. "Faaaiiiittthhhhh." She released a blood curdling scream causing everyone to look at her just as bullets began to fly, and all hell broke loose.

Rich pushed her down to the ground as he pulled his gun to return fire with the rest of Zoo. At that moment he didn't know where everyone else was as tunnel vision took over. As if he was invisible, he ran after the car until his clip was empty. Suddenly, there was an eerie silence that covered the area. Looking over to the building, he could see mouths moving, but he couldn't hear anything. His feet were moving, he knew it because he was getting closer, but he still couldn't hear any sound. There was a crowd of people and it was like suddenly, he remembered Lynette was there.

Finding his voice, he choked out her name. As loud as he could, he screamed her name. "Nett! Shit! Move, move. Lynette!" he shouted, pushing his way through the crowd. He didn't stop until he saw her and at that moment, he had never felt so much relief. Nearly running out of his shoes, he went up to her and pulled her into his arms.

"Give me your burner!" Echo ran up to him and snatched it out of his hands before he disappeared into the crowd.

"You okay?" He pulled back and gave her a once over as she nodded her head. Rich saw blood on her but thankfully it wasn't hers. "Hey, hey, Lynette."

Looking him in his eyes, she could barely see him through her blurred vision. "Yes, yes, I'm okay."

While Rich was making sure Lynette was okay, Sam had Janae tucked away in his car. Shit was crazy, and the last thing he wanted was for something to happen to her or his baby. When he came back, he saw Rich, but he didn't see Stacks anywhere. He could here sirens in the distance, but there was so much going on he couldn't focus. Stopping in his tracks, he took in the scene. Mentally he made a head count. As he scanned the area, he saw a pair of shoes behind one of the cars and he knew it was Stacks. Taking off, he ran faster than he had ever ran in his life. But nothing could've prepared him for what he saw when he rounded the car. Instantly, his mouth filled with bile, and he threw up as sweat covered his forehead.

"Sam, help me get her up." Stacks groaned with tears pouring from his eyes. "Faith, come on." On his knees, he held her head in his lap as he urged her to get up. "I gotta get her to the hospital."

Swallowing his own emotions, Sam had to get it together. He didn't know if Faith was alive or not, but it looked bad. He could tell she'd been shot in her head, and that shit didn't look good. "Stacks hand her here."

"I, I…" He shuddered, seeing her like that had Stacks in shock.

"I got her." Carefully, Sam took Faith into his arms and ran her to where the ambulance had just pulled up.

ARABIA

When he looked back, Stacks was passed out on the ground and by then, Rich had come over with some other niggas from Zoo. There was only one ambulance, so they just started loading niggas into cars, and they were out. Once he was sure of what hospital they were taking Faith to, he got Keisha and put her in the car with Janae before he headed to the hospital himself. Like a bat out of hell, Sam flew through the streets. In order to keep his head together, he had to tune out the girls crying. In the backseat Keisha and Janae were hysterically crying and right now, they had to comfort each other because Sam couldn't do it. He was going to take them home, but right now, the safest place they could be was with him.

At the hospital, it was a bloody mess, everyone there was covered from head to toe as they paced the waiting room floor. Faith and Stacks were both shot, and Jay-Tap was gone. That had everybody fucked up. It was like one minute they were just chilling, and everything was good, then bam…Shit just ain't even right. Jay was cool as hell, and niggas knew for sure he ain't deserve that shit. Outside the hospital, Echo, Sam, and Rich stood around smoking cigarette after cigarette, trying to figure out what happened.

"This shit crazy." Rich paced.

"Hell yeah, like, to come on the block and we ain't even fucking with nobody out here like that," Echo added, shaking his head. He and Jay were the closest and to see him shot up like that, had him ready to shoot up the whole city. "Niggas gotta pay for this shit."

"Hell yeah," Sam agreed, ready to take some heads himself.

"We on that shit." Rich nodded. "Soon as the doctors tell us what's up with Stacks and Faith, we need to put the girls up in a hotel and meet up at the spot off tenth."

Upstairs in the waiting room, Lynette sat still with a tear stained face. She couldn't believe this happened. In her mind, she kept replaying the scene in her head and none of it made sense. That car was etched into her mind, the barrel of the gun sparkling in the sunlight, the spark from the blast, it was all on replay. Her eyes weren't fixed on anything in particular, so when she sensed movement on the side of her, her gaze shifted as she jumped.

"It's just me," Rich said as he slid beside her. "You okay?"

Tears came to her eyes as she shook her head before laying it on his shoulder. He kissed her forehead before laying his head on hers. The longer Rich sat there the more pissed he was. Jay was gone, Faith and Stacks were shot up. Rich could say that as prepared as he thought he was for this day, the day when someone rolled up on the set blasting or for them to have beef, he wasn't prepared at all.

"Family of Faith and Landon Bryant!" The doctor called out, and everyone jumped up.

"Here! That's my daughter and son-in-law," Faith's mom said as she stepped up and walked toward the front.

Lynette looked her over and wondered when she'd gotten there. She didn't remember her walking in, but then again, she ain't really remember how she'd gotten there.

"As you all know both Faith and Landon were shot multiple times. Faith sustained injuries to her head and chest, while Landon was shot in his abdomen and shoulder. The good news is Faith will survive. The shot to Faith's head looks a lot a worse than it is. I do want to prepare you for when you see her, it's not going to be pretty. But the bullet didn't pierce her skull at all, and that's a good thing. We were able to successfully remove two bullets from her chest as well. Now as for Landon he's in for more of a fight. The bullet in his abdomen exploded on impact and sent fragments into different organs…Currently, he's still in surgery. Just know that we'll do everything we can and update you as soon as possible." He asked if anyone had any further questions and they didn't. Besides Faith's mom, who was the only one allowed back to see her as everyone else was left in shambles.

Rich fell into the chair, pounding his head with his fist balled. There was no way they could lose Stacks. His whole life they'd been together, and he couldn't imagine doing this shit without him. Lynette wrapped her arms around his head and held him while she cried his tears. Sam stood up against the wall in shock, feeling the same shit Rich was feeling. Janae in front of him with her arms wrapped around his body, and her head laying on his chest.

Echo took a moment to take everything the doctor said in while mourning the loss of Jay, there was no way he could let this shit rest. "Aight, y'all we need to go," he said, pushing himself off the wall as Sam and Rich looked to him. "Now." He tapped his watch just as the cops walked in.

ARABIA

Everyone stood up and walked out, not listening to shit they were talking about. The first rule of the streets was don't talk to the police. That was law, if anything they would hold court in the streets. Downstairs, everyone separated with plans to link up later. Keisha went with Lynette and Rich, while Janae and Sam went to get the baby. Once they had Sammie, Sam took them by the house to get some clothes and met Rich at the hotel, where they had the girls tucked away.

Each of them had their own room, so they'd be comfortable. While they were at the hospital, Tech was busy setting everything up as far as their new living arrangements. They didn't plan on being there long, but the guys knew they'd be safe there while they were out running the streets. Once everyone got settled, they ended up in Rich and Lynette's room. Together they thought about all the potential beef they could've had, and they came up with nothing.

"What about ya nigga? Where was he at today?" Sam asked Keisha.

She looked from him to everyone else and was confused. "Excuse me?"

"That nigga, Nate," Sam said, giving her his full attention.

"What are you asking me?"

"I'm asking you where the nigga at. He popped up on the set the other day and now this shit don't seem like no coincidence to me."

Keisha's eyes squinted as she looked to him. "First of all, don't be implicating my nigga in no shit like this. You don't know him, and he don't know y'all."

"Well, he knew us well enough to pop his dusty ass up on our block the other day asking for work the other day!" Sam yelled back as he stood up. "How we know he ain't come by on some sucka shit because we ain't wanna fuck with him?" Tears welled in Keisha's eyes as she looked at Sam. She didn't know Nate had been down there, and they had words or whatever. He never told her, and Zoo never mentioned it. She looked from him to Tech and then to Rich, who was looking at her with fire in his eyes. "I'm just saying everybody a suspect at this point and if you weren't with him, then we finna pick his ass up."

WE MADE LOVE IN THE 80'S

Rich didn't know if it was Nate, but from what he was hearing, it was definitely worth checking out. "So, what happened when he approached y'all?" he asked Sam as he went through the story, and Tech backed him up. Rich looked to Keisha. "You talk to him today?"

Tears fell from Keisha's eyes as she shook her head. Rich's eyes connected with Lynette's as she rubbed Keisha's back. "He wouldn't do this?" Keisha swore.

"And you willing to vouch for this nigga? You know for sure he ain't have nothing to do with this? I mean if I'm wrong, I'll apologize, but I don't think it's a coincidence that this shit happens now after he start coming around." Sam had a point, and Rich and Tech agreed with him.

"It's worth us checking out." Rich looked back to Keisha, "Where he be at?"

Keisha rolled her eyes as her lips trembled. She didn't want to believe Nate was capable of this, but she couldn't say without a doubt that it wasn't him. "He hustle off fifth," her voice shook as she told them whatever they wanted to know. When she was done, she jumped up and stormed to the bathroom, slamming the door.

"Aight lets, roll," Sam said and was ready to roll. "I'mma take them back to the room, and I'll meet y'all downstairs." Janae stood up with the baby and gave Lynette sympathetic eyes as she looked towards the bathroom. "I'll call you when I get to the room."

They walked out and Tech was right behind them. Rich stood up and rubbed his hand over his head. He was tired as fuck, his mind was racing, and he felt like he needed to be moving. This was the first time anyone had tested Zoo like this, and it was a must they acted quickly. They had to send a message, and that message had to speak to the streets. It had to speak to anyone that ever thought about testing Zoo. Once again, he looked to Lynette, then turned around, and grabbed his jacket, and slid his shoes on. "I'll be back."

"Be careful," Lynette told him as she walked him to the door.

"Always," he swore as he looked down at her smirking. "Tell Keish, If I ain't sure, I won't kill him." Lynette nodded her head as Rich bent down to kiss her lips. She kissed him back, wrapping her arms around his neck, and pulling him closer. "Lock up, don't leave the hotel,

money is in the dresser, and Steve and Chauncey downstairs." She
nodded her head before he pecked her lips once more and walked out
the door.

Lynette closed the door and locked it like she was told before
she pressed her hands and head against it. Taking a deep breath, she
held her tears at bay. Right now, she had to be strong. Rubbing her eyes
dry, she turned around and walked over to the bathroom door. Gently,
she knocked on the door and waited for Keisha to answer it. "It's just
me."

After a while, Keisha unlocked the door and swung it open
with a face full of tears. "He didn't do this," she cried as Lynette pulled
her into her arms. "I know he didn't."

"Okay, okay, just calm down." Lynette tried to sooth her.
"They just wanna ask him some questions. Rich said if he wasn't sure
they wouldn't hurt him."

"He should've told me he came up here to talk to them," she
hissed, pacing back and forth. Even she had to admit it looked bad, but
she knew Nate. At least she thought she did.

Chapter 14

On the streets it took Zoo little to no time to mobilize. They were all ready to hit the streets and bash some heads. At this point it didn't matter who it was, somebody had to pay. Sam repeated Keisha's directions, and they were able to get to his place with no issue. It was clear, Keisha didn't believe her boyfriend was capable of such a heinous act, but the rest of them weren't too convinced. So, to clear up any confusion here they were parked outside his shit. Checking the clock, it was going on three in the morning, and they were up like it was three in the afternoon.

"Aight, let's go," Sam said as he opened the door. "Keep ya head down."

"Nigga, just go'head," Tech joked, pushing him from the back, causing everyone to smirk. Now wasn't the time for jokes, but it did lighten the mood a little.

The streets were empty as they made their way to the entrance of his apartment building. Like a few homeboys coming home after a long night of partying, they casually walked up to the building and when a guy walking out saw them, he didn't think anything of it when he held the door for them to get in.

"Preciate' it," Rich said as he caught the door, and they headed inside.

They took the stairs two at a time as they made it to the ninth floor, and niggas was winded.

"Shit, let me catch my fuckin' breath." Sam huffed as he leaned up against the wall.

"I swear to God, I'm about to stop smokin'." Rich coughed as he held his chest.

Shaking his head, Tech bounced past him. "Y'all niggas weak." He laughed as he checked the numbers on the apartment door. "He down on the other end."

Pushing themselves off the wall, they made their way down to his door. When Tech got to it, he leaned down and pulled out a barbie pin and a small knife. Carefully, he stuck them in the lock and after few tries, he successfully opened the door.

"Criminal ass nigga." Echo laughed as they entered the apartment.

Everything was still as they walked through. You would think they would be trying to be quiet, but no they were walking like they didn't have a care in the world. There was no one in the living room, so they figured he was sleep. At three o'clock in the morning that's exactly what he should've been doing. In the bedroom, they could see him from the door resting peacefully with the light from the TV illuminating the room.

Sam ain't like this nigga anyway, so he did the honors. Walking over to the bed, he took the butt of his gun and thumped him in the head with it. "Get yo' ass up, nigga."

Nate held his head, as he woke from his sleep. He winced from the pain as he tuned over, wondering what the hell just happened. That was when he noticed four men standing in his bedroom. "Fuck y'all niggas want?"

"Get the fuck up," Rich said as he flicked the light on.

The light was blinding as Nate adjusted his eyes and when he saw it was Sam and Tech, he was instantly heated. "Y'all niggas must be out y'all rabbit ass mind." Sitting up on the bed, he shook his head because shit was still foggy from Sam hitting him. "What the fuck y'all niggas want?"

"Hand this nigga some pants, so we can go," Rich said to no one in particular, but Echo tossed him some jeans on the chair and Nate caught them.

"Nigga, I'm not about to go no fucking where…" His words were silenced by Sam punching him all in his shit.

"Just put the pants on." Rich leaned up against the door frame like he had all day. Murder danced as fire burned Nate's eyes. Shaking his head, he snatched his pants off the bed and put them on. Standing up, he looked Sam in his eyes as he zipped them up. "Good, slide them shoes on, grab ya keys, and let's go."

Without another word or any protest, Nate did as he was told. Tech went to grab his arm, and he angrily snatched away. "Don't fuckin' touch me."

Rich had to commend his courage. Even in the face of imminent danger, he wasn't scared, and he could respect that. Downstairs, they put Nate in the car with them, and Echo drove his car to the spot they were going to use exclusively for tonight. They wanted to bring his car because if he made it out, he would be able to drive it home and if he didn't, it would appear as if he'd left town. They had thought of every scenario and were sure this would go off without a hitch. The ride over to the spot was quiet as they passed a joint between them.

Nate didn't know what was going on, but he swore if he got the chance, he was going to knock one of them niggas out. When they finally made it to their destination, Nate ain't even know where they were at. The house looked abandoned; but he could see there was a light on. Inside the house they made it to the basement, and Nate was pushed down into a waiting chair. "Now, can I know what this is about?"

"Shit, you tell us," Rich said, standing before him.

Shaking his head, Nate was lost. "Is this about Keisha?" He was really reaching at this point because outside of Keisha he didn't know anything about Zoo. She was his only connection to them, so in his mind it had to be about her.

"Nah, she's good." Rich looked him in his eyes. "You been on our block lately?"

Nates eyes shrunk. "Hell no, I ain't got no reason to come through there."

"Shit, you had plenty of reason the other week." Sam stepped up.

"Man, fuck you." Nate sneered. "Shit, fuck all y'all niggas."

"See sounds like he did the shit to me." Sam reached behind his back and grabbed his gun, pointing it at Nate.

"Did what? Fuck is y'all talking about? Did Keisha tell you I did something to her because I didn't."

"You came through the block and shot that shit up…"

"No, the fuck I didn't," he protested, holding his hands up. "Why the fuck would I even care enough to beef with y'all like that?"

"Because Stacks ain't wanna work wit ya hoe ass."

"Man, suck my dick," Nate couldn't believe they really thought he was that pressed for anything. "I ain't had shit to do with nothing that happened over that way. Yeah, I came asking to link up on some business shit, and that was that. I ain't even give a fuck the nigga said no to be honest." Sam and Rich looked at each other and honestly, didn't know what to believe. Either he was a great liar, or he was innocent. It dawned on Nate that he hadn't spoken to Keisha since last night. "Where's Keisha? Is she okay?" he asked looking to Rich.

Just then Echo came downstairs and leaned into Rich ear. "Stacks house was just hit."

Rich looked at him with wide eyes. "What?"

Echo went to tell him all he knew about the break-in so far, and Rich's jaws tensed. "Yeah, so unless he's working with somebody else, it ain't him."

"Yo' I don't know what's going on, but I been home all day." He sighed from a lack of anything else to say.

"Let him go," Rich said, and Sam's neck nearly broke, but he didn't care.

Nate looked from Rich to Sam, then back to Rich before he stood up. On wobbly legs he hesitantly walked to the door. Sam mugged him, and he mugged him right back. Shaking his head, he headed out the house and to his car. Thankfully his keys were sitting on the seat, so he was able to quickly get away. Nate was sure this wouldn't be the last Zoo would see of him, and that was a promise.

"What the fuck was that?" Sam based, not understanding why they just let their main suspect go.

"It wasn't him," Rich told him before filling him in on what Echo had told him.

Sam took in all that he'd told him, and he was really disappointed. "Shit, I was looking forward to killing that nigga too." Shaking his head, he put his gun back in his waistband. "You know what, Stacks just had cameras installed at his house."

Rich raised an eyebrow. "They set up?"

"I think he set them up, hell, ain't gon' hurt to check." Sam shrugged, and the men were on another mission as they piled into the car. On the way over to Stacks house, Sam was thinking. "You know we gon' have to see that nigga Nate again, right?" He knew for sure, if some niggas ran up in his shit like they just did Nate's, ain't no way he ain't killing everybody involved.

"Well, we just gon' have to deal with him then," was all Rich said and left it at that. Stacks was right, but he had already given Kiesha his word that he wouldn't kill him if he wasn't sure. Whatever the case maybe later, tonight he had to stand on his word.

At Stacks' house, the neighborhood was quiet, and nothing was moving. All the men stepped out of the car, and when they did, a guy from Zoo named Ty-Ty came out of Stacks' house. "Zoo," he greeted with their signature handshake.

"What's up?" Rich shook up with him, and they stepped on the porch.

"Man, we came to drop big homie car off, and we peeped his shit was kicked in." He reenacted with animation that had them shaking their head. "We pop inside and shit straight trashed. Tables kicked over; shit tossed everywhere…"

"You think they found anything?" Sam asked as they stepped in the house.

"I mean it's a small safe in the bedroom that was hit. Shit, was wide open." Ty told them as they looked around the house.

Sam and Rich shook their heads because none of this made any sense. Who would want to hit them like this, and why would Stacks be a target? Did he have something going on that none of them knew about? There were way too many questions and not enough answers. Sam walked to the garage, and he hoped they hadn't found any of his video equipment. On the shelf, above the doc, there it was. It didn't even look like they'd come into the garage, and Sam was happy about that. He could see the red-light blinking, indicating that it was still recording, and he thanked his lucky stars.

"You got it?" Echo asked as he walked into the garage with Tech and Rich behind him.

"Hell, yeah." Sam slid the tape out of the player and climbed back down to his feet. "Aight, let's get out of here. Ty-Ty, y'all niggas fix that door, and we'll clean this shit up later."

Swiftly, they left Stacks house and headed to Echo spot because it was closest. The sun was creeping through the clouds, and they were tired from running around all night. But sleep was the furthest thing from their minds. Back at the hotel, they all walked into Echo room and immediately went to the TV. They all stood around as he rewound the video. They went back to earlier that day when Stacks and Faith left the house. Just watching the video had all their stomachs in knots. It was crazy how shit was just all good and then it just ended in chaos, for no real reason. Stacks and Faith were just going about their everyday routine and then this, nah, niggas had to pay. The video continued for a while with no activity outside of the house, until Echo fast forwarded it. They could see a car driving down the street and slow to a stop, then the camera angle changed as the men hopped out. It was three of them total, they watched anxiously to see if they recognized anything about the men.

"Get the fuck outta here," Sam said as one of the men came into view, and they all looked at him like he was crazy.

"What?" Rich asked, looking from him back to the video to see if he saw what he saw.

"That's that nigga Solo," Sam answered, rewinding the video to where he noticed him. "Tell me that ain't that nigga."

Every eye in the room squinted and it took them a minute, but they finally saw what Sam saw. Like him, they were all stunned.

"Fuck is his issue?" Tech wondered taking the words out of everyone's mouth.

"It doesn't even matter…That nigga dead." Rich swore as everyone nodded their heads.

"Hell yeah," Sam hissed, ready to fuck some shit up. Shaking his head, he couldn't say he knew this would happen, but he knew he ain't like that nigga. Even before that shit a few months ago, he ain't never cared for him. Niggas always say, Sam don't like nobody, and it wasn't true, he just moved off vibes. If your vibe was off, Sam just ain't fuck with you, and his intuition was never wrong.

"Aight, well, the good thing is he doesn't know we have this video." Tech pointed out.

"Exactly," Echo agreed. "So, we can creep up on that nigga, and he won't see it coming."

"Nah, I want him to see it," Rich nearly growled. "On Zoo, he gon' feel this shit."

While Zoo was figuring out their next move, Solomon was posted with his crew running through the events that had taken place the day prior. He listened to his boys go back and forth tossing, in his two cents every now and then.

"Shit, them niggas out bad now."

His young boy Kenny relished as he smirked. Their mission was to weaken Zoo Crew, and they'd succeeded. While he was sure they were reeling from the shooting earlier, then the break-in at Stacks house, they couldn't get comfortable. Once they hit them, they would have to keep hitting them. The shit with Stacks was too easy, that housewarming party was the way in they needed, and he opened the door for them. The shit with Zoo wasn't even personal, it was strictly business. Like in any other business, you have to knock off the competition. Besides, the city couldn't have two kings', so it was time for King Zoo to go, so his reign could begin.

"Y'all go home, get some rest and meet back here tonight at midnight."

"We gon' hit they spot on tenth, right?" Kenny asked, and Solomon nodded his head. "Aight, catch y'all niggas later."

ARABIA

Solo dapped everyone up and sent them on their way. He didn't hang around much longer, staying behind only to shut down shop. Once everything was secure, he turned out the lights and locked up before heading home. On the drive to his house, Solo thought about the day's events and what all was to come. He still had a lot of work to do, but he felt ten steps closer than he was before.

Just as he was about to turn on to his street, his pager went off. He quickly reached into the cup holder and checked the number, shaking his head, it was his girl. Solo was about to pull up to his house anyway, so the thought of calling her back was gone. Whether he called her back or not didn't matter because he would be seeing her in a minute anyway. Before, making it to his house, he stopped on the corner at the store and grabbed a few loosies and a beer.

"Aight, nigga, I'll get with you later." He dapped the cashier up and proceeded out the door.

When he stepped out of the store, he twisted the top on his beer, and took a long gulp. Nothing at the end of the day felt better than a cold brew. "That shit hit the spot for real." Solo shook his head, before walking over to his car and hopping inside. Once he was situated, he pulled into traffic and headed home. Suddenly, his body froze as urine soaked his pants and seat.

"Keep fucking driving," Tech said as he sat up in the back seat. Firmly, he held his gun to the back of his head. Solo started to say something, and Tech dropped the barrel on the back of his head. "Shut the fuck up and make a left at this corner."

Solo groaned out in pain as his head knocked from the impact. His vision was blurry, and he was scared, but if he was about to die, they were both going to die. "Fuck you." He winced as he pressed the gas.

"Aye, nigga!" Tech yelled as the car went faster, "what the fuck is you doing?"

Solo didn't respond as he pressed the gas harder, flying through a red light. It was clear to Tech that Solo had a death wish, so he went and granted it. Grabbing him around the neck, Tech pushed the gun firmly into his head and pulled the trigger three times before he fell down into the seat and curled up. His heart raced as he anticipated the impact, he was sure would happen. It wasn't long after that the sound of tires screeching filled the air, followed by the impact of metal hitting metal. Tech crouched down as far as he could as he braced himself. The car was spinning, and it seemed as if the car spent forever before it came to an abrupt halt.

The second impact was damn near worse than the first, and Tech was thrown to the other side of the car. "Fuck." he winced as he slammed into the door. "Got damn, shit." His head was swirling as he focused his vision. Whatever he was feeling, he was going to have to snap out of it. Once he was successfully unfolded, Tech held his gun as he opened the back door and stumbled out of the car. He stumbled, ignoring the people trying to help him as he stood up right, being sure to keep his head down. Tech slowly began to hop away from the car before a slow jog turned into a full sprint. Tech hit one corner, and then another before he hopped a couple of fences. He didn't slow down until he felt he was far enough away. No matter what happened, he needed to get the fuck out of dodge. He peeped a pay phone on the next corner and stopped to page Rich. Ignoring the pain, he was feeling in his head, he carefully read the numbers on the phone and entered them followed by his code.

Less than five minutes later, and Rich was calling back. "Fuck you doing at a phone?"

"Later for all that. Come get me off Glendon and Smith. Just beep the horn when you pull up." He ran down the intersection after checking the signs.

Rich didn't know what to think because this shit wasn't a part of the plan. Tech was supposed to get the nigga and drive him back to the house, so what was this? "Aight, stay right there."

Tech hang up and limped over to the side of the building so he could rest out of sight. His back and leg were fucked up, and he really needed to sit down, but he knew if he did, he wouldn't be able to get back up. Desperately, Tech tried to calm his breathing. "Shit," he hissed. He allowed his head to fall back against the building as he clenched his teeth. Soon as he was beginning to feel a little relief, he heard a horn beep twice. Shaking his head, he seriously dreaded having to hop to the car. But he mustered up all his strength and came out of the shadows.

Rich saw him and knew something was wrong. "Fuck happen to you?" He asked as he made his way over to help him in the car.

"Man," Tech shook his head, "everything happened." Once he was in the car and Rich was back inside, he continued. "Who the fuck thought it was a good idea to slide in the backseat?"

"Echo said…"

"I'mma fuck him up yo'," Tech raved. "Solo dumb ass smashed the gas and wouldn't stop."

"What?" Rich looked over to him.

"Exactly, I had to kill that muthafucka and then a car crashed into us, and he spent out until he hit another car. Fucked me all up."

"That shit crazy." Shaking his head, he wanted to laugh out how outlandish the story sounded. It would've been funny had it not been true. "Well, we gon' have to get you back to the hotel and let the girls patch you up because you can't go to the hospital."

"I know." He winced as Rich turned the corner.

"Just hold tight, I'mma send Lynette to the drug store when we get back to the hotel."

Tech heard him, but he didn't respond. When they got to the hotel, Rich got him inside as quick as he could. They tried not to make too much of a scene because the last thing they wanted was the staff minding their business. Upstairs, they went straight to Tech's room, and Rich helped him onto the bed. Grabbing the phone, he quickly dialed his room number and told Lynette to get Keisha and come to Tech's room. Then he paged Sam and waited for him to call back.

"What happened?" Lynette asked soon as Rich opened the door.

"Shhhh," Rich swiftly pulled her and Keisha into the room and closed the door.

"Shit, what happened to you?" Keisha asked as she walked over to Tech.

"I'll explain later. Right now, I need you to help him get settled while me and Lynette run to the drug store."

Nodding her head, Keisha didn't protest as she watched Lynette and Rich head out the door. Just as she was about to walk over to Tech, the phone rung and both her and Tech looked to it.

"Answer it, it's probably Sam," he said, sitting up on his good elbow. "Just tell him the shit is done and to come back to the hotel."

Keisha answered the phone and did as she was instructed. When she was done, she hung up the phone and turned to Tech, "He on his way back." Walking over to the bed, she told him to lift his arms. "Come on lift up."

"My shoulder fucked up, so be careful," he warned, and she just rolled her eyes.

"Man, stop whining. I know what I'm doing." She swore as he lifted his good arm. Keisha was able to pull it off one side and then over his head before slipping it off his hurt arm. "Anything else I need to know before I finish undressing you?"

Tech looked up at her and for a minute, just stared in her eyes. His eyes traced her features, and he thought she was cute. They had been around each other for a good while, but this was the closest they'd ever been. "Yeah, my leg fucked up too."

"Aight," was all she said as she reached for his belt buckle, and Tech's hands flew to hers. "What?"

"What you doing?"

"How else you gon' get undressed?"

"Nah, come on now. You can't be all on my dick like that unless we about to fuck."

"Boy, shut up." Keisha rolled her eyes. "Ain't nobody looking at ya little dick."

"Girl, don't lie on my shit like that," he swore, looking at her like she was crazy. "My bitch a tell you my shit ain't little."

"Well, call ya bitch and have her come take care of you."

Tech looked at her and laughed. "I can't, she ain't even fuckin' with me right now, on some real shit."

"So, you stuck with me, now lift up." This time, Tech did as he was told, and she helped remove his pants. Keisha tried to glance, but Tech covered up. "Shit, you talkin' about how big it is, I was trying to see."

"Nah, you can't see this shit unless I'm about to fuck or you about to suck." He shrugged, looking at her with daring brows.

"Shut up." Stomping away, she went into the bathroom and grabbed some towels. "So, what happened? Why you all banged up?"

"Man, some bullshit, dumb ass plan went wrong." He went ahead and told her what happened, and she was struggling to keep it together.

"So, you just gone laugh at me? Right in front of me like this."

"I'm sorry." she giggled, clearing her throat. "Nah, but for real, that was the dumbest idea."

"That's what I know." He shook his head.

"Ya leg ain't broke or out the socket." She noticed, seeing him move his toes and everything.

"Well, it's something because this shit hurt."

"Maaannn, stop whinin'," she told him again before shaking her head and walking back into the bathroom. Just as she was coming out with a soap filled washcloth, Lynette and Rich where coming in.

Lynette pulled out the medical supplies they'd gotten while Rich reached in his pocket pulling out a bottle of pills, and tossed it to Tech.

"Good look." Tech caught the bottle and read the label. "Oh shit, I'm about to be knocked out."

WE MADE LOVE IN THE 80'S

The girls shook their heads, laughing as they got the supplies ready. Lynette didn't really know what to get, so she got Neosporin, peroxide, gauze and ace bandages. After Keisha cleaned his wounds, they both bandaged and wrapped his leg before helping him into the clean pajamas Rich had bought him. Rich was even nice enough to bring food back for them.

Once Tech took his meds and they ate, Rich and Lynette left. Keisha watched Tech sleeping and wondered what happened to Nate. She didn't think too long because the thoughts alone made her head hurt. But she had plans to reach out to him when all this was over.

Already in her bed clothes, Keisha decided to call it a night as she climbed into bed next to Tech and laid her head on the pillow. He was knocked out sleep on top of the covers, and she was about to comfortably drop her ass under the covers. After tossing and turning for about thirty minutes, she looked over to Tech. Sighing, she scooted closer to him and lay her head on his shoulder. Keisha had grown accustomed to sleeping with someone next to her, and right now, Tech was that someone. Once she was nice and comfortable; she fell right to sleep.

Chapter 15

The next morning, Tech woke up to knocking on his door. Shaking his head, shit was foggy but the pain he felt reminded him of all that had transpired the night before. When he moved his hand, he noticed that he wasn't in bed alone. His arm was wrapped tightly around Keisha's waist, and she was tucked beneath him. Tech licked his lips, looking down at her. He couldn't even front like he ain't like the way she was feeling in his arms, but he had to get up. Not only was someone at his door, he had to piss. As carefully as he could, he tried to move her from under him but as soon as he moved, Keisha turned towards him and lay her head on his chest.

"Aye, Keish," he called out.

"Humm," she groaned, still sleep.

"I gotta get up." Tech slid her off his chest, and she stared at him with low eyes. Looking around, it took her a minute to remember where she was. "I ain't mean to wake you."

After stretching, she looked back at him. "It's okay." She heard the knocking and slid her legs off the bed. "I'll get it."

Sliding off the bed, her shirt came up, and Tech got a nice look at her ass. "Shiiittt." He smirked, grabbing his dick. Slowly, he used the dresser to help him stand from the bed. The pain shooting from his hip down his leg was something he'd never experienced before. He for real, could cry, that's how bad it felt. However, he sucked it up and went to the bathroom.

"Good morning, y'all," Keisha greeted through her yawn as she let Rich, Echo, and Sam into the room. When she came back to the bed, she slipped on her shoes. "I'mma go shower and change my clothes. I'll be back in a few."

Tech came out the bathroom, and his eyes followed her to the door. When he looked back to the guys, they were all looking at him. "I should beat yo' ass," he sneered at Echo as he limped back to the bed.

"Shit, I ain't do it," Echo swore as he laughed. "How you fuck it up?"

"I didn't fuck it up. It was a dumb ass plan, and I told y'all that shit from jump." Shaking his head, he was mad all over again. "We should've done like I said and ran in his moms' shit, then had that muthafucka talking."

"Well, the shit is done now," Sam said, helping him get on the bed.

"Yeah, and we still don't know who was with him." Tech reminded them.

"Shit, that just mean we hit everybody," Rich spoke up. "Drive by that shit and air it out."

"On Zoo, that's the move." Echo was ready for action.

"Y'all niggas." Tech rolled his eyes. "Now y'all wanna do the fun shit when I'm all banged up and can't move."

"Hell, you handled our main problem." Sam reminded him of the good deed he'd done, that nearly cost him his life. "Now, sit ya ass down somewhere."

"Whatever," Tech smirked, "y'all checked on Stacks and Faith?"

"Yeah, we just came from up there," Sam answered and told him that Faith was doing good, and Stacks made it through surgery, but it was still touch and go.

"That nigga gon' pull through." He waved them off, knowing shit with Stacks was going to be alright. He couldn't explain how he knew; he just knew.

"Shit, he gotta," Sam said sadly, and everyone looked at each other not wanting to even think about the alternative.

After a few minutes, Tech changed the subject. "Aight, so when y'all gon' do all this?"

"Give them a couple of days. Once they find out about Solo, you know they gon' all get together somewhere." Rich knew that was for sure as the other men nodded their heads. "And after that we can all go home."

ARABIA

All sounded good to them, besides Sam was ready. Him, Janae, and the baby were getting restless and needed to spread out. Janae was almost five months pregnant, and Sam had moves to make. He'd been looking for a new place because with the new baby coming, the two bedrooms they were in was not going to cut it. Janae officially moved in after they found out she was pregnant, and shit been good ever since. There was no way she was bringing another baby back to her mother's house, so Janae had to put on her big girl panties and become an adult.

While Sam was handling his own business, Rich still had to meet with Taylor, the realtor, to get the paperwork signed for Lynette's store. Even with everything going on, he wanted to make sure they stayed focused. Rich coughed up the money and Lynette signed on the dotted line. She was now the proud owner of her own building. She had even taken the steps to register and trademark her business name. *55th Street,* for her, was going to be more than just the store, but a brand. Even though she'd been in touch with a few vendors to make sure she was stocked with quality merchandise, Lynette also reached out to a few local designers. Dap had already looked out on the custom Zoo pieces, and she had a couple of other designers on board to do a 55th Street clothing line. Once she got her logo back, it would all come together, and she was ready.

Although everybody was handling their business outside of Zoo, Echo ain't have shit to do. So, he took it upon himself to ride around the block and see what the word was. The hood was eerily quiet as he rode through. Nobody was out, not even any kids, and he figured that was a good thing. After hitting a few corners, he ended up around where Solo be at and parked his car on the corner. There wasn't nothing out of the ordinary, no unusual movements, or anything. He wanted these niggas so bad, he could taste it. He had visions of himself spraying the block and all Solo niggas dying. Shaking his head, he started the car and went to the hospital.

As far as they knew, Stacks was still unconscious, and Faith was in and out. After a quick stop at the front desk, he found their rooms with ease. The nurse told him that Faith had been awake earlier but was now sleeping, so he just peeked in on her. She didn't look too bad, he guessed. Her hair was shaved on the side where the bullet hit. He didn't want to wake her, so he didn't want to make too much noise. She needed her rest, so once he was satisfied with seeing her, he headed to Stacks room.

His heart raced as he approached the room. Echo didn't know what to expect; he was just trying to prepare himself for the worst. After a few deep breaths, he opened the door and walked in. Seeing Stacks hooked up to all those tubes and shit had his stomach doing flips. Seeing him like this, made the possibility of him not making it seem realer than it had when it happened. "Damn, Stacks," Echo whispered as he walked closer to the bed. There was so much more that he could say, but he opted not to. Nothing could be heard but the sound of the machines as stillness enveloped them. Echo looked around, and he saw a chair tucked away in the corner. Echo pulled it closer to the bed and went to take a seat, but before he was even comfortable the door opened and in walked Rich and Sam.

"Guess we all had the same thought," Sam said as they walked into the room.

Echo looked up, shaking his head as he stood to greet them. "Fuck y'all doing here?"

"Shit, same as you." Rich added, "Came to kick it with the homie."

They all looked to the bed before getting comfortable. For a few hours they talked like Stacks could talk back. Telling stories and making jokes, they were having a ball and hoping the energy would keep Stacks with them.

Keisha knew the guys would be talking for some time, so in her room she changed clothes and called a cab to pick her up. This was day two of her not hearing from Nate, and she couldn't stand it another minute. Once she got downstairs, she didn't have to wait long for the cab because it was pulling up just as she was walking out the lobby. Quickly, she ran off Nate's address and prayed he was home.

Keisha didn't know what she was going to say, and she was sure Nate had plenty of questions. Hell, he probably didn't even want to speak to her, but either way she needed to see him. It took them about twenty minutes to get to his building, she swiftly slid the money in the change jar and hopped out. Inside the building, it was as if she floated to his door. With balled fist, she knocked a few times and waited. Keisha anxiously looked up and down the hallway, before knocking again. Suddenly, the door swung open and her heart leaped into her chest. "Nate," her voice cracked as she jumped into his arms. "You're okay."

Nate wasn't expecting her to stop by, so he was taken aback by her jumping in his arms. He didn't hug her back and after a moment, he unwrapped her arms from around his neck. "What're you doing here?" he asked, looking up and down the hallway.

"You weren't answering my calls…I was worried." Her voice trailed off as he backed away from her.

"Worried why? Because you sent them zoo niggas to my fuckin' house?" He based as he banged his fist against the wall.

Tears fell from her eyes as she looked at him. "It, it wasn't like that. Can we just talk about this?"

He stepped back from her shaking his head. "Nah, we ain't got shit to talk about, you chose your side."

"There isn't a side, Nate that's my family," she told him, looking in his eyes. "You didn't tell me that you had words or whatever with Stacks and them the other week. Do you know how that shit looked…What was I supposed to do?"

"You should've had my back! As my woman, you should know I wouldn't do no shit like that to you!"

"I did know. Why do you think you're still here?" she yelled over him as she exhaled a deep breath. "Look, I'm sorry about how shit played out, and I'm sorry that you got caught up in this but…"

"Ain't no but's." Biting his lip, he looked away. Nate really loved Keisha and saw a future with her, but he couldn't trust her and after the other night, he couldn't be with her either. "I ain't no Zoo nigga, and I ain't about to be with you and have to question ya loyalty to me." Shrugging, he looked back to her.

Nodding her head, tears fell down her cheeks as she looked up at him. "So, this is it?"

Nate looked down at her. "I guess so."

WE MADE LOVE IN THE 80'S

Keisha had no choice but to accept what he was saying because he was right. Her loyalty to Zoo would always trump whatever they had, and there was nothing that would change that. Zoo had been there when she ain't have shit, Zoo took care of her, and they were her family. Stepping closer to him, Keisha brought her lips closer to his while staring in his eyes. When they connected, she closed her eyes, savoring his taste.

"I love you," she whispered before backing up from him.

Without looking his way, she headed down the hallway and out of his life forever. Needing to clear her mind, Keisha was in no rush to get back to the hotel. If she were being honest with herself, she wasn't even surprised that things with Nate ended. All of her relationships ended for one reason or another. Which was why she rarely did them. Hours later, she was back at the hotel and after stopping at her room to get her bag, she was using the key she swiped to get into Tech's room. When she walked in and down the little hallway, he was sitting up in bed watching TV.

"Did you eat?" she asked, removing her jacket.

"Yeah, earlier," Tech answered, looking at her, wondering where she'd been.

"You hungry?"

"Nah, I'm good."

Keisha nodded and went to use the bathroom. She removed her sunglasses and looked at her face. Her eyes were red and puffy from crying, and she was exhausted. The only thing she really wanted to do was take a shower and climb in bed, but she had to make sure Tech was straight first. After tossing some water on her face, she shook the bullshit off and walked back into the room. "You wanna shower or something?"

Tech licked his lips, smirking. "You gon' wash me up?" Rolling her eyes, Keisha really wasn't in the mood, and Tech could tell. "I'm just fucking with you. But I'm good, I showered already."

"Aight, well, I'mma go shower real quick." Grabbing her bag, she headed back to the bathroom and closed the door. A little over thirty minutes later and she felt a little better. Tech was still sitting in the same spot, watching the same show when she walked back into the room.

"Where you been all day?" he asked, watching her sit on the bed.

"Out," Keisha answered, keeping it short. "I'mma order some room service, you want anything?"

"Nah, but you can hand me one of those beers in that little ass refrigerator." Keisha got his beer and grabbed the copy of the restaurant menu to look over. "You ain't eat while you were out?"

"Pretty nosey, ain't you?" she asked, not bothering to look up at him.

Tech chuckled as he sipped from his beer bottle. "Hell, I mean, if I wanna know, why not just ask?"

Keisha looked up from her menu and into his eyes. "What do you wanna know?"

"What got you in such a funky ass mood?"

"Nate dumped me."

He tried to control his laughter, but it came out anyway. "I mean are you really surprised?"

"No, actually I'm not." Keisha sat up and looked at him. "Aside from y'all beating the shit out of him, no man that I ever date will come before Zoo, Zoo be…"

"Before God," he smoothly finished her sentence, and she nodded.

"That's the motto." She shrugged.

Nodding his head, he understood that. Shit, he was in a similar situation himself. "My girl called herself breaking up with me too. I mean, I ain't never did no bullshit for real, but she doesn't understand how deep this shit with Zoo really is."

"If you ain't do no bullshit, then what you do?"

"Work, this street shit don't have no hours, and you know how y'all women do. If I ain't home at a certain time, I gotta be out fuckin' on somethin'." Keisha nodded her head, agreeing with that. "That shit get old after a while."

"How long y'all been together?"

"Like, three years."

"Dang, who knew you had a girl for that long. You must've had her ass tucked away." She joked as he shook his head laughing. "But for real, that's a lot of time to just be throwing in the towel."

Shrugging, he agreed. "It is, but at the end of the day, she ain't from this world, and she don't understand what it means to be with a nigga like me. She ain't like y'all."

"And who's y'all? What you trying to say?"

"Not like that, you know what I mean."

"I feel you." She giggled. "Well, nobody said this Zoo life would be easy."

"For real," he nodded, "but I'm sure you won't have a problem finding another nigga."

"Man, listen, I ain't even looking." She laughed. "It takes too much to start over with somebody new."

"Who said it had to be somebody new?" He asked, raising a brow, twirling a joint in his hands.

Keisha stared at him as she contemplated the question, but she didn't answer it. In fact, she went right back to looking over the menu to order her food as he watched her.

Once news of Solo's death hit the streets, the news spread like wildfire. Everyone thought he was killed in a car accident, but once his autopsy came back, they knew his true cause of death. His crew was ready to make moves but had no idea who to hit. It really didn't matter because Zoo was on their heads. They still thought they were moving low since nothing had happened since Stacks and Faith had been shot. They were supposed to be laying low and now that this happened, they had to step up. Rich knew they would all make their way to Solo's house; it was a predictable move and with most of the crew being young. He knew they would make it. Just about everybody in Solo's crew stood outside of his apartment building and didn't think twice about the Chrysler New Yorker that circled the block.

On the second run, the back and front passenger side windows came down. Both Rich and Sam leveled their guns with mask covering their faces. Sam's hands trembled as he gripped the trigger. He could feel his heart beating in his throat as he waited for the right moment to pull the trigger. In his head he counted, *one, two, three...Blast*, and gun fire soon followed. The sound of machine guns piercing the air could be heard for blocks as the men in front of the building crumbled. Rich held his arm out the window to control the kickback from his gun as he relished at the sight of bodies dropping. What felt like an eternity was merely minutes before nothing could be heard but tires screeching down the street. Once they were down the block Echo, Rich, and Sam removed the ski mask from their faces as they spent the block. Their adrenaline was sky high, and the men could hardly sit still. If they knew they could do it and get away with it, they would've doubled back.

"That's that shit I'm talking about!" Sam shouted gleefully, hitting the back seat.

"Zooooo," they howled all hyped up.

"Yo' that shit was like that." Sam continued to bounce in his seat. "Like, I been waiting for this shit my whole life."

"We know." Echo laughed with Rich, knowing it was true. Sam was trigger happy as hell and was always looking for a reason to shoot somebody.

"Yeah, yeah, you just drive nigga." Sam smirked, tapping him in the back of the head. They were quiet for a minute before Sam spoke again. "Like, I can still feel that shit." He swore, looking at his hand as he stretched his fingers.

"Hell yeah," Rich agreed as he stepped out the car. They were back at the warehouse they'd began using not too long ago. The warehouse was mainly for meetings, but now it was about to be used to break this car down, and they were going to get rid of these guns.

"Aight, so what's next?" Echo asked, wondering where they went from here.

Rich pondered his question as he looked to Sam. With Stacks still in the hospital, and their operation temporarily shut down, shit for Zoo Crew was looking bleak. He didn't know if they could do this shit without Stacks, most of all, he didn't know if he wanted to. "We get ready for Jay funeral," was all he said before he walked away. The other men were lost, but Rich felt as if the weight of the world was on his shoulders. Zoo Crew was his, he was the leader and what happened to Jay, Stacks, and Faith was on his hands. Maybe not literally, but to him it was all the same.

Back at the hotel, Rich slowly walked the halls. He knew what he'd done was necessary, but he didn't feel any better about doing it. The same grief and pain they were feeling was the same grief and pain they'd caused the families of the men they'd killed. This was the fucked-up part of the game, the part of the game that turned good men into killers, the part of the game that left children fatherless, and the part of the game that came with living this life.

Lynette was sleeping when Rich got in, but she'd awakened at the sound of the door opening. In one of Rich's t-shirts, she slid out of the bed and practically ran over to him. "Baby, you're okay." Rich nodded as he held her in his arms. "I was so worried."

Never putting her down, Rich walked over to the bed and sat down with her in his lap. "I'm good, babe." He held her tight in his arms as she cried on his shoulder from sheer relief. "Everybody good now," he soothed, rubbing her back. "We can go home after Jay funeral, but for now, we just need to lay low."

Sitting up, she wiped her eyes before kissing his lips, slowly at first and then more feverishly. Right now, she just wanted to feel him, she needed him to take her body and make her feel safe and comforted. The day of the shooting, those men did more than kill and injure her friends, they took her piece of mind.

ARABIA

Rich's hands roamed her body before gripping her ass and flipping her over. He knew exactly what she needed because he needed it too.

Chapter 16

Flowers lined the pews of the church as the community gathered to celebrate Jay-Tap's life. Lynette had never been to a funeral and after this one, she swore she would never attend another. It had been a little over two weeks since the shooting that rocked their neighborhood to the core. Of course, there had been killings, robberies, and domestic shit, but never had there been anything like this.

"You okay?" Rich leaned into her as the choir began singing.

"Yeah," she said softly as she looked to Jay's casket with tears in her eyes. Every time she thought of him, their last moments together replayed in her mind, and it fucked with her. Jay was really a good guy and had always looked out, for not only her, but the whole crew. "Damn," she whispered, shaking her head as tears slowly left her eyes.

Rich wrapped his arm tightly around her shoulder as he sat back tuned into the service. Chills ran up his spine as Jay's mother's cries echoed off the church walls. They watched helplessly as she stood over his casket, asking him not to leave, and Rich couldn't look any more. Honestly, he no longer wanted to be there, and by the looks on the rest of Zoo Crew's faces, neither did they. Once the funeral was over, the men stood outside the church just thinking.

"I need a fuckin' drink," Tech said to no one in particular, but everyone agreed, "in the worst way."

"Shit, we all do," Sam agreed as he wrapped an arm around Janae's neck pulling her into him.

"Well, after this, we can all go home and try to get back to business," Rich said, looking to everyone. He ignored the look Lynette was giving him. They had discussed him going back to work and he already knew how she felt, but that wasn't going to stop him from going.

"Now, I'm with that shit." Tech rubbed his hands together already able to feel all the illegal shit between his fingers.

"Boy, you just started walking, you need to calm down." Keisha rolled her eyes as they all chuckled at that one as Tech shrugged.

ARABIA

"Monday morning we'll link up and discuss moving forward," Rich said as he dapped everyone up and prepared to leave. Lynette shook her head as she turned and walked ahead of him to the car. This was all bullshit if you asked her. All eyes followed her, and Rich ain't even feel like arguing about some shit that wasn't going to change. "I'll fuck with y'all later." Loosening his tie, he took a deep breath and headed to the car himself.

In the car, Lynette sat with her arms folded over her chest, waiting for him. Once he finally made it to the car, they rode in complete silence for a while before she turned to him. "So, you just gon' start hustlin' again?"

"What you mean, start?" He looked to her. "I never stopped."

Rolling her eyes, Lynette shook her head. "You know what, I don't even care! Go ahead and do what you want."

"Lynette…"

Turning back around, she cut him off, "Jay is dead!!! Stacks is practically a fuckin' vegetable, and you want to run back and out there…Go ahead, I'm not gon' stop you, I…"

"What? You gon' leave me? You ready to give up on us?" he asked, shaking his head. Rich understood her fear, but this was his life, this was their bread and butter. There was no way he could quit right now. "You think I wanna do this shit? You think I wanna bury my niggas, watch my nigga wasting away, and ain't shit I can do?" Rich had to take a breath because as fucked up as shit was, he had to keep going.

Tears fell from her eyes just thinking of all the things that could and now, she was sure would go wrong. "And what happens to me? What am I supposed to do?"

"You're supposed to be down for me, open ya store, and leave the worrying to me." He grabbed her hand and kissed the back of it. "I got you, and I know shit crazy right now, but that don't mean we stop believing in Zoo."

Shaking her head, Lynette scooted closer to him and laid her head on his shoulder. She was scared for him. Scared that he would end up like Stacks or worse like Jay, hell, even she could be laid up like

Faith. No matter what happened, she made him a promise a long time ago, and she was going to honor it. "I'll never give up on you Tony," she whispered, sniffing back tears.

Tech pulled up to Keisha's house and cut his car off. After two weeks together, this was it for them, and he couldn't even front like he wasn't sad to see her go. They sat there for a minute, neither of them really saying anything before Tech stepped out the car to grab her bags out the trunk.

Keisha watched him in the mirrors before taking a deep breath and stepping out herself. "You got it?" she asked, her two bags weren't really heavy, but he was just getting back to himself.

"Yeah, I got it," Tech answered as he closed the trunk.

Nodding her head, she walked ahead of him entering her code to get into the door. Patiently, he waited for her to open the door and when it opened, he allowed her to step in ahead of him. Immediately, Keisha turned on the hallway light as she walked to the living room and dropped her pocketbook on the couch. Tech looked around and thought the place was decent. He had never been to the money house but even after two weeks, it was clean, and it smelled good.

"You can sit those bags right there, and I'll take them up later," she ordered before walking into her kitchen and cutting on the light.

Tech did as he was told before turning around. "You good?"

"Yeah," she looked at him as she walked back into the living room, "thanks."

"No problem. Walk me to the door and lock up," he said as he walked back towards the hallway. Keisha was directly behind him, ready to say her goodbyes and lock the door. At the door, Tech opened it and then looked down at her. "Thanks for nursing me back to health too."

Smirking, Keisha grabbed her bottom lip with her teeth as she playfully rolled her eyes. "You're welcome."

"Aight, be good," he said as if he was about to walk out but, in the doorway, he still stood there, looking down at her.

Their eyes were connected and even though they were supposed to be saying goodbye, it seemed as if something was pulling them closer together. Stepping closer to her, Tech held her gaze as he leaned down kissing her lips. Gently, he grazed them at first but when she didn't reject him, he grabbed the back of her neck and deepened the kiss. He slinked his tongue into her mouth, and she nearly melted. Keisha pushed her chest up against his, wrapping her arms around his neck. For a moment she let go of all her inhibitions and got lost in him. His hands gripping her ass and trying to lift her into the air was the only thing that brought her back to reality. This was wrong, wrong on so many levels. She was just getting out of a relationship and he was still in one, so whatever this was had to end now.

Tech rubbed his chin looking down at her as she backed up from him, wiping her mouth. Keisha looked back at him and quickly looked away. "I guess I'll see you around."

"I guess so." Looking to his car, he looked back at her. "Lock up," was all he said before he walked to the car, leaving Keisha standing there.

Tech didn't pull away until, he saw her front door close. Looking around the neighborhood, he was sure to commit the house and directions to memory before he left. Tech didn't know when or how but he planned on seeing Keisha again. She plagued his thoughts all the way back to his apartment, and all he could do was shake his head. It had been too long since he'd been home, so long that his neighborhood didn't even look the same. Deciding to leave his bags, he planned on bringing them up later as he walked into his building. Since the accident he walked with a slight limp that probably needed some medical attention, but it was whatever with him. He was doing fine and had been through worse, so he was good. It didn't take long for the elevator to come down and take him to the seventh floor, but he was relieved when it was finally his stop. At his door, he fumbled with the key when suddenly the door swung open.

"TaShawn!" His girl Raheema jumped into his arms, wrapping her arms around his neck. "I was so worried about you." She swore with tears in her eyes. Tech didn't really know what to say and was shocked by her presence. "Come on in the house." She pulled him along when she released him. "I heard about what happened up there where you be at…"

"What are you doing here?" was all he asked, not even fazed by her presence.

"I wanted to make sure you were okay," she said softly as her eyes watered. "I've been waiting for you since I heard about it, paging you night and day."

Running his hands over his waves, he looked away. "Yeah, I lost my pager."

Raheema could tell by his tone, he still wasn't fucking with her and that made her sad. "TaShawn, can we just talk about this." Chuckling, he shook his head. "You know I love you, and I know I get a little jealous."

"For real Rah, I ain't trying to be with you and have to justify every move I make." He sighed because this whole shit with her was exhausting. "Three years and you don't even trust me with simple shit. Like, I can't even go to the store without you accusing me of shit."

"I know and I'm sorry but come on, TaShawn. You leave and you're gone for days, shit, weeks at a time and you just expect me to be cool with that? If you're just working and hanging out why can't I ever come…You gotta admit shit suspect as hell."

"You don't need to be hanging around a bunch of niggas," he said with finality. "My nigga girl nearly got her head blown off, and you questioning why I don't want you on the block?"

Rolling her eyes, Raheema knew he was playing games. "That just happened, so cut the shit!"

"For real, this shit getting old." Tech didn't know if he was done with her forever, but right now he wasn't feeling it. "Look, thanks for checking on me and shit, but we need to pump the breaks on this for a minute."

With watery eyes, Raheema looked at him, wondering if he was really serious. When she didn't see an ounce or an inkling of sympathy. She knew that just maybe this time, she had pushed him too far. Though in her eyes, her behavior was valid, she also knew it was driving a wedge between them. Their last argument got a little out of hand and had even turned physical. She just couldn't help the way she felt, but it was obvious Tech wasn't feeling her right now. Nodding her head, she wiped her eyes dry before she walked over to him and kissed his lips. Tech didn't kiss her back, but he hadn't stopped her either and to her, that meant he just needed a little time. "Call me later," she told him, and he agreed as she turned to walk out of his apartment.

Tech didn't really have any intentions on calling her tonight. No, tonight, he wanted to rest and enjoy being home for a moment. After two weeks cooped up in a hotel room, he wanted to enjoy being in his own space again. On the way to the bathroom, he removed his clothes to prepare for his shower. The hotel was cool, but it was nothing better than being home. In the shower, he allowed the hot water to flow over his head and cascade down his body. Closing his eyes, he allowed himself the time to just be still and relax.

Later on, that night, Tech found himself tossing and turning as his mind raced with thoughts. He laid on his back, smoothing his hands over the sheets beside him. He looked at the other side of his bed, shaking his head. The empty space next to him was depressing. Kicking the covers off, Tech sat up and stretched his arms, tall above his head before he went to the bathroom. While inside, he quickly put on some basketball shorts and a t-shirt. Tech slid his feet into his sneakers, ready to walk out the door and after grabbing his keys he was out.

In the car, he fired up a joint and just sat there for a minute before he started his car and slowly pulled into traffic. He thought about the shooting, and that day played in his mind like a movie on replay. So vividly he could hear the blast of the guns, and see images of Stacks and Faith. Then his mind drifted to his own accident, and even his on and off again relationship with Raheema. He wasn't sure how he wanted to handle the situation with her. If he was being honest, he really wanted to be done with her and all that extra shit she was on. All that arguing and fighting over nothing all the time, wasn't what he was trying to do. Tech wanted peace when he came home, and he thought about Keisha.

Keisha was cool as fuck, and he could kick shit with her all day. Those two weeks they were together, night and day, were like that. He enjoyed talking to her, and he enjoyed her company. More than anything she understood what this Zoo life was about. He wouldn't say two weeks compared to three years, but he was feeling the different vibe Keisha was on. For about an hour he rode around and when he finally checked the clock, it was going on two in the morning. Deciding to call it a night, he hit a few corners and before he knew it, he was back at Keisha spot.

WE MADE LOVE IN THE 80'S

Sitting outside, he tapped the steering wheel not sure if he even wanted to play himself like this. What if she had a nigga upstairs, or what if she wasn't really trying to fuck with him like that? He looked up towards the house and said fuck it. Stepping out of the car, he locked his doors and walked up the driveway. When he made it to the front door, he took a deep breath and rang the doorbell a couple of times, then stepped back and waited for her to come to the door. His heart beat rapidly, nearly leaping out of his chest, as the porch light came on. Soon after, he could hear locks turning before the door swung open, and there she was.

Keisha stood there with a crop tee on, some pajama shorts, and a scarf wrapped around her head. Stepping out the door just a bit, she looked from left to right, expecting to see other people, but it was just him. "Everything okay?"

He licked his lips, looking down at her. "I, I couldn't sleep."

Shaking her head, she rolled her eyes playfully. "Okay, and you're here because?"

Tech honestly had enough shit on his mind, too much for the jokes. Not only that, he was already putting himself out there in a way he never had before, so he was ready to bounce if she was gonna be on bullshit. "Nothing, man." Turning around he was ready to head back home.

"Hey!" She ran out the door and grabbed his arm just as he hit the steps. He stopped as he was going down that first one and turned to her. At his current position they were standing eye to eye. Looking at each other, neither of them said anything. Keisha thought he was really brave just popping up at her spot like this, but she liked it. Wrapping her arms around his neck, she pecked his lips, once then twice before she kissed him again. Nervously, she looked away pushing her hair behind her ear. "I can't sleep either."

Backing away from him, she grabbed both of his hands and pulled him into the house before closing and locking the door. Tech followed her upstairs, loving the house as he made it to her room. Inside, the light was on, and the room was very spacious with purple and red colors decorating the space. "You can put ya shoes over there," she told him as she made her way to the bathroom to cut off the light and, then pulled the covers back on her bed.

Tech did as he was told and removed his shoes, putting them where she said before he took his shorts and t-shirt off. On the other side of the bed, he climbed in and slid underneath the covers. Soon as his head, hit the pillow his whole body relaxed. Like instantaneously, and he loved it. Keisha handed him the remote and he took it, placing it on the nightstand beside him. When she laid back, he pulled her into him, and they both got comfortable. Her head was on his chest with her arm wrapped around his stomach, while his head rested on hers and his arms wrapped tight around her body. This was it; this was what they both needed. There was a level of comfort that Keisha brought him, that he couldn't see himself being without.

Faith sat up in her hospital bed just hours from being released. Running her hands over her hair, she shook her head. That day changed everything she thought she knew and felt about life. No longer did she look the same or move the same. Even though she was going home, walking, bending over and other movements was still hard for her. Her face was no longer swollen, but there were scars from the bullet and her hitting the ground. Most notably was the scar on her head. She didn't like that they had to shave her hair on one side and now she was walking around with a Gumby haircut that she hated. Shit was just all bad, hell, even things with her and Stacks were shaky.

The first chance she got, she was wheeled to his bedside. Over her own health, she made sure he was being taken care of and that he wasn't alone. Practically all day and half the night she was in his room and when he woke up, he didn't even want to see her. That shit hurt the most, even more than being shot. Her mother explained how he might need a minute to adjust himself and how his pride may have been wounded, and Faith really didn't want to hear that shit.

"So, today's the big day." Nurse Pam beamed as she walked in her hospital room. She was all smiles as she pulled the curtains back, letting in an abundance of sunlight. Faith squinted from the light, but she didn't bat a lash or smile. "I know you're happy, even if you don't look it. You need anything?" Pam asked as she turned and checked her vitals.

"No," Faith mumbled as she flinched a little at the probing. "Well, can you check on Landon for me?"

"Sure thing." Pam smiled as she finished up. "I'll get you some breakfast and some juice too."

Faith sat in the bed, not wanting any of the stale ass breakfast the hospital was offering, but she didn't say anything. When they bought her food, she picked over it and drunk her juice before her eyes drifted out the window.

"What's up, bitch?" Lynette sang loudly as she danced through the door with the girls behind her. "Oh, don't look like you ain't happy to see us."

"Nah, I'm just surprised." She half smiled.

"We told ya mom we would pick you up," Keisha said as she plopped down on the bed and grabbed a piece of her toast.

"And she let y'all," rolling her eyes, she faked irritation. "I already got shot, now I'mma be in a car accident."

"Oh, fuck you. I can drive, hoe." Keisha laughed. "This toast is nasty."

"All this shit nasty," Faith quickly agreed.

"I know you ready to go home," Janae said as she looked out the hospital window, rubbing her growing belly.

Faith thought about the empty house that awaited her and nothing about it made her happy. "Not really." The girls at that moment gave her their undivided attention. "Ain't nothing there for me," she said with her voice cracking as tears left her eyes.

Holding her chest, Janae failed to control her own tears. "Aww, boo, don't cry." Walking over to the bed, Janae sat down, hugging Faith as she broke down.

"Everything just so fucked up," Faith swore as her chest heaved up and down.

Lynette and Keisha didn't know what to say. They knew nothing would make her feel better, nothing or no one but Stacks could do that.

"It ain't fucked up," Keisha said, walking over to the bed. "It's just hard, right now. They say God, gives the hardest battles to his strongest warriors."

Lynette's face twisted in irritation as she sucked her teeth. "Girl, shut up." All the girls burst into laughter as Keisha shrugged.

Faith dried her eyes with the backs of her hands as she giggled. "I can't stand y'all."

"We love you too." Keisha laughed. "But you know if you don't wanna go home, you still have your room at the money house. I could use the company."

"Tech is enough company." Janae smirked.

Lynette and Faith's mouths fell open in shock as Keisha blushed sheepishly.

"You and Tech?" Lynette asked, wondering how she missed this.

"Okay, because I thought you ain't wanna mess with a worker," Faith said matter of factly.

"First of all, Tech isn't a worker." She laughed, throwing Faith's words about Tech back at them. "And second of all, I'm not messing with him like that...we just, cool that's it that's all."

"Yeah, yeah, I hear you," Janae begged to differ.

"Besides, he has a girlfriend," Keisha reminded them.

"So, take her man," Lynette said as if she'd solved the puzzle for her.

"Nah, it ain't that deep. He where he wanna be, so I ain't about to go back and forth with him. Plus, after that whole Nate fiasco, I'm chilling."

"Well, you know I think y'all cute together, so I'm rooting for y'all," Faith said just before the nurse walked in.

She told them, they had just started processing her discharge papers and that they would have her squared away shortly. Nodding her head, that was music to Faith's ears. Janae had given her a bag filled with clothes for her to wear, and she was beyond thankful. Even though she was going home, she was still in a bit of pain, and it showed as she slowly walked to the bathroom. All this time she'd been avoiding the mirror and looking at herself, she knew why. Her lips trembled as she got a cloth and gently wiped her face before brushing her teeth, then she dressed in the sweat suit and sneakers they'd brought her. There was also a baseball cap inside, and she appreciated it too because there was nothing she could do with her hair. Not able to take her appearance anymore, she walked out of the bathroom and the nurse was in there.

"Well, look who getting her groove back," Lynette joked, and the nurse laughed.

"We got you all set," she said as she sat her papers on the small table. "You feeling okay?"

Faith nodded her head that she was before she thanked her for everything. The nurse lady was real nice, and Faith appreciated that.

"Alright y'all let's go," Lynette stretched as they grabbed Faiths bag of belongings. While she was in the bathroom, they took the initiative and packed her stuff up.

Looking around the room, Faith said her goodbyes, and they walked to the elevator. "I'mma stop by Stacks' room before we leave." The other girls nodded their heads but didn't say anything as they stepped on the elevator. Faith was on the seventh floor and Stacks was on the eleventh, so she pushed eleven, tuning out the conversation the girls were having. She was in pain, but she couldn't leave the hospital without saying anything to Stacks. When the elevator opened, the girls stepped out and Faith led the way. She counted the room numbers until she reached his. For a minute she stood there, and after taking a deep breath she walked in.

Instantly, Stacks' eyes met hers. "You good?" He asked, worry filling his words.

"Yeah, I'm okay." She twiddled her fingers. "You?"

"I'm aight, I guess," he said, allowing his body to relax back against his pillow.

"That's good," her voice cracked as she looked away from him. Faith refused to cry, so she wiped her tears and looked back to him. "They're letting me go home today."

"That's good," Stacks said as if he could care less, and Faith just rolled her eyes.

"I'mma stay with Keisha at the money house." He looked in her eyes and still he didn't say anything. Shit, with them was so awkward, and Faith hated it. She didn't know why he was so cold with her, but the shit hurt. "Landon, why are you treating me like this?"

"Like, what?" He asked as if he didn't know what she was talking about.

"Like, I'm some bitch on the street bugging you?" Her voice rose, "Like you ain't fucking with me."

Sighing, Stacks could barely look at her. "You know it ain't like that, Faith."

"Well, tell me what it's like because that's how I feel."

Right now, Stacks couldn't do that because honestly, he ain't even know the right words to express all the shit he was feeling. The guilt he felt was causing him to push her away while his anger kept him from expressing that. Faith was almost killed because of him, and that shit hurt him to his core. He loved her, but he felt like she was better off without a nigga like him. He knew she would never leave him, so he was forcing her hand. "I ain't mean to make you feel like that, but ain't shit I can do for you from a fucking hospital bed…I'm shittin' in a fuckin' bag, Faith! A bag…Man." he stopped as he found himself becoming emotional. "Just go, Faith, you don't need a nigga like me."

Tears fell as she shook her head. "Stacks…"

"Just go Faith," he pleaded with her, almost begging.

Faith nodded her head as she watched a couple of tears fall from his eyes. This feeling, she had never felt before. She imagined this would be how she felt if he'd died. He wasn't dead physically, but a mental death was just as worse. Slowly, she walked over to the bed and even though it hurt her, she leaned down and kissed his lips. "I love you, Landon."

Stacks watched her walk out of his room, and when she was gone, he broke down crying. He loved Faith, he loved her more than he loved himself and felt it was better to just let her go. For right now anyway.

Faith wiped her eyes as she walked out of his hospital room, and the girls instantly turned to her.

"What's wrong?" Keisha asked.

Shaking her head, Faith didn't even want to talk about it. "Let's just get out of here."

Nodding their heads, the girls just followed her lead. They didn't know what was going on between her and Stacks but whatever it was, it was deep. Faith was far from the emotional type so if she was crying, it was big.

Chapter 17

Sam picked Janae up from the money house later that night, and she couldn't get to the car fast enough. "What's up, babe?" he greeted as soon as she stepped into the car.

"Tired," was all she said as she leaned over the console and kissed his lips. It had been a long day for all the girls, and extra-long for her. After being gone all day, all she wanted to do was shower and lay up under her man.

"I told you not to be running around that damn store," he said, rubbing her belly. Just then a loud rumble sounded from her stomach, reminding her that she hadn't eaten since this morning. "And you been starving my baby," he shifted gears and pulled off. "Hardheaded ass, you on that bed rest shit from now on."

Janae looked at Sam like he was crazy. "Being hungry is not a reason to be put on bed rest."

"It's gon' be a reason for you," he told her, not caring what she said. "What you wanna eat?"

"I don't know," she yawned. "Let's get some chicken from down by the bridge." Sam nodded, and she relaxed getting comfortable. "Ya mother keeping Sammie?"

"Do you even have to ask?

Laughing, Janae shook her head. "She ain't never gon' give me my baby back."

"Shit, that's her baby at this point." Sam joined her laughing. Between her mother and his, they hardly ever had Sammie. Janae literally had to go and kidnap her own child from them. Though they were grateful for the help and appreciated the support, Sam planned on bringing her home tomorrow.

"Sam," Janae called out to him, and he took his eyes off the road turning to her. "Are you ever going to tell her?"

Sam sat quiet for a minute, together they had promised to never bring up the fact that Sammie wasn't biologically his, but he knew what she was asking, and she had a right to know. "I told her," he said softly, looking over to her for her reaction, but she had none as she continued to look out the window. "I said I wasn't, but a few weeks after Sammie was born, I told my moms."

"What she say?" Janae asked, never looking over to him.

"Nothing, really. She just said that it takes a special kind of man to step up and raise a child that ain't his, and that she would love Sammie regardless."

Just as he finished, he was pulling up to the chicken spot and he parked the car. Janae looked over to him and beckoned him over. "She was right." Smiling, Janae moved till she was just inches from his lips. "Thank you, Sam, for real." Her eyes filled with water as her voice shook. "Since my dad, I ain't never had a man that was down for me, and I just want you to know that I appreciate everything you do for me and Sammie."

Sam smiled at her words because he knew he was that nigga. Not that nigga like the man in the streets, even though he was that too. But Sam was all about this family shit and if he could have a million kids with Janae, he would. Her evil ass was cool as hell, and she was a great mother. Sam didn't mind taking the time to groom her, for him, and it showed in the patience he displayed with her. "I love ya little ass." He smirked, kissing her lips. "You, Sammie and Sahara, ain't shit I won't do for y'all, just know that."

Nodding her head, Janae was knowing. "We love you too," she told him before kissing his lips a final time.

Together they stepped out the car and walked through the guys around the way. Sam said what's up to the men who spread like the Red Sea to grant him and his lady entrance into the dining establishment. Zoo was known and respected all over the city, so Janae was used to the attention when they went out. Gracefully, she walked past the men as Sam held her hand. Inside the chicken spot, Sam sat her in the back and went to place their orders. When he came back, he had two cups of soda. Grape for her and Coke for him. After sitting them on the table, he sat down. While they waited for their food, they made small talk. Mostly about the kids, but they joked a little bit too. A few moments later, their food was ready, and Janae was tearing into her plate like the food could get up and run away from her.

ARABIA

"I got a house for us to look at tomorrow," Sam told her, in between bites of his chicken.

"A house?" Janae perked up a bit.

"Yeah, I was looking for apartments but shit, why not a house? More room for the kids to run around, we could even get a yard."

Nodding her head, she liked the sound of that. "Where the house at?"

"It's out in Laurel Springs."

"Where Keisha and them at?"

"Nah, but it ain't too far." He went on to explain the agent that hooked them up with the money house, had some other properties available and could lookout for them. "You already know the shit gon' be nice."

"For real, I'm excited!" She bounced in her seat.

"Me too, we definitely need to be settled before you have the baby."

"I know right! Plus, I need to finish shopping."

"Shit, she got everything," he said, not seeing the need to buy everything again.

"I know, but I don't want all her stuff to be Sammie's hand me downs. I want her to have a few things brand new."

"Shit, she don't care." Reaching over, he rubbed her stomach and could feel the baby rolling around, and his heart fluttered.

Dinner lasted another thirty minutes before they were packing up to go. True to her word, Janae showered and when Sam was out of the bathroom, she laid right up under him. With her head on his chest and his fingers in her hair, she was out in no time.

WE MADE LOVE IN THE 80'S

The next morning, Janae and Sam were up with the birds, not only did they have to pick the baby up, they also had to go look at the house. So, they didn't mess around at all. They were dressed and out the house before Janae could wake up good. On the way to get the baby, they stopped and got something to eat because as always, she was hungry, and Sam would eat just because. When they were done, Sam went to get Sammie.

"What's going on, Momma?" Sam said as they bent the corner into his parents' house.

"Boy, don't come in here with all that noise." She hushed him as soon as they came into view.

Janae laughed as she walked over to Sam's mom. "Hey, Ms. Teresa."

"What I tell you about that?" She opened her arms, hugging her tight.

"My bad, Ma." Janae smiled as his mom rubbed her stomach.

"Where my baby at?" Sam asked, removing his jacket.

"She in her room asleep." She was barely able to finish her sentence before Sam took off to his old room. When he was out of sight, Teresa turned back to Janae. "And how've you been holding up?"

Janae took a deep breath, before releasing it. "I'm holding on." She smiled. "I mean, I be a little worked up sometimes, but I'm okay."

"I'm sure you are; my Sam won't have it any other way," Teresa said, already knowing how her son was.

"And you already know." When she looked towards the steps, Sam was coming down with the baby in his arms. Sammie was getting so big. In just a few weeks, she would be one, and everyone was overly excited. "Sammie," she squealed as Sam walked her over. "My baby." Janae really did miss her baby girl and it showed.

"Aight, Momma, we'll catch up with you later." Leaning down, Sam kissed his mother's cheek, and they headed for the door.

ARABIA

Outside, Sam quickly buckled the baby into her car seat, and they were off to see the house.

It took them about thirty minutes, but when they pulled up to the house, Janae was in love. The flowers that lined the walkway gave the house curb appeal and it was huge, way bigger than she imagined it would be. "This is the house?"

"Yeah, come on let's check it out," Sam said before he stepped out the car, and got the baby out the back seat.

Janae let herself out and gave the neighborhood the once over. It was nice and seemed to be quiet, she really liked that. Turning her attention back to the house, she followed Sam up the walkway. The house was two stories, and that to her was dope because she'd always lived in an apartment. Inside, the living room was nice and open with a spiral staircase that led to the second level, and beyond the staircase was a small hallway that led to the kitchen. "This is so nice," she marveled, smoothing her hands over the counters that appeared to be glistening with different colors.

"Hell yeah, I'm ready for you to cook already." He smiled. "Shit, put a table over there, and we good to go."

Janae nodded her head agreeing. She could already see them eating breakfast in the mornings, sitting by the window. "Is that the backyard?" She asked, walking over to the window.

"Yup." Sam followed but walked over to a door and opened it. It led out to a screened porch, and the porch led them to the backyard. "This shit tight, for real."

"Yes, it is, I love it." She smiled as she peered out the door, not wanting to walk all the way out. She just wanted to see what the yard looked like.

"Come on," Sam walked over with Sammie in one hand and grabbing Janae's hand with the other. Together they walked the three-bedroom house, two bathrooms, and the finished basement. Everything was so perfect Janae wanted to cry. "Cut it out."

"I can't." She wiped her eyes. Never had she ever imagined living in anything close to this.

WE MADE LOVE IN THE 80'S

They had covered every inch of the house and were back in the living room, Sam put the baby down on the floor and turned to Janae. Reaching inside his coat pocket, he pulled out a card. He handed it to her and just watched her.

"What's this?" She asked, twirling the card in her hands, Sam encouraged her to open it, and she did. Inside was a card that read *Welcome Home* with a house key attached to a purple ribbon. It took a minute but after reading the card a couple of times, it registered. "Sam."

Sam wasn't good with all the sappy shit, but if nothing else, he was a man of his word. "I told you before, I got you and the kids, forever."

Tears fell from her eyes as Janae wrapped her arms around his neck. He held her tight around her waist. "Thank you, Sam."

It warmed his heart to hear those words at this moment. Sam wanted to be the type of nigga that provided for and supported his family. The kind of man his father was, and he was doing that. "Nah, thank you."

Janae wiped her eyes smiling as he palmed her stomach. This was it; this was her family and a start to her forever. "So, we can move in?"

"Whenever you ready," he told her before kissing her lips.

"Good," leaning down, she picked Sammie up, "I'm ready to live here."

"What I tell you about carrying her like that?" Sam asked, taking Sammie from Janae's arms, and she rolled her eyes. Here he was back on his bullshit, but she loved it.

All the way back to the house Janae went on and on about furniture, what colors she wanted to decorate with, and how she wanted to do the girls' room. Because they would be so close in age, she thought they should share a room until they got older, and Sam agreed.

"What you want for dinner?" Janae asked, and Sam shrugged. "I wanna cook something, I'm tired of eating out, I know that."

ARABIA

Sam pulled up to their building and parked his car. He half tuned Janae out because all her ass did was talk about food. "Here, take her bag."

Janae did as she was told and together, they walked towards the building. She was busy running her mouth while Sam was watching the man sitting on his stoop. He wasn't doing anything per say, but niggas ain't chill like that in front of his building. As they got closer, the man turned around, and Sam's blood started to boil.

"What're you doing here?" Janae asked shocked to shit to see Kevin.

Kevin looked from Sam, to Janae and back to Sam before his eyes fell on Sammie. He took in her features and she looked so much like him. "I just wanna talk."

"We don't have shit to talk about." Janae fumed at the audacity of him. "You wanted me to disappear, right? You didn't want a baby, remember?

Kevin wanted to see Janae and his little girl, but the last thing he expected to see was her with Sam. He remembered him all too well. He could still feel his fist drilling into his face, and it had him stumbling over his words. "She's my daughter…"

"Take Sammie and go upstairs," was all Sam said as he handed Sammie to Janae. She took the baby but was hesitant to leave Sam with Kevin, and he could sense that. "It's cool, I'mma just talk to him." Leaning down, he kissed her lips. He watched as Janae gave Kevin an evil eye and turned to leave. The both of them watched until they couldn't see her anymore, and then Sam spoke. "You got a lot of balls showing up at my house."

Almost instantly, Kevin's hands flew up in surrender. "Look, I don't want any trouble. I didn't even know you and Janae…" he stopped himself from rambling to take a breath. "I just wanna see my daughter."

"Listen to me and hear me good," Sam squared his shoulders and stepped closer to him as he spoke, "this family and every person in it, is mine. You ain't got shit over here. The pretty ass little girl you ain't want, got my last name." He pointed to his chest as he held eye contact with Kevin. "That beautiful woman you played, taking my dick every night and is about to have my baby." He smirked. "You fucked that up, nigga. You wanted ya wife and other kids, and you got them."

"Please…"

"Get the fuck off my stoop." Quickly, Sam snatched him up by his collar and stared in his eyes. "If you ever come around here or step to Janae again, I'll fuckin' kill you." From head to toe, Kevin trembled in his hands, and Sam let his punk ass go with a push that landed him on his ass. "Get the fuck outta here." He watched as Kevin scrambled to his feet and ran off to his car. "Punk ass nigga." Turning back to the building, Sam headed up the stairs and opened the door. "Didn't I tell ya hardheaded ass to go upstairs." Reaching down, he took a sleeping Sammie from Janae's arms and kissed her cheek.

Janae heard him, but did she ever listen, no. She was watching and listening from the door, she wanted to be there just in case shit got out of hand. "Where he go?"

"The fuck away from here," was all Sam said as he walked over to the elevator.

Janae looked back towards the front door before they stepped on the elevator. She didn't know why, but the thought of Kevin popping up didn't sit right with her. "You think he gon' try to take her from us?" she asked with tears in her eyes as they stepped into the apartment. "What if he calls the police?"

"And I'll kill his ass," Sam said without a hint of laughter in his tone as he laid Sammie down. "Look just calm down, he ain't coming back, aight."

"But…"

"Ain't no but's!" he yelled, grabbing her. "Sammie is mine, and that nigga ain't coming around here claiming shit." Nodding her head, a few tears fell, and he calmed down. The last thing he wanted to do was upset her or the baby. "Look, I ain't worried, so you shouldn't be either." He dried her tears with his fingertips and pecked her lips. "You already know how I give it up, so let's focus on real shit, like packing all this shit up."

Nodding, her head she sniffed back the rest of her tears. "Okay, okay."

ARABIA

"Aight, now go cook because I'm hungry." He popped her ass and she was off to the kitchen.

Tony had been feeling like he was being pulled into a million directions lately. He was still in the streets, even more now that Stacks was out, helping Lynette with the store and keeping up with his own home. There was a lot on his plate, but like they say *heavy is the head that wears the crown,* and Tony now knew it to be true. Even though he was tired, there was still work to be done.

"Babe," Lynette called out to him from the loft of the building.

"Yeah?" he yelled back as he went over the paperwork for the contractors.

"Come here."

He heard her but didn't respond right away. They had been busy painting and getting furniture and things together, for the grand opening which was a little over a month away. Like, Lynette he liked the building and was sure the store was going to be dope as well. "Aight, give me a minute." Once he was finished going over the papers he was looking at, he sat them on the counter and headed up the steps.

"Ta-da!" Lynette waved her hands in front of her like it was magic as she revealed her new office space.

Rich nodded his head in approval as his eyes roamed the space. "This is tight, real nice." He looked at the desk, covered with picture frames and a calendar while the walls were covered with quotes and sayings that meant a lot to her. On the other wall was mural she had painted of Zoo and he loved how it all came together.

"Right." she danced bopping her hands as she smiled. "It's so cute!"

"Yeah, he killed it with these paintings tho." Walking over to the wall he admired the piece of art. Downstairs on one of the walls was another mural of 55th street and it was just as nice. It was so dope, he planned on having something painted in his house when he moved. "Well, the painters are done, and the floor is refinished."

"Good! Now all I have to do is go over the inventory and stock the shelves," Lynette said proud of all her progress. "That shouldn't take long, then I got Keisha and Faith working on the party."

"Yeah, tell them don't go crazy." He mugged her, already knowing how they got down.

"Shit, nigga, we going all out." She laughed as he play-boxed her. "Sike! Nah, I gave them a budget in cash and told them that was it."

"How much?"

"Only twenty thousand."

"Only, huh?" He shook his head. "Yeah, yeah, well, let's blow this joint. I got a stop to make before we go home."

"Well, go ahead and pick me up afterwards because I got a few more things to do." Rich eyed her, not knowing if he wanted to leave her in the store alone. "Go ahead, I'll be fine. I'll set the alarm when you leave."

"Aight, I'll be back in twenty minutes or so."

"Okay," Lynette stood on her tippy toes kissing his lips.

"Aight, watch out." He popped her ass, and she moved to the side while adjusting her hat.

Downstairs, Rich walked out the door and waited as he watched her set the alarm and go back upstairs to the loft. He didn't like the idea of her being in the store by herself, especially after what happened to Stacks. But he figured thirty minutes wouldn't hurt. In his car, he waited until traffic was clear before he pulled off. Rich didn't believe in loose ends, and he had one in particular that he needed to tie up.

After mentally giving himself directions, he pulled up to the apartment building and grabbed the bag he had sitting in the back seat. Carefully, he checked his surroundings before heading to the front door and to his surprise it was open. Inside, he found the apartment he was looking for and went to the door. This time he knocked politely as he stood back and waited for someone to answer.

ARABIA

"Fuck you doing here?" Nate asked as he stepped up with a gun, pointing it directly at Rich's head.

Rich wasn't moved nor scared of Nates actions, besides, if he was going to shoot him, he would've done it already. "I just wanna talk, no bullshit."

Nate's better mind told him to shoot Rich for having the nerve to come back to his house after what he'd done. However, as conflicted as he was, he allowed Rich into his home. "You got five minutes." In the apartment, Rich walked in and stopped in the dining room where he sat the bag he was holding on the table. "What's that?" He motioned towards the bag.

"A peace offering," Rich shrugged. "I know how shit went down was fucked up."

"Fucked up?!" he yelled, shaking his head. "That shit cost me my girl." It cost him a lot more than Keisha, but he wasn't about to confess that he no longer had a peace of mind.

"I know, and I can't do shit about that, but I figured we could call a truce before you get any ideas."

"Nigga, fuck you," he swore, ready to take off on Rich. "You nearly fucking kill me, and what you thought a few dollars would make up for it?" He unzipped the bag and his mouth fell open. Never had he ever in life seen this much work. Shit, if he was being honest, he'd never touched a brick. And here he was looking at four of them.

"You wanted to be put on, and now you're on." Rich smirked. "That should be enough to clear the air, right?"

Nate ain't really know what to say as he looked back to the contents in the bag. "What's the catch? A price on my head? You want a percentage off each brick? What, this puts me in debt with you?"

Shaking his head, Rich was about ready to go. "This makes us even." Stepping past him, he headed for the door. Nate knew what he meant and nodding his head was him giving Rich his word. "When you get that off, hit my jack.".

Smirking, Nate shook his head and looked back to the bricks in front of him. He still couldn't stand Zoo, but now he figured he could let the shit go. His life was about to change forever, and he knew that was all thanks to Zoo. Even after they ran up in his shut, there was no way he was turning down four bricks of pure cocaine with no strings attached. Nah, Nate was about to take this shit and be next level with it.

Rich walked to his car feeling like a good deed had been done, and he could breathe a little. The way he saw it, Nate was one less nigga he had to worry about coming for Zoo. After stepping into his car, he sped back to the store and scooped Lynette. Together, they rode home pretty much in silence. She was tired and as always, he was busy thinking. They were just walking into the house when the phone rang.

Lynette was walking in the house first, so she answered it, "Hello." The woman on the other end of the phone asked for Tony by first and last name so she figured it was important, "just a minute." She told her before she passed the phone to Tony.

"Yo'," he answered as he watched her walk down the hall.

"Hi, Mr. Ricker this is Melissa Farrington, I'm a nurse here at Jefferson Hospital. I'm sorry I'm calling to notify you that your father passed away this evening. He had instructed us to call you and only you when the time came." Rich's heart fell to the pit of his stomach as he listened to the nurse talking. He could believe it, but he couldn't believe it. Since he left his father in the restaurant that day, he hadn't thought of him again. "I'm really sorry to tell you this, umm do you have any questions?"

"How long was he in the hospital before…"

"He'd been here with us on and off for years, but this last time he was here for three months."

Rich really didn't know what to say. "Thank you, for calling," he said just as Lynette walked back in the front room.

"Of course, you do have to come, and claim his body, and have the funeral home you choose come get him for his final arrangements."

"Thank you," was all Rich said as he hung up the phone. Leaning against the wall, he ran his hands over his face as he took a deep breath.

ARABIA

"What, what happened?" The first thing Lynette thought was that something happened to Stacks. She stood in front of him, and the glassy look in his eyes frightened her. "Tony?"

"My pops died," he told her with a far-away look in his eyes.

"Aww, babe," she wrapped her arms around him. "I'm so sorry to hear that." Laying her head on his chest she allowed him to use her body as a vessel for his pain.

"I don't even know how to feel about it neither," he said, shaking his head. "I don't wanna care…"

"And it's okay if you do," she told him as she looked in his eyes. "I know he wasn't there for you, and you had to go through a lot of shit because of that. But just maybe him staying away was the best thing he could've done for you."

Rich nodded his head as he wiped a lone tear from his eye. It was one thing for him to move like he ain't have no parents, but now he really didn't. He wondered if he had helped him back then if it would've made a difference. He didn't know and now, Rich would never know. Standing up right on his feet, Rich removed Lynette's arms from around his neck and headed for the bathroom.

Chapter 18

Together Sam and Rich had gone to the hospital to visit Stacks. Rich had been in a funk since finding out his dad died and Sam had been busy moving, but they made time to see Stacks every chance they got. Since the shooting, a lot of shit had changed. Tech had basically filled in for Stacks and Sam, and Rich had been busy in their own lives. They couldn't wait for the day shit went back to normal and for them it didn't look like it was any time soon.

"What up, fool?" Rich asked as they walked into the room.

Stacks was sitting in the bed watching tv when he looked over and saw them at the door. "What up?" His voice lacked any type of enthusiasm, but he welcomed the company.

"You looking like ya self today nigga." Sam noticed the change in him and hoped it was for good.

"Shit, I feel better too. Finally got that fucking shit bag off me."

"That's what's up," Rich clapped it up. "So that mean you'll be coming home soon, right."

"Yeah, the doctor said in about a week or so."

"Hell yeah, Zoo back together again." Sam clapped it up for them.

"Shit, I don't know about all that."

"What you mean?" Sam asked, confusion covering his face.

"You ain't coming back?" Rich asked wanting to know.

"I don't know," Stacks sighed, "shit just different now."

"Them niggas ain't even out there no more, you clean now." Sam tossed in.

Shaking his head, they ain't get it. Nobody did, because it wasn't even about that. "Every time I close my eyes, I see Faith with her fuckin' head blown off. I can't unsee the shit…" he said softly, "that shit fuck with me so hard, like all I can think about is her dying."

"But she ain't dead," Sam told him, like he ain't know that already. "Focus on that."

"I wish it was that easy." Stacks was mentally tired. "I can't even look at her, because the type of nigga I am is why this shit happened in the first place. It's all good when we making money and then some shit like this happens and ain't none of it worth it. I don't know, I guess I'm seeing shit for what it really is, seeing myself and I ain't feeling it."

Sam and Rich just sat there, listening because there was nothing they could say.

"Well, take all the time you need we got Tech filling in, in the meantime," Rich said as he sat back in the chair.

"So, what's going on with you and Faith?" Sam asked, wanting to know.

"I don't know," he sighed missing her but knowing right now it was best they be a part. "I just ain't what she need, right now."

"Y'all engaged?" Sam said not seeing at all where this was going. "It's one thing for you to walk away from us, but Faith too."

"I ain't walking away from nobody, I just need time to figure this shit out." They were all quiet for a minute, before he spoke again. "How she doing?"

"She aight, she been keeping busy at the store with Lynette and them," Rich told him.

"She been chilling but since you ain't really feeling her, I'mma tell sis to go and get her mack on." Sam shrugged and the look Stacks gave him if it could've it would've killed him. "What?"

"Don't play with me like that."

"Well, shit you better act like you want her. Faith ain't no poo-putt, niggas be checking for her. How long you think she gon' stay faithful while you figure this shit out?"

Stacks didn't know what he expected her to do, but seeing other people was far from his mind. He loved Faith he just had some shit he needed to deal with on his own. They spoke a little while longer before the guys left Stacks to his thoughts. He was sitting there about an hour before he decided to call Faith. Reaching over he picked up his phone and dialed the money house number. Twisting the cord around his fingers, he waited to see if someone was going to answer.

"He-llo," she answered as if the word was two. Stacks didn't say anything, and she spoke again. "Aight, well I'm about to hang up."

"Hey," he said softly, not knowing what else to say.

Tears welled in her eyes at the sound of his voice. "Hey." They were both quiet for a moment before she spoke. "How're you doing?"

"I'm okay." Tears silently fell from his eyes. "I just needed to hear your voice."

She nodded her head as if he could see her. "I love you."

"I love you too," he cleared his throat and hung up.

Faith held the phone to her ear as the dial tone sounded. Slowly she put it back on the hook and headed back to her bedroom. She didn't know what was going on with Stacks, but she was so happy he'd called her. Day and night, she prayed that he would, but he never did. It had been a few weeks since she'd been home from the hospital, and she hadn't heard a peep from him. Rather than sweat him, she gave him space like he'd requested. Back in her room she climbed in bed and for the first time in a long time she didn't cry. Just a few words from Stacks had her feeling a little better. Just as her head fell against her pillows, she promised herself tomorrow was going to be a better day.

The next morning, Faith woke up with a little pep in her step. After getting dressed and handling her morning hygiene, she headed downstairs. "Morning, Tech," she smirked as she passed him, and Keisha all hugged up at the door.

"Sup, sis.?" He nodded before looking down to Keisha. "Aight I'll see you later, you coming to the block?"

"Nah, I'll be at the store." She told him, before she looked towards the kitchen.

"Aight, hit me later." Leaning down, Tech pecked her lips a few times before he left and got in his car.

When he pulled off, Keisha closed the door and went to find Faith. "Make me some."

"You don't even know what I'm cooking?" Faith laughed shaking her head, "greedy ass."

"Thank you," Keisha got comfortable and noticed Faith was moving a little different, "what's up with you?"

Looking up from the pan Faith didn't know what she was talking about. "What you mean?"

Keisha cut her eyes at her trying to figure out what it was, but she didn't know. "I don't know, you just seem different, shit happy I guess."

Faith giggled as she went back to cooking, "I am happy," she said, thinking a little before she continued. "I can't even lie, being shot and this shit with Stacks got me fucked up. But I'm tired of crying and I can't make Stacks do anything he don't wanna do." Tears came to her eyes. "So, right now I just gotta take care of me."

Everything she was saying, Keisha felt in her soul. Faith was one of her best friends, and she wanted nothing but the best for her. "Right on, bitch! Right on!" She screamed pumping her fist in the air.

"I fucking hate you." Faith laughed because her friends never took anything seriously.

"I'm laughing, but I feel you."

Nodding her head, Faith continued cooking breakfast and for an hour her and Keisha sat at the table eating and talking shit. Faith may have been having a hard time right now, but one thing she was grateful for was the love and support of her girls. When they were done, together Keisha and Faith rode over to the shop and met up with Lynette.

"Where Janae?" Keisha asked, sitting her purse down on the counter.

"They moving today," scratching her head, Lynette was in desperate need of a stylist. In the past months, she had to get ugly on them while she focused on her business and it was all paying off.

"That's right," Keisha shook her head. It had totally slipped her mind.

"Yup, but I ain't doing shit just adding some final touches. Y'all like the fresh flowers?"

Both Keisha and Faith looked around and had to admit it was a nice touch.

"Yeah, I love it, make it look all fresh and shit." Faith nodded taking in the store.

"So, grand opening is this weekend." Lynette smiled, hoping they would be willing to budge on the details and by the looks on their faces they weren't. "Y'all get on my damn nerves."

"I'll tell you this, you gon' love it." Faith smirked knowing she was.

"Right, and we have to start setting up Thursday, so that means you can't come back until Saturday evening." Keisha tossed in. "The party starts at seven, but we're going to do an official Zoo Congratulations thing at five…So, I don't wanna see you pop up before then.

"Ooooh, two parties!" Lynette squealed. "Shit, it's been so long since I been out, I'mma think this a real club and shit."

"Hell, you and me both." Keisha laughed as she did the whop in her seat. "I'm beyond ready."

"Okay, Zoo back on the set is going to be epic."

ARABIA

Lynette and Keisha continued to talk their shit as Faith sat back listening. This would be the first public event, party, or anything Zoo would attend since the shooting and she was nervous. Her nerves were all over the place, but she was working hard to fight it. Planning this event was a great distraction, but now that it was here, she didn't know what she would do next.

After the shooting Rich, Sam, and Tech stayed posted. On any given day, you can find either of them in the streets on the frontlines. Before all this, they were out there but they were comfortable. Kicking shit, rolling dice and all that was fun, but it was a distraction. They figured if they established presence what happened with Solo wouldn't happen again. Rich knew Solo didn't grow balls like that overnight, which meant that they weren't paying much attention. For a minute, Zoo was feeling as if they were untouchable, like every nigga that knew of them, knew not to try them and they were wrong. They were moving on from the incident, but they planned to move smarter.

"What up, Zoo?" Tech greeted as he bopped over to where Rich was leaning up against the gate.

"Zoo," was all Rich said as he shook it up with him. Together they sat back just observing, keeping their eyes on everything moving. Rich was holding shit together, but honestly, he was tired. The shooting with Stacks, his dad, shit was just weighing him down. Since that talk they had with Stacks the other day, the more he was able to feel where he was coming from. They were so ready to come up, that they never thought about the consequences or the severity of what they were doing. Just looking at the neighborhood right now, all Rich could do was shake his head. Zoo Crew was one of the most famous, most notorious crews to come out of their area.

They had more money than they knew what to do with and that was exactly what Rich wanted. If only he had known his community, his people, the mothers, and fathers he watched as he grew up would pay the price. Like, just watching how far a dope head was really willing to go for a hit of crack, was sickening. There was no limit to what they would do and over the years Rich had seen it all. Just for a moment he was still long enough to think about it, and it was then, he knew exactly what Stacks was saying. Hell, all this time he'd been on Lynette's ass about having more and doing better and never once did he see himself making a living outside of the drug game. Lately, just the thought alone bothered him.

Without taking his eyes off the streets, he spoke. "You ever think about what you gone do after this?"

Tech, heard him, but he wasn't even paying attention. "What you mean?"

"Like, when this shit is over."

For a moment, Tech sat and pondered his question. The thought had crossed his mind before, but he hadn't given it much thought. "Nah, not really. I mean, I know this ain't gone last forever, but my only concern is the right now…And right now, this is what's putting food on the table."

Nodding his head, Rich could respect it, because he shared the same sentiments. "I don't know, but we gotta do better than this." Taking a deep breath, Rich finished the cigarette he was smoking and flicked the butt in the street. "I'm out, I gotta go scoop Lynette."

"Aight," Tech and Rich quickly shook hands before Rich got in his car and pulled off. He didn't know what was going on, but everybody was in a messed-up head space. Shaking his head, Tech couldn't think about that shit right now, because his mind was on the money.

Tech stayed on the block with the rest of the crew, until the wee hours of the morning. He was tired as hell and all he wanted was a hot shower and a warm bed. Then he thought of Keisha, he for sure enjoyed her company, and he would rather be headed to her place after a long night, but his girl Rah was at his place. Honestly, Tech couldn't tell you why he was still with Rah or what they were doing. He thought about just leaving, but then he thought about the years they'd been together, and he stayed. Once Tech made it home, he entered his apartment and immediately noticed how quiet it was. Rah usually had the TV or something on, but he didn't hear anything. *Maybe, she left…*He thought as he moved toward the back of the house and just as he was walking into the bedroom, she was coming out the adjourning bathroom.

"Hey," she smiled happy he was home.

"What's up?" was all he said as he removed his shirt and then his jewelry. "What you been up to?"

"Nothing, really…Went to work earlier and been waiting for you to get home. I missed you all day."

"All day," he smirked.

"Yup," smiling she leaned up and kissed his lips.

Tech kissed her back before he stepped pass her and walked into the bathroom. It was crazy he was here with his girl, and all he could think about was Keisha. After setting his shower water, he stood back and removed his clothes. When he was completely naked, he placed his dirty clothes in the hamper and stepped into the shower. A hot shower after a long day was just what he needed to relax. As he washed up, he thought about what he was going to wear to the Grand Opening party. He knew Keisha was going to be there, so taking Rah was out of the question. She was still on his ass about him bringing her out around his peoples, and he still hadn't budged on that.

Even though, he and Keisha were just friends, in his heart he knew it was more than that, so he for sure wasn't going to disrespect her by bringing his girl where he knew she would be. Nah, he definitely ain't need those kinds of problems. He took his time washing up and drying off, hoping that Rah would be sleep by the time he was done and to his dismay, she was wide awake.

"So, what you do all day?"

"Nothing for real," was all he said as he climbed in the bed. "I'm tired as hell." Rubbing his eyes, he reached over and turned out the lamp. "Lay down." he turned her around and wrapped an arm around her waist.

Rah wasn't really as sleepy as she was horny, but she turned around and got comfortable. For the past couple of months, they'd been trying to work their relationship out, but it just wasn't the same. She could feel the rift between them and instead of them getting closer, it felt like they were growing father a part.

WE MADE LOVE IN THE 80'S

"Alright, I know you ready to run up outta here." One of Stacks nurses joked with him.

Stacks didn't know how he felt about finally going home, but he was ready to get out the damn hospital. "Yeah, something like that." He chuckled.

She smiled as she made her way over to him. "Ya fiancé coming to get you?"

"Nah," Stacks didn't even wanna think about the state of his relationship. "My homeboy gon' carry me to the house."

"I know that's right," she said as she continued to unhook his cords and remove his IV.

Stacks sat there and thought about what he was going to do when he got home. He was already feeling weird, and he hadn't even left the hospital yet. When the nurse was finished, she walked out the room, and Stacks sat back rubbing his arm where the needle was. Licking his lips, he figured he would get up and shower, so when Sam and them came, all he would have to do was get dressed. He stood to his feet while holding on to the bedrail taking deep breaths. Walking for him was no walk in the park after being bed bound for over a month. Stacks felt like he was a fish out of water, right now.

In the bathroom, he moved pretty slow, but he was determined to push through the pain and shower. He slid out of the hospital gown and stepped into the shower. Needing to feel something other than depression, he stood under the shower head and turned on the cold water first. Stacks allowed the water to fall over his head and he nearly screamed the shit was so cold. After a few minutes he added hot water and proceeded to shower.

"Stack Dollas!!" Rich yelled as he walked into the room. He tossed the duffle bag he was carrying on the bed and noticed the room was empty. He could hear the shower going and knew that's where Stacks was, so he plopped down in the chair and grabbed the remote. For about fifteen minutes he sat flipping through the channels before Stack's came out. "What's up?" he stood up and they slapped hands the Zoo way, before he stepped back. "I got ya shit right here."

"Good look," Stacks smirked as he took the bag from Rich and went back into the bathroom. He was happy Rich ain't pick him out no real clothes. Just a pair of sweats, a t-shirt, some sneakers and underclothes. Looking in the mirror the little get up, had him feeling a little better. "I definitely need a cut." He rubbed the side of his face, "Welp, time to roll."

"You ready?"

"Yeah, let me get this paperwork and I'm good."

"Aight, I'mma pull the car up and meet you downstairs." Rich grabbed the bag Stacks had and went to the elevator. Just as he stepped on, he checked the time it was almost twelve. He was still good on time and could relax a little. The 55th Street Grand Opening was in two days and everyone was scrambling to make sure shit got done. He also had to get with Sam and get Lynette's gift. Rich was so proud of her, there was nothing he could buy or nothing he could do, to show her how proud of her he really was. But, he had to at least try. It didn't take him long to get to the car, and before he knew it, he and Stacks were pulling off into traffic. "So, what you wanna do? Ride through the block, get something to eat, see ya girl…what?"

"None of that, just take me to the crib." He shook his head.

Rich was quiet for a moment as he got his words together. "So, you still ain't talk to Faith?" without Stacks saying anything, he knew that was a no.

"I just," Stack stopped and looked out the window. "For real, I don't want her to see me like this. This shit, ain't even me. I nearly fucking died…I ain't never felt that weak."

"Yeah but you didn't," He guessed he understood what Stacks was saying, but Rich ain't get it. "Stacks Faith been rocking wit you for a minute. Through whatever, she always had ya back. And to be real with you, it's fucked up how you doing her…you left her out here naked my nigga." Rich took his eyes off the road to glance his way. "Like I understand you feeling a way about being shot and what you had to go through, but just think about how she was feeling, and you left her to go through all that shit alone."

Nodding his head, Stacks couldn't even deny it. He knew he was wrong and there wasn't really shit he could say. "I know."

"So, what you gon' do? You know she ain't just your homie no more. She ain't even ya girlfriend, that's ya fiancé nigga. I'm sure when you asked her to marry you, you meant it." Stacks nodded his head, "And now you gotta stand on that." He finished just as he pulled up into Stacks driveway. "But, I ain't gonna beat you in the head about it." his eyes drifted over to Stacks and they both laughed, because he had knocked his head clean off his shoulders. "I'm happy you home and I know you gone be back on ya shit in a bit."

"Yeah, I just need a minute."

The car fell silent for a moment before Rich stepped out the car, and grabbed Stacks bag from the back seat. Stacks was opening the passenger side door as he pulled his keys from his pocket. Together, he and Rich walked to the door and he let them inside. It looked nothing like it did after the burglary. Zoo had come together and cleaned his shit up while Stacks and Faith were in the hospital. "We went food shopping and shit, got you right for a minute."

"Preciate' it," Stacks dapped him up as he looked around, the house. It had been so long since he'd been home, he felt like a stranger in his own house.

"Aight, I gotta go handle some shit for Lynette," Rich said as they walked to the door. "I'll hit you later to check up on you."

"Bet," was all Stacks said as he bid Rich goodbye and closed his door. Even though he hadn't done anything but leave the hospital, he was drained. A nap was calling his name, but he promised himself that tomorrow was a new day and he was going to be on some shit.

Soon as Rich left Stacks house, he rode over to Sam house to scoop him. Pulling up to his house, the shit was nice as hell. Nigga had flowers and shit out front. It was crazy all his niggas were growing up, getting money, starting families and shit. Both Stacks and Sam had moved into houses and he didn't plan on being too far behind them. Stepping up on the porch, Rich knocked and stepped back waiting for someone to answer.

Janae opened the door and wasn't at all surprised to see Rich. "What's up?" she spoke as she moved to the side, and let him in.

ARABIA

"Shit," Rich said as he stepped out of his shoes. Janae ain't play that shoes in the house shit, especially since Sammie was all over the floor. "Where ya nigga at?"

"Downstairs," Janae answered as she took her spot back on the couch and propped her feet up. Her beef with Zoo was nonexistent these days. She had way too much going on to keep the bullshit going, and not only that, her nigga was head Zoo in charge, so what could she say?

"Zoo!" Rich yelled walking into the basement. "Fuck you ain't even dressed."

Sam looked up from the joint he was rolling like he ain't know what Rich was talking about. "What you mean? I just gotta put a shirt on, and I'm ready."

He swore and Rich just shook his head. "Man hurry up." Plopping down on the couch, he grabbed the remote just as Sam stood up.

"I'll be back in a minute." Sam took the steps two at a time as he made his way back to the main floor of the house. They had only been moved in for a few weeks, so they were still getting things together, but he was happy with the progress. In the living room, he found Janae rocking Sammie to sleep. "What's up?" he walked over to them and peeked at Sammie all nestled into Janae's chest.

"Nothing, she ready for a nap." Janae told him gently rocking Sammie while rubbing her back. "Where you going?"

"To pick some shit up with Rich."

"Ooooh, he got Lynette something?"

"Nunya business, nosey ass." He laughed, leaning down kissing her lips.

"Yes, it is, what he get her?" She asked too excited for him.

"Calm down," he laughed, "he ain't get her shit. It's something we gotta get for the crew." Twisting her lips, she ain't believe nothing he was saying. "You want me to lay her down?"

"Yeah." She handed him Sammie and prepared herself to get up. At nearly eight months pregnant, Janae felt like she couldn't do shit.

Sam took the baby into his arms and placed her on his shoulder, then he reached his free arm and helped Janae up off the couch. He allowed her to walk ahead of him and together they went upstairs, and into their bedroom. Gently, Sam laid the baby down in their bed while Janae went to the bathroom. She had her own crib and stuff in her own room across the hall, but he didn't like Janae having to reach over the crib to get her out. Sam stepped over to the dresser and quickly grabbed a t-shirt out and put it on. When Janae came out the bathroom, he was holding his shoes in his hands.

"Aight, I'll be back in a few." Janae was a little over seven months and looked as if she was ready to pop.

"Okay." Stepping on her tippy toes, she kissed his lips and he was off.

"Aight, nigga let's roll," Sam said, smacking Rich's foot off his damn table. When they got to the door, they put their shoes back on and stepped out the house. Sam locked up and Rich went ahead on to the car. "So, what we gotta pick up?"

"I got Lynette a car."

"A car?! Look at you, she gon' love that shit."

"That's what I know. She been on her shit lately, she deserves it."

Sam nodded his head because he agreed. "Yeah, she been on it, for real. The store is dope as fuck."

"It is, I was shocked at how good it really turned out." He sat back for a moment before he spoke again. "We need to start investing in some legal shit too. I mean this shit good for now, but we both know this shit ain't gone last forever."

"You on that shit Stacks was on now?" He smirked, looking over to him.

Rich shrugged, "I mean, he wasn't lying. Shit out here fucked up."

Looking out the window, Sam listened as he continued. Since that talk with Stacks at the hospital, Sam had been thinking of the end for him too. He had had kids now, and a family to think about. "For real tho, I been thinking the same thing. I mean the game been good to us, but I got kids now and shit just different." Adjusting himself in the seat, he got back comfortable and turned to Rich. "So, what now? What's the move, King Zoo!"

Laughing, Rich ain't even know. "I don't even know, we been Zoo so long, shit got so big, it's like what's after this."

Sam thought about it and shrugged, "I mean, I can still wrap." Rich looked over to him and they both burst out laughing. "Shit, nigga I got bars. Let me dust off my old notebook. Niggas really getting money now in the rap game, we could have our own label and shit."

"Shit, you never know," Rich said, voice full of thought as he pulled into the car dealership. Together he and Sam stepped out of the car and Rich hit the alarm. After the shit they pulled with Solo, he wasn't taking any chances at all. He stepped inside the dealership with Stacks on his heels. "What up, Frankie?"

"Rich my man," Frankie smiled greeting him with a handshake and then Sam. "I got you right over here." He led the way through the dealership and out the back door, where a car sat in the middle of the parking lot covered in tarp. "You're gonna love it." Frankie said in his heavy Italian accent.

Rich nodded his head as he lifted the tarp off the bottom and moved around the car pulling it off. When the sun hit the wax, it caused the paint to sparkle and Rich couldn't help but smile. The red 1988 Mercedes shined like a new penny as Rich walked over to it. It was a two-door coup, with a phone and power seats in the inside, it was really the gold BBS rims that set it off with the butter interior. Lynette had been asking him for a car for a minute, so her ass was gonna hit the floor when she saw this.

"Got damn," Sam walked over opening the passenger side door and hopping inside. "Shit I wanna ride myself."

"This shit tight, right?"

"Hell yeah, nigga, I'm jealous." He laughed but he was only half joking. The car was nice as hell and putting all their cars to shame.

"It's fully loaded, everything you need. Plus, I threw in the tints you asked about, the rims, tape deck, hidden compartment in the door." He pulled open the door and showed them the compartment. "That's ill, right."

"Right," Rich said as he started the car, and the engine purred. "That shit smooth. Damn, I want one now." He laughed.

"No offense but this a female car." Frankie laughed. "Y'all big dogs now and I got something for you, just got it in." He walked away and waved them over. "Brand new, black on black, factory rims…1988 Range Rover."

Both Rich and Sam's mouths dropped when they saw the truck sitting before them.

"I gotta get this," Sam nodded his head. It wasn't even up for debate; this truck had his name written all over it.

"I got this one and two more coming in next week." Frankie told them running his hands together.

"Same color?" Rich asked as he opened the passenger side door, because Sam big ass had already claimed the front seat.

"Another black one and a red one."

"Shit, we'll take them." Sam let him know with no hesitation. "Write that shit up for me and we'll be back with the money."

"You got it," Frankie said as he ran to his office.

Sam was in love with the truck already and he hadn't even driven it. He was just thankful that he had the money to get whatever he wanted, and his kids could sleep in a nice house. They may have been ready to stop hustling, but the money was good.

Chapter 19

The day they had been preparing for was here and everyone was running around like chickens with their heads cut off. Keisha and Faith was putting the final touches on the store, while Lynette trying to make sure all the new equipment was setup and working. Rich made sure she had the best of everything, but none of them really knew how to work it and had spent the last two days testing it out. She hoped and prayed everything went off without a hitch. The plan was for Lynette to work the crowd as the owner, Keisha and Faith were going to make sure the catering, drinks and music were good, and Janae was going to run the register. The guys were going to be there for security and to represent Zoo, so, they prayed everything went well.

"Let's get this party started right." Janae walked into the store extra hype and ready for tonight's festivities. This was the closest she was going to get to a club, and she was beyond ready. "Aww man, DJ Red Alert!" She ran over to him all groupie down, and she didn't care.

"Girl, bring ya ass over here." Faith walked over snatching her up while rolling her eyes.

"Damn, y'all ain't tell me it was going to be real people here." She jumped up and down. "Who else gon' be here? Just tell me now, so I can get it outta my system."

Keisha shook her head laughing while Faith went back to what she was doing. "McLyte, Rakim, and Big Daddy Kane."

"Mmm, his fine ass." She stomped her feet. "Girl, let me go get dressed. Where Lynette at?"

"She'll be on her way in a few." Faith said tying the last of her balloons. "We're going to have to go outside and walk my little red carpet and take pictures."

"Okay," Janae had her little bag in hand. "Why you looking like that?"

"Because what y'all gone do with y'all hair? Ain't no scarves on my red carpet."

WE MADE LOVE IN THE 80'S

Janae and Keisha looked at each other, before shrugging. Together, they removed their scarves and Faith's heart fell to the pit of her stomach as tears sprang from her eyes.

"What you don't like it?" Janae asked as she fingered the haircut, they all got to resemble Faith's.

"I mean it grew on me," Keisha said, rubbing her hands down the back of her head. "Lynette cut hers too, but you'll see it later."

Faith didn't know what to say as she cried. She hated her haircut so much, and the fact that her girls went out and got the same cut just to be ugly with her was an act of love she couldn't describe. "I love y'all, man." She walked over hugging them and they hugged her back.

"All I know is, my hair better grow back." Keisha laughed but she was serious. The cut was cute on Salt-N-Pepa, but she didn't like it. Faith and Janae laughed hoping and praying for the same thing.

"Aight, that's enough of all this sappy shit, we have a party to get ready for," Faith said, drying her eyes.

"Okay, I'm going to get dressed for real now." Janae grabbed her bag and headed to the loft to put her clothes on.

While she was upstairs, Keisha and Faith opened the doors, and Red Alert started spinning. The caterers came out with glasses of champagne on trays along with finger foods ready to greet all the guest and the girls were excited. About thirty minutes later the first of their guest arrived. Keisha and Faith didn't want this to be an exclusive event. This shop was for the community and Lynette wanted to make sure they felt connected, so it was open to any and every one that wanted to have a good time. First come, first served was how the flyers read and she meant it. So, as the people arrived Faith and Keisha greeted them with a smile. It wasn't until Zoo started to arrive that shit really turned up.

Tech parked his car in the parking lot across the street and walked over. He was glad they had designated Zoo parking because shit out here was crazy. Looking at the building all lit up, with cameras flashing and shit, it was like a movie. From the street he could see Sam and a few other guys from Zoo had arrived. They were on the red

ARABIA

carpet flicking it up and he was ready to jump in himself. Stepping up on the sidewalk he pushed his way through, "Zoo!" he yelled, almost in a chant, as he posed with the rest of the crew. They took a few pictures before Sam moved and his eyes fell on Keisha. Smirking, he licked his lips as he walked up behind her and pulled her into him. "You look good as hell."

"Boy, don't be grabbing me like that." She quickly swatted her hand at him, not really trying to hit him. "Scared the shit out of me."

"Scary ass, give me a hug." He held his arms open and without hesitation she fell into them. She looked up into his eyes and he pecked her lips, making her blush. "Nah, don't act all shy now."

"Cut it out," she smiled as he wrapped his arm around her shoulder, and they posted up talking and making sure people were getting in without an issue. Just as they were making their way back to the entrance, they heard a horn, and everyone turned to see who it was. Once they saw it was Rich, they all started clapping and shouting Zoo. "Alright, camera people, camera," Keisha said, pointing them to the car as everyone stood back.

In the car, Lynette couldn't believe all these people had come out for her. "This is crazy," she marveled as the flashing lights sparkled in her eyes. "Can you believe this?" she asked never taking her eyes off the crowd.

"Shit, you Ms. Zoo." Rich smiled as she continued to look out the window. Rich pulled right in the front and parked his car in her reserved parking spot.

Snapping out of her trance, Lynette took a deep breath and looked over to Rich. "Thank you." Was all she said as her eyes watered.

Shaking his head, Rich didn't feel she owed him that. "Nah, this all you." Stepping out the car, he fixed his clothes saluting his crew as he walked around the car and opened Lynette's door. When she stepped out of the car, the applause she received seemed to come in waves as she smiled. With Rich at her side she took a deep breath and together they walked the red carpet. Smiling and waving, Lynette looked beautiful and graceful as she made her way to the store. "Mom!" she nearly yelled as she ran over to her wrapping her in her arms. "You made it."

"I wouldn't miss it," she choked out through her tears. "I'm so proud of you."

"Thank you," Lynette mouthed, fighting tears. For so long, Lynette felt as if she didn't cause her mother anything, but grief and it felt good to finally see happy tears in her eyes.

LaVelle looked to Rich and nodded her head approvingly. He was happy she was able to make it and that everything for them seemed to be falling into place. They continued on their walk and as soon as they made it to the door, the crew started howling and getting rowdy. Looking at her mom, Lynette just shook her head laughing. Yeah, they were crazy and even a little wild, but Zoo was her family and she loved it.

Inside the lights were a little dim, the decorations seemed to shimmer, and the music was pumping. All the clothing was on display looking nice, even her Dapper Dan pieces were on full display. There was no doubt that they would sell out, and he would make her more. Once Lynette was able to get her bearings together, the show started and the grand opening of 55th Street turned into a real party. The girls danced to every song and performance with no breaks. It was truly a celebration as they snaked their bodies and did The Whop. The guys weren't stuck holding up the wall like usual either, they were right there with them cutting up on the dancefloor. Everyone was celebrating because this store was truly a win for them all.

By the end of the night, it was time to cut the red tape that separated them from the register area. The red tape that would officially open them for business, and Lynette was nervous as hell standing in front of everyone with a huge pair of scissors in her hand. "Aight, everybody quiet down, I wanna say something before we open this register." She laughed and everyone else did too as they quieted down. "I just want to say thank you for coming out and supporting the event and supporting the store. This isn't only for me, this is for my crew, my love, my family and my hood. So, with that said, let's cut this damn tape." she laughed, and everyone cheered.

Lifting the scissors, she gently cut the red tape. It was official they were open for business. Going back to her cashiering days, they were so fresh in her mind that she moved around the register like a pro. Lynette checked out every customer while the girls and her mom helped her bag and keep the line together. The guys worked as security and kept the crowd in order and made sure wasn't nobody stealing. That was one perk of having a crazy crew of niggas behind you, you didn't need security.

It was after two in the morning, when the last customer left the building, and everyone was beat. Faith locked the door and turned around smiling, "We did that." She slapped hands with Keisha as they laughed.

"But for real, you know how many people asked me if we did event planning?" Keisha asked as she pulled business card after business card out of her pockets.

"You too." Faith did the same and they continued to laugh.

Keisha shrugged. "Yo', word, Zoo Party Planning and Events could really be a thing."

"Shit, I'm with it!" Faith high fived her again. "Ain't no party like a Zoo Crew party cause a Zoo Crew Party don't stop!" They sang and the rest of them joined in liking the idea. "Shit, as much as we go out, we should've been planning parties."

Rich looked around at everyone dancing and laughing, and he couldn't describe the sense of pride he felt. He was sure Sam was feeling the same way. They were just talking about starting legal businesses and trying to think of what they could do, and here the girls were making the shit happen.

"Aight that's enough, time for y'all to call it a night," Sam said, knowing it was way past Janae's bedtime. In the corner she sat tucked away using Sam's jacket as a blanket.

"I second that," Lynette stretched. "This mess gon' have to sit until tomorrow." She shook her head too tired to even care about cleaning up.

Everyone started grabbing their belongings as they prepared to leave. Lynette and Rich were the last ones to walk out the door because they had to lock up and set the alarm. Rich wrapped an arm around her neck as they walked out, and Lynette immediately stopped in her tracks. Rich's car was gone, and in its place was the car he bought her with a big red bow on it. Immediately, Lynette's mouth fell open as she looked from Rich and back to the car. Reaching in his pocket, he pulled out the keys and dangled them in front of her face.

"Congratulations." Turning into him, she buried her face into his chest crying her eyes out as Rich held her tight. He whispered into her ear, how much he loved her and how proud of her he was before lifting her head and kissing her lips.

Nodding her head, Lynette kissed him back as his eyes connected with hers. She wiped her eyes as she handed him her bag and took the keys from his hand. The car was so cute and better than she thought it would be. For over a year, she'd been asking for a car and this was beyond a car. This shit was sexy and screamed she was THAT BITCH! "I fuckin' love it!" she screamed as she jumped in the driver seat. Playing with all the buttons and starting the engine, she ain't know what she was going to do with herself now.

Keisha and the rest of the girls looked on happy for their girl. Tonight, was Lynette's night and Rich made sure it was memorable. Standing back Keisha was genuinely happy for everyone. Their whole crew had come up and she was happy she got to witness it.

"So, what you about to get in to?" Tech asked as he slid behind Keisha.

She smiled as he wrapped his arm around her waist and pulled her into him. "Nothing, the party is over and it's time to go home."

Leaning down into her ear, Tech licked his lips. "Can I come home with you?" he asked in that husky voice that gave her goose bumps.

"Tech," she whispered as he gently nibbled on her earlobe before his tongue slid behind her ear. Keisha's heart began to jolt at the feeling of his soft kisses. They may have kissed here and there, even fooled around a little bit, but they had never had sex. She more than him, didn't want to cross that line because he had a girlfriend. The idea of her fucking behind the next bitch just didn't sit right with her. But, tonight, tonight, she was game. Keisha turned around facing him as she pressed her body close to his. So close that her chest was pressed up against his. Looking up into his eyes, Keisha didn't hesitate to seize his lips with hers. With as much passion as the moment would allow, she slinked her tongue into his mouth as his hands gripped her ass.

When they finally came up for air Tech's dick was so hard, he could knock a hole in the wall. "So, I'm following you?"

"Nah," Keisha shook her head as her lips once again grazed his. "I'm riding with you."

"Well, let's go," was all Tech said as he grabbed her hand in his, and they said their goodbyes.

Keisha was supposed to ride with Faith, since that's how she got to the shop, but her plans had changed. While they were saying their goodbyes, she told Faith what was up, and everything worked out well because Faith wanted to crash at her mom's. So, either way it worked out for both of them. When they got over to Tech's car, he opened the passenger side door for Keisha to hop in and then he closed it behind her. Tech walked over to the other side of the car, adjusting his dick. For months he'd been wanting to fuck Keisha and now, after all the flirting, all the kissing, and fake arguing it was going to happen. He was drunk of course, he'd been drinking, but he wasn't drunk enough to not know what they were about to do. Shit, the anticipation alone was enough to sober him all the way up.

They didn't say much on the ride over to the Money House, but soon as they pulled up into the driveway, they didn't waste any time going into the house. Soon as Keisha unlocked the door, Tech tossed her ass over his shoulder as she yelped in surprise. "Boy, put me down."

"Shit, I got ya boy." He flexed his arms as he supported her weight taking them upstairs. Tech twisted the doorknob and once he entered her room, he threw her on the bed. "I got ya boy right here." He smashed his lips into hers as he slid her clothes off. Keisha didn't put up any resistance as Tech slid her clothes off and tossed them on the floor. She sat up pulling at his shirt and Tech moved her hands. Then she reached for his belt, and he popped her hands. "Don't touch shit, I got this." Looking in his eyes, she let go and allowed Tech to do with her what he pleased.

At the top of the bed, Tech stood there looking down at her as he began to remove his clothes. As he moved his muscles flexed, and her eyes outlined every crease and curve of his physique as her mouth watered. Tech was so fine to her. She probably didn't see it before, but she damn sure saw it now. Their eyes stayed connected as the passion grew between them. Tech didn't plan on wasting any time with Keisha, and she didn't want him too.

Once he was undressed, he licked his lips and climbed on the bed. Tech grabbed her by the ankles and spread her legs taking in the sight of her glistening pussy. He grabbed his dick as he looked into her eyes. Falling between her legs, he slid the head of his dick up her opening, and his eyes involuntarily closed as he sighed. Just the feeling of the wetness between her legs nearly caused him to cry out.

Keisha held her legs wide open and once she felt the head of him at her opening, she sat up on her elbows and began to move her hips working herself onto his dick. "Sssss," she hissed, biting her bottom lip as she continued to roll her hips.

"Shit," Tech looked down at her and began to gently pump into her matching her thrust.

Gripping the sheets, Keisha was not prepared when he began to fuck her back. "Oh, wait…" she began but was cut off by him going deeper.

"Nah, ain't no wait," he said, breathlessly as he began to dig into her. Tech wrapped her legs around his back as he lay on top of her. Gently he kissed her lips, before feeding her his tongue while stroking her deeply.

"TaShawn," she crooned as her nails raked up and down his back. He went deeper thrusting into her so hard her body rocked as sweat splashed off their skin. A tingling she could feel in her soul, a yearning for release…One that she'd never felt brewing inside of her.

Tech could feel her walls tightening around his member as he thrust in and out of her. "Shit." he leaned down kissing her lips again as he fought not to cum with her. Pumping in and out of her, she held him tighter as cries of pleasure filled the room. Tech looked at her, and she had real tears in her eyes, and it blew him away. Never had he ever experienced this type of connection. "I love you, Keish," he whispered before bending his head down into the crook of her neck. "Fuck…"

Hearing that he loved her caused her to cry a little harder. "I love you too." She wrapped her arms around his neck and allowed her body to succumb to the explosion of their love making.

As hard as he tried, Tech couldn't hold out any longer. In her arms, his body spasmed as he filled her up with his finish.

When they were done, neither one of them knew what to say. Confessions of love had been made, and they didn't know where they went from here. Once she was able to catch her breath, without a word

Keisha slid out of the bed and headed to the bathroom. Tech watched her until the bathroom door closed, and he focused his eyes on the ceiling more confused than ever.

Rich stood at his father's grave, not knowing if he should say something or not. Lynette stood calmly at his side, ready to support him in every way possible. Right now, her presence was all the support he needed. When the hospital called him and told him that his father had passed, Rich honestly didn't know how to feel. But he felt it was his duty to at least give his father a proper burial and that's what he did. Before they closed his casket, he was able to look at him one last time. He was skinnier than the last time he'd seen him, his face almost sunken in. The man before him, didn't look anything like the man that sat across from him a year ago, Rich barely recognized him.

Lynette walked over to Rich and gently placed her hand on his back as she stood next to him. "You okay?"

Nodding his head, he wrapped an arm around her neck. "Yeah, come on, let's get out of here." Together, they walked back to her car and got inside. After buckling their seatbelt's, they were off. "Take me to get my car."

"Aight," was all she said as she headed for the shop.

His car was parked up there because he'd rode home with her the night before. They didn't think about what having two cars meant but often times, one or the other would leave their car parked somewhere and ride with the other. Just to later find themselves where they were now. Lynette had to go into the store anyway, to relieve Janae from register duty so she quickly headed over there. They opened at 9am, it was only noon, but she was sure Janae ass was already complaining. Lynette had reserved parking on the side of her building and she quickly whipped her car in the spot. Swiftly, she pulled her club from under the seat and secured her steering wheel before she stepped out.

"Girl, bring ya ass." Rich shook his head laughing at her.

"Whatever, they won't steal my shit." She laughed with him as she set her car alarm. Lynette was crazy, but she wasn't stupid, and she didn't play about her car. Laughing, they walked around the building hand and hand. When they got to the store, Rich opened the door and held it open while Lynette walked in.

"You're late." Janae waddled from around the counter.

"Dang, let me walk through the door first." Lynette laughed.

"I did." She sighed taking a seat. "I'm tired."

"You ain't even do nothing." Lynette giggled just as a customer walked in. "Tony, can you run the register while I put my stuff up."

"Shit, I ain't no cashier either." He rolled his eyes talking his shit, but he hopped behind the register like she asked.

"Oh, hell no," Lynette roared as she walked into her office. Keisha was sitting at her desk on the phone, while Faith was kicked back on the couch writing in her planner. "Y'all need to get out."

"Why, you said we could use the space for our business." Keisha said just as she hung up.

"No," Lynette knocked Faith's feet down off her table as she walked by. "I said y'all could use the back room for your office."

"But it's so much nicer up here." Keisha smiled as Faith laughed.

"I'mma start charging y'all ass's rent." Lynette joked as her phone rung. "55th Street this is Lynette." Rolling her eyes, she pulled the receiver from her ear and held the phone out for Keisha. "The backroom." She swore.

Just then an alarm sounded, and Faith jumped up and ran into the bathroom. Lynette sighed as she sat back stretching out. "Oh, shit!" Faith screeched causing both Keisha and Lynette to jump up. Running into the bathroom they pushed their way through the door. Turning to them her eyes were wide and a pregnancy test was in her hand. "I'm pregnant," she whispered before she broke down crying.

"Aww, shhhh, it's gonna be okay," Keisha and Lynette both said at the same time as they hugged her.

Nodding her head, she sniffed back her tears shaking her head. It was like her life just kept going from bad to worse. After a moment she got herself together and wiped her eyes dry. "I know. I just hate that it happens now, when me and Stacks..."

"He'll come back around, I'm sure when you tell him..." Keisha began, and the look Faith gave her shut her right up.

"I'm not telling him shit." She rolled her eyes pushing past them. "And y'all ain't either."

"Ain't what?" Rich asked as he walked up on them.

"None of your business." Faith clasped the pregnancy test in her hands pushing past Rich and down the steps.

He looked to Lynette and she shrugged. "What's up?"

"Shit, I'm about to go?" he looked to Keisha who walked out the bathroom first and then to Lynette. She walked up to him and hugged him tight as he leaned down and kissed her lips. "What's up with Faith?"

"Nothing, just a bad day," she said as her phone rung. Her eyes squinted as she looked around him and at Keisha who answered. "Bitch, downstairs."

Rich chuckled before pecking her lips once more. "I'm out."

"Where you going?" Lynette asked as she walked with him downstairs.

"The block," was all he said before waving his hand at the other girls and walking out the door.

Lynette walked behind the register and took over while Janae took a seat. Faith was assisting a customer with clothing and she figured Keisha was still upstairs tying up her damn phone line. This was her knew life, their new life and she was tired of it already. From one until five she worked the register while the other girls kept busy.

"We booked our first event!" Keisha came flying down the steps as everyone turned their attention to her. "A month from today."

"Are you serious?" Faith asked, not believing they were really doing this.

"Yes, and they're paying big money. Five thousand dollars for us to plan and host their event and all event cost."

"Five thousand American dollars?" Lynette asked, not believing it either.

"American, bitch!" Keisha screamed, dancing around the sales floor.

"That's what's up!" Lynette danced behind the counter, truly happy for her girls. "Now y'all can get ya own damn office."

"Nah, I like the one we have." Keisha shrugged, and Lynette mushed her laughing.

Lynette checked her watch and rolled her eyes. "I need to hire a cashier."

"I second that," Janae said from her chair. "Because I'm about to quit."

"Fuck you," Lynette joked. "But I'm about to stick a *Hiring* sign right up in the window."

"That's cool, but I'm ready to go." Standing up, Janae headed to the phone that hung on the wall.

"Go where?" Lynette asked ready to throw a fit.

"Away," she laughed picking up the phone.

"Me too," Keisha said as she flipped her hair. "I feel like celebrating."

Lynette was not having it. "Well, I'm going to."

Faith laughed as she watched her lock up and flip the closed sign over. "What're you doing?"

ARABIA

"Closing early." She laughed as she headed upstairs for her bag. "Faith empty the register and put that in the safe." In her mind, she would come in early and do the paperwork for the daily count but right now she was about to go have fun.

Instead of closing at eight, Lynette shut the shop down at six without a care in the world. The girls all decided collectively to roll through the block and pop up on Zoo. Together, Lynette and Janae got in her car, while Keisha and Faith rode in hers. Revving up their engines, they sped through the streets, racing to see who would be the first to arrive. After bending a few corners and nearly running lights, the girls came to a screeching halt grabbing everyone's attention.

"And I fuckin' won!" Keisha hopped out the car yelling.

"Because you almost ran me off the road at the corner hoe." Lynette rebutted shaking her head. "I almost smacked that damn pole, bitch."

"Glad you didn't." She laughed as they all walked to the back of the buildings where the courtyard was. "I forgot you still new to this, you ain't ready for all that yet."

"Girl, fuck you!"

Keisha and Lynette went back and forth as Faith and Janae walked behind them. When they finally made it to the back, the guys were all posted up. Just one look and Keisha immediately spotted Tech, then it clicked that he didn't come alone. He was leaned up against the bench with some chick tucked underneath his arm. Keisha's words became lodged in her throat as her legs stopped moving.

"If niggas don't have nothing else, they have the audacity." Lynette huffed as she shook her head and walked over to Rich.

Echo peeped Keisha walk on the set and shook his head. He told Tech stupid ass not to bring Rah around the way. The girls popped up all the time, so he should've known better. Walking over to Tech, he nudged him to get his attention and then he nodded in Keisha's direction. "You better get ya girl up outta here."

Tech's eyes locked with Keisha's, and he could see the fire burning in them. Smoothly, he moved Rah from up under him and put a little space between them. Rah looked up and wondered what he was doing. "What's up?" she asked, never taking her eyes off him.

Shaking his head, Tech couldn't even say anything. Keisha was coming his way, and he ain't even want shit to go that way. "Echo, clear the way nigga."

"Shit, the fuck you want me to do." He sucked his teeth, but he went to do as he asked. "Keish," he smiled as he walked over to her meeting her halfway.

"Don't fuckin' Keish me, he better get that bitch outta here!" She screamed loud enough for the whole courtyard to hear. "Now!"

"He taking her home, chill out."

"Ain't no chill out, he shouldn't have brought her here in the first place." Keisha was pissed. Yeah, okay, she knew Tech had a girlfriend or whatever, but to bring her around her way was mad disrespectful. "I'mma beat his ass."

Faith walked over laughing and shaking her head. "Girl, calm down."

"Girl, fuck him!"

"I know that's the fuck right!" She laughed as they slapped hands. "I wouldn't fuck with him no more either after he done brought that bitch up here around all ya people…"

"Whoa, let's not get crazy." Keisha cut her off. "I didn't say all that. I'mma still fuck with him, but he better get her ass the fuck from up here." She quickly clarified. Faith was talking crazy. One thing she would admit was that she and Tech had a lot to talk about. Never had she ever been a side chick, and she wasn't about to start. Tech was either going to be with her, or he had to step.

When Tech saw Echo walk Keisha away, he grabbed Raheema's hand and led her out the courtyard and to his car. He ignored her questioning eyes as they got inside, and he ain't waste no time pulling off. Rah had heard everything the girl said, and the way Tech practically ran her up outta there at her request had her pissed.

"Who was that?" Tech sighed before adjusting his body in his seat, he thought about how he wanted to answer her. Taking longer than she liked, she yelled at him, "Hello, you deaf now?"

"You don't really wanna know who she is," was all he said as he glanced her way.

That response gave her all the answers she needed as she sat back in her seat. Licking her lips, she willed back the tears. All this time, she knew Tech had been cheating on her, she felt it. He convinced her that she was tripping, and she went against her gut because she wanted to believe that what they had was solid. "How long?"

"What?" Tech asked as if he didn't know what she was talking about.

Chuckling, Rah wasn't even in the mood to play with him. "TaShawn, don't take this moment to insult me. I think at the very least you owe me the truth. Is she the reason you never wanted me to come around?"

Swallowing hard, Tech wanted to argue and lie, but he wasn't even that type of nigga. The last thing he wanted to do was hurt Rah, but it was bound to happen. Whether it was today or three months from now, it was going to happen because Keisha was who he wanted to be with. "No," he answered honestly. "I never wanted you to come around the way because that ain't for you. This whole lifestyle ain't for you."

"Is that what you like about her? She's the opposite of me..."

"Rah..."

"How long?"

"Since that last time, we broke up, after the accident." Tech felt like shit listening to her cry, but she wanted to know, so he told her. "Rah, I never even looked at another woman like that. The last three years, I was with you and only you...Shit just ain't there no more."

Now it all made sense. She felt he was becoming distant and no matter how hard she tried, it just wasn't working. Now she knew he never planned on being with her, he was just going through the motions. Nodding her head. "Just take me home."

WE MADE LOVE IN THE 80'S

Tech put his blinker on and bent the corner headed to her house. He didn't know how things with Rah would end or when it would happen, but he was relieved that the truth was out. Hurting her was never his intentions, but there was no way to avoid it. So, when he pulled up to her apartment building and she hopped out without so much as a goodbye, he didn't blame her. Pulling back into traffic, all he could think about was how he was going to smooth things over with Keisha.

He didn't go to her house right away, nah, he took a moment to get himself together. Tech went home, had a beer showered, and changed his clothes. Since shit with him and Rah were officially done, he went ahead and cleared all her shit out too. He ain't wanna just toss her things in the trash, so he put them in the trunk and planned to take them to her.

On the drive all the way to Keisha's house, Tech went over what he would say. True they weren't official, but Tech knew shit went all bad this afternoon. He was afraid he had fucked shit up with her before it even started. He wanted her and only her, so he was going to have to prove it. Tech just knew with Keisha the shit wasn't going to be easy.

Outside of Keisha's house, Tech sat parked in his usual spot. All of the lights in the house were out, and Tech was praying she was home. Stepping out of the car, Tech adjusted his clothes and walked to the door. Without hesitation, he rung the bell and stepped back.

Upstairs, Keisha thought she heard something, but there was no mistaking that loud as bell. Walking over to her window, she peaked out the blinds and could see Tech's car parked out front. Smirking, Keisha was ready to play madder than she really was just to get on his nerves. Pulling her hair out of her ponytail and slipping her nightgown over her panties she looked in the mirror. She was bedtime cute and was sure it was just enough to have him drooling. After adjusting her breast in her nighty, she went downstairs. Sleepily, she prepared her voice, "Who is it?"

"It's me, Keish," Tech said once he cleared his throat.

Stifling her laugh, she turned on her attitude face and cracked the door. "The fuck you want? Don't you gotta bitch to entertain?"

"Keisha, can we just talk about this?" He sighed.

"You bring that bitch around the way, around my friends and family, and now you wanna talk. I'm done with whatever the hell this is…"

"I broke up with her." Keisha fell silent at his words, and he continued, "I'm sorry about earlier. I swear that was just some dumb shit, and it won't ever happen again. I love you, and I only wanna be with you."

Smiling, Keisha bit her lip as she listened to Tech confess his love for her.

"Girl, let that nigga in like we both know you're going to, and stop making all that damn noise."

"You not even supposed to be here, you shut up." Keisha and Faith both laughed as she walked into the kitchen and came out with a bottle of water. Keisha waited until she was walking back upstairs to tune back into what Tech was saying. Sliding the chain off the door, she opened it and looked at him. "You broke up with her?"

Nodding his head, he grabbed her face and kissed her lips. "I did, I love you, babe."

"I love you too." She kissed him back. "But I'm still mad at you."

"I know, and I'mma make it up to you."

"Whatever." She rolled her eyes locking the front door back. Leaning her back up against the door, she looked to him with her arms crossed at her chest. "So, now what?" she asked needing them to be clear from this point on about exactly what they were doing.

"What you mean?"

"You broke up with ya girl now what? Is that supposed to make me happy?"

Shaking his head, Tech ain't know what the fuck she was on. "Hell nah, that's supposed to make you mine…Fuck you mean?"

"Well, breaking up with her, doesn't mean that I automatically win some type of prize. You wanna be with me, then you ask me, nigga. You tell me what that shit gone mean, right here, right now, or good night."

"You for real?" he asked, and she tilted her head eyeing him, and he knew she wasn't playing. Tech took in a deep breath as he stepped back from her. He wasn't really good at all this mushy shit, but if Keisha was asking the least, he felt like he could do was answer her honestly. "Keish, we've been fucking around for a few months now and I know I was dead ass wrong for how shit with us started, but shit, I know you feel it. Like you got me out here making love and shit…" he paused as he looked down at her and into her eyes. "I love you."

"You love me?" she asked trying to conceal her smirk.

"You know I love you." He walked up to her and leaned down kissing her lips. After unwrapping her arms, he placed them around his neck and lifter her in the air while she wrapped her legs around his waist. "So, you good with that, or I gotta tell you how I'm take care of you and eat ya little pussy every night."

"Hell yeah, tell her that shit too!" Faith yelled from upstairs causing both theirs eyes to look up to the staircase.

Neither one of them could hold their laughter as they shook their heads. Tech was sure Faith would never let him forget how he was down here begging like a bitch, but he had his girl now, so fuck it. He was willing to be whatever they called him as long as they added Keisha's Nigga too.

Chapter 20

When Stacks came home from the hospital, he stayed in his house avoiding the world. He felt he needed time to rebuild his strength and his mind. Night and day, he worked out in his garage pacing himself. He also changed his diet and it helped him cleanse not only his body, but it replenished his soul. The stronger he got, the better he felt and the more he felt like himself.

On this day, nearly a month after Stacks had come home from the hospital, he was finally ready to emerge. He couldn't front like he wasn't a little nervous because he was. But he was going to go see his crew and his girl. In his garage he jumped into his car and started the engine. The feeling of the car beneath his fingertips as he gripped the steering wheel, was almost foreign to him. Swiftly he switched gears, and then opened his garage. Stacks took his time backing up, but once he was safely out of his garage, he spent tires down the street. The weather had definitely changed, and fall was here. The air was crispy, and it was quite chilly, he wished he'd brought a jacket, but his long sleeves would have to do.

It took him about thirty minutes to get back to the city, and he was torn. Stacks didn't know if he should go see his crew first or if he should go see Faith. He wanted to go see Faith, but he knew the shit with her would take time. That situation wasn't something he could do in ten or twenty minutes, so he opted to go see his crew first. Stacks pulled his car up in the front and parked. His eyes traveled around the neighborhood as he stepped out looking around. He hadn't been around the way since the shooting, but nothing seemed out of place or out of the ordinary. Tapping his waist, he felt for his pistol and relaxed a little bit. He knew now it was better he get caught with it than without it, and he didn't ever plan on the latter.

"Zoo, look who finally came up for air!" Echo said loudly as he clapped it up for Stacks grabbing everyone's attention. "My nigga."

Smiling, Stacks was glad to be back. "What's up?"

"Shit, you know how it is out here," Echo said as he pulled him on for a brotherly hug. "Shit, glad to see you back."

"I know, right?" He looked around and nodded to the rest of his crew. "Where everybody at?" Stacks asked when he notice Rich, Sam and Tech weren't there.

"Shit, I don't even know. Sam been laid up with Janae, you know they baby about due now. And Rich he back and forth, between here and the shop, niggas be ghost."

"Right, right!" He nodded before he hit Echo with another question, and they began chopping it up for a minute. Every other minute someone was welcoming him back, and he appreciated all the love.

"So, what you bout to do now? You trying to step out?" Echo asked because he was ready to slide if he had to.

"Nah, I'mma go check Faith out."

Echo knew a little about their situation, and he also knew Stacks had fucked up. "Good luck with that," he said, and they both chuckled.

"I'mma need more than luck." Stacks shook his head. "Aight, well I'mma get outta here." They slapped hands and said their goodbyes before he was off. On the way over to the shop, Stacks' biggest worry was Faith's reaction to seeing him. He knew she was going to chew his ass out, yell, and scream. So, he prepared himself for what he figured was the worst-case scenario. At the shop, he parked around the building and walked over. No one knew he was coming and a part of him wanted to hold that element of surprise. He took a deep breath and released it just as he walked into the shop. Nodding his head, he was really impressed. The store turned out way better than he could've ever imagined.

"Welcome to 55th Street," Janae said from behind the counter as she handed a customer their bags.

Stacks peeped her and smiled. Janae was pregnant again and big pregnant at that. He didn't remember they were having another baby, but he hadn't seen her in so long it seemed new to him. On his way to the checkout counter, he noticed Lynette in the corner helping a customer. "Miss, can I get some help over here?" he asked just to fuck with her.

"Yeah, I'll be with..." her words stopped as she looked up and saw it was Stacks. "Oh, shit!" she yelled rushing him. "About damn time, man, shit."

Lynette hugged him, and he hugged her back. "I missed you too."

"Right," she smiled with a few tears in her eyes. "I should beat yo' ass." She popped him on the arm as he released her.

"I know, I know. Where she at?" He asked, looking around for her.

"She in the back office," Lynette pointed him in the right direction, and he was off.

Janae waved, actually happy to see him too and he hit her with a head nod. In the back, he stepped to the door and knocked. Come in, he heard her say and he stepped in. Soon as he walked through the door, she looked up and stopped whatever she was doing.

Keisha sat in a chair on the side of the room, feeling the same shock she knew Faith was feeling. "Ugh, I'll wait for you outside," she said before standing up and gathering her things to take with her. "It's good to see you Stacks." Keisha smiled before opening her arms for her hug that he warmly returned. Faith didn't take her eyes off him as they both stood there quiet until Keisha left.

"Hey," Stacks said looking her over. It seemed as if he hadn't seen her in forever. She appeared to be older and more mature than he remembered. Her hair, her clothes, everything was different.

"Hey," was all she said after clearing her throat and blinking back tears.

The moment became awkward as she looked at him standing there. "Give me a hug or something. Ya man back." he smiled, trying to ease the tension, but Faith wasn't budging, nor was she smiling. After a while he cut the shit. "I know I got a lot of making up to do..."

Chuckling, Faith shook her head. "Making up to do?" Tears burned her eyes at the audacity of him. "I nearly get killed, you haven't spoken to me in months, and to top it all off, you drag ya tired ass in here and tell me *you got some making up to do?*"

Stacks' eyes got wide, not expecting her outburst. He didn't even know how to respond, for real. "Faith…"

"I'm so pissed I could kill you right now." She stomped as she began to pace.

"I know…"

"No, no, you don't know." She stopped and looked at him as tears slowly fell from her eyes.

Licking his lips, Stacks was stuck. He knew what happened with them was all on him, he had to sort some shit out within himself but how did he tell her that. How did he tell her that he was broken, the fact that he wasn't able to protect her had him feeling like less than a man, that in order for him to get better he had to step away? Stacks wasn't good with words, but he was good with action and until now that was always enough.

"Don't cry babe," he soothed as he stepped closer to her causing her to take a step back. "Faith, you're mad right now, and I get it, but let's talk about this…I'm here."

"Nah, I don't have time to talk, I have to go secure a venue." She pushed past him and began to gather her things. This was too much for her. The stress she was feeling at that moment couldn't have been good for her or the baby. "After you." She looked him up and down, waiting for him to get out her office.

Nodding his head, Stacks couldn't process what this meant. "Whoa, hol'up," Stacks stopped her as she walked past him. Exhausted and over this whole situation, Faith turned to him. "So, you're really not going to talk to me? After all we been through, I…"

"We?" she asked as if she didn't know what he was referring to. Their eyes met and she continued, "This ain't about you…For the first time in my life, it's about me." She pointed her nail into her chest as her lips trembled. "I've been hanging on to you like a lost puppy all my life, cool with whatever you wanted to do and making whatever you did okay…And it took for me to be shot to realize what a selfish asshole you really are." Snatching away from him, Faith stormed out the store, leaving Janae and Lynette's mouths on the floor.

Slightly embarrassed, Stacks flicked his nose with his index-finger. Looking around, he smoothly walked out of the store and to his car. When he was inside, Stacks sat thinking as Faith's words echoed in his head. Starting his car with a heavy heart, he headed home.

While Stacks was confused, Faith was inconsolable. In the car with Keisha, she broke down crying harder than she ever had before. Her heart was literally in a million pieces and pouring out of her body in tears. Tears that she wouldn't allow herself to shed for months were coming faster than she could wipe them. "I fuckin' hate him," Faith choked out.

Keisha just sat and rubbed her back as she allowed her the moment of release. "You don't hate him, and that's okay."

Shaking her head, Faith begged to differ. "Yes, I do too. He ain't never gon' see me or my baby." She swore, and Keisha bust out laughing. Looking over to her, Faith sucked her teeth. "Shut up," she giggled.

"I hear you, girl." Keisha continued to laugh knowing Faith wasn't going nowhere. "If for nothing else make him earn all that love back."

Faith knew she was right, and that's exactly what she was going to do. Her time and her affection weren't going to be as easy as it was or as easy as it's always been. This new Faith came with demands, expectations, and priorities. A lot had changed in the past few months, and the biggest change of them all was growing within her womb. She had to be better not only for herself but for her child.

Once she got herself together, they continued with their plans to go secure the venue for their upcoming event. Faith had to put all her shit on the back burner and get to work. With Keisha by her side, she was ready.

It was crazy how one by one each of the girls were finding their way. Whether Lynette knew it or not, she sparked a fire inside the other girls, and it made them want to be more, made them want to do more. Before her, neither of them had thought of opening or running a business and now, shit was practically falling into their laps. Faith was on her way, and she was going with or without Stacks.

WE MADE LOVE IN THE 80'S

I Got It Made by Special Ed played loudly in the club as everyone rocked to the beat. The club was packed, and money was flowing like water. Every other minute Nate was making a sell and life couldn't have been better. A new city, more drugs than he knew what to do with and an endless supply of women…he couldn't ask for more. Looking out at the crowd from his section, he smiled as they switched up the song and Biz Markie *Just a Friend* came on. Bopping his head, he stood up with his large rope chain swinging.

"Oh, baby yooooouuuu," he sang loudly before tossing a handful of money in the air. Like rain, it fell down all around him as he held his arms up, and the crowd around him cheered. This was it; this was the life he'd always wanted, and it was all his. Nate was definitely feeling himself and he wasn't the only one. Looking over, he eyed his company for the night, and it was clear she was feeling him too. "You about ready to go?" He leaned over and spoke into her ear.

Smiling, she licked her lips. "I'm ready when you are."

Nate liked the sound of that, "Aight, we out in thirty," was all he said before turning his attention back to the crowd.

Over the past couple of months, Nate had really reinvented himself. Everything he was, everyone he knew he left it all behind when Rich gave him those four bricks of cocaine. Nothing was the same for him after that night, and he loved it. For all he felt that was going right in his life, he still couldn't shake thoughts of Keisha. Every now and then, he would think about her. Some night she was all he could think about, but on those nights, he just bedded a different woman until he fucked her out of his thoughts. This was Nates life now, living in the fast lane. He let about three more songs spin before he decided to call it a night. Together he and his friend for the evening gathered their things and headed for the door. "You wanna get something to eat?" He asked pulling out of his parking space.

"Not really," she flirted.

Nate didn't miss the sex dripping from her tone as he smirked, but he ignored it. "I do." He decided they were going to get something before they made it back to his place. Besides, he hated to drink on an empty stomach. At the light, Nate went to make a left and not even a minute later he saw blue lights flashing behind him. "Fuck." His heart rate increased as sweat covered his forehead.

ARABIA

"What you do?" Ole girl asked checking her review mirror.

"I ain't do shit." Trying not to panic, he was just going to play it cool. "I'm dirty, shit!" Shaking his head, he couldn't believe he got caught up like this.

"Aight, hand it to me, and I'll put it in my bra or something." He looked over to her not sure if he wanted to take that route and she could sense his hesitation. "They ain't gon' search me, we good…Shit, nigga, hurry up." Nate saw the cop open the door and quickly tossed her the rest of the drugs he had on him. "Damn, this a lot. I thought you had a couple of bags." She fussed as she tucked the drugs in her clothes.

Before either of them could say anything else, there was a knock at the driver's side door. Nate looked over before manually rolling his window down and squinted into the light that was blindingly shining into his face. "Yes officer?"

"Step out the car for me?" He ordered, and Nate's face twisted in confusion. "Now."

"You not gone tell me why you pulling me over?" Nate asked, not understanding what was going on.

"I'm not gonna tell you again, I know that." The officer replied smartly as he pulled Nate out of the car. Just then four other squad cars pulled up, and Nate began to panic. "Detective, you can step out too."

"With pleasure." Nate's friend stepped out and his mouth fell open. She half glanced his way as she walked over to the police car and hopped inside talking on her cellphone.

Suddenly, Nate's head started spinning, and he felt as if he was going to pass out. He thought of how they had met, how they kicked it. Tonight, wasn't the first time they'd hung out, he had met her a few months ago. A few weeks after he came down and now, he was kicking his ass for not being more careful. Then he thought of how he'd passed her his work just a moment ago and was sick to his stomach as it began to churn. She sat right beside him as he made sales, not only this day but other days, and now he was going down. He didn't have any more questions; he knew what this was about. After he was hand cuffed and patted down, he was led to another squad car. They walked Nate past another police car and saw them examining his bag of drugs, all he could do was shake his head. As he walked, he looked for his date, but he didn't see her anywhere.

From the backseat of the police car, he watched them literally tear his car to shreds. They were looking and they were looking hard, but that was all he had on him. Shit, what he had was enough for him to do some serious time. With that *Just Say No* bullshit, they were giving niggas real time out here and he knew he wouldn't see outside for a long time. At the police station, he just sat in the interrogation room waiting. Minutes turned into hours and hours into some time the next day.

"Nathanial Walker," The detective called out causing him to steer.

He heard his name called through his sleep mixed with the motion of people entering the room, caused him to steer. Sitting up he wiped his mouth and looked to the two detectives. Nate didn't plan on saying much of anything since he knew he was going to jail no matter what he said. "Y'all ready to book me?"

"No, not just yet."

"Well, I ain't got nothing to say." He stretched ready to go upstairs.

"So, you don't want to explain this?" The detective sat the bag of crack he had on him at the club on the table.

Shaking his head, Nate damn sure ain't have nothing to say about that. "Nah, I gave the shit to an undercover. I know what that mean."

The detectives looked at each other and the one closest to the door spoke. "How about telling us where you got it or this?" From his briefcase, the detective pulled out a brick of cocaine, and Nate almost wet his pants as his eyes ballooned. "How about I start because I got this from underneath your bed. It was in the back by the wall in a Nike box."

"See how this works is, we tell you where we got this, and you tell us where you got it?"

ARABIA

Nate was stuck wondering how he went from partying enjoying life, to being caught with an eight ball of dope, and now he added a brick of cocaine to his list of charges. Like, there ain't no way this shit was really his life.

The detective could sense he was still hesitant, so he had to put this in perspective for him. "You got two choices kid. You can stay quiet and go to jail for the rest of your life, or work with us and you can go home."

"You want me to snitch?" Shaking his head, Nate couldn't believe he'd even said the word. "Hell, nah, I work with y'all and niggas will have my head. Shit, I'd rather go to jail."

"Protective custody ain't too bad now a days." The detective said matter of fact. "All we want to know is where you got it, and all this goes away. You can go home today, or you can go to jail and do fifty years. Seventy years old isn't too old, might have a little left in you to have some kids or something."

Sweat beads began to form on the top of Nate's head as he weighed his options. On one hand, he wasn't no snitch ass nigga...He would never snitch and had condemned anyone who had. He took loyalty and brotherhood seriously, but on the other hand Zoo was no kin to him. In fact, they didn't deserve the thought he was giving to the situation. They did try to kill him, and he didn't doubt that they would have. So, the way he saw it, it was payback. "Down bottom, in the LowLands, crew name Zoo."

"Zoo?" The detectives questioned looking at each other. "What is that?"

Sighing, Nate shifted in his seat. "It's a crew of niggas. Dude name Rich Tony brought me the work."

"How much did he bring you?"

"He gave me four, but I...I sold the rest," Nate answered honestly. Shit, he'd come this far there wasn't no point in lying now.

"So, he just gave you four keys of coke?"

"Basically, yeah. He owed me a favor and that was it. Four keys, no strings and bounced."

"So, this is your last key, when did you plan on getting more?"

"I hit him to reup a few weeks ago, and I been waiting for him to get up with me."

"Okay, call him again and get him to meet you somewhere."

Nate wasn't about to meet with them, nah that was taking shit too far. "You said all I had to do was tell you who gave it to me?"

"And we need to verify this guy is who you say he is before you get any kind of deal from us." He grabbed his stuff, and both of the detectives stood up. "You let us know what you wanna do?"

Nate had gone back and forth with himself enough, "I call him and then what? Do I have to meet him?"

"You call him, get him to agree to the sell once the transaction is made, we'll get him."

Looking away, Nate was sure he would hate himself for what he was about to do, but there was no way he was about to do fifty years in jail. Shit, anything with years on the end of the number was too much for him. "Okay."

Just one word sealed the deal and the rest of his life. With a heavy heart and his head low, he walked out of the police station a snitch. His car was still parked where they'd pulled him over, so he caught a cab and was off. Over the next couple of days, the cops had come into his home and bugged his phone. Let them tell it, he had a month to make something shake or he was going back to jail.

A week after his release, Nate began reaching out to Rich. He would page him, and Rich would never respond. He didn't want to seem too pressed, so he didn't sweat him. Usually, he would page him once a day or once every two days because he knew Zoo wasn't dumb and would detect any foul shit going on. Nate was on week three and growing more nervous by the day. Then he got a little angry because Rich specifically told him to hit him when he got the work off. So, what if he was really calling because he wanted to reup? Now, he was feeling like Rich was playing games, and that nearly made him want to pull up on his ass. But he wasn't even tripping, he planned to reach out to Keisha if he had too. He told himself this was the last time, he was going to page Rich and if he didn't call back, he was going to take another route. Imagine his surprise after paging him for over a month, the phone rung not even five minutes later.

"Yeah, somebody page Rich." His deep baritone came over the phoneline, and Nate sat up.

"Uhh, yeah it's Nate."

"Nate?" he asked as if he didn't know who he was.

"Yeah, you know Keisha ex. I was calling to get..."

"Nah, not on the phone. I'll meet you around your way, down the street in about an hour."

"Oh okay..." before Nate could finish, he heard a dial tone sounding in his ear and before he could make it to his bedroom, there was a knock on his door. Doubling back, he went to answer the door. Peeking through the peep hole he saw it was the detectives and rolled his eyes. He opened the door and they pushed past him holding up wires in their hands. "What's all this?"

"We gotta get you wired."

Nate was over this shit with them and a part of him wished he'd never agreed to it. But instead of saying anything he stood with his arms up and allowed them to wire him. Once they were sure the device was on, they were gone just as quickly as they had come. There was no time for him to dwell as he had to get to the meeting site. Nate was nervous as he walked around the corner. He could've drove himself, but he used the time to think and try to relax.

"Get in," Rich said as he pulled up next to him, nearly scaring the shit out of Nate.

He was so lost in his thoughts that he didn't even see Rich pull up beside him. Without hesitation, Nate hopped in and Rich rode around the block. Rich didn't say anything, so Nate thought he was waiting for him to speak. "Yeah, like I was saying. I need..."

Rich silenced him and handed him a piece of paper. Strangely, he looked to him before taking the piece of paper and unfolding it. Written on the piece of paper was a price and a minimum purchase of three bricks. "So, I gotta buy three bricks to purchase?" Still Rich didn't speak, he just nodded his head. Nate ain't know what he was supposed to do next. Rich wasn't willing to talk, and he was wired. If everything was on this paper, how were they supposed to record it. "Okay, so how do I get it." Before, he knew it they were pulling back up to his house.

"We'll be in touch," was all Rich said as he double parked in front of the building and waited for Nate to get out of his car.

"And when is that? I already been paging you for a month, just to get this meeting, and now you can't even come through with the product. I need that asap," he said, purposely stalling trying to get something on tape. "You gotta let me know something."

Nate was practically begging as Rich listened to him and from what he knew about Nate, this wasn't his style at all. He didn't even beg for his life when they were going to kill him, but here he was practically on his hands and knees and that rubbed Rich the wrong way.

"So, what you think he was doing? Maybe the money to good, and he don't wanna run out." Tech thought out loud as Rich ran down how he was feeling about the whole link up with Nate.

"First of all, he a hoe ass nigga anyway." Sam shrugged against the whole thing with Nate from the beginning.

Stacks listened to them go back and forth for a minute and sat quietly. He was really just getting back into the fold of things and felt a little out of place. But he was working through those feelings. Sitting up in his seat, he spoke as he lit his joint. "If you gotta question it, don't do it."

Rich looked to him, and he agreed. Something with the whole Nate thing just didn't sit right with him, and his gut was telling him not to do it. "Well, that situation is done."

"Good," Sam said as he stood up, and the guys chuckled. Just as he was about to go to the bathroom his pager went off. He quickly pulled it from his waistband, and he could see it was Janae's number followed by 911. "Shit," he cursed as he quickly moved to the phone. Dialing the number back he waited.

"Yes, ya girl in labor, and her water broke all over my damn floor…" Lynette answered the phone, rolling her eyes.

Janae snatched the phone, threatening to beat her ass. "You gotta come quick."

"Aight I'm on my way, y'all at City Hospital, right?"

"Yes," she strained as a contraction hit her. "You gotta get out," Janae screamed at Lynette.

"Just calm down, I'm on the way." He hung up and felt his pockets for his keys. "Janae in labor."

"That's whats up," Tech said as the other men congratulated him.

Stacks knew more than likely Faith was at the hospital with Janae and them, so he stood up to leave too. "I'mma ride with you?"

"Aight, we out then." They walked to the door. "I'll catch up with y'all later," Sam said before he and Stacks got in the car and went to the hospital. Sam was kind of mad Janae went into labor at the store. He had already told her about being up on her feet all the time and now look. What if they baby would've came out on the damn floor? Then he would've had to beat her ass.

Soon as they got to the hospital and upstairs, Sam suited up and went into the delivery room. Stacks looked around the waiting room and saw Faith and Keisha sitting in the corner. After taking a deep breath, he walked over and sat next to her. She looked up just as he sat down causing her to immediately suck her teeth. "So, you just ain't wearing ya ring?" He hissed grabbing her left hand.

"I'm not engaged, so why would I?" She replied, snatching her hand out of his.

Stacks chuckled. "So, what you just gon' ignore me forever? You wanna see other people? What?"

Tears burned her eyes. "Fuck you, Landon," she cursed him before punching him in his chest. Quickly, she stood up and stormed off.

WE MADE LOVE IN THE 80'S

Exasperated, he just shook his head. Since he tried to talk to her at the shop, he'd been calling, paging, coming by, and she wasn't trying to fuck with him at all. He looked up, and Keisha was looking dead at him. "Why don't you talk to ya girl?"

"I talk to her every day," Keisha joked.

"Come on, you know what I mean. Get her mind right, and tell her ass she needs to go home."

"Faith ain't trying to hear that shit." Keisha adjusted herself in her seat. "She ain't really go into detail about what's going on, but whatever you did, you really fucked up this time. I ain't never seen Faith like this."

Stacks couldn't do anything but shake his head. He knew if he wanted her, he was going to have to try harder.

At eleven thirty at night, Janae and Sam welcomed baby Sahara Nicole into the world. She weighed in at seven pounds, three ounces and looked like the perfect mixture of her parents. While everyone stood around the bed practically drooling over baby Sahara, Faith was looking at Janae and Sam. He was so happy and so supportive. She knew for a fact Sam would've never carried Janae how Stacks did her, Rich either. In her eyes he fucked everything up, and now she was going to be a single mother, struggling to make ends meet. Maybe a little dramatic, but it wasn't going to be all beautiful like this, and that was depressing. "Aight, I'm about to go," she said, causing everyone to look her way.

"Alright, thanks for being here." Janae smiled as Faith leaned down and she hugged her.

"I'll talk to y'all later," her voice cracked, and she covered it up with a slight giggle. Faith could feel Stacks burning a hole into the side of her head, but she refused to look his way.

Stacks stared at her. His eyes traveling her frame from head to toe. This shit was killing him, having to be away from her, seeing her but not being able to touch her, this shit was worse than him being shot. Now, Stacks knew how she felt, he got it now. His face contorted in confusion when she leaned over the bed and her shirt came up. Nah, Stacks knew he must've been tripping. He studied her intensely and when she walked past him, he followed her out. "Faith," he called out and she kept walking. "Fucking stop," he pulled her arm and slung her against the wall.

"What Landon?" she asked, refusing to look at him. Faith did her best looking everywhere but at him as he studied her.

He didn't say anything, Stacks just stood there quietly. He took his hand and smoothed it over her cheek and down her chest. Stacks kept going until he palmed her stomach. Only then did their eyes meet. His hands slid under her shirt and with both hands, he felt her stomach. Her stomach wasn't big, but it for damn sure wasn't small and had it not been for the oversized shirt she is wearing; he would be able to tell. "You pregnant?" He asked softly as he looked in her tearing eyes. "You pregnant, and you weren't even gon' say shit to me about it…That's foul, Faith."

Rolling her eyes, she shrugged away from him. "No, how you did me was foul." She angrily spat as she wiped her eyes. "You don't get to enjoy this with me," she said pointing to her stomach. "Hell, you ain't even the type of nigga I need, if you telling it."

Anger burned his eyes, but he didn't react. "Aight, I hurt you, I been apologizing for that shit. What you wanna do now, hurt me back? That's what you wanna do? Hurt me by keeping my baby from me?" She didn't answer, Faith just looked past him. "Aight," he nodded his head, "I see the type of shit you on." Stacks stepped back from her with disgust written all over his face as her eyes squinted.

Faith watched him as he walked away from her, and she ain't really care how he was feeling. Well, she cared but she wasn't about to tell him that. This wasn't how she planned on him finding out about the baby, but it's how it played out and he got exactly what he deserved. All that hurt he was feeling right now was only a fraction of the pain she'd been feeling for months.

Chapter 21

After Janae had the baby, shit for Lynette got hectic. No longer did she have help running the register or the day to day store operations. Faith and Keisha were there, but they weren't any help. From the back office they were running their event business and was actually making a little buzz for themselves. Lynette was happy for them, but hell she was tired. Out of desperation, she had even asked her mom's to come work a couple of times.

"This is just not the business." Lynette sighed as she leaned over the counter.

"At least it ain't busy today," Keisha said as she flipped through the racks of clothes.

Lynette looked at her shaking her head, "Stop stealing my clothes." Keisha looked at her, and they both bust out laughing. "I'mma start charging yo' ass."

"I love you too." Keisha wasn't seeing what she was looking for, but that Dap area was calling her name. "Lynette you know I love you right."

Squinting her eyes, she already knew where this was going. "Hell no!"

"Come on please!!! Just this one time?" She practically begged and she didn't care.

"You know the rules, you can have anything in here but that."

"I know that's why it's a favor! Just this once, come on it's our first event and it could be promo for you also!" Keisha threw in. "Just look at me as a walking billboard. Turning around she strutted down the aisle. "Keisha what are you wearing. Oh, this is Dapper Dan for 55th Street all exclusive line."

Lynette listened to her go on like the fool she was, but she gave in. "Just this one time." Rolling her eyes, Lynette was tired of standing up. Grabbing a seat on the stool, she watched Keisha go through the Dap section and pick out an outfit to go try on. While she was off, Lynette flipped the pages of one of the many magazines behind the counter as a young woman walked in. "Hello welcome to 55th Street." She greeted before looking up from her magazine. Quietly, she watched the girl shop and she was cute with a little style. Going back to her magazine, Lynette was flipping the pages when the girl walked up to the counter. "Can I help you with anything?"

"Yeah, this store is really nice! Is the owner hiring? I mean I'm in school or whatever, but I been looking for a job and ain't nobody hiring." She huffed.

The more she talked the Lynette was serenaded by her words. "Looking for a job, huh?"

"Yes, I can use the extra money to help with my tuition and stuff."

Lynette smiled loving the way this conversation was going. "What hours are you looking to work?"

"I can do whatever for real, my classes are at night…three days a week from six to nine. Well, I don't know what time y'all close, but I can work all day."

"Well, shit you're hired." Lynette continued to smile.

"What?" the girl looked surprised. "I don't need to talk to the manager or fill out an application?"

"I'm Lynette, the owner." Extending her hand, Lynette waited until she shook her hand. "What's your name?"

"Michelle," she smiled looking around the store. "So, I really got the job, just like that."

"If you want it, it's yours." Lynette moved from around the counter. "I was looking for a cashier anyway, but I really haven't had the time to really sit and interview anyone. So, it's like you just fell into my lap."

"I can't believe this!"

"Me either, you're a life saver, literally." Lynette laughed, thanking God for his small blessings. "Well, we'll talk about your salary and the job itself later, come back Wednesday morning at 8am sharp. I'll have your salary, and uniform shirt," she pointed to her chest at the 55th Street logo on her baby tee. "You can wear pants and shoes of your choice. No short shorts or anything like that though."

"Got it, oh, thank you so much, Ms. Lynette."

"Oh, please none of that miss stuff, I'm not that much older than you."

"Okay, well, I'll see you Wednesday morning at 8am."

"Alright, I'll see you then." Lynette smiled as they shook hands again and Michelle was off.

Just as she was walking out, Rich was walking in. "Who was that?" He asked before kissing her lips.

"My new cashier." She smiled, wrapping her arms around his neck. "I missed you all day."

Rich blushed trying his hardest not to. "You ain't miss me, did you?" Slowly, she nodded her head up and down as she kissed his lips again. "Who here?" He asked after pecking her lips once more.

"Keisha in the dressing room stealing my damn clothes," she rolled her eyes, "and Faith is upstairs tying up my damn phone."

He chuckled, "Take a ride with me real quick."

"I think this the one," Keisha said, walking out of the back in one of Lynette's most expensive pieces.

"Keisha watch the store while I run out for a minute." Letting Rich go, she saw Keisha pout, "You owe me."

She pinched the outfit as she walked past, and Keisha guessed it was the least she could do.

"We'll be back in like an hour or so," Rich said as he walked to the door.

"Aight, let me change my clothes back."

ARABIA

"And don't leave the front unattended!" Lynette shouted as she walked up the steps to her office. "Oooh, nice flowers, they should be downstairs in your office."

Faith laughed as she twirled in her seat. "Where you going?"

"I don't know, Tony want me to ride with him somewhere, and I'm fucking going." She laughed ready to run up out the store.

"I know that's right," standing up, Faith tossed the flowers in the trash and adjusted her clothes. Now that Stacks knew she was pregnant, she wasn't trying to hide it anymore. At nearly five months, she was nice and round showing her pudge off. "I'll help Keisha on the register while you gone, you know she be half paying attention."

"Okay!" They both laughed as Lynette grabbed her things, and they headed downstairs.

"You coming to the party Saturday, right?"

"Of course, I am! You already know I'm not going to miss y'all first event! We in there like swim wear!" After a little small talk, Rich and Lynette were saying their goodbyes. Together they walked hand and hand to his Range Rover, and he held the door open for her to get inside. Once she was seated, he jogged over to the driver side and got in. "Where we going because I'm hungry?" She asked once they pulled into traffic.

"Yo' ass always hungry." Not even laughing she stuck her middle finger up to him as she dug through her bag for a piece of gum. "We got the place."

Her eyes were wide as she turned to him excitedly. "Which one?"

"I ain't telling you, you just gon' have to wait and see." Pouting she sat back in her seat before smirking. Lynette looked over to him before excitedly bouncing in her seat. They had narrowed their house hunting down to three properties; a condo and two houses. Rich wanted to do shit like Stacks and Sam had and just surprise her, but Lynette's detective ass would find out. So, they looked together, and he made the final decision after they agreed on the top three properties.

"So, is this my anniversary gift?"

WE MADE LOVE IN THE 80'S

Laughing Rich just shook his head. Lynette ass was spoiled as hell, and he could admit it was all his fault. "Only you would think a house was an anniversary gift."

"Well, is it?" She asked not caring what he was talking about.

"Yeah, it's one of them." He shook his head as they laughed. Rich was a sucka when it came to Lynette and he knew it.

"Ahhhhhh, I knew it!" She took off her seatbelt and leaned over the seat kissing his cheek. "What else you get me?"

"I ain't tellin' ya big head ass shit else."

Lynette kissed his cheek once more before mushing him upside his head. "You wish my head was big." Back in her seat, Lynette put her seatbelt on. "Aight, stop up here at that White Castle."

Shaking his head, Rich did as she asked. "And don't be spilling shit in my car." He let her know as he pulled through the drive thru.

"Boy, shut up." She rolled her eyes. "Ain't nobody gon' mess up this raggedy car," she joked.

"Yeah, aight, you heard what I said," he said, just as he grabbed the food from the cashier. Happily, Lynette took the bags into her hands. Before Rich could put his change up, she was tearing into one of her burgers. "Shit, you ain't pregnant, are you?"

"Nah," she moaned in between bites. "You know I just had my cycle."

"And what that mean?"

"That I'm not pregnant." Rich looked out the window before looking back at her. "What?" she asked still eating her food.

"Nothing." He shrugged.

"Yes, it is. What is it?"

Rich thought about how he wanted to ask his question before he asked it. "We would make some pretty ass babies."

"Because of me!" She laughed.

"So, when we gon' make that move?"

Lynette looked at him to see if he was serious. "You're ready to have a baby?" It wasn't like they were trying not to. Lynette wasn't on birth control, and Rich only strapped up half the time.

"I mean it ain't no perfect time. We just get ready when it happens." He looked over to her. "You still want kids with me, or you one of those workin' women now?"

Lynette laughed knowing she was far from that. She was proud of her business and her store was going well, but she wasn't Ms. Independent. "Nah being a wife and a mother are still on my list."

"Aight, so no more strapping up?" He asked just so they were clear about this next step in their relationship. "We fuckin' with a purpose now."

Laughing she guessed he was right. "Yeah, we fuckin' with a purpose," she agreed as he grabbed her hand and kissed the back of it.

Rich drove to one of the houses on their list, just to fuck with her, before he made his way downtown and parked in one of the many parking garages. "Aight, come on."

"Nah, you ain't tricking me again."

Chuckling, Rich leaned over. He would never forget seeing her running up to the house trying to open the door. Rich hated to do her like that, but that shit was funny. "Nah, for real this time, come on."

Lynette didn't know if he was lying or not. "Babe, you got the condo, for real?"

He continued to laugh. "On Zoo." Rich held his right hand up, and she knew he was serious.

Happily, she jumped into his arms and he held her up. "This the one I really wanted too."

"I know," he smiled, kicking the car door closed. Rich held her up by her ass as they walked from the parking deck to the main building.

"Hello, Mr. and Mrs. Ricker," The concierge greeted them, and Lynette smiled, liking the sound of that.

"How he know who we are?" Lynette asked as Rich nodded his head greeting the man.

"It's his job to know who lives here, ain't that right, Frank?"

"Absolutely." He smiled, tilting his hat as the elevator doors opened.

"Aight, get ya heavy ass down," Rich said nearly dropping her on her feet.

Sliding next to him, Lynette wrapped her arms in his and laid her head on him. She loved Rich so much, like, she didn't see herself ever living without him. Them moving together was just the beginning, she planned to do and share everything with him. Finally looking up, Lynette noticed the twentieth floor was highlighted. "Oh, top floor." She squealed.

"Shit, damn near." He thought of the extra money he put out just to make sure they had one of the best views in the building.

Smiling Lynette stood on her tippy toes and kissed his cheek. "Thank you, Tony." He smiled, and she got serious. "Nah, for real because you really be making shit happen, and I love you for that."

"You know whatever it is, you got it." Leaning down, he pecked her lips just as the elevator doors opened. They stepped out of the elevator and on opposite ends of the hall was a door identical to theirs.

"It's only two apartments per floor?"

"I guess." Rich shrugged as he pulled out the key and handed it to her.

ARABIA

Lynette's eyes lit up as she snatched the keys out of his hands. Rich wrapped an arm around her waist and kissed her neck as she unlocked the door and opened it. "Ooohh wow." She smiled with tears coating her eyes. The space was so grand and even bigger than the model they saw a few months back.

Rich kissed her cheek and grabbed her hand, leading her through their new home. From room to room, he covered every inch of the four-bedroom, three-bathroom condo. Everything was clean, and the hardwood floors in the front were so pretty. This was literally the best place Lynette or Rich had ever lived in. The view from their bedroom overlooking the city was fit for a royal couple, and Lynette loved it.

"This shit really gon' be crazy." Rich was still shocked himself. To come up how he did and survive all that he'd been through, he was a walking testimony. When he was coming up, he used to think his life would always be full of bullshit; fighting, crime, and violence, but he took all the negative things around him and turned it into this. Before either of them could say another word, there was a knock at the door. Rich looked to her and she looked to him before they both looked towards the front.

"Now who could that be?" Lynette asked, not wanting to answer it or investigate.

Shrugging, Rich let her go and walked away. "Probably Frank."

"And he just be popping up like this?" she asked, not liking that shit at all.

"Maybe he wants something." Rich shrugged his shoulders as he walked with Lynette on his heels.

When they made it to the living room, Lynette immediately noticed her mother. "Ma, what you doing here?" Walking over, they hugged each other, smiling.

"Ya man invited me." LaValle smiled, winking at Rich.

"Oh, y'all think y'all friends now?" She playfully rolled her eyes.

LaValle laughed causing them all to laugh with her. "Well, Tony asked me to come." There was a man there standing with her, but Lynette didn't pay him any mind.

She didn't start paying attention until Rich stepped up. "Oh, did he." Lynette glanced his way.

"Yeah, I did." Lynette looked back to him and their eyes met. "I asked her to be here." Taking a deep breath, Rich reached in his pocket and pulled out a small black box. Looking down at her, he continued. "When I first met you, I knew you were going to be mine. In fact, I put that shit on Zoo."

"Oh, my gosh." Her hands flew to her mouth as she covered her face crying.

Smiling, Rich moved her hands and held the left one, looking in her eyes. "When it comes to you, no matter what, I show up. Whatever you need, I make sure I provide, and whatever you want I'm gonna make sure I get it. You wanted this house to be ours, and it is. I wouldn't stop trying, even when they denied me...I found a way because I knew you wanted it." He looked down at the box as he opened it and removed the 4ct princess cut ring out of the box. "Now I want something from you. I want us to move into this place, raise babies, and live as husband and wife. Lynette Beatrice Parker, will you marry me?" Just then LaValle cleared her throat and nodded her head pointedly and Rich knew what she was saying.

He stepped back and dropped down to one knee and asked her to be his wife again and LaValle smiled. She could see the love they had for one another. Even on that day a few years back when he sat in her kitchen, she could see it. Rich was a good man, and he took great care of her daughter. What more could she ask for? So, when Rich came to her asking what she thought about them getting married, she gave them nothing but blessings on top of blessings.

"Yes," Lynette choked out, wiping her eyes so she could get a good look at her ring. Her fingers trembled as Rich placed the ring on her finger and stood up. Jumping into his arms, Lynette didn't waste any time kissing his lips and all over his face.

LaValle clapped and they cheered, before Rich placed her on her feet. "Well, let's do it, right now. Melvin is an officiant and your mother is our witness."

"What?" she looked between the three of them stuck and lost for words. "Right here, right now?"

"Why not?" he said, so sure of himself and full of confidence.

"Oh-kay," Lynette shook her head not believing that they were really going to do this.

LaValle pulled the wedding rings from her purse and held them as everyone got into position. On their anniversary, in their big ass living room, wearing a baseball cap and jeans, Lynette and Rich said *I do.* Their wedding wasn't anything that she'd ever imagined, but it was perfect. After they placed their wedding bands on each other, they were pronounced husband and wife, and neither of them could've been happier. Melvin was a magistrate, so he had them sign their marriage license and promised to have it filed and the actual license mailed to them, and he was off. LaValle wasn't too far behind him. After both Lynette and Rich showed her their new home, they were left to consummate their marriage by fucking all over their new house.

"You look fine, babe," Tech said as he leaned back on the bed with his arm covering his eyes.

"You're not even looking," Keisha whined.

"Shit, it ain't but so many ways you can swoop that shit." He joked but he was serious. Rolling her eyes, Keisha stuck her middle finger up at him and went back into the bathroom. Shaking his head, Tech knew they ain't have time for this back and forth shit she was on. "Come on, man, we gotta go, or you gon' be late."

Keisha heard him, but she still picked up the comb and swooped her hair to the other side. Why she cut her hair into this ugly shit, she would always blame Faith. Looking in the mirror a final time, she just said fuck it and went back into the room. "Aight, I'm ready. You got my bag?"

"Yeah, I got it." He held up her bag and grabbed his keys and wallet. Keisha walked ahead of him out the door, and he locked up. Since they made their relationship official, things with them had been great. Of course, it wasn't perfect, but they were adjusting. Tech more than her because he wasn't used to checking in and making time for dates and things, but he was getting there. His relationship with Keisha was so much different from Rah because he was actually trying. Tech really didn't know what held him back from his previous relationship, he just figured she just wasn't the one.

"We still doing good time. Faith is there, and we set most of the stuff up last night," Keisha said as she sat in the car.

Tech was half listening to her as his pager went off, and it was Rich. He was on his way to him, so he wasn't about to run in the house and call him back. Just as he was about to step in the car, he changed his mind. "I gotta run back in the house right quick," he said, and took off for the door. With his key, he opened the door and headed straight for the phone. Quickly, he dialed Rich back, and he answered on the first ring.

"Where y'all at?" His voice boomed over the line.

"Shit, we was on the way; I came back in to call you back."

"Oh, aight, the girls just wanted to know. I'll tell them you'll be pulling up in thirty," Rich said loud enough for them to hear.

After ending the call with Rich, Tech went back outside and hopped in the driver's seat. They didn't do much talking on the drive over, they just listened to the radio. It took them a little over thirty minutes, but once they arrived, it was straight to work. Faith handed Keisha her walkie talkie and a clipboard. Zoo worked as security so a few of the guys were at the door, while the others were inside making sure things went smoothly and watching the girls. The event was a birthday party, and the woman was turning twenty-five. They wanted a ballroom style party with glitter, and the girls delivered. Everything from the décor, to the decorations, balloons, the food, the music everything was so well put together and on point.

Together, Faith and Keisha had that place running like the military. They were hoping this party led to many more. Since the grand opening of 55th Street, they had gotten plenty of calls. Calls with people just wanting information about booking, to vendors wanting them to book with them exclusively, to artist looking to perform…It was just nonstop, but this was the only party that actually came through. So, they were hoping to keep up the momentum. As the night was winding down, everyone was standing by the door talking amongst themselves as the party goers kept partying. It was only midnight, so the night was still young as Faith thought about what she was going to get into once the party was over. She wasn't quite ready to go home, and neither was the rest of the crew.

"So, what's the move?" Echo asked, ready to cut up. "Shit, lets slide to Leroy's for ole time sake?"

"Boy," the girls said in unison, knowing damn well he had lost his mind.

"Shit, I'm with it," Rich chimed in. "Leroy's used to be jumping."

"Yeah, when we were teenagers." Lynette shook her head.

"I don't know y'all, I'm with it." Keisha shrugged. "Leroy's was the spot on a Saturday night."

Faith and Lynette just rolled their eyes. Clearly, they were outnumbered.

"Well, the party is over in thirty minutes…"

"Can I talk to you for a minute?" Stacks asked, walking up behind Faith.

Sighing loudly, she was not in the mood. "Now is not the time or the place."

"It ain't never the right time." He went to grab her arm, and she shrugged away.

"This is my business, okay?" Faith tried to keep her voice down as everyone else stepped away to give them some privacy.

"Go ahead and handle that," Keisha said as she and Tech got ready to shut the party down. "We'll get everyone out."

Finally, Faith turned to Stacks and he was standing there dressed to the nines with a bouquet of flowers in his hand. "I got these for you, to congratulate you on your first event." He smirked, handing them to her.

Reluctantly, she took them before staring up at him. "Thank you. So, why are you here?"

"Because you won't talk to me any other way." At this point Stacks was exhausted and running out of options. "So, can we go somewhere and talk, or do I need to show my ass right quick?" he asked, raising his voice as her eyes got big.

"Shhh, keep your voice down," Faith whispered loudly.

Stacks looked at her not really caring one way or the other how it played out. "You gonna talk to me or not?"

Looking around, Faith just shook her head. "Just let me get this party situated, and we can talk." Stacks nodded his head, agreeing. "Here, hold these?" She handed him her flowers before walking back into the party. While she handled her business, Stacks walked over and kicked shit with the rest of Zoo.

"So, what he say?" Keisha asked when Faith made it over to where she was.

Shaking her head, Faith rolled her eyes. "He wants to talk."

Keisha ain't want to say it again, but she did. "Y'all need to." She knew Faith didn't want to hear it, but she told her anyway. "Faith y'all are about to have a baby, and I know Stacks fucked up, but you and I both know how he feels about you."

Blinking back tears, Faith didn't care. "Well, he has a real fucked up way of showing it."

"I know, but you gotta tell him that shit. Because for real, Stacks has always been Stacks. He didn't change, you did. So, now you gotta get his ass in line."

Faith knew she was right, but she was still mad. "Well, I told him I would talk to him when we left here."

"What, so you're going to miss Leroy's?"

"And I'm glad too." Faith laughed. "Something is wrong with y'all."

ARABIA

They continued to work as the lights came on, signaling the party was officially over. Keisha jumped on the mic and yelled, "Y'all ain't gotta go home, but y'all gotta get the hell outta here!" And the crowd fell into laughter. Their first event, outside of Zoo, went off without a hitch. They were so proud of each other, and they were five-thousand-dollars richer.

"Ain't no party like a Zoo Crew party cause a Zoo Crew party don't stop," Lynette, Faith and Keisha sang in unison as they danced and laughed, basking in their success. At this point, it was almost tradition that they do this after every event.

Faith lollygagged and bullshitted around as long as she could, and Stacks was just patiently waiting, standing in the lobby against the wall as if he could wait forever. Sucking her teeth, she hated that he looked so good. She gave him one last look from the balcony before she rolled her eyes and went downstairs. The rest of the crew had left so it was only them and the cleanup crew left in the building.

"You ready?" Stacks asked as she approached him, and Faith just nodded her head. He smirked as he watched her walk ahead of him. Tonight, she was wearing her little baby bum proudly, and he was proud of that. Yeah, she hated him right now, but he knew she loved his baby. Outside, he held the passenger door open for her. She went to get in, and Stacks stopped her. She stared into his eyes with a questioning look, and he just looked at her. Stepping closer to her, he kissed her. Just a gentle graze against her lips had his heart racing. "Go ahead, get in."

In the car, they didn't really say anything as he drove. They let the music play filling up the space that was seemingly empty and quiet. Stacks bent a few corners and before she knew it, they were riding around their old hood. It had been years since they had laid eyes on the neighborhood, but it sure brought back memories. Pulling into the parking lot of the park they used to hang at, he parked the car and looked to her.

Faith didn't know what he was thinking or planning to say to her, but she was prepared to shoot the shit down. Out of nowhere a man came out of the shadows of the building and started walking over to the car and immediately, Faith grew nervous. It was two in the morning, dark as hell outside, so what could his ass want. Looking over to Stacks, he sat back, cool as a fan. Rolling his window down, he smiled. "What up, Nephew?"

WE MADE LOVE IN THE 80'S

Reaching his hands up, the young man bumped his fist. "Nothing for real, dead as hell out here."

Slowly, Faith was able to relax seeing Stacks knew the man that had approached them. She remained quiet as they exchanged pleasantries and was happy when the man finally left. She didn't know Stacks still came around this way, but she wasn't really surprised. Zoo was everywhere and they knew just about everybody. Even though she was far from sleepy, she was getting hungry. They had been at the park for about thirty minutes, and she was growing impatient.

"When I need to clear my head, I come out here. Just sit out here and think about us, about work, about when we were young," he said softly. "Back then, my day wasn't complete if I ain't talk to you. All the shit I was going through, I only made it out that shit because I had you." Stacks looked over to her, before looking back to the park. "I needed you then, and I need you now." Stacks shook his head, "I'm sorry about how I carried shit after we were shot. Being shot, being weak like that, feeling that type of helpless...did something to me. Something to me that in turn made me make you feel the same way. I know I fucked up, but Faith you gotta know that I ain't just some selfish nigga out here just using you. I didn't know you felt like that, and that shit hurts me more than being shot ever could."

He paused to think and then looked back over to her. "You've always been so much stronger than me, stronger than anyone I've ever known. So strong that it never dawned on me that you needed me just as much as I needed you." Tears fell down her eyes as she sat there listening. Of all the things she expected him to say and of all the reactions she'd prepared in her mind, this wasn't one of them. "I'm here for you, our baby, and I'm here to support your business. I'm really proud of you by the way...Just tell me what you want me to do, and I'll do it."

Faith shook her head as she wiped her eyes getting herself together. "I just wanna be happy. I wanna know that no matter what, what happens, what you're feeling that we're in this together. I need to know that I can depend on you." Sighing she closed her eyes and placed her hands on her stomach. "I don't want to have this baby and then you just leave because shit really get hard."

"Faith..."

"I never in a million years thought you would turn ya back on me like that, and it made me think. I didn't have nothing for myself, nothing I could call my own…Everything I had, I got from you or its yours. And, that's fine, but for the first time in my life I had to think of what I would do without you." She looked to him, and he was staring right at her. "I love you, Landon…"

Reaching over he grabbed her hand and kissed the back of it, silencing her. "I love you too, more than anything," he said, words dripping with honesty. After a moment, he let the tension die down a little. "So, where we go from here? I mean I want us to be together, get married, and all that shit, but if that's not what you want, I ain't gon' like it, but I'll accept it."

Her lips twisted as she looked at him. "Yeah right."

Stacks looked at her and cracked a sexy smile. "What? I mean if that's what you really want. Is that what you want?"

"No," Faith answered honestly while shaking her head.

"It better not be, I'll snap ya damn neck," he joked, and they broke into laughter.

Now that was the man she knew and loved. "Talking about some you gon' be cool with that."

"Aight, so what we doing? You coming back home?" Stacks asked, looking for some type of clarity.

"No," she told him adamantly. "Not right now, I just think we should date and get to know each other again. A lot has changed in these past months for you and me."

Nodding his head, he could accept that. "You right a lot has changed." He palmed her stomach, and he could feel the baby moving around. Stacks was happy that she was carrying his baby. "Give me a kiss." Faith side eyed him, and he snatched her ass right up. "Stop playing." When she was close enough, he pressed his lips to hers, and they shared a long passionate kiss.

In all the years they'd been together or whatever they were doing, this was the longest they had ever been at odds. Even when she wasn't fucking with Stacks, or he was seeing some bitch somewhere, they were always still at least on speaking terms. But this fall out showed

Stacks what it would feel like to lose her, and he ain't like that feeling at all.

Chapter 22

The past couple of weeks for the girls had been eventful to say the least. Janae had given birth to the newest Zoo Baby, Keisha and Tech finally getting their shit together, Stacks and Faith were right behind them, and Rich and Lynette had practically eloped. Since the event last week, Zoo had even taken the event business to the next level and started offering security services. Zoo Events and Planning was coming along nicely and something the whole crew was in on. Now they seemed to all have a route to be legit and it was definitely something to be proud off.

"Ms. Lynette, you want me to put these up?" Michelle asked as she walked from the back, holding a handful of clothes.

"Yeah, you can," Lynette said, barely turning her way.

"How long you sit staring at those damn rings?" Keisha mushed her in her head as she walked by.

"Jealousy is a sickness," she said as her head bounced on her shoulders.

"Yeah, well, I'm still salty about not being invited." Faith rolled her eyes and Keisha cosigned.

"Well, I ain't do it." Lynette laughed as she walked out from behind the counter. "Rich surprised me too." Smiling, she held her hand out in front of her, marveling over her ring. Nowadays, it was her favorite thing to do. Just as they were talking, the guys walked in with Janae and the kids. "My babies." Lynette ran over kissing on them.

"Dang, let them get in the door first," Rich joked before snatching her up and kissing her lips. Something about being married had him wanting to fuck her all the time.

"Ugh, y'all need to get a room," Keisha said as she grabbed baby Sahara.

Rich slid Lynette back down to the ground as he moved past her. "Whatever." she flipped her middle finger as she picked Sammie up. "What y'all doing down here?"

"Nothing, we just came to get out the house, and I don't know what they want." Janae shrugged pointing to the guys.

Stacks walked to the back office where he assumed Faith was, and everybody else chilled in the front. Michelle busied herself and continued to put the clothes up as she tried not to look at how fine these niggas really were. Like for them to be young and everything, they were into some real shit. The store was beautiful, the cars were fresh, and their clothes were top dollar. She didn't know what they were doing, but she wanted parts.

"Now that everyone is here!" Keisha stood up with excitement dancing in her eyes. "We are working on throwing the biggest party of the century."

"For what?" Lynette asked.

"Duh, New Year's is like right around the corner." Rolling her eyes, Keisha was not in the mood. "Now, since the grand opening party, we've started planning everything. Venue, entertainment, and food will all be available for our Zoo Year celebration."

"Zoo Year," Lynette slurred, liking the sound of it.

"I know. That part was my idea, and this shit about to be epic."

Sam listened to everyone talk about the New Year's party before his pager went off. Checking the number, he didn't recognize it, but it was followed by 911, so he knew it was urgent. Standing up, he stepped away from the crew and walked over to the counter using the phone. "Yoooo, somebody page Sam?"

"It's me Echo; we got a problem." Echo went on to tell Sam some shit about his sister, he really wasn't trying to hear. His blood boiled as he listened to Echo tell him how the product was coming up short. "So, she stealing?" he asked, his voice rising.

"Nah, I think she getting high." Echo gave him the real.

"Where she at now?" Sam asked, ready to knock her damn head off. This was shit he expected from random niggas in the street, but his sister. Nah, she knew better.

"I don't know; she dipped then I think she got picked up."

"Aight, I'll be over that way in a few. Lock everything up and shut that shit down," Sam ordered before he hung up.

"What's up?" Rich asked.

Shaking his head, he ain't even want to repeat this shit. "Latifah stupid ass getting high."

"Getting high!" Everyone said in unison.

"Right, that's what Echo said. I don't know what's going on."

"Well, where she at now?" Janae asked really concerned. Not only was she Sam's sister, but her kids' aunt, and she was just over the house the other day.

"I don't know. Echo think she got picked up." Reaching in his pocket, he pulled out his car keys and handed them to Janae. "Here, take the car. I'mma ride with Rich."

The girls watched Rich walk to the back to tell Stacks they were leaving and just as quick as they came, they were gone. Getting back comfortable, the girls continued their conversation.

"That's crazy." Lynette shook her head.

"Right. It seems like everybody getting high nowadays," Janae tossed in. "But Tee know better."

"Shit, temptation a muthafucka," Keisha added, and Faith quickly disagreed.

"Nah, when I was…Shit, just know I ain't never think about trying that shit." Faith caught herself and tried to quickly clean it up. She thought Michelle was cool, but she ain't know her like that.

"This too much." Lynette stood up. "Michelle you can go ahead and clock out if you want, I'mma get ready to close."

"Okay," she said softly as she quickly finished the last of the clothes she had been putting up. "Later ladies." Michelle waved goodbye and walked out the door.

On the next corner, she bent the block and crossed a street. Soon as she stepped on the curb a car rolled up and she quickly got in. "Sam has a sister named Latifah, street name Tee, she was picked up not too long ago."

"Got it," the detective said as she buckled her seatbelt, and they were off. "So, what else you got?"

"Not much, they real tight about stuff around me."

"And for good reason," he laughed.

"Yeah, yeah." Looking out the window, she kind of felt bad because she thought everyone was really cool for the most part, but she had a job to do. "I think one of the girls, Faith, used to cook up the work for them...She started to say it but back tracked. If we can get his sister this would be huge."

"If we can get her to talk, we don't need Nate."

"Hell, we really don't need either of them." Michelle shook her head. "The more people we can get to talk the better case we have."

"You think we'll be able to flip his sister?"

She thought about it for a moment. "Well, supposedly she's on drugs, so we'll see."

When Sam, Rich, and Stacks got to the house where the work was kept and whipped up, all they wanted to know was what happened. Intently, they listened to Echo run down the events that had taken place earlier. Sam still couldn't believe his own sister was getting high. A little weed was one thing but crack, that was just unacceptable.

"And how you know she got picked up?" Sam asked as he paced the floor.

ARABIA

"One of the little homies told me. Shit it wasn't too long after she ran up outta here."

"And she had work on her?"

"Honestly, I don't even know. The packs been light these last few times I came to pick up, so today I popped up, and she was sitting in here smoking."

Sam was furious, nothing could explain the amount of anger he was feeling right now. "Aight, I'm about to call downtown and see if she got bail." He didn't want her to sit for too long, because if she was high, she was liable to talk, and if she talked, that put all their lives on the line.

"Aight, and I'll handle the shit here," Echo swore as they shook it up, and the men separated.

They headed downtown and into the police station where they were told they didn't have any file on his sister. Sam knew that meant either one or two things. Either she wasn't picked up, or they were holding her to talk to her before they booked her. He was willing to put his money on the latter of the two, leaving him no choice but to wait until she resurfaced. Sam dropped the guys back to their cars and they said their goodbyes before heading home.

It took Sam a little over thirty minutes to get home and when he pulled up into the driveway, he took a deep breath and let it go. When he and Janae moved in together, he promised himself that he would never bring none of that street shit home. After a few minutes he got out the car and headed into his home. When he walked in, Janae and his sister where in the living room sitting on the couch talking. Almost instantly all that leave the street shit in the streets shit went out the window. In seconds he had snatched his sister up by her collar and slapped fire from her ass.

"You a fuckin' dope fiend now?" Crying, Tee couldn't even answer him before he struck her again and threw her ass up against the wall. "A fucking fiend."

"Sam," Janae called out grabbing his arm. "Let her go."

Sam heard her, but he wasn't trying to hear that. "Where the fuck you been? You got picked up?"

WE MADE LOVE IN THE 80'S

"No," she choked out. "They…Didn't take me."

"Why the fuck not? You talked, and they sent ya crack head ass over here?" he shouted with spit flying as the base in his voice rocked the walls.

Tee was scared and her feelings hurt, sure she smoked a few times, but she was far from a fiend. "I'm not a crackhead, I don't even smoke like that."

Shaking his head, Sam rammed her into the wall once more before he let her go. "Tee we out here, we know what this shit does to people. If you ain't a crackhead now, you'll be one later." Disgust was written all over his face. "You fired, and as long as you on that shit, you ain't welcomed in my house or around my kids."

"But, Sam…" her voice shook with tears.

"Ain't no but's." stepping back from her, his decision was final. "Fuck out my house."

"Sam, please. Sam," Tee called out to him, but he was up the steps. Janae came over and helped her up off the floor. "You gotta tell him I wouldn't snitch, he gotta know that." She cried.

Janae pulled her close and held her as she cried. "I'll tell him," she soothed, "But you gotta get ya shit together, Tee. Getting high, you already know how Sam is when it comes to shit like that."

"I know, I just…" She didn't know what to say because there was nothing she could say.

After Janae walked Tee out, she headed up stairs to find Sam. He was just coming out of the shower. In the room, he stood by the dresser with a towel wrapped around his waist. She looked him over, her eyes trailing his body.

"You knew she was getting high, and you let her in the house," Sam said, interrupting her thoughts.

"Babe, she's your sister."

"I don't give a fuck. A fiend don't give a fuck about blood!" He shouted, still angry. "All they care about is their next fix…"

Janae listened to him go on as she sat on the bed. "She's not a fiend and had you let her explain, you would know that."

"There ain't shit for her to explain. She got caught smoking crack and then her ass got picked up. You know when I went to go pick her up from downtown, they didn't even have her in the system...You know what that shit mean."

"Maybe it means she was telling the truth, and they didn't take her downtown." It was clear, Janae was the only one of them willing to give her the benefit of the doubt. His silence let her know that he was listening, so she continued. "She said they picked her up and was asking her questions about Zoo. She denied knowing anything and said, after about twenty minutes they let her out of the car, she ain't even have shit on her."

He thought of what Janae was saying and what Echo had told him, and it all seemed like lies. "Well I don't know, and I really don't care. I don't want her over here or around me if she on that shit," Sam said those last words with so much finality that Janae didn't dare to challenge him.

She said what she had to say, but that was Sam's sister not hers. So, it was whatever he said. Sam was so pissed he wanted to break Tee fuckin' neck. He was so mad that if Janae kept talking to him, he was going to snap hers too. After putting on his bed clothes, Sam went downstairs and grabbed a beer out of the refrigerator. Leaning up against the counter, he twisted the top and took a long swig. Sam rubbed the fine hairs growing on his chin before he put the beer bottle back to his lips. As he was drinking, Janae walked her little fine ass in there, and their eyes connected. He watched her walk over to him as he removed the bottle from his lips.

Janae smirked as she stepped up to him and grabbed the beer from his hands. They watched each other as she took a sip and sat the bottle on the counter. Licking her lips, she ran her hands up his bare chest, allowing her fingers to brush up against his nipples before she kissed the middle of his chest once and then again, before standing on her tippy toes and kissing his lips. Sam's tongue was so warm and smooth, she fell more in love with every twist of it. Reaching in his pants she massaged his dick, gripping it in her hands.

"Come on, you know I ain't got no rubbers down here," He spoke as his head fell back, and she kissed his neck.

"So." Down his chest, she kissed until she was face to face with his dick. Just looking at his thick member standing proud and ready to salute her, had her mouthwatering.

"Sssss, fuck," Sam hissed as she took him into her mouth. Each time she came up and took him back down, her mouth got wetter and wetter. He gripped her hair trying to control the speed at which she was sucking him up, but she wasn't having it as she snatched her head away. Janae bobbed up and down on him as he moaned out curling his toes. This was just the nut he needed, and he was right there. A loud moan belched from the pits of his soul as he filled her throat with his kids.

Janae French kissed the head of him as she stood back up to her feet, licking her lips before she kissed him. Sam wrapped his arms around her waist and deepened the kiss as he turned her around and put her on the counter. Janae wrapped her arms around his neck getting lost in everything that was Sam as he stood between her legs. He slid his fingers under the shirt she was wearing, and her fast ass wasn't wearing any panties. Sam shook his head as his fingers dipped into what felt like a puddle of water. "Ya little ass." He slid into her slowly and she wrapped her arms around him tighter.

Once he was all the way in, he began to move in and out of her, causing cries of pleasure to fall from her lips. "Samuel," she moaned breathlessly. Her center began to throb with each stroke as he worked her body just right. Closing her eyes, Janae could feel the pressure building in her soul, every part of her body was tingling, so much that when she came it was like an explosion, and Sam was right there with her.

Heavily, Sam panted as he pushed himself into her as far as he could go. There was nothing on this earth that could compare to the feeling of him being inside of her. It was a connection, a bond, something that was deeper than love, and deeper than the sacrifice they were making to each other. When their breathing was back to normal, they looked at each other. Sam looked down at his dick and watched intently as it came out. Her walls tickled his sensitivity as he pushed back into her. "Yo' ass gon' be pregnant again."

Leaning back on her elbows Janae allowed Sam to hold her legs open as he moved in and out of her. "And you gon' take care of us."

Sam chuckled knowing it was all truth. He could feel his little man's growing inside of her and then, then, the baby started crying. Immediately, they stopped moving and looked at each other before they burst out laughing. Sam pulled out of her and helped Janae off the counter. He put his dick up before wrapping her in his arms and kissing the back of her neck. Together they walked up stairs, him to tend to the baby and her to clean up.

The next couple of days the shop remained closed and none of the guys were really in a rush to get shit back moving, especially with the cops snooping around. They didn't know where the heat was coming from, but it was getting hot. Them sniffing around and asking questions meant they were already on their radar.

"So, you just let Tee walk?" Echo asked, not understanding.

"Tee on her own with her bullshit." Sam shook his head. "She better stay the fuck away from me."

"But what if she talked?"

Sighing, Sam really didn't know. "Well then, she talked, and I'll deal with that shit when it comes," was all Sam said as he tightened his tie.

"Maannnnn," Echo dragged, not liking his answer or his shit being left in limbo. Sister or not, he thought she had to go.

"What, you got something to say?" Squaring his shoulders, Sam didn't like feeling challenged. And, he wasn't going to be challenged by a nigga that worked for him.

Echo's eyes met Sam's and they looked at each other for a second before Echo looked away. "Nah, it's nothing, man."

"Good. I get what you saying, but she's my sister, and I'll handle her how I see fit." The underlying message was his sister wasn't to be touched, and Echo heard him. "Now relax, it's Zoo Year, nigga. Let's go party and have a good time…We can worry about that other shit later."

WE MADE LOVE IN THE 80'S

Before they could say anything else, Tech walked in, and they slapped hands. "It's done," was all he said as he passed Sam a set of keys. Under Zoo orders, last minute they decided to move some shit around, and Tech had spent most of the day moving all the work to another spot. None of them wanted to give the police any more ammunition then they already had if they were being watched. They had to move smart.

"What's up?" Echo asked, wanting to know what the keys were for.

"Party tonight, work tomorrow," Sam said, slapping a hand on his shoulder as he walked out the room.

Tonight, was the night, and Zoo Year was in full effect. Keisha and Faith had really out done themselves this time. They had rented a ball room, and it was decorated in silver and black, with animal figures strategically placed throughout the venue. The party wasn't supposed to start until 10pm, but the girls had a dinner planned on the second floor of the venue, for the crew. Of course, they had the food catered, and the drinks were plentiful. The huge rectangular table was set to perfection as they dined, talked, and laughed.

Rich looked at everyone grateful for the role they had all played in Zoo's success. Even the girls because they were single handily responsible for making Zoo legit, and Rich knew it. Standing up, he fixed his suit and held his glass in his hand as he garnered everyone's attention. Rich didn't speak until everyone was looking at him. "This shit feels like the last supper," he joked, and everyone laughed because it really did have that feeling. "The only thing missing is the betrayal. But we don't have to worry about that because I personally vouch for everyone at this table," he spoke nothing but facts, and no one could argue with him. When it came down to it Zoo was as solid as they came.

"If I had any doubts," he corrected himself, "If we had any doubts about any of you, you wouldn't be here with us…Getting money with us, eating with us, building with us. Building," he paused and turned to Lynette and then looked to the other girls. "Shout out to the women of Zoo…Faith, Keisha, yo' ass too Janae." Everyone laughed as she smiled shaking her head. Yeah, they had some bumpy days, but they were cool now, Janae ain't have no beef. Rich chuckled and continued, "and my beautiful wife, Lynette. Because y'all don't know it, and we probably don't say it, but y'all the ones really out here making shit happen. I mean we made the money, but y'all took it and really did something with it. Y'all the ones really giving Zoo a name out here, and I respect that."

Rich took a deep breath and glanced at everyone at the table. "I ain't gon' take up too much more of y'all time with this sentimental shit, but I gotta thank my niggas. Y'all been holding shit down and pushing this Zoo shit since we were snotty nose little kids. Together we made this shit bigger than we could've ever imagined. Bigger than, shit, I ever thought it would be, and if it wasn't for y'all, this never would've happened. Lift ya glasses up," he encouraged everyone, and they did. "I love y'all. 1989 was one hell of a year, and 1990 gon' be even better. Happy Zoo Year!!!"

Everyone in turn stood to their feet and yelled Happy Zoo Year as loud as they could. After clinking glasses, they hugged and kissed each other to end their early celebration. Echo didn't have a girl to bring to the dinner, so he wasn't trying to see all this kissing shit. "Aight, aight, that's enough. I'm ready to party."

Lynette kissed Rich once more as he hugged her. "Ain't no party like a Zoo Crew party cause a Zoo Crew party don't stop!" The girls chanted hyping themselves up as the guys yelled Zoo and started taking shots. They bounced down the steps just as the doors where opening and the rest of the night was a movie.

The dress code was black tie, so everyone was dressed to the nines while they listened to rap music and drank vodka and Hennessey all night long. The smoke machine blew smoke all over the floor had the whole place looking foggy, but it was sexy under the low light. The disco lights bounced off the walls and confetti sprinkled the air as they jammed till the ball dropped. The ball dropped signaling that it was officially 1990. Black, white, and gold balloons fell from the ceiling as everyone screamed. It was officially another year, and they were ready to party the night away. Just as the DJ switched up the song, a loud commotion could be heard coming from the front.

"Everybody get down on the ground, now!"

"It's a stick up," Echo yelled as he pulled his gun.

Quickly, Rich held his hands up stopping him as DEA and undercover cops swarmed the building. Lynette looked up to him. She didn't say anything, but he could sense the worry and fear in her eyes.

"Babe, listen to me, don't worry about shit. You know what to do?" Nodding her head, she knew what he was asking. "Good, I love you."

He kissed her lips and only then did a tear fall. "I love you too, Tony…"

"Get the fuck down." Lynette was pulled back by her hair and thrown to the ground.

"Muthafucka," Rich snapped, and punched the officer as many times as he could before he was knocked to the ground himself. "Lynette!" He called out as he lifted his head trying to see her.

"I'm okay, I'm okay," she said as she was being lifted up and taken away in handcuffs.

By now, it was total chaos. None of them had ever expected to bring in their new year celebration in cuffs, but the game was full of surprises. Within the hour, everyone was in cuffs and hauled down to the police station. In separate rooms the girls where held while the men were booked immediately.

"Fuck," Sam screeched before punching the wall of the holding cell. "I'mma call my mom's to get the girls out."

"Aight, you do that, and I'll call this lawyer nigga," Rich said, worried about Lynette, but he had to focus. If they were brought in and booked immediately without any questions, shit was all bad.

Stacks sat with his hands on his head, thinking about Faith. She was a little over six months pregnant, and he ain't even want to think about her spending the night in jail.

"My pops on his way," Sam said as he finished his phone call, and told the other guys what was up. His parents had the kids, and one of them had to stay with them, so his pops was coming to save the day. Not being able to see his kids or Janae any time soon, fucked with Sam the most.

"The lawyer on his way too. So, if nothing else, the girls gon' be good," Rich said once he wrapped up his conversation.

ARABIA

Neither of the girls had anything to say and exercised their fifth amendment rights to the fullest. Hell, Lynette was married so her answering any questions or testifying about Zoo or Rich was out of the question. After hours of being detained, the girls were finally allowed to leave. Lynette didn't know what everyone else did, but as soon as she could, she called her mother.

LaVelle was asleep but getting that late-night call from her baby crying got her ass up quick and in a hurry. When her daughter walked out of the jail, she was right there waiting with open arms. Distraught and exhausted from the night's events, Lynette fell into her arms crying.

"Aww it's gone be okay," she soothed, rubbing her back. She stepped back and looked at her, immediately noticing a bruise on her face. When they threw her to the ground, she hit her face on a shoe or something. Lynette didn't even know but that shit hurt like hell. Together, they walked to the car and got inside. "So, where you wanna go?" Her mom asked as she bent the corner.

"Home," Lynette's voice shook. "I need to shower, call the lawyer, and wait for Tony to call me."

Nodding her head, LaVelle did as she was told and took Lynette home. When they arrived, she parked in front and offered to come up, but Lynette declined.

"Nah, I'm okay. I just need to get myself together. Thank you for picking me up."

"Anytime." Reaching over, she hugged her only child and promised to check on her later.

When Lynette got upstairs, she walked into her home and just looked around. It seemed so empty without Tony. Slowly, she removed her clothes leaving a trail leading to her bathroom. After a nice hot shower, she was drying off when she heard the phone ring. Quicker than her damp feet would allow she made it to the phone, "Hello!" She listened to the operator and pressed five to accept the call when prompted. "Tony," she said, barely audible as she choked on her tears.

"Babe, you okay?" He asked as his jaws flexed from anger.

"Yes." Lynette nodded as if he could see her. "I, um, just got home. How are you doing?"

"Long as you good, I'm good." He sighed into the phone. "The lawyer just left…"

"And?"

"And, right now it ain't looking too good. He got some more shit to go through, but it looks like they been building this case for a minute." Tony listened to her cry into the phone and was silent for a minute.

Once she was able to get herself together, she focused. "I'll be down there later to put some money on y'all books…I think I got the lawyer's number in the office somewhere. I'll call him later and figure this out."

She began to run off all that she was going to do, and Rich was proud in that moment. He trusted that Lynette would hold him down. "I love you."

"I love you too," was all she was able to say before the line went dead. Looking at the phone, she took a deep breath, before hanging it up. Lynette promised herself that after she took this nap, she was going to handle her business. It seemed as if she had just closed her eyes, and the phone was ringing again. Thinking it was Rich, she answered, "Hello."

"Get ya ass up and get down to the store now," was all Faith said before she hung up.

Looking at the clock on the dresser, it was a little after two in the afternoon. Sliding from under her covers, Lynette went to the bathroom to get dressed and handle her hygiene. Within the hour, she was in the car and on her way to the store. After parking in her regular spot, Lynette walked to her door, and her heart dropped. Taped to the door was a warrant to search her property, rolling her eyes she snatched it off the door. Inside the store, everything was trashed. Stuff knocked over, her office and the back office was ransacked. All her hard work was just destroyed, and all she could do was shake her head.

"This shit is crazy." Keisha came out of the back office shaking her head.

"Well, whatever it is, they ain't gon' find it." Lynette knew that for sure because Rich, nor any of the other guys, kept illegal shit at the store. Taking a seat at her desk Lynette was at a loss. Holding her head in her hands, she could feel the tears brewing.

"Aht aht, we not doing that," Faith chastised as she walked into the upstairs office. "Come on, Janae just got here."

"Where we going?"

"Well, first we gone clean this mess up, then we have to get this money together, and then we gon' eat," she laughed, "because I'm hungry."

Shaking her head, Lynette giggled. "Faith," she cried, "I don't know if I can handle this. What am I supposed to do without him?"

"Aww babes," Faith walked over, hugging her tight, "I know it's fucked up, shit, I'm pregnant, Janae has two kids, and we all out here naked right now. But you know just like I do that Zoo prepared us for this. You may seem overwhelmed and lost right now, but Rich gave you the game." Lynette dried her eyes, and Faith continued, "He made you Ms. Zoo for a reason, and now you have to stand on that."

Lynette listened to her and she knew she was right. She didn't know how, but she had to do it. Closing her eyes, she nodded her head and silently prayed that Zoo would guide her.

The Trial

Six months after the cops burst into the Zoo Year party and turned their lives upside down, the founding members of Zoo sat in court. With their heads held high Sam, Rich, Stacks, and Tech sat together as co-defendants with their families not too far behind them. From what they knew, Echo was sent to another prison after requesting separate council. Apparently, he felt his chances of getting out were better if he was tried separately. Neither of them felt any kind of way about it, he made his choice and as men, they had to respect it. However, the members of Zoo that were really down, stayed true and stuck together. Whatever the odds, whatever the consequences, they would face them together.

Rich straightened his suit, before looking back to Lynette. *I love you*, she mouthed, and he smiled before mouthing it back. He loved the fuck out of her, and these past six months made him love her even more. She held shit together. All the girls stepped up in a major way. Even silently keeping their drug empire together but keep that on the low. If he could, he would marry her ass ten times over. It was hard not being able to see her every day or touch her, but they managed. Daily phone calls and their weekly visits was the best they could do, until he made it out or to the feds. Rich turned around in his seat just as the bailiff read off the case and docket number. Respectably, the people in the courtroom stood up from their seats as the judge walked in.

Everyone sat lost in their own thoughts as the judge read their charges and turned to the prosecution. None of them were half paying attention until the prosecution called their first witness. The courtroom door opened, and everyone but the guys turned to see who it was, and to all their shock, it was Michelle.

Keisha was the first to see her and squinted her eyes in confusion as she turned around and leaned into Lynette. "Ain't that the cashier hoe?"

Shaking her head Lynette couldn't believe it either. Had she played a part in her husband's demise? "Stupid bitch," she hissed, anger radiating from her pores. "I paid that hoe in American money to work in my store! I'm fucking suing…"

"Shhh," Keisha tried to tell her to lower her voice as she giggled, but Lynette wasn't having it.

Rich turned around, giving her just one look that told her to chill and reluctantly she did. After turning back around he looked to Sam who was right next to him. Sam was trying to remember if they'd ever had any conversation around her about their business or anything and he couldn't remember. He couldn't recall one time, not even a slip up. However, she got up there anyway and told all she knew; who was who, about the operations in the store, and she also mentioned the phone call Sam received about his sister being arrested, which only corroborated the prosecutor's story of them being Kingpins.

When she was done, the prosecutor called another witness and then another, so many they had lost track. They impatiently sat through a slew of witnesses, some they knew, and some they'd never seen in their life. The feds were playing a dangerous game with these people, and they ain't even know it.

After two hours of testimony, they finally took a break. Court was in recess, and the guys were left with their heads spinning. In addition to testimony, they had tape recordings and pictures. Nothing that really showed them doing anything, but if the jury could read in between the lines they knew what was up.

"I know it looks bad," their lawyer started before they could say anything.

"Shit, it looks worse than bad," Tech said as he leaned up against the wall, with his head back.

"It doesn't matter what they say, it's what they can prove. Where's the evidence?" He asked looking to each of the men. "They don't have any?"

They listened to the lawyer as he spoke, and neither of them were really convinced they would walk. It could be because they knew they were guilty. Guilty of everything they were accused of and more.

Court was in recess for an hour, so the girls decided to go and get something to eat. At a diner down the street, the girls sat at the round table, a ball of nerves. Everyone was on edge and didn't know what turn the case would take next.

WE MADE LOVE IN THE 80'S

"I just want all this to be over," Janae pouted. "I mean, at least if we knew how much time they were getting, we would know what we were facing, you know?" She sighed with a heavy heart. It was killing her just as much as it was killing Sam with him being away. Being a father was his greatest accomplishments, and him not being able to be there was worse than being shot. Thankfully, both of their parents stepped in to help them out because Janae honestly didn't know what she would do without their help.

Nodding her head, Lynette agreed. "This is just crazy," she said as the waitress came over. Life without Tony hadn't been a walk in the park for her either. In a lot of ways, she felt slighted. Like, after all they'd been through, the business, moving, and getting married that's where their story ends. Lynette wanted to have kids, travel, and make memories. Now it was like she wouldn't be able to do any of that, and it pissed her off. Most days it felt like she had the weight of the world on her shoulders. Keeping up her business, the house, and Rich's affairs, Lynette was burnt out. All of the girls had their struggles moving forward without the men, and like the others, Lynette made do.

After they ordered their food, Faith stood up and straightened her clothes. "I'mma check on LJ," she said referring to her and Stacks five-month-old son. Landon Jr. was the apple of her eye, and Faith's life today was completely devoted to him. She still had the event business, but LJ came first.

She never saw herself actually being a single parent but here she was. Stacks had missed the last few months of her pregnancy, he missed the birth and was missing him grow. In a way, the time her and stacks spent apart, made her stronger and independent. She felt capable of making decisions on her own, and she wasn't like that before. Though she was stronger in many ways, she still needed Stacks to be there. Plenty of nights, Faith cried herself to sleep but when you saw her, she was well put together and handling her business.

While Faith went to make her phone call, the other girls sat at the table discussing the case until their food came. By then, Faith was back, and the girls hurriedly ate their food. They knew they were on borrowed time, so they finished eating and made it back to the court room with just minutes to spare. The judge walked in just as they made it to their seats. Once everyone was seated, the prosecution began to speak. They were just about ready to wrap up their case, but they had one last witness to call. All day they'd been calling witness after witness and just about everyone was over it.

ARABIA

"We call our final witness, Terrence Latham," The prosecutor said, smugly before glancing over to the defense table.

The courtroom doors opened, and bile filled Lynette's mouth. So much that she jumped up and ran out of the courtroom and to the bathroom. Rich's eyes followed her until she was out of the room, then he focused his eyes back on what was going on in front of him as his jaws clenched with anger.

"Objection," Zoo's lawyer stood up. "This witness, nor his testimony, was in the discovery."

"For fear that harm would be brought to the witness, he is cooperating with us and has offered testimony under a new agreement. As long as he is cooperating, his testimony and identity up until trial was anonymous."

The judge sat back and looked between them. "I'll allow it."

"Please state your name for the record?" The prosecutor asked.

"Terrence Latham, but I go by E...Ec...Echo." He stuttered as his voice shook.

"And, what's your relationship to the defendants?"

For a minute, he looked over at the table but turned away and focused back on the prosecutor. Sweat bubbled on his forehead as he tried to steady his breathing. He knew eventually this day was coming, and for as prepared as he thought he was, he wasn't. "I'm a friend and former member of Zoo Crew." A deep breath followed that statement, and he shook his head.

He always thought he was too real a nigga for what he was doing, but not too long after the grand opening, he got pulled carrying work. So much work that he would never see the light of day again. Echo was sick, but when they put the deal on the table, initially he said no. When they added relocation and money to blow, he reconsidered. It was fucked up, true indeed, and there was nothing he could say that would make it any better. In his mind, the time he was facing was guaranteed. No jury in the world would let him walk, but Zoo had a better chance of getting off. A lot of stuff Echo knew or had taken a part in, he didn't even tell, and he knew some shit that could put everybody under the jail.

Sam scoffed not believing this shit was happening, while Rich's jaws clenched, and Tech's leg bounced in anger. Stacks sat there stoically looking directly at Echo. He wanted him to look him in his eyes. Stacks wanted to see the bitch in him, but never once did he give any direct eye contact. On the stand Echo pointed each of them out and told them story after story, dates and times of drug transactions, everything. With the recordings playing, he filled in the blanks putting all the pieces together for the jury. Echo even went as far as to drop names of guys from other crews.

Rich sneered at him with nothing but death in his eyes. For all the lessons Rich felt he'd learned, or for all that he'd prepared himself for, betrayal wasn't one of them. Betrayal in all honesty was the furthest thing from his mind. Not betrayal from Zoo anyway, Zoo came before God. That was the motto, it's what they lived by and looked up to, and to go against it was to go against God. As he sat there thinking about the night they were all arrested, it dawned on him that Echo was Judas. Instead of silver they promised him freedom, and he took it. Shaking his head Rich couldn't believe the irony in this situation, but rest assured just like Judas, he would die but by the hand of Zoo. In his mind, Rich had already killed Echo a million times over, and if he had the time, it would've been a million and one.

They were all sure at this point that their reign as the biggest crew to ever do it in their city was over. And, it didn't end by the hands of a stranger, by Nate, or Sam's sister but by a snake. One they would've seen if their grass was lower and they were paying attention, but they weren't and now they were paying the price.

After the most damaging testimony of the evening, they all sat and waited for the verdict. If there was an ounce of optimism, it was replaced with every ounce of doubt there was. Rich wasn't supposed to but since he was there, he turned around and leaned his head on the rail as Lynette held on to him for dear life. Never had she ever prayed so hard in her life.

Next to them, Keisha sat talking to Tech. Their shit was cut down before it could really get started, and it was sad because they had so much potential. A relationship for them was completely up in the air, but she was here for him to do whatever he needed.

ARABIA

It seemed like hours had passed before the jury came back. In all actuality it was only a little over thirty minutes, and that wasn't good at all. The room was silent so silent you could hear a pin drop as they delivered the verdict. Lynette closed her eyes and held her breath as the words guilty rung in her head. Like a bell, the words rung louder and louder so much that it became painful to hear. Rich looked back at her and they held eye contact, before the bailiff came over and told him to face forward.

The leaders of Zoo were found guilty of all charges, Tech ended up only getting three years for his crimes. They couldn't really prove shit on his end but being locked up violated his probation, so he was sent up state to do his time. Stacks got five years, and that was a slap on the wrist to him. Thankfully most of the surveillance took place while he was in the hospital, but they got him on some shit when he came home, so he took his time on the chin. However, Sam and Rich weren't so lucky. They each got fifteen years for their role as what the prosecutor considered organized crime and gang leadership. Because they were the leaders of Zoo, they got the most time, and Rich could accept that.

What he couldn't except was being gone from his life, his wife, and his Zoo family that long. That was going to be hard…But in this game, it was better to be judged by twelve than to be carried by six, so, he wasn't even tripping because one thing for sure, and two things for certain, his legacy would live on forever. Nobody could do in the streets what they had and live to tell about it. Their name and their legacy would live forever.

WE MADE LOVE IN THE 80'S

The End

ARABIA

If you enjoyed this book visit http://www.trapfiction.com/ for other reads by Arabia

<u>SERIES</u>

Coke Dreams Reloaded 1-4

New Money: A Coke Dreams Novel

From the Beginning It Was Us 1-2

<u>STANDALONE</u>

G-CODE

Money Is the Motive: Trilogy

The Plug Chose Me

WE MADE LOVE IN THE 80'S

CPSIA information can be obtained
at www.ICGtesting.com
Printed in the USA
LVHW031505241220
675096LV00002B/172